The Telling of
ANGUS QUAIN

I myself have seen the ungodly in great power:
and flourishing like a green bay-tree.
Psalm xxxvii, *Book of Common Prayer*

The cult of success has replaced a belief in principles.
GEORGE SOROS in *Atlantic Monthly*

The notion that because somebody is filthy rich,
he must also be ruthless and devious is complete
nonsense and pure Hollywood. Many of my friends in
the business world are committed altruists whose only
desire is to make the world a better place and create
jobs for our people. It often comes as a terrible shock
to them when they find out how much the share price
of their company has risen or discover that their free
share options are worth another R10-million.
DAVID BULLARD, 'Out to Lunch'
Business Times 3 August 1997

The Telling of

ANGUS QUAIN

A novel

JENNY HOBBS

JONATHAN BALL PUBLISHERS
Johannesburg

Published by
JONATHAN BALL PUBLISHERS (PTY) LTD
P O Box 33977
Jeppestown 2043

ISBN 1 86842 052 3

Design by Michael Barnett, Johannesburg
Front cover painting (top): John Meyer – Old Jeppe, 1974
Cover photographs: Image Bank
Typesetting and reproduction of cover by RT Sparhams (Pty) Ltd, Johannesburg
Typesetting and reproduction of text by Book Productions, Pretoria
Printed and bound by National Book Printers, Drukkery Street, Goodwood, Western Cape

INTRODUCTORY NOTE

All the characters in this book are fictional. So is the 'Johannesburg Club'. Having intended to use the Rand Club as a background for some of my scenes, I requested permission from a distinguished member for an official tour so I could get the details right, but did not receive a reply for over two years – probably because the prospect of being scrutinised by a woman novelist was too ghastly to contemplate.

So I invented my own club, based on a single brief visit to the Rand Club some years ago, news clippings and memories of meals at my father's Victoria Club in Pietermaritzburg. As well as protecting me against libel actions, this allowed a great deal of licence and the imaginary club flourished as a result, to the point where it almost took over – and certainly improved – the background.

ACKNOWLEDGEMENTS

Those who did answer my queries or gave me generous help and encouragement include: Jane Dugard for the original spark of an idea; Shelagh Watts of *The Star* library for insight into the art of filing news clippings; John Leach for sharing his expert knowledge of classic hunting rifles; Dr Selma Braude for checking the details of cancer treatment and pain control; a number of business informants who wish to remain nameless; Jenny Dereham for editorial advice; Jonathan Ball and Nicholas Combrinck – old publishing friends – for their vote of confidence; and my agent Dinah Wiener for continued professional and moral support.

*Dedicated to the memory of
a man who epitomised honour and excellence:
our incomparable friend,*
RAYMOND HASSON

1

*A*ngus Quain had been my best friend for
fifteen years, but during the months before he died I discovered that I hadn't known
him at all. Or to be more exact, I had known only the facets he chose to reveal.

As I sat by his side and later by his bed listening to the people who came to
say goodbye, it gradually became apparent that 'King' Quain, one of the doyens
of the South African accounting profession, chairman of a dozen boards of directors, distinguished member of business councils and the Inner City Forum,
TV panellist, patron of the arts, founding trustee of the Market Theatre and benefactor of worthy charities, was a far more complex and devious man than anyone suspected. And so nimbly had he danced from one compartment of his life
to the next that I could be the only person who has ever learnt the truth about
him. Perhaps I should say, a reasonable percentage of the truth. Baring all wasn't
his style.

It was the ultimate accolade from a friend, to let me into his secrets – though
of course he had an ulterior motive. Angus's reasons for doing things were as many-
layered and convoluted as the strips of rubber inside a golf ball.

Unlike his health-obsessed peers, however, he scorned golf and all forms of activity besides a purposeful walk which grew more and more impressive as he rose
in the business hierarchy and acquired a trail of minions. He used to boast that
his heart was in fine form, his cholesterol level below the norm, and his chief form
of recreation carrying the coffins of his more athletic friends. 'I've got a strong
life force,' he'd explain with the smug conviction of those who take their good
health for granted. 'That's the most important asset a person can have: a strong
life force.'

A month before he learnt of his fatal illness, he told me of an impending takeover
that would guarantee him a seat on the board of one of Africa's biggest conglomerates for a decade after his retirement, 'Whenever that may be.' Radiant with

7

unquestioned power, he dismissed the very idea of stepping down. I had no inkling then of his secret lives; not the slightest indication that I would spend the following year investigating and writing about men who created and controlled some of South Africa's biggest companies. With growing dismay, I might add. What began as a social history turned into an overview of corporate malfeasance down the years.

But this is one exposé you won't find on the back page of the *Sunday Times*. It's going into a bank vault where it will stay until everyone who features in it is dead and gone, and then it will be published by the Witwatersrand University Press as part of their Business History series. Angus Quain will be immortalised as he wished: 'Warts and all, rags to riches, no punches pulled – but only when I'm gone. Promise?' And so I present this man of chameleon talents and wide-ranging interests, brilliant and scheming, dismissive of the laws that bind others, yet loyal to a fault – the twentieth century Renaissance man.

Joburg Renaissance. Johannesburg. Jozi. Egoli. City of Gold. Gauteng. Whatever you like to call the parvenu mining camp whose stumpy skyscrapers now rear into the highveld sky, don't laugh to hear it coupled with Renaissance. Brash Joburg has its pride, as can be seen by the phallic upward thrust of its Civic Centre on the hill near the old jail. Joburg is the place where highways and financial aspirations meet, hustling engine room of Southern Africa, squatter mecca, street-smart metropolis, conglomerate city ... perfect milieu for Angus Quain. Viva the Big Naartjie, viva.

He was the first person I heard call Joburg the 'Big Naartjie', long before the journalists and stand-up comics latched on and yammered it to death. The occasion was a rugby test match at Ellis Park during the polecat years when no self-respecting nation would come and play South Africa, so we had to lure opponents with promises of visits to posh game reserves and wads of petty cash under the table. Angus's firm had a hospitality suite where the partners could male-bond in style with their clients, and he had asked me to come to the pre-match luncheon and the game itself to provide company for a recalcitrant wife who would not be fobbed off with tickets to a theatre matinée.

'Besides getting a decent bite to eat, you'll be doing us a favour, Faith,' he'd said. 'The bloody woman insisted that she wanted to come and watch the test, and one of us will have to hold her hand if you don't.'

'You want me to be a nanny? Forget it.'

'Please come. You may actually learn something about rugby.'

'What for?'

He gave me an exasperated look. 'Indulging the acerbic today, are we? Because rugby is the king of sports. Most red-blooded South African women would thrill with flattered pride if they were asked to a test match.'

8

'Not this one. I detest the sight of sweaty, grunting men running after balls.' I eyed the paunch swelling under his waistcoat. 'Don't tell me you used to do it too? I'd find that hard to believe.'

'I've done a lot of things you wouldn't believe.' It was the first hint he gave me of the secret dimensions behind the gleaming facade of his career. His gaze lingered on me as though considering whether to enlarge on some of them.

'Like what?' I prompted. Angus was as tight as a duck's arse about his private affairs.

But I had got too close and he said, 'Oh, things,' with a dismissive gesture then, 'If not for the rugby, come for the food and the atmosphere. At the very least, I promise you a diverting experience.'

How could I resist? I had nothing better to do that Saturday and Angus was persuasive. He dominated the party: clapping blazered shoulders, comparing rugby Springboks going back to the thirties, and pontificating over a succession of Castle Lagers which I knew he detested. He had a great sense of occasion and would never have drunk a sissy wine before a rugby match. He had asked his awful secretary (of whom more anon) to look up some virile jokes which he told with aplomb in the course of a short speech, ending with the rallying cry, 'Up Ellis Park! Up the Big Naartjie!'

The now-mellow guests surged off to their seats muttering that his firm must be doing damn well to put on a show like this; better keep an eye on their shares. The wife and I trailed in their rear with nothing in common but mutual dislike on sight.

But sitting shoulder-to-shoulder among thousands of animated men in the pale sunshine was, I have to admit, unexpectedly pleasant. As I watched the shadow of the western stand crawl across the field of combat, ink blue on lion pelt grass, I thought at first, How clever to turn aggression into a game, and then, It's damn exciting. As the end of the match drew near with both teams even on points, I was on my feet with the rest of the crowd cheering our boy in green and gold home as he sprinted down the wing to score a diving try with frantic opponents clawing at his legs. It was a glorious climax: brave, single-minded and triumphant.

'Converted, are we?' Angus murmured when I went to say goodbye after the post-match exultation over more Castle Lagers and kudu biltong.

'I can see the attraction now. Rugby is a much better spectacle than throwing Christians to the lions: there's minimal blood, and players can say sorry to each other with mass hug-outs between hostilities.'

He laughed. 'You'd come again, then?'

'Not as a nanny. For the adrenaline rush.'

'Aha. A fan is born. I shall have to organise tickets more often.'

'Don't go overboard.'

'Certainly not. I am the captain of the ship. My place is on the bridge,' and he plunged back into the thick of convivial post-mortems that would go on for hours. He was on a pinnacle that day; at the height of his powers.

My first and easiest task is to describe Angus before he ended up holding court on his mahogany deathbed, magnificent in his defiance of pain and regret.

For the fifteen years I knew him, he lived like an Edwardian gentleman in a suite of rooms on the third floor of the Johannesburg Club in Fordyce Street, just off Market. When his wife Hannah had left him to return to England with their children, he had sold their large Saxonwold home and moved into the Club where he'd done most of his business entertaining anyway. Hannah was a potter and no social butterfly, he would say in the early days, followed by the amused rumble that became famous during his years as a financial pundit on TV. The word got around that she wasn't good with servants (being English), couldn't care less about cooking and had a sharp tongue that made dinners at the Quains' house an ordeal. Even the keenest young executive, programmed to hold his drink and fawn on his superiors for hours, would cringe at Hannah's leathery soufflés and clunky hand-thrown dishes and uncomfortably bald questions.

The Johannesburg Club became the ideal setting for Angus after she left. To see him arriving in his chauffeur-driven black Bentley and surging up the sandstone steps through the ornate carved doors and across the airy marble hall into the main dining room, usually with an entourage of trim eagle-eyed men in dark suits and discreet ties, was to understand the enduring glamour of big business.

Angus himself was an imposing six foot two, but far from trim with the bulk and belly of a once-muscular man gone to fat. His head could have been the model for a ravaged Roman emperor: balding with a frieze of silver curls, thick black domineering eyebrows, a broken nose that had healed skew, bags of flesh sagging under his eyes and chin.

But his physical defects were eclipsed by the booming force of his personality and the power of his charm. Angus played his instinct for people like a church organ with an infinite number of stops. He could win over the most sceptical opponent in five minutes. Ambitious young men hung on his every word. Women found themselves wanting to drown in his rich vocabulary and candid blue eyes. Even government officials, congenitally distrustful of businessmen and their tax-avoiding financial expertise, would end up eating out of his hand.

Angus usually wore navy, I suspect because he knew that it deepened the colour of his eyes. He had a venerable Lithuanian Jewish tailor in End Street who made him two hand-stitched suits a year – always with pocketed waistcoats to accommodate his gold watch and chain – and a shirtmaker with a subtle eye for cut and cambric. His shoes were made by Lobb of London, from a wooden last shaped to his foot; his ties were Italian silk, his blazers navy cashmere, his socks pure new wool. He was profligate with socks: Hannah counted seventy-two pairs in his drawers after he died. All navy.

'Everything of the best' was one of the rules he lived by, and that was how he had his suite of two rooms with an adjoining bathroom furnished. First he prowled the Club's attics and found a trove of mahogany furniture that had been out of fashion in the fifties when the building was refurbished. Then he called in a decorator who created an interleading bedroom and sitting room that would have done Napoleon proud: plum velvet curtains flowing from tasselled pelmets, Regency striped wallpaper, sofa and easy chairs re-upholstered in burgundy leather, a massive desk and oil paintings in important gold frames.

The king-sized bed that he died in had a high carved head-board, a hillock of pillows, a paisley eiderdown of epic proportions and bed linen of the finest cotton percale embroidered with his initials, AQ. During his periods of intermittent sleep towards the end, I would sit fingering those initials and thinking about the places he had taken me and the visitors I'd seen and heard coming to say their last goodbyes. Thinking of the Angus I had thought I knew, and the Angus who was being revealed to me.

How little we really know of each other. How little it matters when the chips are down. As Albert Camus said: 'We are made to live for others. But one really dies only for oneself.'

He also said, 'Meaning of my work: so many men lack grace. How can one live without grace?' Angus had it. He may have been flawed but he moved through his life with the majestic assurance of an ocean liner, taking the brunt of heavy seas as he swept people along in his wake. He had the twin graces of generosity and humour to offset his many sins. He was unique.

My second and more onerous task is to introduce myself: Faith Dobermann, a writer-historian who lives in a national monument, one of the few remaining Parktown mansions.

I'm tall and too thin and on the wrong side of forty and divorced. Besides my collection of African carvings, I enjoy reading, hiking, art movies and small owner-run cafés like Sam's in Melville where the food and wine are more important than the decor. I also confess to secret passions for biltong, chocolate and Pieter-Dirk Uys, and have an explosive laugh which ruins the scholarly image I try to cultivate. Angus often said that it should be bottled or canned for sale to depressives on their bad days.

That was a typical compliment, tossed off in the middle of a conversation before he plunged on to the next thing he wanted to say. Talking and arguing our way through whole afternoons without getting heated was a talent we shared, augmented by a mutual fondness for unusual words, irony, limericks and puns. I enjoyed rubbing my mind against his, generating the static electricity of new ideas.

We weren't lovers. Just friends. Every Saturday for fifteen years if neither of us had anything else on, I would lunch with him at the table in the bay window of the almost empty Club dining room, a 'lady guest' who at first was only allowed in by the side door, and certainly not up to the third floor. But the rules were relaxed as women became fiercer about their rights, and by the time he lay dying I was allowed to sit by his bed and sleep on the sofa in his sitting room when the night nurse came on duty.

He wanted to die in his own lair, he said, and the Club management couldn't deny such an eminent resident his final wish. *Éminence grise* would be a better description. How I miss the old fraud.

2

When Angus learnt that the nagging pain in his lower belly which he had tried to ignore for months was a cancerous tumour in his colon, I was the first person he told.

He broke the news at our regular Saturday lunch over the Club's speciality: roast Karoo lamb, new potatoes, braised pumpkin and garden vegetables. I remember the late summer sunlight angling through the window on to starched damask and silver and crystal, and the vinegary tang of mint sauce, and the noisy street bazaar on the pavement outside.

Joburg is all black shoppers on Saturdays, when the white lemmings of weekday business hours withdraw to their safe suburban shopping centres and the executive class rolls about its trout farms and private game reserves in Range Rovers. The Club had objected many times to the city council about the street vendors who sold overripe fruit and plastic shoes and cheap watches and gimcrack African masks on either side of its stately entrance, leaving tides of litter in their wake, but to no avail. Civic shoulders were shrugged, and it was intimated that a club whose members were capitalists to a man should be encouraging rather than complaining about the new breed of entrepreneurs. Less and less of the members were willing to brave the teeming proletarian heart of Joburg at midday on Saturdays, which meant that the Club dining room was almost empty and explained why Angus needed my company.

He liked people around him ... 'Intelligent people who make stimulating conversation,' he said at the beginning of our friendship, knowing how seductive it would sound to a lone woman with big ideas. He must have learnt to manipulate people from his cradle because he had it down to a fine art.

We met several times at those pointless parties given for prominent visitors from overseas, where local celebrities they don't recognise are trotted out to try and impress them. But he only really noticed me when I had a sharp exchange with an ignorant amateur book critic and stomped away from her to an open window, fuming.

He manoeuvred his way to my side and picked up my hand and said, 'I hadn't realised what a genuine pearl you are, Faith.'

I hate being pawed and snatched my hand away. 'What do you mean by that?'

'Opaque and secretive, with an irritant at your core.'

God, the man had brass. 'The irritant is that stupid woman who thinks she knows all about books.'

'No.' He gave me a considering look. 'I think there is something chafing you inside – some dolorous injury to your psyche as a child, perhaps? And I'd very much like to discover what it is.'

People who think they can psychoanalyse you after a brief meeting are pests. I muttered, 'I'm just prickly. A typical nitpicking historian,' and began to move away.

He followed me. 'I find you interesting. Will you come and have lunch with me at the Johannesburg Club on Saturday? They're somewhat stuffy about women guests but I can guarantee a fine table and an excellent cellar.'

I was so surprised at being asked to lunch by a distinguished businessman that I agreed. But going up the Club steps to my first encounter with the revolving glass door, I was thinking, If he's got ulterior motives, I'm leaving. I may be single but I'm not desperate.

So the first thing I said to him when we met at the hall porter's desk, after I had been warned by a shocked flunkey to use the side entrance next time and before Angus signed me in, was, 'I presume there are no strings attached to this lunch?'

'None at all.'

'Or obligations?'

Looking down his skew nose, he huffed, 'Relationships can only flourish if they're allowed to develop naturally. Minus strings and obligations.'

'Then you got me here under false pretences, Mr Quain. I'm not looking for a relationship.' The heels of my new Italian leather shoes squeaked on chequered black and white marble as I walked back towards the revolving door.

A plump hand wearing a signet ring came down on my arm. 'Look here, I asked you to lunch so we could enjoy some intelligent conversation. I don't want to bloody ravish you. Could you sheath your prickles long enough for us to have a simple meal together?'

I turned and we stood glaring at each other, two people who habitually spoke in sentences beginning with 'I'. It was a critical moment for me, during which I weighed my dignity against my curiosity and a peremptory growl from my stomach brought on by the delicious smells wafting out of the dining room. I don't like being bullied or forced to make instant decisions; I need time to consider things before committing myself. But I took an uncharacteristic plunge that day, and have been grateful for the impulse ever since.

'Just as friends, right?'

It was the first time I felt the full blast of his card-sharp's smile. 'Good friends, I hope. Since my wife Hannah left, I've lacked an intelligent companion to bounce ideas off. Unlike my contemporaries who recoil from the least sign of female intellect, I revel in clever women.'

Now, fifteen years later, I saw that smile's shadow across the table as he put his fork down parallel with the knife on his plate, having eaten only a few mouthfuls. 'I have something to tell you.'

'What is it?' I expected to hear of a business coup, or some insider gossip. His boardroom tales were well-informed and his advice on shares always worth listening to. I'll be able to retire in style one day, thanks to Angus.

'I have cancer.' It was typical of him to come straight out with it.

'What?' The shock was so great that I could only repeat myself, butter knife poised in mid-air. 'What?'

'The Big C. I suspected as much when my quack referred me post-haste to a specialist for tests yesterday. He phoned this morning to tell me that the biopsies were positive. I have a large tumour in my colon.'

Behind his face, lit from below by the sunlight on the white tablecloth, the almost empty dining room receded down a rushing dark tunnel.

'How serious?' They were the only words I could force out between rigid lips with the taste of mutton gravy congealing on them.

'They're being cagey and won't commit themselves. Each case is different, they say; there are various treatments and patients react in different ways to them. But their eyes keep sliding away when they talk to me. I think I'm done for.'

I was horrified by the resignation in his voice. 'You must fight it! They have amazing cancer drugs now. And there's surgery and radiotherapy...'

'Of course I'll fight it, tooth and bloody nail. I'm not a good loser, as you know.' He was folding his starched white table napkin into a cube. 'Though equally, I'm not good at convincing myself things are better than they really are. The operation's on Monday but the doctors have warned me that the cancer may already have spread. And I can't say it's unexpected. My father, God rot the old bastard, died of mice in the basement.'

'Mice in the basement?'

'His euphemism for cancer of the prostate. He knew when he was done for too.'

'But you have to believe you'll get better! A positive mental attitude is crucial when you're fighting cancer.'

'Belief in anything beyond my control has never been easy for me. That's why

Hannah left.' He placed the cubed table napkin on the table, laying one of his knives across it so it wouldn't unfold. Even inanimate objects submitted themselves to Angus's will. 'But I'll try to maintain a positive mental attitude, of course. And I'd be grateful if you didn't mention this to anyone else. I need to attend to my affairs before I'm incapacitated, and I don't want any interference.'

'Angus...' What do you say to a best friend who has just told you that he is almost certainly dying? I'll miss you? Don't go? For God's sake don't leave me?

'Listen, old girl.' He leant across the table and took my hand. 'You don't have to say anything. I can see it on your face. You've been a marvellous friend to me, and that's what matters.'

I wrapped both my hands – cold bony fingers – round his plump white one. 'You too, Angus. Oh, hell.'

To my intense discomfort, hot springs were welling up in my eyes. The last time I'd cried was with rage when my husband Kurt, seventeen years before, had said he had no use for a barren wife.

'No libations, please.' Angus disengaged his hand from my bone trap and fished out a handkerchief ironed in sharp creases; the Club prided itself on its laundry. 'I'm conceited enough to have expected some distress, but hoped it would be a hoot of disbelieving laughter.'

I shook my head as I dabbed at my eyes. 'You've always had a warped sense of humour. This is – shit.'

'The same thought has been running through my head in a continuous loop since I heard the fell tidings,' he admitted. 'It's a strange feeling, knowing that you can't buy your way out.'.

His last remark surprised me. I had never thought of him as a man who bought his way out of situations. He had seemed so powerful that problems unknotted themselves and people naturally gave way or bowed down before him.

I tried a probe. 'When did you last have to buy your way out of a situation?'

His answer was a dismissive gesture. He looked tired and haggard that afternoon; assailed by doubt in a way I had not seen before.

'You can't drop hints like that and not explain what you mean.'

Irritated at being quizzed, he said, 'If you must know, two weeks ago. And don't ask me the whys or wherefores. I'm not ready to bare my soul yet.'

'Don't be offensive. I've never made any such demand on you.' I sat back in my chair, fighting anger. The basis of our friendship had been the mutual respect of two people who keep their own counsel, simply enjoying what the other chose to offer and a few laughs together.

'No offence intended. Struck the wrong note there, what?' He had these moods sometimes when he would act like the older Club members, sprinkling 'whats?' at the end of sentences and waffling his chins and pontificating about what the world was coming to, but they never lasted long. He'd suddenly notice what he was saying and break off with a bellow that made his paunch shake all over like the Club's succulent brawn when you cut off a slice.

'Don't try and jolly me either.' I arranged my butter knife in the exact centre of my side plate. It's odd how discord at table seems to engender a need to organise cutlery precisely. 'What are you going to do?'

'Beyond cursing fate and railing at the gods? Go through the motions, of course. Have the operation, endure the chemotherapy and attend to my affairs as well as I can before…' He checked the thought, then said, 'When everything's in order, I'll let the family know.'

My brief surge of importance at being taken into his confidence faded. Of course his ex-wife and children would have prior demands on him. 'Shouldn't you tell them straight away so they can make plans to come out and see you?'

He shrugged. 'All in good time.'

'How long is it since you last saw them?'

That was when I first began to realise how secretive Angus was about the different compartments of his life. He looked down to flick away an imaginary crumb on his lapel. 'Oh, a couple of months ago at Hannah's pottery in Suffolk. I helped her to set it up and I like to check on the investment every now and again.'

We had been lunching together for fifteen years, and he had never mentioned seeing Hannah or his children. I shivered. Angus had deceived me by omission, and now I would lose him even before the death he foresaw, to his unknown and probably grasping family.

I had to put up a fight. I blurted, 'Let me look after you when you need nursing. My time is my own. My work can go on hold.'

His cheeks flushed maroon. 'What an appalling idea. Wouldn't dream of it. There were no strings attached to this relationship at your request, remember?'

'At least let me come and sit with you. That's something friends do.'

'I can pay for nurses.' His eyes were a fathomless blue that day, intensified by his navy blazer and blue Club tie; the lower lids gaped from the weight of the fleshy bags sagging beneath them. Angus was sixty-four, and looked older.

'But you can't pay for friends any more than you can buy your way out of this mess.' I had trapped him in his own logic; a favourite ploy in our verbal skirmishes over the years.

'Touché.' The shadow smile was back. 'You're a bonny opponent in an argument, old girl. I'll miss your debating style in the eternal pit.'

'What do you mean, pit?' Under the circumstances, I didn't make my usual crack about businessmen's perks. If we had been talking about another man's death, I would have said, Surely there's a guaranteed paid-up membership in Club Heaven waiting for him?

'Hell is my undoubted destination.'

Was that curious note in his voice self-pity? I said, 'It's not like you to get melodramatic.'

'I mean it. I've done some bad things and I always knew I'd have to pay for them.'

'What bad things? You're one of this country's foremost businessmen.' My own voice was becoming shrill – a frowned-upon misdemeanour in this male sanctum, even on Saturdays when there were more waiters than members – but I was too upset to care.

'That's not saying much. The concept of honour among thieves is a myth, believe me.'

'You've always seemed the epitome of honour to me.'

He sat looking at me for a long moment, then said, 'I've chosen to show you only my good side because I wanted to keep your friendship.' The folds of flesh under his chin were slack now where they had once been rotund with good living. 'I needed someone to like me. I needed contact with a clean conscience.'

The confession gave me a sickening jolt. I had seen our friendship as something fine and rare, a meeting of true minds above the mundane affairs of the world. Now he was telling me that he had cultivated me for selfish reasons: to have his ego stroked by a woman who was naive enough to be flattered by his attention and occasional favours, probably paid for out of company funds. I had given him fifteen years of Saturdays in return for a mess of free lunches.

I'd been well and truly had. Laughter came hissing like caustic soda when you pour boiling water over it. I laughed and laughed as he sat looking at me and the waiters stood looking at me and the sun twinkled on the table silver. Then I wiped away my tears with his now-crumpled handkerchief and handed it back to him before reaching for my bag. 'You really had me fooled, Angus. I believed in this friendship.'

His voice was steady. 'So have I.'

'But you've just said…'

'I was trying to be honest about my initial motives for inveigling you to lunch on Saturdays. When you're staring the Grim Reaper in the face, an honest reckoning with those you care for is imperative. And I have come to care for you very much, Faith. I value our friendship. I'd be honoured if you came and sat with me as my sun sinks slowly in the west.'

It was typical of him to temper serious sentiments with a joke – part of his genius for manipulating the people around him, I realise now. But it's unimportant when set against what he gave me. He may have taken but he also gave, and I suppose that is the true nature of friendship: that it be mutually pleasing and rewarding.

A two-way trade.

18

Of course I relented and stayed for the Club trifle and coffee in the library afterwards. And we talked until the sun and the pavement vendors had both gone and the entrance hall was as cold and still as a marble tomb.

3

*H*e spent ten days in a private ward at the Kenridge Hospital where I was allowed brief visits. And even that was a major concession; he hated people seeing him at a disadvantage and would not let anyone from the firm or the Club come near him, though they sent banks of expensive flowers.

For the first week he lay grey and deflated with drips in both arms, though he began to brighten after the drips came out. When he was moved to the oncology centre for his initial course of chemotherapy, I too was banned.

'Got to face this lot on my own,' he growled. 'No spectators.'

'If you let me come, I promise to look the other way.'

'No. Mind's made up. I'll call you when I'm fit to be with again.'

It was no use pleading. He was adamant and I had to settle for bulletins from his doctor's receptionist. Then he left the oncology centre and disappeared.

I called his office after I had heard nothing for over a week. His secretary Prunella (well-named; she was fifty-something with a mouth and a temperament like a dried prune and raven hair courtesy of Clairol) said he was out of town, adding, 'And don't ask me where he's gone to, Mizz Dobermann. I'm not permitted to say.'

It was a minor coup for her in our on-going hostilities. She prided herself on organising his business affairs with robot efficiency; she wore office suits whose cut and trim and padded shoulders were in slavish accord with the prevailing word on power dressing. When she hinted during our first contact by phone that I was just one of many status-seeking bimbos who had pestered him since his divorce, I told her that being paid to skivvy for him at work didn't give her any rights over his private life.

'But I don't even know you,' she bleated.

'I am his friend.'

20

'Not…?' Her voice was pregnant with conjecture.

'Just plain friend.'

I don't think she believed me. Generally I won our verbal clashes on the phone and she won on points when he had gone away leaving instructions that he was not to be contacted. There were a lot of times like that. Angus had perfected the art of disappearing for a week or two, then slotting back into his life as if nothing had happened, without a word about where he'd gone or what he'd been doing.

Two days later he phoned to ask me to lunch, unusually on a Friday. When he shuffled forward to meet me in the entrance hall of the Club using a walking stick, his face drawn and his already sparse grey curls thinned to spider silk, I was appalled by the change.

He tried to make a joke of it. 'No oil painting, eh? You'll have to help me into my seat too.'

'Angus, you're…'

'Cut the cackle, old girl. Let's get there first.'

Our halting progress through the dining room was silent except for subdued greetings from other members whose heads turned to follow us. Men, I was learning, did not discuss their ailments with each other and saw illness as a sign of embarrassing weakness.

When I had settled him at last in his chair at the table in the bay window and sat down myself, he sighed, 'I feel bloody awful. That's the longest walk I've had since they let me up.'

'Was the chemotherapy bad?'

'Worse. Foul and hideous. Now I've plumbed the heaving depths of nausea, I'm not sure I can take any more.'

'You can't mean that.' I sat down facing him, squaring up for battle. 'Why didn't you let me know where you were?'

'Didn't want anyone to see me laid out like a harpooned whale.' He turned to hang his walking stick on the back of his chair, moving gingerly. It was heartbreaking to see that urgent man slowed by illness.

I said in a sharper voice than I intended, 'Surely vanity is the least of your worries now?'

'Vomiting isn't. Most undignified bloody activity known to man. Makes you pong like the lavatories in a cheap pub.'

As he looked up to give his order to the waiter, I saw that his waistcoat was gaping. Angus was losing weight, eating titbits and bread crusts like a scavenging street pigeon instead of going through the menu as was his habit. He made up for it, though, by demolishing a bottle of 1984 Kanonkop Cabernet Sauvignon while I sipped my usual glass of riesling.

21

After lunch I helped him up to his rooms and bullied him until he took off his jacket and tie and shoes and got on to his bed. Pulling up the folded eiderdown to cover him, I said, 'Have a rest while I sit here to keep you company.'

'Go away. Don't need company.'

'I think you do.'

'Interfering women. Always think they know best.' He lay on his back, glaring up at me.

'When it comes to illness, we do.'

I ignored his answering growl and went next door and brought back the seat he used at his desk, an old dining chair with a curved backrest and a worn black leather-and-horsehair seat. Though I live with the starkest of modern furniture, I am powerfully attracted to old chairs dented by generations of behinds; that sag in the middle tells of family continuity and long convivial meals, home comforts I never had.

'This isn't necessary,' he kept repeating. 'For God's sake, Faith, it's not necessary to hang around. I can handle this bloody business on my own.'

'You'll handle it better with a friend to lean on.'

'Never leant on anyone in my life, and I'm not going to start now.' Thinning curls limp with sweat, his head moved about on the pillow seeking a comfortable position. His cheeks had a wine glow deepened to crimson with the effort of coming upstairs.

'What, never?' One of my father's old jokes.

He gave me a half-smile. 'Well, hardly ever.'

'So I don't have to teach you how?'

It was another probe. Ever since he had told me about his cancer, Angus had been dropping hints like this as though he wanted me to follow them up. Hints about the aspects of his life he had never mentioned and I had been careful never to ask about: his childhood and growing up, his family, his career, his social network.

How can you have a fifteen-year friendship and not discuss any of these things? Easily. You talk about books and films and plays and the critics who savage them in the press, seeming unable to confess pure enjoyment. You discuss business and politics and world affairs, and gossip about leaders' indiscretions. You pull arguments to pieces and reshape them. You barter words and ideas and jokes back and forth. You eat and drink and talk and talk, and the waiters lean against the walls and the coffee dregs grow cold leaving beige tidemarks on the Club's crested porcelain cups.

'My mother taught me that adults know best.' His voice was slowing. 'She was half wrong, of course. Fathers are notoriously deficient. I'm the living proof.'

'Surely…'

'Oh, I looked after my lot financially: a comfortable home and trust funds when the children turned twenty-one. I taught them to believe in my motto: Never fear, Quain is here. But I wasn't there physically. Hannah had … Hannah had to…' He began mumbling and fell asleep before I could probe any further.

When his lips started plopping with each exhaled breath, I got up and prowled. I'd sometimes been asked up to his sitting room next door for coffee or brandy after a lunch that had stretched into the late afternoon, but the parameters of our friendship had excluded his bedroom. Now, encouraged by his breaches of the unwritten rules, I felt I could at least look at the things he lived with.

The decorator had striven hard to live up to the Club's exacting standard of male comfort zones. The huge mahogany bed had a matching wardrobe with bevelled mirrors, and there were Persian carpets, a dumb valet, a military chest and oil paintings similar to those in the sitting room – done by a protégé, perhaps? Angus was often photographed with groups of socialites at art exhibitions and charity first nights, and he was a generous patron of young artists.

I had expected a grand bedroom in keeping with this public style, but long occupation had worn the grandeur to the mellow ambience of an old tobacconist's. Angus's aura of sandalwood and cigars and venerable leather came from his lair, I now realised. As do most people who live alone, he had developed his own scent like a hibernating bear.

The details reminded me of my father when he grew old: a spotted silk dressing gown hung on the back of the door; a row of pigeonholes for paired shoes, each with its wooden tree; a rack of ties in the darkly rich designs that complement bespoke suits; cufflinks in a silver tray flanked by a pair of tortoiseshell hair brushes. There was a tall bookshelf near the window where Kipling jostled with Galsworthy, O Henry, PG Wodehouse, Damon Runyon, Alastair Maclean, Dick Francis, John Le Carré and other classic thriller writers.

I left the framed photographs on the military chest till last, then picked them up one by one. First a big woman in a messy striped apron, clay-covered hands on her hips, bird's nest hair scooped back and tied with a bandana, confident smile for the camera; this must be Hannah. The next ones were of three children at various stages: wispy blond toddlers; a boy on a bicycle and later in a cricket team photo; two girls in school uniform and as teenagers. The sepia photo next to them must have been the mother Angus had mentioned: a grim woman in a pre-war nursing sister's uniform with his wiry black eyebrows meeting in the middle under a veil tied low across her forehead.

The last photo was a surprise: a posed studio shot of an elderly coloured woman with a child on her lap – his nanny, perhaps? One of the few facts I knew about his early life, because it was usually mentioned in interviews, was that he had been born in the Cape.

Hanging on the wall behind the family photographs were his corporate trophies: framed certificates and press photos of him giving speeches and receiving awards and sitting amid phalanxes of business executives wearing expressions that announced their conviction that huge profits would be achieved in the next financial year – due entirely to their extraordinary acumen, industry and foresight.

I was moving from one to the other, marvelling at all the level stares and firm jaws, when there was a tap at the open door. Turning towards it, I whispered, 'Come in.'

'Madam, excuse, please?' It was Boniface, the Club's senior manservant who looked after Angus's needs. A fervent Catholic, Boniface stalked the tall passages looking as dignified as the Pope in his starched white suit and red cummerbund, and ruled the service staff with a rod of iron.

I put my finger over my lips. 'Shhh, he's sleeping. You know he's ill, Boniface?'

The close-cropped head gave a lugubrious nod. 'I make the prayers for Mr Quain every day. He is a great man.'

Was he a great man? He'd made more than one comment about bad things he had done. But I agreed and went on, 'He doesn't need anything at the moment, thanks. I'll ring down for tea when he wakes.'

'You look after Mr Quain very nice. I am thankful, Madam.' Nobody could be more gravely complimentary than Boniface. 'But no, it is not why I come. There are some visitors downstairs to see him.'

'He can't see anyone now.'

'They say they will wait. It is an important matter.'

'Would it help if I came down and saw them?'

'I think not, Madam. They say they must see Mr Quain, urgent. I will serve them tea in the visitors' lounge until he wakes up.' As befits a relic of the British Empire, the Club only served coffee after meals though tea could be ordered at any hour.

'It may be a long time.' Who were they? Had word of his illness got around already?

'They say they will wait, Madam.' Boniface turned and squealed away in his impeccable white tennis shoes.

As he closed the door of the sitting room with a click, I heard Angus mutter, 'Bloody vultures gathering already.'

I went towards him saying, 'You're not in a fit state to see anyone. Let me go down and send them away.'

'Not necessary. I'll be fine in a moment.' He rolled on to his side and began to push himself up, looking flushed and rumpled and breathing hard. When I moved to help him, he said crossly, 'Get away, woman. I can manage. There's life in the old dog yet.'

I stood my ground. 'The old dog has a stiff neck.'

'He's also used to his privacy.' Angus's feet in their navy socks landed on two worn places in the Persian rug beside his bed. 'Would you kindly leave the room while I change?'

'Do you have to? Why don't you just…'

When he roared, I jumped; it was so unexpected. 'Will – you – get – the – fuck – out – of – here! I can't stand clucking women. Why do you think I live alone?'

Furious, I snarled, 'Because nobody would put up with you.'

'Get!' He flung his arm out.

'Keep your hair on. I'm going.'

I stomped out and stood raging next door. I'd never realised that my suave lunch companion was a misogynist. I'd imagined that after his divorce, he had either not found the right person to marry or become so caught up in his complicated business affairs and so comfortable at the Club that he had not felt the need of a wife. So where did this leave me? Making a fool of myself, blundering into his private life in the belief that I could offer a lonely dying man my support. St Faith the Gracious to the rescue. What a joke.

I picked up my bag and was on my way out when he grumbled from the interleading doorway, 'Where are you going?'

'I'm getting the fuck out, as requested.' I kept walking.

'You know I only meant out of the bedroom while I got changed. Please don't go. Sorry. Lost my rag.'

The Grand Panjandrum apologising? Wonders would never cease. Slowing down but still with my back turned, I parried with, 'I'm not used to being sworn at.'

'Don't be mad, old girl. I plead extreme provocation.'

This was a definite climb-down. I relented and turned to face him. 'You know I only meant to be helpful.'

He had changed into an unfamiliar checked shirt and comfortable trousers and slippers, and stood in the doorway leaning on his stick. 'I know. It's just that my mother used that excuse to try and organise every aspect of my life. She nagged at me day and bloody night after my father pushed off with a floozy, so I wouldn't be like him when I grew up. Made me allergic to being bossed around. I swore when I was sixteen that I would be my own man one day so nobody else could tell me what to do, and I'm not going to capitulate now.'

I thought of the grim-faced nursing sister in the photograph – an abandoned wife struggling to bring up her son and determined that he would have a better future – and of the fatherless boy trying to cope with an angry rejected mother. It was a common experience for broken families, yet it drove some to drink and drugs and others, like Angus, to achieve conspicuous success. Why do similar circumstances have such different results? Is that why the cancer doctors were being

so cagey about his prognosis? I thought, There are advantages in having a difficult childhood. It can steel as well as damage.

But I said only, 'You've never told me any of this.'

'I've never wanted to. It's too raw. My mother still haunts my dreams thirty years
after the stroke that killed her.'

There was a discrepancy too. 'I thought you told me that your father died of
mice in the basement. How could you know that if he ran away with a floozy?'

'Doubting my word, eh?' There was no mirth in his smile. 'Because the old man
reappeared when I got successful. Saw my name in the papers and came sniffing
round my office week after week asking for handouts. He had a prodigious
cheek matched only by his thirst; he was a hopeless drunk by then. Eventually I
had to put him away in a private clinic. Couldn't have my reputation sullied by
an alcoholic paterfamilias intent on squandering my hard-earned money on
rotgut brandy.'

High dudgeon hasn't a snowball's chance against curiosity. I said, 'Does this
qualify as one of the bad things you were talking about?'

'Among many. He died a few years later, in a lot of noisy pain because they
wouldn't let him have the brandy he asked for, so he pushed away their morphine.
I try not to think about it.' Angus started to shuffle towards his favourite club
easy chair. 'Mind if I sit down? Get tired if I stand around.'

He had pulled out all the stops and skilfully charmed back my sympathy. So
I dumped my bag and rang the bell for tea, which we sat drinking in silence.

I was thinking that we would have to examine the terms of our changing friendship; it would falter if we kept misunderstanding each other like this.

He must have been thinking something similar, because he was saying, 'You
have to understand, Faith, that it takes a while to adjust to the idea that one's life
is basically beyond one's control. I always believed…' when there was a knock at
the door.

4

*A*ngus called out, 'Come in.'

Boniface ushered in a large tweedy man followed by an Al Pacino clone, closing the door behind them with a louder click than usual, his way of indicating that they could be trouble. He was adept at the subtle hint and the art of showing wordless affront, as black servants have always had to be.

Angus said, 'Well, I'm blowed. Jumbo and Hugh.'

He began to struggle upwards but the large one blustered forward with his hand out saying, 'Don't get up, Gus, old man. How are you?'

The visitor had broken veins in his cheeks and big yellow teeth and the battered ears of a former lock forward, lumpy with scar tissue. The look on his face said that he had heard a rumour of cancer, which meant it would be all over town by Monday morning. I thought, Gus? That's a new one on me.

'Cat out of the bag already?' Angus looked annoyed. 'In that case, I can tell you I'm feeling bloody awful.'

'Bad luck. I'm sorry.' The Al Pacino clone could have been a gambler: slick dark hair, black trench coat, gold watch strap, noncommittal eyes.

'Needn't be. Quacks are optimistic they've caught it in time. I'm down but far from out yet.'

Were the doctors spinning him a line when they told him that? I wondered. In my limited experience as a patient, you can't trust doctors to level with you. If they can bullshit you into believing the situation isn't as bad as you fear, they will, aided and abetted by grovelling nurses who are supposed to be on your side. I'd love to know where doctors and business executives get the idea that they're superior to the rest of humanity. It must be infectious, as they all seem to catch it eventually.

The large man rumbled, 'Glad to hear that, Gus.'

'Yes, indeed,' the gambler echoed.

Angus flapped his hand. 'Stop hovering like constipated fish eagles and sit down, won't you? Faith will ring for more tea.'

For an instant I felt like a wife: 'Faith will...' instead of, 'Faith, would you please...?' I didn't like it, for all its implied cosiness. I said, 'They're probably awash with tea, if I know Boniface. Wouldn't whisky be more appropriate?'

The look of relief on both visiting faces was instantaneous.

'Very well, we'll make it whisky. Soda and ice?' He raised his black eyebrows at the visitors, who nodded, then turned back to me. 'Better ask for a bottle.'

Nettled at his abruptness, I said, 'You haven't introduced your friends yet.'

'Friends?' His laugh was half snort. 'Wouldn't go as far as that. These are two of my colleagues on the Business Initiative board: Walter Urquhart, the travel agency chief – commonly known as Jumbo – and Hugh Softley, who is a financial wizard. Gentlemen, Faith Dobermann.'

We exchanged handshakes and I went to the desk to phone down to the bar. Hugh took off his trench coat, laid it with care over the arm of the sofa and sat down next to Jumbo.

Settling back into my usual chair I thought, They look as though they're sitting on cactuses. And said, 'Would you like me to go, Angus? The worst of the rush-hour traffic should be over.'

He gave me one of his considering looks, then said, 'No, stay. We'll order some wine too.'

'I'd rather join you in a whisky.'

He nodded. 'I'd like that.' When I glanced sideways, I caught the visitors looking at each other in dismay.

Small talk filled in the wait for Boniface to appear with the whisky. Jumbo had recently taken a group of corporate clients golfing in Spain and Scotland. Hugh, accompanied by his wife and daughter, had just returned from a business trip to Taiwan, Singapore and Australia which had included a week at a famous hotel resort on the Great Barrier Reef. It was clear that both travelled widely and often – first class, of course. Ordinary mortals like me who have to travel steerage, packed in like sardines, could only listen and envy.

When Boniface knocked at last and stalked in bearing a bottle of J & B in the middle of a loaded silver tray, Angus looked relieved and said, 'Thanks, Bonny. Put it down on the table here. I'll pour.'

'Are you sure, Mr Quain?' Disapproval etched deeper lines on the severe dark face. 'You are not well, sir.'

Angus's chins did a shimmy as he barked, 'I'm well enough! Don't you start trying to mother-hen me too.'

'Oh no, no, sir.' Boniface put the tray down in front of Angus and went out again looking pained.

'You live in a place more than a few years, they begin to think they bloody own you.' Angus poured us each a whisky and soda with a neat double tot on the rocks for himself, then sat back in his chair. 'Nectar of the gods, what?'

'Great stuff,' Hugh agreed.

Jumbo harrumphed into his crystal tumbler. 'Whisky and golf, both great stuff.'

'But I vote trout-fishing a close third.' Softley.

'No argument there. Been to Millstream recently?'

'Last month. And you?'

'Couldn't. Had to trot a visiting VIP out to Mala-Mala for a few days before returning with him to London.'

'Coincidental with the second Test at Lord's?'

Jumbo exposed his tusks. 'Pure coincidence. Only just remembered to pack my MCC tie at the last minute.'

Angus cut into their one-upmanship ritual with, 'I find it ironic that you dour Scots, Jumbo, should have invented two of life's greatest pleasures. I'd have expected you to stick to haggis making and tartan weaving in that foul climate.'

'Why?' After my years as his arguing partner, I couldn't help rising to the bait. 'Scots are far too ingenious to stick to such boring occupations. Look how many Scottish engineers there are, for example. They emigrated all over the world and took their favourite pastimes with them. That's…'

I stopped. The visitors' faces had swivelled towards me and I knew that look: women were supposed to be decorative, it said, not have opinions or butt in on important male conversations.

Angus murmured, 'You're right as usual, Faith. I defer to your hypothesis.'

The faces turned back to Angus with identical pitying expressions for the sick man who was already having to abdicate some of his autonomy. Poor bugger's as good as finished already, I could see them thinking. In which I knew they were making a grave mistake.

Jumbo harrumphed again and began turning his glass round and round in awkward fingers. 'We – er – we…'

'Another drap, Jumbo?'

'No thanks.' He gave me a significant look, then said, 'We've come on confidential business, old man.'

Angus treated them to the full card-sharp's smile. 'You can speak in front of Faith. We've been friends for many years. I trust her discretion.'

'Oh. Well. I see.' Jumbo took a noisy gulp that emptied his glass. 'In the matter of that – er – financial undertaking we agreed on, could we expect a resolution in the near future?'

'Specifically by the middle of next week,' Hugh put in.

'Which undertaking was this? I'm involved in a number of negotiations at the moment, as you can imagine. Affairs to settle and all that.'

'The – er – initiative we discussed over our lunch at the Country Club a month ago. Remember?'

'Amalgamated Couplings,' Hugh prompted.

'You said, "Give me twelve mill and I'll guarantee you a rise of twenty rands at least." This was a month ago and we're getting a wee bit concerned about delivery.' Jumbo's glass was covered with large damp fingerprints.

'More than a wee bit, if you must know.' Hugh ran a hand over his slick hair. 'The futures close-out is only a few weeks off.'

'I used that vulgar word mill? Surely not.' I'd never seen Angus in such a playfully sarcastic mood.

'Maybe it wasn't mill. What does it matter? We're worried about delivery, Gus. There's a lot riding on this arrangement.' Jumbo was beginning to look desperate at having to think up new synonyms.

'Money markets drying up? Overdrafts shrinking in the wash?' Ice cubes jangled as Angus swirled the whisky in his glass. 'You must keep the faith, gentlemen. If I say I'll do something, I do it, but in my own good time. I have been somewhat preoccupied these past few weeks.'

Jumbo blurted, 'That's exactly what's worrying us. Can you still deliver?'

Angus's mirth vanished. 'For Christ's sake, I'm not six feet under yet. Of course I can deliver. Have I ever broken any of my promises?'

'There's always a first time.' Hugh's gambler's eyes left his face and moved down towards his slippers, sign of an ill man who has begun to care less about his appearance.

Angus slammed his glass down on the tray and lunged forward. 'You fucking little worm! I've a good mind to leave you wriggling on the hook.'

'And break one of your sacred promises?'

Transfixed, I watched Angus's face go brick red and the two visitors rise to their feet as if pulled up by invisible strings. It was Jumbo dropping his glass that broke the tense silence; it bounced on the carpet and smashed into crystal fragments against the desk.

'Get out!' Angus roared. 'And don't come near me again. I'll do what I undertook to do, but I'd advise you to keep away from me and your bloody quacking mouths shut. Do you hear?'

'Yes. Thanks. And sorry, eh? About the glass. About – everything.' Jumbo bared his tusks again and lumbered for the door.

Hugh Softley said, enunciating each word, 'I hope you don't end up rotting in hell, Quain, but it's a distinct possibility.' He picked up his raincoat, gave me an ironic bow and left, closing the door with a precise click behind him.

'And so you get to meet some of my less reputable colleagues.' Angus sat back in his chair trying to calm his breathing. 'The sour cream of the Joburg business community.'

'I suppose I shouldn't ask what you're up to with them?'

His answer shook with a vengeful need to let off steam. 'You shouldn't, but I'll tell you. Why not? Strictly off the record, agreed?'

I nodded, and he reached for the bottle of J & B to pour himself another double tot.

'It's quite simple. Those two unmitigated shits – no other word for them – own large blocks of shares in Amalgamated Couplings. They lend twelve million to a nominee shareholding company which I control, to purchase more Amalgamated Couplings shares. The sudden spurt of interest plus the imminent futures close-out pushes up the price so they can sell theirs at a profit. Then I trickle off those bought with the twelve million, pay the capital sum back and pocket the difference.'

'Isn't that illegal?'

He shrugged. 'It's a common enough practice and difficult to prove because nominee companies are allowed by law to keep their identities secret. Did you know that more than twenty percent of the shares on the Johannesburg Stock Exchange – worth nearly 200 billion rands – are held by just four nominees? Four. This means there are hundreds of South African companies whose managements are not able to establish who owns large chunks of their shares. In consequence, there are good pickings to be had by investors with flexible principles.'

I sat looking at the acknowledged doyen of the accounting profession. My friend King Quain, manipulator of share prices.

'You seem surprised?' He wore a sardonic half-smile.

'I'm appalled. Morality apart, you're saying that one fifth of our country's industry is owned by nameless rich men?'

The smile broadened. 'And I'm one of them. Though not in the billionaire class, I hasten to add.'

What did he do with it all? Stunned by the revelation but keen to know more, I dredged up my researcher's voice and said, 'How did you get involved with those two?'

'When Softley came up to me at a party and said of a company in which I had a large interest, "You need to do something about the share price." His meaning was unmistakable and I wasn't averse. Creative dealing is an irresistible temptation, and of course it snowballs. Always told you I wasn't a saint.'

'You didn't tell me you were a crook.'

'Call that crooked?' He let out an amused rumble. 'My dear innocent Faith, don't you know about the chancers who rise to the top in the business world? Ambitious executives with no scruples are like politicians: first they get power hungry, then they get money hungry. It's the virus of entitlement that seems to infect everyone in this self-centred age of ours. With millions passing through their hands, they begin to think they're entitled to a percentage. And if they increase profits and get the share price moving nicely upwards, nobody questions them about how it's done. It's results that count.'

'What about the workers? To coin a phrase.'

'Use your logic. Workers are the diligent bees of our society whose labour is wasted without direction. The less ethical executive sees himself as the mastermind who creates the beehive and keeps it humming; therefore he deserves a proportion of the resulting honey, which he doesn't hesitate to extract. Sometimes at the expense of profits and even wages.'

'Surely the unions keep an eye on fair pay for...'

'You're not listening to me. Masterminds operate at far more elevated levels than wage negotiations. And fairness is a wonderful principle, as is affirmative action, but neither is realistic. To quote the *Sunday Times*: "Affirmative action might make you feel good but results are what create wealth." That's the bottom line. Results generate the conditions that make life easier for everyone. Fair pay is pie in the sky.'

I studied my empty glass. 'That's not what I'm trying to say.'

He forged on with his argument, ignoring me. 'The concept of fairness is socialism's big flaw. If people would only accept inequality as a fact of life, they could focus their efforts on improving their lot so as to get ahead of everyone else. That's how I succeeded: by hard, unremitting work.'

It was a standard Angus speech and he was getting off the point; I wanted to know more about the shadowy masterminds. I said, 'You talk about the chancers. Who are they? And how do they operate without getting caught?'

'Control is all.' His hand moved to grip the arm of his chair. 'If you will permit a change of metaphor, the man with control over the financial tiller is admiral of all he surveys. Here's another statistic: more than a quarter of the directors of the Top 100 companies on the Johannesburg Stock Exchange are chartered accountants. Money men. In today's business world, short-term profits are the thing; loyalty and the concept of companies as providers of jobs for life are out. Forget about skills and long-term training. If there's a downturn, middle managers can be retrenched and workers fired. And if the admiral doesn't get enough of the honey he feels he deserves, he hoists anchor and sails on to a more lucrative position.'

'You make it sound so cynical.'

'It often is. Though I have to add that the vast majority of our business leaders are veritable pillars of the community: defenders of the capitalist faith who are consulted by government, fêted by the media, held up by society as role models, envied by all. Which lofty position provides, of course, all the honey they feel they deserve: stock options, posh executive cars, first class travel, company flats, club memberships, gourmet restaurants and fancy wines. All justified as oiling the wheels of commerce, though the rare ascetics in this town do twice the amount of business for a fraction of the cost.'

'You're not doing too badly yourself when it comes to honey.'

The teasing interjection was rewarded by a black frown. 'I earned every last drop by working harder than most. Damned hard.'

I thought, A lot of people work damned hard and don't get rewarded at all.

'Spit it out,' he challenged. 'I know that look.'

I said, 'Why is the honey harvest only enjoyed by those at the top? Surely there's enough to spread around more evenly.'

'Because those at the top have to take the risks, so they deserve the...'

'Using other people's money? That's not what I call a risk.'

'They put their reputations on the line every time a decision is made,' he insisted, growing pompous. 'In law, a company director can be jailed for a wrong decision made by an employee, because he is the responsible person in charge. Running a company takes its toll in executive stress.'

'Stress happens at all levels, not only at the top.'

Now the smile was pitying. 'Be realistic, old girl. You can't compare the enormous burden an MD has to carry with the petty problems of his staff.'

'Petty problems?' I was getting angry. 'They're not petty to the people struggling with them. What about all the lowly managers and filing clerks who are battling to pay off their bonds and lucky if they can take their families out to a Spur Steak Ranch once a month? Why don't they get any honey?'

'Come, come. You're being naive. That's not how the system works. You can't equate worker bees with queens.'

'It's a lousy system, then.'

He shrugged. 'It's a human system, full of flaws but operating well enough to keep the wheels of industry turning. Executives are well paid because the good ones are few and far between. It's a simple case of demand outstripping supply.'

'But can't you see...' How could I get through the barrier of his smug righteousness? 'Can't you see that what upsets ordinary working people is the obscene discrepancy between the pittance they're paid for blood, sweat and tears and the six-figure annual salary a top executive creams off for sitting behind his desk all day in an air-conditioned office? Not to mention the honey harvest and what they make on the side with their stock options.'

He chuckled. 'There've always been lords and peasants. The only thing that's changed is that peasants like me can climb the ladders on the castle walls now if they're ambitious and work hard enough.' He indicated my empty glass. 'Have another? We haven't nearly plumbed this subject yet.'

'No, thanks. I don't feel like plumbing any deeper. What you're saying is too upsetting.'

'Don't be so prissy. You asked what I'm up to with Jumbo and Softley, and I'm telling you. This is how life is at the top. Cream and honey, not always honestly come by. As Shakespeare put it: "We few, we happy few, we band of brothers".'

He reached for the bottle of J & B to pour himself another double tot, added several ice cubes and leaned back to take a contemplative sip.

It's hard to explain how extraordinary these revelations were. Throughout our long friendship, Angus had been tight-lipped about his business affairs and I had never questioned him, respecting the taboo. Now he was telling me that he and his colleagues sometimes indulged in fraudulent transactions and that the whole system may be flawed, but it worked. And quoting Shakespeare to bolster his argument.

I said, 'This is the first time I've heard you expound on the iniquities of your profession.'

He gave a sarcastic snort. 'Those are just the peccadilloes. The iniquities begin with greed. What a greedy man has is never enough; he always wants more. Having achieved the first million, he wants a second, then a third, then five, then ten. When you get a really greedy bastard running a company, he milks it from every orifice.'

'But aren't the company's auditors supposed to pick up discrepancies? There are strict legal requirements, I know.' I wanted to show him that I wasn't ignorant in financial matters, but all I got was a look that would have blistered paint.

'Auditors are paid by the companies they audit, which doesn't encourage whistle-blowing. On the contrary, we acquire useful knowledge of the companies' cash-generating capabilities on the one hand and cover-ups on the other. Play our cards right, and a grateful client rewards us – if not in cash or kind, then in more business steered our way.'

'Are you saying that all auditors do this?' By now I was so aghast that I would have believed anything.

He let out a rich guffaw. 'God, no. Didn't mean to give you that idea. The accounting profession sees itself as a model of rectitude, bound by a set of gilt-edged rules. But there are too many elective accounting practices which have left windows of opportunity for the unscrupulous. Even I'm surprised at the number of colleagues who've confessed to making accommodations.'

'Is that what fiddling the books is called now? "Making accommodations"?'

Again he shrugged. 'The rearrangement of figures is only the final lick of paint on a whole can of worms. The methods used to conduct all the schemes and fiddles in this town are as varied as they're ingenious. You know about the foreign exchange scams, I suppose? Round-tripping and over-invoicing?'

'A little. People let things out at parties when they've had too much to drink.'

'Bloody fools. A zipped-up mouth is rule number one for the successful fiddler, but secrecy too often succumbs to the need to impress. Get-rich-quick men enjoy boasting about their acquisitions. Each new toy, each company takeover or block of shares, each simpering beauty queen bought with thirty pieces of jewellery represents another notch on the stick. Or should I say prick?' He spoke the last word with savage mockery.

'Are you trying to impress me, Angus? If so, I have to tell you it's not working.'

His black frown descended. 'Balls to that. One of the reasons I'm taking you into my confidence, as I've explained before, is to make a clean breast of things before I shuffle off. And don't get on your high horse again about being used, because the other reason is that I wish to provide you with useful tips on how to survive financially when I'm gone. You're too unworldly.'

'Oh, rubbish. I'm a historian, remember? My forte is analysing trends and teasing out hidden motives. It's part of my job to find out what makes people tick.' I was annoyed at his condescension.

'You sit there in your ivory tower and think you can figure out what makes people tick?' His face, which in the way of once-overweight older men was like a peach wrinkled from being left in the sun too long, began to redden again. 'Forget it, my dear. You need to get your hands dirty, to start on a factory floor or greasing engines or down a mine, so you can understand the power of envy before you forge your way up through hard work and sweat and discipline to a place where you can get those hands on to the sources of commercial power. The drive to acquire money isn't only the prerogative of the greedy. It can be a positive force which will enhance your life if you learn how to channel it properly.'

'Did you start on a factory floor?' It would explain a lot about him. Though he enjoyed his club life and looked every inch the part, Angus had never claimed to be a gentleman.

He nodded. 'Tell you about it one day.'

'Why not now, seeing you're in a confessional mood?'

'Because I'm trying to open your eyes to the way business is done and how the crafty businessman scores: he uses his expertise to enrich himself along with the company. He keeps his ear tuned for rumours of takeovers and deals, employing confidential information to his own benefit. He puts some assets into his wife's name and spins off a bevy of trusts and closed corporations for the rest that he doesn't want her to know about. He encourages friends and relatives to set up companies in a complementary field, then supplies them with information that enables them to bid successfully on contracts, some of whose profits find their way into yet more secret accounts. He practises insider trading with the infinite care he takes when practising safe sex with the high-class call girls he is offered by people who want to impress him. This is known in less elevated circles as setting up a *pomp*, and it's highly effective with older men whose enlarged prostates demand more skill in sexual encounters than the aging lady wife at home can usually muster.'

From the derisive curl of his mouth I guessed that he had been offered *pomps* and wondered whether he had accepted them. Sex was a subject we had avoided; greeting each other with a peck on the cheek was as far as our physical contact went. I had sometimes wondered what he did about sex after Hannah left, then pushed the thought away as an intrusion on friendship.

Now I pushed it away again. 'To go back to your deal with Jumbo and Hugh: aren't the Stock Exchange computers programmed to pick up insider trading?'

'What if they are? There hasn't been a conviction yet.' Angus was on a high now. I sat marvelling as he thundered on. 'The law isn't enforced because the authorities lack the sophisticated manpower to track down offenders. Criminal scams can run for years before they're detected: cases where computers are used to shave small amounts off money transactions and siphon them into private bank accounts; where bogus employees inflate wage bills; where goods are whisked out through security gates as guards look the other way.'

'Commonly known as shrinkage.'

'That's it. The old and ancient game of stealing from the company. And it's vastly profitable. I happen to know that the shrinkage figure for last year for just one of the big local banks was R247 million.'

'What? I don't believe it.'

'You'd better because bank clients end up paying, and that means you. I should add that a fair percentage of that shrinkage figure was paid out to the safe deposit clients of a down-town Joburg branch whose stashes of Kruger rands had been replaced with lead washers by persons unknown. They were the lucky ones who could prove with specific receipts exactly what was in their safe deposit boxes. The unlucky ones got nothing: no proof, no payout. To avoid future mishaps, the bank in question replaced every person in that branch within twenty-four hours.'

'I had no idea.' What a soap bubble I had been living in, believing that people were basically honest. 'But why doesn't the public hear about these things?'

'When dirty tricks are discovered, nine times out of ten the companies involved won't prosecute because they're either too embarrassed to admit they've been defrauded, or afraid that disclosure in court will give people ideas and lead to copycat crimes. Big business has a goodly share of rotten apples and it's a world phenomenon not confined to Joburg – or business. Civil services are even more notorious for bureaucrats with sticky fingers.'

I murmured, 'Who was it who talked about the ugly face of capitalism?'

'It was the unpleasant and unacceptable face: Edward Heath's description of the Lonrho deal back in the seventies. But I don't think the blame should be laid at the door of capitalism. The saintly Gandhi himself said: "Capital as such is not evil; it is its wrong use that is evil." That's exactly the point. Money isn't the culprit – greed is. It's a human failing exacerbated by today's rampant selfishness.'

'And you're trying to tell me that hard-earned money like yours is different?' I didn't try to hide the sarcasm.

He sighed, shifting in the armchair. 'More honestly come by in the beginning, but I admit the distinction blurs. You have to understand that life can be damn sweet for a big cheese like me with a tame conscience. At the end of our long and lucrative stints in charge, we retire and live happily ever after – at least, for as long as we can keep debility at bay – on healthy fortunes swelled by untaxed capital gains from the stock options we voted ourselves while in office. A good proportion of which fortunes we whisk into the global marketplace to be pumped up by financial experts based in the Bahamas or the Isle of Man, locked into trusts so our kids can inherit without onerous death duties to pay. Which of course perpetuates greed and the culture of entitlement.'

For a moment I didn't know what to say. He looked livid, as though the cancer in his body was flooding it with poison. Then I ventured, 'Are you guilty about the way you've acquired your wealth?'

'The odd twinge. But I only have to remember what it was like to be poor and how bloody hard I've worked to get here, and the feeling soon goes away.'

'Just how many rules have you flouted?'

'No more than others have.'

'You're evading my question.' I felt like an inquisitor: shocked but avid for details.

'Enough to put me in the top bracket,' he admitted. 'You wouldn't believe me if I told you what I was worth.'

'I don't want to know.'

'Ah. You have the English disease: the idea that it's not quite nice to talk about money. Which is bollocks. The subject of money and its acquisition is a conversation-stopper in all languages, at all levels.'

'You mean, greed rules?'

'Not at all. If that's what you think, you've misconstrued what I'm trying to tell you. To acquire money is not dishonourable; most people spend their lives doing just that in order to survive. But like alcohol, money can be a drug that drives addicts into realms where the law and concepts like trust and honour become irrelevant. Look back in history and you'll find that most great fortunes were founded by men who drove hard, often unscrupulous, bargains: pirates and robber barons whose wealth became sanitised by their more law-abiding descendants.

Who could afford to be, of course, because they were already rich.'

'Like you.'

He unleashed the card-sharp's smile again. 'There's no need to sound so bleak. I'm not the devil incarnate, just your average slightly tarnished businessman. And I must point out that you've benefited handsomely from my advance knowledge of share movements.'

I hated that smile; he used it either to mesmerise people or to charm them so he could get something out of them. At that moment, I was damned if I was going to give him the absolution he was trying to wheedle out of me. I said, 'My share portfolio is a fait accompli that I don't feel too comfortable about right now. Though I took your advice in good faith.'

'As it was given. I think you're a valuable person with a solid contribution to make to society, and I want to make sure that you continue to enjoy the financial ease which enables you to go on writing your excellent books. Is that such a bad thing?'

'Does the end justify the means?' I flung back at him past the lump growing in my throat. I seemed to do nothing but argue with Angus now that he was mortally ill. Our friendship was evaporating to bitter dregs as it approached its inevitable end.

'That's another whole debate,' he said with the smile fading to sadness and his now flabby body sinking deeper into the chair with sudden exhaustion.

I got up and took the empty whisky tumbler out of his hand to put on the tray, then knelt down next to him. 'I don't want to go on arguing with you, Angus.'

Heavy eyelids lifted enough for me to see into the enigmatic blue beneath. 'Then listen and learn,' he mumbled. 'I don't have much time left to make amends. Besides sorting you out…'

'What do you mean? I'm perfectly well sorted.'

'No you're not. You're a bright, capable, attractive woman leading a bloody dull life. Got to fix it.'

I was outraged. 'That's rubbish. You hardly know me!'

'Know more than you think.'

'My life is none of your damn business, anyway.'

'Got to fix…' he mumbled '…didn't see it before. Lot more to get off my chest too.'

'I am *not* your confessor.'

'…asking you nicely.' His voice was only just audible. 'Quid pro quo at the pearly gates, what?'

It wasn't like him, to abandon an argument in the middle. He was growing weaker as he grew thinner, and the sight of him slumped in his chair like an old man stilled my turmoil of anger and irritation at his glib assessment. He knew nothing of Faith Dobermann, successful author and academic, beyond what I had chosen to tell him. Our friendship had been a thing apart from our daily lives; a space ship we entered every Saturday to explore new and different regions of the galaxy of ideas. A space ship that very soon, by the look of him, would dock at its last resting place.

I left him sleeping and went downstairs to alert Boniface so there would be someone to help him into bed later. The staff at the Club tended him with devotion during his dying months and being Angus, he made sure that each one received a substantial bequest.

He could well afford it, of course.

5

What a strange mixture Angus was: good and bad in parts, like a company chairman's report that struggles to gloss over deficits with fine words about staff loyalty.

Loyalty was a word we had argued about often. He said it was a dogged, unimaginative quality and usually misplaced. 'Loyal people are boring. Among employees, they're the ones who stick around looking noble as they volunteer for all the dull routine jobs no one else will do. Then they get offended when they're kicked out because they're long past their sell-by date, having not had a new idea in years.'

'How can you say such things about decent people?'

His laugh was caustic. 'Loyalty is using the same brand of marmalade all your life and thinking the Queen of England is doing a damn fine job. Loyalty is sticking to a person or company you've outgrown because it's the easiest option. It's the least of the qualities I need in a person I'm hiring. I look for originality and spunk and a drive to succeed that out-paces mine, not a faithful basset hound with mournful eyes who'll dog my heels in the hopes of a pat on the head for being so honest and true.'

I had to laugh too; he had painted an exact picture of at least three people I knew. 'What about loyalty in an employer or a spouse? Surely that's important? You have to be able to depend on people.'

He thought about it for a while, swivelling the stem of his empty wine glass in his fingers. We were sitting replete after a lunch at which the new assistant Club chef had excelled himself – smoked trout roulade followed by a veal roast stuffed with nuts and dried apricots and served with glazed onions and a delicate winter salad, and had flattened a bottle of honeyed Vin de Constance in tribute. It hadn't been a universal verdict, though: several of the older members had sent their veal back to the kitchen grumbling that fruit didn't go with meat and salad was pansy food and onions disagreed with them and where were the roast potatoes?

The new assistant chef was told at the following management meeting that members expected (and paid for) meat with three veg and gravy, and the meal was not repeated.

Angus said, 'I think strong, flexible leadership backed by a prosperous balance sheet is more important than loyalty in an employer; it'll get you further in life than a dependable but prosaic fellow will. Of course, you need a good, watertight contract too so you can access that balance sheet if you get fired.'

'You haven't answered the bit about a spouse.' I wanted to hear what he would say about Hannah, whom he seldom mentioned, and their failed marriage.

But he evaded my probe with a question. 'You never talk about your ex-husband. Why?'

'He was an overbearing bore – far worse than your basset hound. Can't think why I married him.'

'We take extraordinary decisions sometimes, don't we?'

I was remembering this conversation as I drove home after leaving Angus asleep in his chair. He was thinking the same things about me now: a bore with a bloody dull life. Was it true?

No, dammit! He didn't know me outside the sedate confines of the Club. I worked alone but had plenty of friends – mostly academics. We had parties and braais, played word games, laughed a lot, ate out, went to movies, and had hiked most of the well-known trails. There'd been lovers too, though nobody special enough to want to live with. I was choosy about my companions.

It was a vast improvement on my earlier life as an only child of aging parents. Free of their cluckings at last, I had gone to Wits University to study history then foolishly compromised my new freedom by marrying a complete opposite. Kurt Dobermann was on an extended sabbatical from his German art college, a huge, hairy, noisy painter of swirling abstracts whose massive self-confidence attracted me like a pheromone. He was very conscious of his duty to the family name, however; when we were informed after three years of increasingly desperate lovemaking that I couldn't have children, he divorced me and went back to Germany to find a more fertile mate.

It was a great relief. I had begun to loathe the smell of oils and turpentine he wore like a malodorous aura, and resented being expected to pick up his trail of socks and shirts and underpants and snot-encrusted tissues (he had a sinus problem; par for the course in dry, polluted Johannesburg). His leaving was the only thing we ever agreed on. He liked hot curries and Mexican dishes laced with chillies; I like French cuisine. He could sink tankard after tankard of foaming draught beer and never get drunk; I sip wine and get tiddly after two glasses.

After he left I started to call myself Ms again, though I kept his doggy surname. Both my parents had died by then. With no ties and nothing better to do, I went back to Wits and studied for an MA in history. Thanks to a timely commission from a publisher, I started writing social history books that people seemed to enjoy reading and this pleasant activity became a full-time career. I earned an excellent living working from home and giving occasional lectures, and had enough money to indulge my eccentricities and travel overseas often.

Travel is a passion fed by a profound curiosity as to how people live today as well as yesterday. I have marvelled at god-haunted Jerusalem and the Taj Mahal and Kyoto temples and the busy souks of North Africa; danced with the gypsies in Granada caves and the square-dancers in American country towns; listened to a brass band on Paddington Station and a kilted man playing the bagpipes under the northern lights in Skye; sipped coffee on the Champs Elysées and wine under the gum trees in Australian vineyards and Irish whiskey in Dublin pubs to the music of fiddles and flutes and tapping shoes; cycled through New York's Central Park on a weekend summer morning watching buskers and fire-eaters and mimes and joggers and people making love on blankets under the trees.

It's a good diversion for single people, travel; you're never alone unless you want to be.

The Parktown Edwardian building I lived in was an ornate red-brick edifice with wooden fretwork balconies whose syrupy embrace I tried to neutralise by making my flat on the upper floor as spare as possible: fabrics in minimalist greys and beiges, black leather and chrome chairs, perspex tables, halogen uplighters, modern lithographs and a collection of antique West African carvings. No clutter. No mementos; my travel memories live in my head. I like clean lines and orderliness; things in their places and parameters to live within.

Driving home in the car I thought, Does that sound like a dull life? Perhaps I'm a basset hound too? And then, Impossible. My friendship with Angus would never have lasted if I had been. Our regular lunches were enjoyable not because we agreed but because we struck sparks off each other. I have an analytical point of view: reason buttressed by factual research. He was ever the pragmatic businessman, able to read the future in balance sheets and to make shrewd guesses and conjure up profit from loss situations.

In other circumstances we could have been the ideal couple; our skills and temperaments were well-balanced and we agreed on core issues. Except over the question of loyalty. I still think it's an important quality but Angus would jeer at the story of the dog that stood guard over his master's grave until he died. 'You can't hang around grieving over what's gone. You have to move on,' he insisted during his long months of dying. 'Nobody's indispensable, least of all me. Move on, Faith.'

Yet he was the most loyal of friends, a paradox to the end.

6

As Angus grew sicker, his hectic life had to slow down. He still went away on his mysterious trips for a week or so at a time, but when he was in town he worked mornings only at the office and slept for several hours after lunch. Sometimes he'd phone at four to invite me to tea and early drinks at the Club, and we'd sit chatting in the lounge or in his rooms, insulated from the honking rush hour traffic in a time capsule modelled on an English country house at the turn of the century.

The Johannesburg Club was established in 1904 by a group of mining magnates who needed a haven where they could congregate to enjoy their new wealth unhampered by women. On the advice of Lord Milner they commissioned Sir Herbert Baker, hot architect of the moment, of the Union Buildings and later – under Sir Edward Lutyens – of New Delhi, to design the building in Fordyce Street.

It's a grand example of Edwardian classicism: four storeys of dressed sandstone, Ionic colonnades, tall bay windows, cast-iron balconies, cornices, architraves and pediments topped by a central domed roof pavilion. Pass under the leaded fanlights and carved scrolls of the front doors and through the revolving glass door into the entrance hall, and it's a symphony of marble and teak, curving balustrades, brass fittings, sombre panelling and parquet floors spread with Persian rugs and runners, many of which look worn enough to pre-date the Crimean War. Other creature comforts include an arthritic lift in a wrought iron cage that rises up a central well around which the main staircase curls, and dumb waiters that shuttle between the basement kitchens and wine cellar and the ground floor dining room, bearing legendary meals and vintages from around the world.

Also on the ground floor are the members' lounge and bar, the ladies' bar, the billiard room, the library and the office. On the second floor are the gym, the steam room, the barber shop and private rooms where members may entertain, and on the third floor, the resident members' suites and facilities for reciprocal club members visiting from other cities. The fourth floor, which has a plebeian corrugated iron roof not visible from the street because of cost overruns during building, is devoted to attics and servants' rooms.

To enter the Club is to be enveloped by tradition and formality; to be subtly reminded that the British Empire lives on, albeit largely in the hearts and minds of businessmen who would once have been looked down upon as In Trade.

If Angus was in a sociable mood, we sat in the lounge with its hum of retired members playing bridge or taking tea with elderly wives in knitted jersey suits and clenched grey perms and pearls. In his usual corner Monty Steyn would be puffing at his shaggy hand-rolled cigarettes and slurping Old Brown sherry, shreds of tobacco chasing the soup stains down his front, scabs flaking off his ears, cheeks and nose ablaze, an embarrassment that could not be tidied away as he had been a member for too long.

Angus was fond of the large panelled room with its gloomy oil paintings and leather armchairs and rosewood table with newspapers and imported magazines ranged in tidy rows: *Country Life*, *Field & Stream*, *The London Illustrated News*, the *New Statesman* and *The Spectator*. There was a fireplace that looked as though it belonged in the great hall of a castle, and a trophy corner with mounted skulls and horns and rows of engraved silver cups in glass cabinets.

At other times we would sit in his living room up on the third floor. We never went near the ladies' bar, a pink brocade grotto that had once been a butler's pantry and he called a modern abomination. 'Why should members be forced to sit in that poncey jumped-up parlour if they want to drink with women?' he would fulminate. 'Nothing wrong with the main pub.'

I had peered through the door of the members' bar once. It had a worn wooden floor and there was an overpowering smell of beer.

'Women aren't wanted in there,' I said.

'Bloody nonsense. I enjoy female company when I'm drinking. They set a tone, stop the boneheads from getting too drunk.'

'You enjoy female company?' This I hadn't heard before.

A reminiscent look that I had never seen before appeared on his face. 'I like women a lot.'

'You seem to be a man of wider-ranging interests than you've let on all these years.'

But he was roaring on as he always did when he got carried away with an idea that had struck him. 'Pubs should be for convivial drinking, not exclusive enclaves. Christ, male bonding rituals can be boring. When I think of all the stag parties I've had to sit through, all the poor buggers having liquor poured down their throats and their noses rubbed in the horrors of getting married, I wonder how the hell I put up with them.'

'Did you…' I was venturing into new territory, and put the question with care. 'Did your friends organise a stag party the night before you and Hannah were married?'

He snapped his fingers. 'Hannah. That reminds me. Spoke to her on the phone last night. She's decided to fly out and should be here on Saturday week. Says she's looking forward to meeting you.'

My morale plummeted. He had evaded my question and dealt a body blow in the same breath. I had just begun to imagine I could be a real comfort to him, and now his ex-wife was coming and would shut me out. I mumbled, 'I'm looking forward to meeting her too.'

'No, you're not. You're afraid she'll monopolise me and stop you from carrying on with your Lady of the Lamp act.'

He could be cruel too. I looked away so he wouldn't see that he'd scored another body blow.

But he was barging on, 'We have to be honest with each other. The closer I get to the edge of the pit, the more I value straight talking. Your view of me has changed since I became ill. I'm no longer the once-a-week good friend you had lunch and arguments with; I'm a mortally ill man and therefore an object of pity. But I don't want that from you, can't you see? I want your understanding and your toughness and your humour, not your condescending ministrations. Don't change tack on me, please.'

It took my breath away because it was true. I had begun to pity him and it was curdling our friendship. I wanted him to need me and lean on me; I had gilded a long-suppressed need for someone to mother with a fragile layer of what I had imagined was tender loving care. I hung my head and said, 'Sorry.'

I heard him heave his body forward in his chair and then the warmth of his cheek near mine. 'No offence intended, right? I don't want to lose you now.'

'No offence intended' was a code phrase we had used to take the sting out of arguments that got too heated. I shook my head and managed to croak, 'None taken. My fault.'

The chair creaked as he sat back again. 'Well, that's a relief. I've been meaning to clear the air. Glad we didn't get into a slanging match.'

'Does this mean that you don't want me to come and visit you any more?'

'Not at all. Not at *all*. I look forward to your company. Just, could you try to look less like that long-suffering basset hound we were talking about and more like the feisty Dobermann I'm used to? I need cheering up, not commiserating with.'

He was right and I felt a fool. The worst thing to bring to a sick person is a long face. Angus was a fighter. He needed a fellow warrior, not a nurse.

I forced a smile. 'Mea culpa. I'll try to give you a better run for your money from now on. What shall we argue about? Crooked business practices again?'

He was wearing one of his beautiful navy suits and a vivid silk tie that afternoon, in preparation for a cocktail party in his honour. The gold chain of his watch seemed to sag a little lower every time I saw him; his waistcoats were loose where they had once strained. I saw his hand move to ease the still-niggling operation scar as he said, 'I find I'm increasingly indifferent to my business affairs. Bloody bad timing when I need to get everything stowed away ship-shape in case…' He broke off, then went on with a determined effort, 'But it seems more important now to deal with the loose ends in my life. Know what I mean?'

I nodded. 'Tidying up.'

'Just so. I've caught myself recently wishing I were a Catholic so I could exculpate my sins with a confession and some Hail Marys, but of course I'm not, and I can't.'

'I'm aware that you're trying to set me up as your confessor.' My words came out like prickly pears. We were back to normal again.

And I was rewarded by an appreciative smile. 'Trying and failing. Should have known you wouldn't be putty in my fat old hands.'

'They're not fat.' Any more, I added silently.

'Or old, really. Sixty-four. Too bloody young to die. Dammit, Faith.'

I could see his mask slipping and said quickly, 'Have they done tests to see if the chemo's working? When is your next course due?'

'The Monday after Hannah arrives. They'll do the tests beforehand. It's one of the reasons why the business community is holding a cocktail party for me this evening – in case I'm too incapacitated to function afterwards.'

'Promise I won't offer to come and hold your hand again.'

His eyes were wells of ink in the darkening room. 'Will you come if I ask? In spite of what I've just said?'

I shook my head. 'Hannah will be here.'

'Not for long, just a week. She has commitments she can't break.'

'Angus,' I said, 'if you want me at any time, anywhere, I'll come. But if you call me a long-suffering basset hound or joke about my Lady of the Lamp act once again, you can forget it.'

'Agreed. And here comes my first request: be my partner at this cocktail party.'

'What?' Besides the rugby match, I had never been invited to his business functions.

'Please come with me this evening. I'm going to need moral support.'

'But I can't. I'm not dressed for it.' I'd dropped in on him that afternoon after a meeting with my publisher.

He put on a cozening expression I had never seen. 'Go home and put on your glad rags. A night out together will be fun for both of us. I'll appear with a new woman on my arm, astounding the doomsayers who expect me to be on my last legs, and you can pass the time working out which ones are the millionaires, and why.'

My old laugh exploded, released from the bonds that had constrained it over the last few anxious weeks. And of course I agreed: dashed home, washed my hair and blow-dried some bounce into it, donned my sequinned jacket over a black velvet sheath that I had been told made me look like Lauren Bacall when she was young and tigerish, and was borne off by Angus in the chauffeured Bentley.

Cocktail parties may be a necessary bore for business executives, but for a lowly scribbler like me that one was unheard-of luxury. The palatial hotel room had gold columns and a scarlet carpet and a firmament of downlighters and crystal chandeliers. The Soweto String Quartet, resplendent in their zebra jackets, played with zest amid the potted palms. Attentive waiters circulated with trays of champagne flutes charged with Moët & Chandon, to which I did full justice. The most enjoyable thing about French champagne with its bouquet of dry chalk caves and wavering threads of tiny bubbles is that it doesn't make you drunk, just high on life.

My high that night was intensified by the surprised faces that kept turning to Angus and me, the whispers of 'Who is she?' and the confidence-inspiring knowledge that I looked ravishing.

Angus told me so before we braved the assembled throng. 'You look ravishing tonight, Faith. Where does the wondrous sparkle come from?'

'Your life force must be catching.'

'I've never seen you like this.'

Hilarity was close to the surface that evening. I tossed my head to make my hair swing round my face and said, 'It's the fun of doing something unexpected. I don't often have a chance to attend big smart occasions.'

He stopped me before we went through the door. 'Why not? Why don't you get out more? You work alone in that flat of yours far too much, hiding your light under a bushel.'

'Oh, rubbish. I'm always going out.'

'You've never told me about it.'

'My life isn't as glamorous as yours. I didn't think you'd be interested in faculty dinners and hiking trails.'

He stood looking down his skew nose at me; always a danger sign. 'What about boyfriends?'

'I'm not a nun.' Big false smile.

'But nobody special, or I'd have heard about it.'

'Good men don't grow on trees.' Favourite line of single women.

'It's a howling waste. I command you to find a boyfriend.'

'Here?'

He barked, 'Never know your luck. Even Joburg businessmen are said to have hearts,' and swept me into the room.

He kept me next to him for a while as people queued up to greet him, introducing me as 'my friend Faith Dobermann, the historian', while Prunella glowered from a distance. She was wearing a pink suit crowned by an intricate arrangement of jet-black curls glued in place by hair lacquer that gave off polymer glints every time she moved. It was clear that she was used to being at Angus's side and, denied her moment of glory, was loathing me with every fibre of her well-organised being. How sweet it was to triumph over The Prune; how graciously I smiled and shook hands and chatted with my other hand tucked under Angus's arm in tacit support. He seemed to be enjoying himself too, causing a stir with my presence and later sitting in a chair of honour while speeches were made.

I noticed that he ate nothing though there was a whisky glass in his hand most of the evening. Before the speeches, he released me from his side saying, 'Have a go at the feast before it's demolished. This is an excellent example of honey-gathering.'

It seemed a cynical remark for a guest of honour but he was right; I had never seen such a lavish spread. Hillocks of fresh Knysna oysters; mountains of pinkly moist prawns and crayfish chunks; whole fillets of smoked salmon; platters of fresh asparagus tips swaddled in Parma ham; mounds of steak tartare surrounded by all the trimmings; sumptuous displays of cold meats arranged on mirrors; steaming silver bains-marie filled with sausage rolls and fat little smoked sausages like children's toes (I was reminded of the game I played with a friend's child: 'This little piggy went to market, this little piggy stayed at home'); quails' eggs; devils on horseback; crumbed mushrooms; pâtés; sushi; spiced samoosas; tiny kebabs ... an assortment of multicultural delicacies that guaranteed indigestion for the unwary.

The buffet would have fed a squatter camp for a week, even without the pyramids of profiteroles and battalions of éclairs beckoning from the far end of the draped and swagged table. And it was demolished in an hour by a hundred and twenty well-fed businessmen and their consorts, even though they knew it would go straight on to their stomachs and hips and clog their arteries.

With hypocritical gusto I joined the demolition process, lurking next to a gold column with a heaped and re-heaped plate, trying to guess who was who in Angus's pantheon by tuning in to the conversations around me.

'Did you hear what happened at National Nut last week? Their database was completely wiped and...'

'We first have to get our ducks in a row...'
'Simpson never outgrew his box, that's why ...'
'He didn't!'
'He did! It was all over Plett...'
'The Old Man expects us to parade every morning at seven for a prayer meeting. God, I'm tired of...'
'Taking the matter to arbitration...'
'The bottom line is...'
'Offshore funds...'
'Long bond rates…'
'The Reserve Bank…'
'I'm telling you, the Minister's about to abolish all exchange controls...'
'The P/E ratio is pathetic...'
'Gilts are going to hell...'
'The gearing's all wrong...'
'The parameters are far too...'
'Over-capitalised...'
'Under-utilised...'
'Grindley's is going under...'
'Tenders close on Friday...'
'Confidentially, we're using it as a cash cow...'
'Then he threw all his toys out of the cot and...'
'My stockbroker says...'
'My gynae says...'
'Susie's orthodontist says…'
'It's the Italian disease all over again...'
'We're looking for a win-win situation but...'
'The synergy's not right...'
'He's way out of his comfort zone. Way out.'
'A quantum leap…'
'A paradigm shift…'
'Get the unions and government working with us, and we'll have a virtuous circle that'll...'
'Impress the stakeholders...'
'The money markets...'
'Number-crunching...'
'Hedge funds...'
'A brown-paper exercise…'
'A greenfield project…'
'Blue chips…'

'The Dow Jones...'

'The London fixing...'

'Pumping profits...'

Buzzwords. Buzzwords. The remark I most enjoyed was made by a disgruntled wife whose diamonds did not succeed in distracting the eye from the fine plastic surgery scars along her hairline, who passed me saying peevishly to a friend, 'Next time he has an erection, I'll bring it to you on a plate.'

I couldn't wait to relay this gem to Angus but he was hidden from sight behind a wall of dark-suited backs, including those of Jumbo Urquhart and Hugh Softley, both of whom had greeted me with frosty smiles. So I returned to the feast for another éclair.

Behind me, a voice grated, 'Hungry, eh?'

I turned to find a facsimile of Rumpelstiltskin in a shimmery dinner jacket leering up at me, and said, 'It's just greed. I don't often get a chance to plunder such a royal feast.'

'King Quain getting mean in his old age?'

'Not that I've noticed.' I gave my finger a surreptitious lick. I'd forgotten that éclairs are an inelegant choice at a party because the chocolate icing melts all over your mouth and whipped cream oozes out each time you bite.

'Where did he find you?' Voracious eyes were roaming my face for the answer.

'Oh, Angus and I met long ago, at a dinner party. We're old friends.'

'Can't be. I'd have noticed. Come clean, my girl.'

'Honestly. I've known him for fifteen years.'

'Bull. He hired you to distract attention from his appearance, right? What's your rate? Any more where you came from?' He began edging closer.

I have to admit that I giggled; he was so obviously annoyed that Angus should have got one up on him by finding a new source of presentable – if somewhat long-in-the-tooth – callgirls.

'Name of your agency?' he was insisting. 'Got a card? Phone number? See me right and I could put a hell of a lot of useful business your way.'

'Listen, Mr...?'

'Just call me Carl.' He leaned even closer. His breath smelled of over-ripe Gorgonzola.

'Sorry to disappoint you, but I'm neither an escort nor a prostitute. I'm a respectable...'

'Not another friggin' moonlighting housewife,' he jeered. 'Two a penny nowadays. Nothing to do when the kids push off, so you flog your fanny for a bit of extra pocket money and tell the old man you're going to Ladies' Night with a friend. Right?'

He was bouncing from one grey suède shoe to the other, delighted at having blown my suburban cover. Restraining the urge to give the little lecher a knee in the crotch, I hissed, 'Wrong. I'm a historian with a Master's degree from Wits. And if you don't sod off, I'll scream.'

It was the threat Violet Elizabeth Bott used to make in *Just William*: 'I'll thcream and I'll thcream until I'm thick!' – one of the echoes of my bookish childhood that carry flooding memories of my old bedroom at home. But right then I was flooded with rage and he got the message, because he slunk off without another word and tacked himself on to a group of haw-hawing cigar smokers at the far side of the room. When I managed to get back to Angus's chair and catch his attention during a lull in obeisances, I pointed out Rumpelstiltskin and asked who he was.

'Why do you want to know?' The downlighters threw cruel shadows; Angus's eye-bags were melting down his face and the old break that had skewed his nose was exaggerated, giving him the look of a tragic ex-boxer.

'Because he propositioned me. Thought I was a callgirl, for some reason.'

The tragic look vanished. 'It's your penance for looking so gorgeous tonight. That's…' And he named a famous magnate who was said to be the fifth richest man in South Africa. 'He's worth a billion or more, Faith. Play your cards right, and he'll set you up in a penthouse of your choice with a gold card and a poodle and a Ferrari convertible.'

'No thanks,' I shuddered. 'Sis.'

'Sis? I didn't know you used such common language.'

'Expressive, I call it. Creepy little runt.'

'Everybody knows he's got the morals of a hyena, but they kowtow to him because his money makes him all-powerful. It's the name of the game.'

'Not my sort of game.'

'Are you having fun, though?'

'Great fun. I haven't eaten so well in years.'

He nodded. 'It's a good spread. They've pulled out all the stops tonight. Must have decided that it's the last one I'll be fit to attend. See the old bugger off in style, what?'

The only eyes Angus never tried to pull the wool over were his own.

7

*T*he following morning I had a call from Angus on his cellphone on the way to work.

'Did you enjoy it?' He sounded chipper, quite recovered from his subdued mood at the end of the cocktail party. He had fallen asleep against some cushions in the back of the Bentley on the way to my flat, an ailing emperor exhausted by his efforts to maintain the facade of power.

'I had a wonderful time – felt like Cinderella at the ball. Hope I didn't disgrace you by eating and drinking too much.' I was paying penance with a mug of black coffee for breakfast.

'Nobody was holding back. Excess rules when someone else is paying.'

'Having French champagne on tap was the best part. Your colleagues must think a lot of you.'

'Hogwash. That was a public expression of the old-boy network code: you scratch my back and I'll scratch yours.' He paused a moment, then went on in the dry voice he used when he knew I wouldn't like what he said, 'There wasn't a man in the room last night who didn't owe me, one way or another. It's the modus I've employed from the moment I realised how effective it was. You do people favours, keep them in your debt rather than the other way round, so that whenever you need something you have a range of creditors to choose from. When – if – I go, they're absolved of their obligations. Hence the air of convivial relief and the Moët.'

'That's so cynical.'

'Shocked and horrified, are we? Ivory tower rocked to its foundations? As I've said before, there's no need. I'm just one of many pigs with their snouts in the trough. Getting on now, too. Younger pigs on their way up have far more audacious schemes tucked under their curly tails. They call it life in the fast lane and every one of 'em has a BMW and a cocaine habit to match.'

I tried a charitable thought – There's something bothering him this morning – but the hangover prevailed. I gulped another jolt of caffeine and said, 'I'm not interested in your porcine activities. If this is the prelude to another bout in the confessional, please desist. I have work to do.'

'You sound more stuffy than the Club's retired colonels.'

'Heaven forfend. I'm just not in the mood right now for more sizzling disclosures about dirty doings in the boardroom. Phone Jackie Collins.'

His rumble of laughter made the cellphone crackle. When it subsided, he said, 'I don't know anyone else who would dare say heaven forfend in this day and age.'

'Mother always said I was old-fashioned, but how could I help it with two aged parents? They spoke like Edwardians.'

'No bad thing, I'd have said. Historians need to understand the verbal conventions of the past, surely?'

'Verbal conventions, hell. I left home sounding like a dictionary. Took me years to learn to talk like my contemporaries.'

'Perhaps that's why we've understood each other so well.'

'Perhaps.' I felt another groan coming on and said, 'What historians need to know is when to draw the line at parties.'

'Ah. Do I detect morning-after remorse?'

'Excess. You detect signs of gross excess and its aftermath. I have to tackle an important chapter today and I feel mentally sluggish.'

'Suppose it's all my fault?'

'Compounded by my greed. But I wouldn't have missed the party for anything,' I added in case he thought I was being ungrateful. 'Thanks for taking me. It was fun.'

His answer was an abrupt, 'You should go out more. That's why I'm phoning.'

I didn't want his pity any more than he wanted mine. 'To wave your magic wand again and whisk me off to another ball, Fairy Godfather? No thanks. Mustn't go gadding about too much if it means I can't think straight the next day.'

Even over a crackling cellphone, Angus could pick up nuances; it was another facet of his formidable way with people. He said, 'Sheath your prickles, woman, and listen. I decided while I was shaving this morning that you are one of the major loose ends in my life, and I wish to secure your future before I go. This call is a formal announcement that as from now, I am officially on the hunt for a suitable boyfriend. You need someone to complement your considerable talents.'

Monumental arrogance, was all I could think, telling me that what's missing in my life is a man. I snarled, 'I refuse to be a loose end and the last thing I need is a boyfriend.'

'Companion, if you prefer. I blame myself for not thinking of it before, but you've always seemed so...'

'Spinsterly?' I was furious. 'Reclusive?'

'Contained and self-sufficient, I was going to say. But last night I saw a different Faith: a vibrant, interesting woman going to waste because she's drifting along doing her own quiet thing in a backwater. You're living a half-life, old girl.'

What could I say? He was partly right and he wouldn't even listen to opposition in this mood.

'The point is,' he rumbled on, 'I am in an excellent position to find and vet potential companions. The corporate world is seething with eligible men who are so busy pursuing their ambitions that they haven't the time to pursue partners. I know a number of extremely able lawyers and accountants who...'

'Haven't you forgotten something?' I didn't care if it sounded bitter. 'I am no longer young. I'm damn nearly forty-four and enjoy my life the way it is. Furthermore, after what you've just told me about the pigs with their snouts in the trough, I have no intention of tainting my life by getting involved with one of them.'

'I didn't mean to imply that all businessmen are pigs, nor would I dream of introducing you to someone unsuitable. Besides...'

'Angus, can't you hear me? It's none of your damn business.'

'Besides,' he went on in the impervious way he adopted on the phone, as though it were yet another slave paid to do his bidding, 'you've managed to associate with me for long enough without apparently feeling tainted.'

'You're different.'

'Am I?' From the tone, I could picture the caustic smile that accompanied the words. 'If that's a compliment, vive la différence. And I tell you now that your diatribe won't deter me from my task. You can expect more invitations to corporate functions as my partner while I investigate the market.'

'Please lay off,' I begged. 'Stop being such a bully.'

'I'm just getting started.'

His voice was fading. I imagined the Bentley rolling in its stately way down the ramp into the parking basement of the city-centre building which housed the Quain & Associates offices. We'd lose contact soon. I said, desperate for him to understand, 'You don't really expect me to go round parading myself as available?'

'You don't have to. Just come with me when I ask and enjoy the food and the company, and I'll handle the technicalities.'

'This is ridiculous!' I shouted. 'I won't do it!'

But he was gone leaving me with a hammering headache, glaring down at my coffee dregs.

Thus began my foray into the exclusive social stratum of the Joburg business world. Angus would not take no for an answer and I capitulated on the understanding that I was not committing myself to anything, merely acting as his partner for friendship's sake and the occasional square meal. I have to confess that there was an ulterior motive too: I wanted to annoy Prunella, who had embarked on a campaign of passive resistance. When I tried to phone Angus at work now, he always seemed to be 'in a meeting' or (more impressively, using a hushed tone) 'in conference'. Prunella was a natural minion – as devout in her worship of Angus as she was in carrying out the duties she performed for him – and could be relied on to work until all hours for just one medium-voltage smile of thanks.

During the following week I accompanied him to a luncheon at the Carlton Hotel addressed by the Minister of Finance, the opening night of an art exhibition at the Goodman Gallery, a presentation of company results at the Park Hyatt followed by another sumptuous cocktail party, a glittering dinner in Pretoria at which he presented an award for business excellence, and a charity ball at the Sandton Sun in aid of a Tembisa youth centre. I met scores of well-dressed, well-heeled men, jewelled wives and socialites, some impressive women executives and a flotilla of hopeful girls in gleaming plumage who were clearly on the lookout for security and fortune.

Angus primed me in advance of each introduction. Apart from his enjoyment at dropping names, he had an encyclopaedic knowledge as to who was what, how they rated financially and socially, and who was sleeping with whom. When he tired of circulating, we would sit together at the edge of the crowd and he would pick out people and tell me about them.

'See that chap over there? He was a building group executive until he was caught rogering his secretary on his desk at lunchtime, and fired. Best thing that could have happened, as it turned out, because he started his own business and made a fortune exporting galvanised roof bolts.'

I saw a mournful man with jug ears, and tried without success to imagine him being carried away by lunchtime lust. Mother used to say, darkly, 'You never know what goes on behind the bedroom door,' but for me the matter of sex boils down to: how do you find another person who enjoys doing the same things as you do without going through a lot of humiliating experiments? My post-Kurt lovers were intelligent, amiable men but there were no fireworks in bed and inevitably the relationships faded. I hadn't met anyone recently who inspired me to try again.

Jug-Ears' transgression against company mores was only the first of many exotic tales that Angus told me. He directed my gaze to a thrice-married wife whose two previous husbands had died leaving her a million each; she was now hanging on the arm of a third millionaire, an ebullient cattle farmer from the Free State. 'People aren't quite sure whether to warn him or egg her on,' Angus murmured.

There was a forex dealer recently convicted of contravening exchange control regulations, out on bail because his case was on appeal. 'They've given him five years, poor fellow, but it's his own damn fault. He overspent his salary by a factor of ten and someone blabbed. It's anathema to excite jealousy among your contemporaries.'

Angus pointed out the reticent bachelor brothers who had built a fortune on coal dust briquettes and devoted all their profits to a haven for stray dogs called Paws Awhile, and a woman with blonde tresses and metallic eyes whom he described as one of the best business brains in the country. He whispered in my ear about charity queens, cuckolds, tragic mistresses and a military-looking group accountant who had been caught kerb-crawling for street boys in Hillbrow.

His pet celebrity was an elegant old woman with pencilled-on eyebrows who often attended civic and business receptions, always dressed in the same black suit worn with a marcasite brooch, different turbans and a voluminous handbag. 'Watch her,' he said behind his hand when we first spotted her. And I saw her manoeuvre towards a buffet table while people's attention was held by a speaker, then start expertly whisking food into the open maw of the handbag held below table level.

'Her husband killed himself some years ago when the bank foreclosed and she's too proud to admit she's destitute,' he explained when she had drifted away towards the door. 'So we let her nick a few square meals while we pretend we're not looking. You've got to admire her style.'

'Oh, I do.' And I thought, The largesse gives them a nice glow inside when they climb into their limousines to go home to their indigestion mixtures.

Rumpelstiltskin was another regular presence. I watched him scrutinise groups of women in search of prey, then sidling up to his targets with ferocious tenacity. He avoided me, as did Jumbo and Hugh.

You couldn't miss Jumbo, who cut a vivid dash among the sober suits in his dark green and blue Urquhart kilt, his velvet jacket with silver buttons, his buckled shoes and lace jabot frothing below whisky-fuelled red cheeks. There was even a dagger handle sticking out of one sock, flirting coyly with the pleats of his hem as he moved.

Angus murmured, 'Jumbo is as South African as I am but since he rediscovered his origins during a visit to Edinburgh a few years ago, you'd think he was born doing the highland fling. Calls that ridiculous knife in his sock a *sgean dubh* and goes around boasting he's descended from Robert the Bruce.'

'My mother put me off ancestor worship.'

'A good thing too. Nothing worse than people who preen themselves on the past glories of their ancestors.'

'Only present glories count, then?'

'Only personal achievements.'

'The credo of the aggressively self-made man. As in, Never fear, Quain is here,' I mocked.

He swung on me. 'What's wrong with that? It's a joke motto I made up for the children to hang on to when they went back to England. They needed to know they could rely on their father, even if he wasn't around.'

'You may have had the purest motives but it has a ring of overweening vanity, you have to admit.'

I watched Jumbo across the room raising his whisky glass with a hectic flourish and calling out, 'Scots wha' hae where Wallace bled!' Several of the women standing nearby tittered.

'That's a bloody sour remark,' Angus grumbled. 'Urquhart fits the description far better than me.'

'I don't think so. The way self-made men assume all the glory for themselves negates all the people who've make contributions along the way – their employees and wives, for example.'

'We've had this argument before.'

'And I argued last time that claiming sole credit verges on hubris. To quote John Donne: "No man is an Island, entire of itself."'

'I am entirely self-made, old girl, and I demand sole credit,' he said with a complacent smirk. 'Now cut the cackle and let's get back to business. Which one of those executives swopping inside information over there do you fancy?'

Out of curiosity, I was following the share price of Amalgamated Couplings; within a week it had edged up five rands in what the Stock Exchange report called 'medium to heavy trading'. Angus's undercover operation appeared to be working. I wondered whether he had agreed to it in order to put Jumbo and Hugh in his debt, or for other reasons.

The thought was always with me now: What was I doing consorting with a less-than-honest businessman and his cronies? Images kept running through my mind of Michael Douglas with his weak chin and petulant mouth fulminating in *Wall Street*, and widows losing their life savings, and men jumping out of New York skyscrapers on Black Monday. But then I'd remind myself that the man who had been my friend for fifteen years had not changed, only my point of view since I had learnt more about him. The real question was: if you weigh fifteen years of friendship against a revelation of occasional cheating, which tips the balance?

It wasn't a difficult decision and I enjoyed the social whirl, though the strain on my minimal wardrobe became a problem and I was forced to consult a more knowledgeable friend. After quizzing me about the functions I'd be attending, she whistled and said, 'Nice going! I hope he's rich and gorgeous.' Then whipped me through a series of boutiques from which I emerged flat broke.

The most expensive item was the slender column of pale grey silk that I was persuaded to buy for the charity ball. Its aura of shimmering moonlight made me stand out from the profusion of stiff bright taffetas like a mermaid in a jungle of parrots – an unexpected coup which had Angus uttering fulsome compliments and my photograph on two society pages.

It also attracted dancing partners. I spent the evening in various black-tie embraces as Angus sat watching, benign as the nodding porcelain Buddha that had once sat on the mantelpiece at home. When I joined him after each dance he would give me a rundown on my partner, awarding a rating which ranged from Excellent Potential through A Good Bet and Worth A Try down the scale to I Hear He's A Poofter, Bats For Both Teams – Avoid At All Costs, Safely Married And Not Available and No Bloody Use At All.

He was very funny about what he began to call 'the quest for zero defect' after a current advertisement, and I could see that the idea of getting me paired off was diverting his mind from his growing weakness and fatigue. He began to spend less time at the office and more at the desk in his sitting room going through his private papers. Once I arrived to have lunch and found him talking to a lanky man with a harassed look who knocked his chair over as he stood up.

'Leo's my lawyer and the son of one of my oldest friends,' Angus said, introducing us. 'Older than you even, Faith.'

'Whaddaya mean, older than me?' I was making an effort to be bright and jokey now when I came to see him.

The lawyer smiled, then looked embarrassed as though he shouldn't have.

Angus said, 'Tom Greyling and I started our first jobs together just after the war, working for a ships' chandler in Cape Town. He was in the transport section and I was the warehouse tally clerk who checked outgoing deliveries. We were two wild boyos then, I can tell you. Mixed with the ex-servicemen home from Up North, and they knew how to live it up.'

I was staggered. 'A tally clerk? I thought you studied commerce at university.'

'Me, at university?' His expression was radiant with derision. 'No chance. I had to leave school after Junior Certificate to go out and work because there was no money. My father lost his railway job at the beginning of the Depression, a year after I was born, and we moved into a backyard room in Woodstock. He used to tell me about the doctors and lawyers, professional men, shovelling coal with him down at the docks to earn a few pence to keep their families going. We lived on porridge and soup and bread and dripping, and my mother made me embarrassing clothes out of Union Mills flourbags because she wouldn't accept cast-offs. It was bloody rough then and it didn't get much better for struggling poor whites like us. We understand how the blacks have suffered in this country because we went through it too. Including having to grit your teeth to accept as charity what you know damn well to be your birthright.'

The exalted King Quain came from a poor white family? I said in a voice gone feeble with shock, 'How did you qualify as an accountant, then?'

'One of my old man's favourite expressions was, "There are more ways of killing a cat than sucking its brains through its ear'ole." I was good at maths. Got my Matric by going to night school after work, then wangled articles and slogged for seven years as a general dogsbody, during which I rose from tea boy to tickbird to chartered accountant. Came up the hard way, as did Tom Greyling. I made up for my social and academic deficiencies by reading everything I could lay my hands on. Also by learning to play chameleon, changing my spots to blend in with my background. It's easy when you know how. Having a strong life force helps too.' His chin went up, a deflated cascade where there had once been prosperous curves. 'And there you have it: the humble origins and early career of Angus Quain.'

He sat looking pleased at having produced another revelation. I wondered whether it was a mischievous fairytale he had dreamed up; if he was as un-scrupulous as he had been implying, he could equally well have made up a colourful past. But the lawyer Leo Greyling was standing with folded arms show-ing no surprise, so it must be true.

Scrabbling for sarcasm, I said, 'Who would have guessed at humble origins in one so distinguished? I'll raise you on a rotten childhood, though, if you have time to spare.'

'Haven't, sorry. Leo's going to join us for lunch because we have a lot more busi-ness to get through this afternoon before he leaves. There are still a number of loose ends to be tied up.'

'Please don't carry on about loose ends, Angus. Maybe some of them want to stay untied.'

He unhooked his stick from the side of the desk and began to get up, moving with slow care as he did all the time now so as not to aggravate the pain. I went to help him, but he waved me away with a testy hand saying, 'Don't you start with the mother-henning. I'm quite all right. Much better today.'

But he didn't look it. His eye sockets were as hollow and purple as sucked grape skins and he shuffled along the carpet as he made for the door. There were two days to go before Hannah arrived, and four until the next course of chemother-apy began. While he gathered his resources for the onslaught I would have a respite from the quest for a potential partner, and I wasn't sure whether to be relieved or sorry.

It had been an agreeable week. Life at the top seemed less and less decadent the more I enjoyed it.

8

*H*annah was to arrive on the British Airways flight on Saturday morning and Angus phoned to invite me to dinner that evening.

I declined, saying, 'Surely you'll have too much to say to each other to want a stranger present?'

'Hardly a stranger.'

'Stranger to her. To your marriage.'

'Ex-marriage.'

'Nevertheless. Not even you can ask me to play gooseberry.'

'That's nonsense, and I'm asking you to abide by your undertaking. "If you want me at any time, anywhere, I'll come." Remember?'

'I didn't mean that I'd be at your beck and call on a whim.'

'It's not a whim. More like a last wish.' He was pulling out all the stops, including blackmail. 'It would please me very much to have two of the most important women in my life to dinner. And you'll like Hannah. She's direct and warm-hearted, as you are. I'm a sucker for the type.'

He had not said 'the two most important women in my life'. Were there others? I remembered him saying 'I like women a lot,' and he was an unusual South African male in that respect.

I blurted, 'Do you collect us, Angus?'

He evaded my question with one of his own. 'Grumpier than usual today, old girl?'

'I'm not grumpy, just more suspicious of your motives. You have to admit there are good grounds.'

'Not at all. I'm asking you to come to a respectable dinner in the Club dining room with my ex-wife, not to join my harem.'

He was in a cheerful mood and I wondered if it was from the thought of seeing Hannah again or because he had managed to tie up more loose ends with the help of his lawyer. The lunch with Leo Greyling had not been a success. He had been preoccupied and uncommunicative, not the suave city attorney I would have expected Angus to use but a small-town lawyer in a rumpled suit and a hurry to get back to Nelspruit where he practised. It was clear that Angus felt he could only discuss his confidential affairs with someone outside his usual ambit, the son of his old friend.

I repeated, 'I'm not grumpy. Just pissed off.'

'The writer of all that elegant historical prose is *pissed off*? Why, might I ask?'

'Because one of my student researchers has let me down and I can't go ahead with the section I'm working on. So I'll be twiddling my thumbs all weekend.'

I had reached a crucial point in my latest book and was angry at having to wait for information I had commissioned and paid for weeks in advance. It was agony to be held up by a feeble little student who hadn't kept his fervent promises to submit the material on time.

Angus said, 'All the more reason to come and have dinner with us on Saturday. I shall expect you at six-thirty for drinks in the lounge,' and rang off before I could make any further objections.

Trying to decide what to wear for dinner, I thought of the Hannah of the photograph: a big woman in scruffy clothes with a confident smile. How should I present myself to her – as artsy-ethnic or academic-intellectual? My caftan and heavy Ethiopian silver necklace, or the black polo-neck and skinny corduroy pants that make me look intense and brainy? Or should I cover my bets by combining artsy-ethnic (Ethiopian necklace) with intellectual (black polo-neck)? First impressions are important and I wanted Hannah to see me as a person of substance: a successful writer who was Angus's friend, not one of his circle of society women. Had he played around while they were married? I wondered. Did he still?

Artsy-intellectual prevailed, and I had to brave a barrage of disapproving elderly stares as I entered the lounge. Women who wear pants (especially in the evening) are still considered fast at the Club.

Angus had come out to the entrance hall to sign me in. When we reached the lounge he gestured with his walking stick towards a group of armchairs near the fireplace where a display of proteas was standing in for the log fire which was lit every year on the fifteenth of May. Nobody knew, he had said when I'd asked, why the fire was always lit on this date; it just was, with Boniface performing the ceremony and port all round afterwards for those present. It was yet another of the rituals which made Club members more secure in their belonging and kept outsiders outside.

Enthroned in a leather club easy was the woman of the photograph: an earth mother with abundant curly pepper-and-salt hair held back in combs from a round sensible face, a generous body and heavy thighs under a tweed skirt. The soles of two large brown lace-up shoes rested side by side on a footstool. She looked more homely than I'd expected of Angus's ex-wife. He had always taken a dandy's care over his appearance.

'Hannah, this is my friend Faith Dobermann. Faith, this is Hannah.' Angus stood leaning on his stick; if he was apprehensive about the meeting, he didn't show it.

I reached down to where she was sitting, dredging up my formal English manners. 'How do you do?'

'Hullo at *last*, Faith.' She raised her arms and drew me down next to her and into a hug. 'I'm so glad to meet you. Please forgive me for not getting up, but my ankles are swollen from the flight and I've been told to keep them elevated. I'm not sure if one should use such a superior word for common old ankles?'

Hannah had a way of including you in her life from the moment you met. In the following half-hour, as we sipped our sherries and Angus sat watching with a proprietorial expression, she told me about their children, her life in the Suffolk village, her work as a potter and her pleasure at being back in Johannesburg again. 'It's a changed country,' she said as we rose to go into the dining room. 'The children and I left in the late seventies when the system was horrendous, and now look what you've achieved under President Mandela's wise guidance.'

How pleasant for South Africans to be able to bask in praise for a change, I thought as I followed them. We won't mention the squatter camps and the hijackings and the bank robberies just yet. Angus was holding on to her arm with his free hand. He had a marked stoop that night.

Over the convivial dinner that followed, with the conversation between the three of us flowing as smoothly as the rich dark brown gravy ladled over the roast beef and Yorkshire pudding, I began for the first time in many years to feel part of a family again. But it would be a brief belonging, I thought, watching Angus eat little and drink less wine than usual. He also said no to his usual snifter of cognac and looked tired as we said goodbye in the entrance hall afterwards.

Hannah was to be driven to the Carlton Hotel a few blocks away in the Bentley after she had seen him settled in his rooms. I would be speeding home in my own car with locked doors and my self-defence spray in my lap, ready to jump any red traffic lights with dark figures loitering nearby. Joburg streets are deserted at night, an urban moonscape of stark concrete and blowing litter. As with so many cities, the town planners succumbed to commercial pressure and allowed the blight of offices to soar and spread, pushing homes further and further outwards. Now the few people who live in the city centre are too frightened to go about at night: the indigent elderly and poor families crammed into tenement flats, the pavement dwellers who live in cardboard cartons, and the ragged street children huddled in shop doorways sniffing glue and paint thinners out of plastic bags.

Angus was saying, 'I'm glad you two have met at last. I knew you'd like each other.'

'You've always had good taste in friends.' Hannah turned to me. 'Faith, if Angus is well enough after his chemo treatment to be left alone by Wednesday, would you have time to take me round a bit? From what I've seen today, Johannesburg's a very different city to the one we left.'

'Go. Go anyway. I'll be fine,' he insisted.

She turned to him with a brusque, 'I'll be the judge of that, all right? I've come to be with you, not gallivant around sightseeing.'

'Bloody women, give them an inch and the interfering begins.' He was trying to make a joke of it but I saw his hand trembling on the stick. There were old tensions here.

I said, 'Of course I'll take you round. I'd love to.' Hannah's conversation was salted with humour and I would enjoy being her companion.

She put her hand on my arm: thick square fingers, short nails and an embedded gold wedding ring. 'Are you sure? I hate asking people to interrupt their work, knowing only too well how it breaks a train of thought.'

'Quite sure. My car has seen better days but we're both at your disposal.' It was a seven-year-old beige Toyota, ever-reliable but useless as boyfriend bait according to Angus. He had been trying for weeks to persuade me to sell it and buy a convertible, saying he would help with the difference. Which proposition I was resisting with vigour, since I have never wanted to drive a Venus flytrap and would not stoop to taking money from him. Furthermore, I had explained, serious writers don't drive convertibles.

'That vehicle of yours is a jalopy. My driver Praise can take you about in the Bentley,' he cut in now. 'He'll be free as long as I'm laid low.'

Even as his health failed, Angus kept trying to organise the people round him. I said, 'No thanks. I'm perfectly capable of...'

'This time I insist. It'll be far easier on Hannah's ankles if you're dropped off where you want to go, rather than pounding the pavements to get there.'

His usual weapon for getting his way, a truculent glare under knotted black eyebrows, was not even half-strength that night; I remember it as a poignant marker in his decline. Behind his shoulders, hunched that evening inside a blazer that drooped in front where it had once swelled, the Club's staircase rose in a graceful sweep of carpeted teak steps and brass railings. And I had a vivid flashback of sitting in the old café-bio on Main Street drinking tea with Mother as we admired Georges Guetary dancing up a flight of stairs in *An American in Paris*, outrageously debonair in white tails, each step lighting up under his feet as he sang:

63

'I'll build a stairway to paradise
Wiz a new step every day,
I'm gonna get zere at any price
Stand aside, I'm on my way...'

It could have been Angus's theme song. But the lights were dimming for him now; he needed to conserve his energy for fighting the deadly enemy within, not his friends. So I conceded that being driven round was a good idea, and he looked pleased at having prevailed and went slowly off with Hannah to the lift in its cage with the staircase coiling upwards round it. As I listened to the rubber tip of his walking stick squealing on the marble floor, I thought, He always knows exactly what to say in order to get his way. Is it an innate skill, or did he have to learn it? Can I learn it from him before he goes?

Angus was sicker after his second course of chemo and lost the rest of his hair. 'Poor old thing, he's flattened,' Hannah said over the phone. 'Could we make our jaunt on Friday instead?'

I thought, 'Poor old thing' – Angus will be furious if he's listening. And said, 'Of course. Friday's fine. Give him my love.'

We met on the front steps of the Club with the Bentley purring by the pavement. Angus was a little better that morning, she said; being ministered to by Boniface and drinking weak orange juice.

She wanted to begin at the Art Gallery. 'It was always one of my favourite places. I love Rodin's calm, creamy Miss Fairfax,' she said as we bowled down Market Street behind the ever-silent Praise.

He was in full regalia that morning: black jacket and tie, white shirt, dark glasses, peaked and corded black hat set well forward on a head with neat ears. He seemed young to be the driver of such an expensive car, though he handled it with smooth expertise. Perhaps there was a school for executive chauffeurs, I thought, like the school for butlers in England. One felt like a celebrity being driven in Angus's svelte limo because people would turn and stare and sometimes wave in a hopeful way because the windows had one-way glass so anyone from a queen to a soccer star could be inside.

Hannah said, 'Typical of Angus to own such an over-the-top vehicle. He has an instinct for the trappings of power. I believe he's become quite an important personage since I left?' She was shaking with laughter. 'Probably because I left. You can't imagine what an unsuitable business wife I was. Clay under my fingers, hair in a mess, no dress sense, intolerant of fools, allergic to red wine and a lousy cook on top of it all. No wonder he booted me out.'

'Did he?' I was surprised. He'd said that she had left him.

'That was unfair,' she admitted. 'It was a mutual thing. We got along fine in

64

the beginning, but after a few years it became apparent that our ambitions were poles apart. Angus was desperate to be what he called A Top Man before he was thirty. I wanted to astound the art world with my brilliant ceramics. He was promoted to bigger and bigger jobs that absorbed all his emotional energy and took him away from home a great deal. I became obsessed with manipulating the blobs of clay spinning on my wheel, to the point where the children could barely speak English because they spent more time with their Zulu nanny than with me. When they grew past childhood, it got worse: now there were five of us revolving round the house like angry electrons, all with monumental egos. There had to be a big bang at some stage and when it happened, Angus and I decided that we were better apart than together. And so it has proved.'

She fell silent, looking out at the busy street. That day, she was wearing a voluminous trouser suit and a sling bag woven out of hairy brown jute and thick-soled brogues that would have looked at home on a grouse moor. Her taste for Wagnerian shoes alone would have meant social death as a Joburg executive's wife.

I said, 'You don't know how much I envy you, having those electrons buzzing about. I was an only child and my parents were elderly and polite with each other, so my childhood was a long quiet boredom alleviated only by school and books. Which is probably why I made such a disastrous mistake when I got married straight after university. I couldn't have chosen a worse escape hatch than Kurt.'

'We make so many mistakes that seem obvious later.' She spoke to her reflection in the window.

I had a sudden urge to explain my unconventional relationship with Angus. It seemed the right moment, and I wanted her to like me as much as I already liked her. 'My mistakes have been compounded by having no family to fall back on since my parents died. That's what Angus has been to me: a family friend. We haven't…ever…'

She turned to me and took my hand. 'You don't have to explain, Faith. He's been telling me about you for years. You've been as good as a family friend to him too, and I'm grateful for it. Made me feel less guilty about leaving. He needs people around him. Needs to feel that he's in control: making things happen, heaping up profits, bestowing advice and running everybody's lives for them, which was another reason why I had to leave him. It just got too much. I need space. I can't create in a maelstrom, and that's what Angus is.'

Up close now, I saw that her face had a furry golden sheen like the moths that blunder in through open windows on summer nights. In the intimacy of that plush back seat, I asked the question that had been hovering ever since Angus had begun hinting about his other lives. 'Does he have many friends like me?'

'You mean women?' She gave me a veiled look. 'How well do you know him?'

'Hardly at all, I'm beginning to think, though we've had Saturday lunch together for fifteen years. It's always been a conversational thing, you know? Talk and argument, puns and word games, nothing too personal. But the ground rules have changed since he told me about the cancer. He keeps talking about bad things he's done, hinting at secrets and saying that he wants to tie up his loose ends and I'm one of them. I feel that I'm being treated as a kind of confessional.'

'He wants absolution now? Again, how typical! What is he offering in exchange?'

I was about to say, 'He hasn't offered anything,' when I realised that of course he had. He had bribed me with parties and dinners and the dangled carrots of a suitable mate and a convertible. Most seductive of all, he had hinted at letting me into other compartments of his life.

Wanting to be honest with this sympathetic new friend but reluctant to let her know how tempted I was to try winkling out his secrets, I said, 'You know Angus. He offers friendship on his own terms – generous, but with obligations attached. I try to resist his blandishments, but it's hard.'

'Specially for a lonely person with no family ties.' She was still holding my hand, and I wondered if she was reading pulse messages from my inner being. I spent a lot of time trying to persuade myself I wasn't lonely.

I began to stutter, 'I'm – well, I – I suppose...' when I saw that Praise was conducting the Bentley through the Art Gallery gates and said, 'But here we are,' in a hearty tour guide's voice. 'Did you know that they've added a wing and changed the entrance so that it faces north on to Joubert Park instead of south over the railway tracks?'

She let my hand go with an understanding smile and my sense of propriety was saved. The moment of self-revelation did not happen again though we spent the whole day together roaming the streets and seeing the sights and visiting places she remembered. 'I want to get re-acquainted,' she said. 'It's all so different. The pavement vendors everywhere, for one thing.'

I remember it as a day of contrasts. The Bentley edging past patient queues for minibus taxis like a dowager negotiating an unemployment bureau. The graceful oriental curves of the new mosque on Sauer Street dwarfed by anonymous office buildings. Walking up Diagonal Street with its renovated Edwardian balconies above muti and blanket shops and fruit stalls, and the fast-food carts from which the aroma of sizzling boerewors wafted up the prismatic glass cliffs of No 11 and the Stock Exchange. Smooth-talking Zairean traders with French accents and sacks full of impressive African masks – 'Genuine tribal antiquities, madame!' – and wondering whether they had been plundered from AIDS-ravaged villages or made and aged on jungle assembly lines. The Oriental Plaza where she bought vivid silk saris for her daughters and a bag of samoosas because she said she could never find them as good in England. The refurbished MuseumAfrica tucked into what she remembered as the old Market sheds, where rock paintings rub shoulders with Struggle memorabilia and relocated shacks through which we walked in shamed silence, listening to the sounds of poverty and overcrowded squatter life. At a special display of African food, she sampled dried mopani worms – braver than me.

Sitting at a café table in Rockey Street afterwards, drinking beer and sharing the samoosas, Hannah commented on the lunchtime strollers: 'I'd never seen a mixed couple on the street till we got to London, yet look at this lovely relaxed scene.'

'Don't be taken in. Half of them are drug dealers or their clients. Another third are waiting to mug us.' One of the Hell's Angels hired to patrol the street throbbed past on a Harley Davidson, flexing the tattooed biceps bulging out of his T-shirt, and a group of young loiterers melted into an alley. 'See?'

'Yet look at those two.' She pointed to a black woman helping an elderly beard-ed man in a yarmulke over the street on his way to the Yeoville synagogue. 'Apartheid seems to have vanished.'

'Not yet, I'm afraid. The elections may have changed the balance of power but racism and inequality have by no means vanished,' I warned, and asked Praise to drive us north for more contrasts, past suburban shopping malls and Alexandra township and the burgeoning slums known as 'informal settlements' (as if that will dignify them) and through suburbs Hannah would remember. It was a crash course in Joburg domestic architecture, where crude shelters of rough packing-case timber and plastic and old metal signs poxy with rust can erupt overnight next to pastel cluster homes and the imposing nuclear bunkers of the rich with their dish antennae and manicured gardens. I pointed out the high walls and remote-controlled security gates and razor wire coiling everywhere, and took her to parking lots to listen to the doleful bleating of faulty car alarms.

'Enough of paranoia,' she said, looking shaken, and Praise drove us to Hillbrow ('I can't believe how sleazy it's got') then past the Civic Centre and the modern mausoleum that calls itself the Joburg General Hospital ('Monstrosities! They've spoilt the lovely ridges') and down to the motorway where we turned south.

There was a long silence as we rolled along the elevated section above unlove-ly commercial buildings and between nibbled-away mine dumps. 'Joburg doesn't look the same with motorways snaking everywhere and half the mine dumps gone,' she complained as we pulled up under the gum trees at Gold Reef City. But that didn't interest her either. 'It's tourist candyfloss. I'm not a tourist, I'm a former resident who wants to see what's been happening since I left. Could you take us to Soweto, Praise?'

He turned round in the driver's seat and faced us for the first time: a contained young face, firm lips, eyes unreadable behind the dark glasses. 'I would not like to do that, Madam. This car is too conspicuous.'

I hadn't heard Praise speak more than monosyllables before; he'd been a man in uniform opening and closing doors and standing next to the car, nodding when Angus gave his instructions. So his precise diction was a surprise – another of Angus's mysteries. And I thought, This man must know more about him than anyone else. Praise drives him to where he goes when he disappears.

Hannah was saying, 'Oh, how disappointing! I'd really like to visit Soweto. It's a part of Joburg I've heard so much about but never seen, hidden away for too long like a family skeleton.'

'I could take you to Chris Hani Baragwanath Hospital, which has a view from the footbridge over Soweto,' Praise conceded, and the last sight of our day's tour was the huge red sun subsiding into a smog of coal smoke and dust above patchwork tin roofs.

'Thank you both so much,' Hannah said as Praise double-parked at the Club entrance and we got out. She went round to his open window to shake his hand. 'I really appreciate the trouble you've been to, driving us about.'

'It was a pleasure, Madam.' The dark glasses angled up at her.

She fished for her purse among the parcels in her sling bag and took out five new hundred-rand notes. 'It's a small gesture, but I'd like to thank you particularly for the good care you take of Mr Quain. He's going to need it more than ever now, you know?'

The peaked cap jerked a nod. 'I know. But this isn't necessary, Madam. I am well paid.'

'It's my personal thank you. Please.'

After a moment he took the notes, flashed a boyish smile of thanks and the big black car pulled away in a smooth surge, gliding down Fordyce Street.

As we went up the steps and through the revolving door together to go and sit next to Angus's bed for a while and tell him what we'd seen, she said, 'Who is that reticent young man?'

'Praise Ngcobo. He's been driving the Bentley since it was delivered.'

'I must ask Angus about him. He always tried to hire people whom he owed or who owed him something; it ensured their loyalty, he used to say. I'd love to know which cranny of his past Praise comes from.'

I had to laugh. 'He's always insisting to me that loyalty is a dogged, unimaginative quality and usually misplaced.'

'Angus is adept at changing his tune to suit his audience. It's one of the secrets of his success.'

'Chameleon style?'

It was her turn to laugh. 'Exactly.'

Waiting for the lift, I said, 'What do you think of Joburg now?'

'Badly planned. Dirty. Appalling contrasts: beautiful old buildings fallen into neglect, civic decay cheek-by-jowl with treasures like the Art Gallery, people burrowing into covered malls to shop when they live in a God-given climate with year-round sunshine. This is a crazy city. I'm glad the children and I left when we did.'

In my driest voice I said, 'So it's a hopeless case?'

'Not at all. There's a huge vitality which is lacking in most European cities. I have the feeling that the people crowding the pavements are looking beyond the problems, saying to themselves: This is our city at last, and there are better things to come. It's as though Joburg's shiny commercial epidermis is being rubbed away to reveal its African bones.'

She went on in that vein as the lift creaked upwards and I followed in her wake down the passage, drooping with fatigue. Much as I welcomed her as a friend, Hannah was an exhausting companion to be with for a whole day. She fired questions and demanded answers, and kept picking at the scabs we South Africans have tried to grow over our sore places. When I saw that Angus was sleeping, I excused myself and slipped away to my quiet flat and a deep hot bath.

I lay there thinking, I wonder what the son and daughters are like? Whether they have suffered from the divorce and missed their father, or simply see him as a source of income. Hannah doesn't. Looking at the two of them, and thinking what fond and civilised friends they are, makes me realise the enormity of the mistake I made with Kurt. I was so naive when I married him, so fuzzy about who I was and what I wanted out of life... I must remember to tell Angus to drop the quest for zero defect because I'm a terminal klutz with men...

When I woke, the water was cold.

9

Hannah left a week after she arrived, disappearing into the airport weighed down by parcels of jazzy cotton fabrics in African designs for her pottery showroom. As we hugged goodbye, she said, 'Our eldest daughter may be flying out to see Angus in a few weeks, but I'm not sure about Benj. Like God, he moves in a mysterious way.'

'Benj?'

'You know, Benjamin, our son. We don't know if he's heard of Angus's illness yet.' She had explained that he was earning his way around the world with his guitar, collecting folk songs as he went.

'Where is he at the moment?'

'Somewhere in India. He doesn't communicate very often. He set off saying he wanted to learn about life, but the girls and I think it's a reaction to the pressure from Angus to enter a profession. Benj loathes being told what to do.'

'Like father, like son.'

We both laughed.

'It's been good to meet you, Faith. Thanks for the conducted tour round Joburg.'

'I enjoyed it. You made me look at familiar things with new eyes.'

'And thanks again for being so good to Angus. He really needs you now. Don't let his overbearing ways get you down.' There were tears in her eyes. 'I'll try to come back again before he – before…'

I said, 'He'll be well looked after between his doctors and me and the Club, don't worry.'

'You'll keep in touch?'

'Reuters won't be a patch on the Dobermann e-mail service.' I touched her mothy cheek. 'Tot siens, Hannah.'

During the drive in the Bentley back to Joburg, I sat looking at the back of

Praise's head and wondering what his connection was with Angus. But there were no answers in the softly spoken, 'My pleasure. Goodbye, Madam,' in response to my thanks for the drive.

By Saturday evening Angus, now totally bald, had recovered enough to get dressed and come down to the dining room for a light meal of consommé and the chef's cinnamon-scented rice pudding, a great favourite with the older members who had a sentimental fondness for nursery food.

When we got into the lift again I must have pressed the wrong ivory button, because it creaked up past the third floor to the top floor where I'd never been before. Beyond the lift cage a narrow passage stretched away on both sides, its utilitarian linoleum and wan lighting in stark contrast to the deep-pile carpeting and creamy paintwork and elegant wall sconces of the passages on the lower floors. I slid aside the concertina gate, held it open with my foot and put my head out. 'What's up here?'

'Attics and staff quarters. This is where I found the furniture for my suite.'

'Is there a lot of stuff in the attics?'

He nodded. 'Nine decades' worth. Club policy is never to throw anything away. Joburg antique dealers would sell their grandmothers to get behind some of those doors.'

I felt a thrill of lust, not for the hoarded antiques but for the historical perspective I could glean from rooms full of discarded social objects going back to an Edwardian mining town. 'Do you think the Club management would let me look around from a professional point of view? They must be full of Africana.'

'I could ask. Not sure how they'll respond. Stuffy lot.'

Angus's speech was more staccato than usual and I saw from the way he hunched into the corner of the lift that he was close to exhaustion again. I pulled my foot back so the gate could close and pressed the third floor button and said, 'Never mind. It was just a thought. Let's get you back to your rooms and into bed.'

'Don't bloody nanny me, woman,' he warned.

'Sorry. Keep forgetting.' As the lift jerked to a stop, I drew his free arm through mine and walked him slowly along the passage to his room. 'We'll just make believe I'm a callgirl.'

'Would that you were.'

'Is that a proposition?'

'Wishful thinking, alas. I…' He stopped, then said, 'No undignified confessions tonight. Just deposit me at my door and I'll see what I can do about your having a look at the attics.'

'Can't I help you into bed?'

'Not a foot over my threshold, trollop. I shall be fine. Feeling much better than yesterday. Going back to work on Monday.'

'Angus, you're not well enough.'

There was a feral gleam in his eyes as he turned to me in the doorway into his sitting room. 'I'll be the one who decides that. Off with you, now.'

I hated to leave him wrestling alone with his weakness and fear and rage at being sabotaged by disease, but I was a friend, not a wife or a lover, and there was nothing more I could do for him. So I said, 'Take care,' and walked away.

True to his word, he spoke to the Club management and I was summoned to appear before a members' committee to plead my case. From long experience at looking the part of an academic historian, I wore my grey suit with a prim white blouse, my most earnest pair of hornrims and an important black leather briefcase.

The meeting was held late on Wednesday afternoon. Angus met me in the entrance hall looking as imperious as he always had – paler and thinner, but walking upright without the stick. He whistled when he saw me and said, 'Excellent camouflage, my dear. I couldn't have done better myself.'

The hall porter had lifted his head at the whistle and was watching us with interest, so I made a decorous response. 'You're looking good today.'

'The chemo must be doing the trick. I feel like a new man,' he said, hustling me towards the library where committee meetings were held. 'I've given them your credentials and explained what you'll be looking for. Just lay on the discreet charm and I'm sure they'll give you permission.'

We entered the library which I had only been allowed to peep into before. It was on the same baronial scale as the main lounge: shelves of books lining three walls rising up to a decorative pressed steel ceiling, bay windows with deep window seats along the fourth wall, tall library ladders on runners, desks lit by green-shaded brass lamps, and more leather armchairs. On the floor was a vast carpet that looked as though it had come from a Turkish brothel, a riot of what must once have been lush scarlet and crimson flowers faded to a sinuous intermingling of salmon and claret.

I felt a surge of furious envy and for a moment wanted to throw down my briefcase and howl, 'Why should all this splendour be reserved only for Club members? What about the rest of the human race?'

But what was the point? Clubs at all levels justify their existence by pointing to the principle of free assembly: you are just as much at liberty to choose your friends as we are to choose our members. Prison gangs and township self-help groups are as much exclusive clubs as are associations of golfers. And the Johannesburg Club had, in the spirit of the New South Africa, begun gingerly to admit women and black members from those realms of business and society as had provided a leavening of Jewish members when they had at last been admitted.

What really got my goat, though, was the fact that the white Anglo-Saxon males who formed the Club's core continued to have a stranglehold on so many of our country's physical assets: time-hallowed buildings and academically excellent schools and old boys' bursaries as well as important jobs and beautiful libraries. How infinitely more enraged the majority of black South Africans must feel, I thought, if they believed all the election promises.

Angus was nudging me forward hissing, 'Concentrate, old girl. This is your only chance.'

Planted on the enviable carpet were six pairs of polished black lace-ups. Their owners sat in a semicircle of armchairs. Six concerned male faces turned towards the female interloper who wanted to delve into their past and discover God knows what dangerous secrets.

'Ah – Miss Dobermann,' a plummy voice began, and the inquisition was on.

I must have acquitted myself well enough. After Angus and I had left the room and they had deliberated for a while with the aid of a bottle of Spanish sherry, I was called in and given reluctant permission to explore the attics. The chairman of the committee took pains to explain that this was a special concession to one of their most valued residents, and made possible only by my standing as a historian. I would be allowed to search drawers and packed containers with the proviso that I replaced things as I found them, disclosed any unusual finds and removed nothing from the building. If I wished to copy a document, I was to do so in the Club office under supervision. I would be allowed into the attics only on Saturdays as it was a quiet day for the staff, and someone would have to accompany me – either a member or a member of staff.

'We trust, Miss Dobermann, that you are not seeking to wash our dirty linen – if indeed there be any – in public?' he concluded.

I stifled a snotty retort and said like a lamb, 'Of course not.'

'We also require you to sign an undertaking that anything you may wish to publish relating to the Club must be vetted by this committee.'

When I agreed, he produced two pages of close typing which I signed, followed by two witnesses, as Angus sipped a proffered glass of sherry. There were not enough glasses for me to have one too; my permission to rootle about in the Club's past must have been considered favour enough for that day.

Angus said as we walked down the passage towards the entrance hall, 'I had to move heaven and bloody earth to convince them that you're interested in the history of the place, not just poking around out of curiosity. Even if you are.'

'Gee, thanks, pal.'

'You won't let me down? Rummage where you oughtn't? I've laid my reputation on the line for you.'

Irritated that he should think he had to spell it out, I said, 'I haven't let you down yet, and I'm not going to now. When can I get started?'

'I volunteered to make myself available as your supervisor this Saturday.'

That stopped me in my tracks. I hadn't expected him to become involved, and he wouldn't be able to do so often, I knew. Having to find someone with the time and the inclination to be a watchdog was going to be a problem. Perhaps I could pay one of the staff to do it?

'What do you say to my generous offer?' he prompted.

Flustered, I said, 'I wouldn't dream of imposing on you. It'll be a horrible dusty exhausting job.'

He let out the amused rumble I hadn't heard for weeks. 'You will be doing the horrible dusty work, old girl. I will be reclining in an easy chair making sure you don't steal the family silver.'

'But...'

He held up his hand and the signet ring gleamed. 'No buts. I'm on top of the world this week, fit and bloody-minded and raring to go. Been in the office for three days and everyone's complaining about the work load, lazy sods. I will expect you on Saturday morning at about ten, and we can discuss what you've found over our usual lunch. Right?'

He was his ebullient old self, calling the shots in the office and ordering me around. Maybe the chemo really was working, I thought, waving goodbye from the far side of the revolving door. Miracles do happen.

The attics were my Rosetta Stone: an extraordinary key to Joburg fads and fashions and foibles since the Club was founded. Management must always have been a conservative affair. As each period's furnishings and utensils and pastimes declined from out-of-date to unwanted, they had been consigned to the attics in case they were needed again, as had the effects of members who had died in residence without a traceable family.

On that first morning, as Angus lolled on a chaise longue under a cobwebbed window with the latest *Economist*, I prowled the main attic giving off subdued shrieks of delight. (It had been stressed that my investigations should be unobtrusive and not disturb the members).

Under dust sheets was an army of heavy old chairs and tables and desks, beds with coir mattresses on sagging bases of interlinked wire, worn tapestry stools, rolled-up carpets, marble washstands, lidded enamel buckets, calico screens, folded curtains and counterpanes and eiderdowns, mosquito nets gone sepia with age, archery targets, croquet and backgammon sets, piles of odd crockery and kitchenware, memorabilia from the two World Wars, boxes of 78 rpm records and books in foxed paper jackets, hand-wound gramophones, brittle Bakelite radios (their dials reading Daventry and Hilversum), photograph albums shivering with fishmoths, top hat boxes, tea chests, bundles of fishing rods and strapped gun-cases and the heavy canvas safari equipment you see in old hunting photographs, leprous with mould.

From the number of cabin trunks and shabby leather suitcases, it seemed that there had been many solitary clubmen over the years. Younger sons and black sheep banished to the colonies, perhaps; mining engineers come to the Reef to make their fortunes; lone ivory and trophy hunters, professional soldiers with no family ties, bachelors and widowers.

It was the richest historical treasure trove I had ever seen, and it was all mine to explore and annotate. Angus had to coerce me into the lift to go down to lunch and afterwards, seeing my disappointment when he wanted to rest, tipped Boniface to accompany me as overseer.

From his austere expression, it was clear that Boniface disapproved of my meddling in the past. At one point during the afternoon, having watched me go through a mahogany wardrobe and a gentleman's compactum, he said, puzzled, 'What is the madam looking for, please?'

I answered, 'I'm looking for history,' but he didn't understand. He thought I was turning over stones in search of scorpions and it offended him. His life had been devoted to the welfare of the Club's members and the keeping of their secrets, and my prying could only damage the protective shell he had constructed during his tenure. The disdain for women that he shared with so many of the members was close to the surface during that long dusty afternoon. I could never look at Boniface later without seeing my father and the headmaster at my primary school rolled into one: the disapproving paterfamilias.

10

The following Monday, Angus took me to the opening of an exhibition of West African art at which I bought an exquisite carved ebony head from Ghana, fending him off as he tried to pay for it.

'Why won't you let me give you a small present?' he demanded. 'I chose this exhibition because I know you like African carvings.'

Hannah had warned me. I said, 'No more bribes,' and bent to sign my credit card slip.

'What are you insinuating?' He spoke in a low hurt tone, pulling out the organ stop marked 'Quaver'.

'No offence intended, you know that.' I stood up again and turned to him as the gallery assistant wrapped my purchase in tissue paper. 'It was understood from the beginning that I'd act as your partner out of simple friendship, not for benefits conferred.'

'God, you're a prickly individual.' He swung away from me to scan the overdressed glitterati who stood chatting to each other over slopping wine glasses, paying scant attention to the artworks.

'Angus,' I said to his huffy back, 'please try to understand. I want our relationship to remain as uncomplicated as it always has been, with no obligations on either side.'

'You want the moon. Everything's changed. My life has become a seething mass of complications.' He spoke with a bitterness I had not heard before.

I took the wrapped carving in its chic plastic carrier bag from the gallery assistant and walked round to face him. 'What are you saying?'

'I'm saying that I'm getting into deep water and need a diverting companion, not a virago who stands on her dignity every time I try to make a gesture of appreciation.'

There was a rage in him now that went much further than the odd flash of cruelty in our conversations. I wondered if it stemmed from fear of the deadly disease he was fighting or if there was another cause: one of his deals about to go wrong, or worry about possible exposure. As a man of high repute in the public eye, Angus had a lot to lose if someone blew the whistle on him. I thought of the line from the old song – 'Pyramids crumble, Gibraltar may tumble...' – and put a contrite hand on his arm.

'I'm sorry. I see that I did offend you and really didn't mean to.'

'You're too proud, Mizz Dobermann.'

'Guilty.'

'And I demand an apology for having the purity of my motives questioned. A small gift to a friend, I wish to point out, is a mosquito bite to a Southern Right whale like me. Do you know how bloody rich I am?' This last was flung at me in a voice so tight that I barely made out the words.

'I don't want to know.'

He slammed his open palm against his forehead. 'Fool. I forgot. Academics don't like to talk about money.'

'This isn't about money. It's about self-respect. I'm not as other-worldly as you seem to believe.' ·

'You're worse. You're holier than thou.'

'And you're an overbearing bully. This going around together isn't working, Angus. I'm no more a social butterfly than Hannah was.'

'I have no use for vapid social butterflies.' His scorn bit like acid. 'And stop using Hannah to evade the issue, which is a matter of accepting gestures of friendship with good grace.'

'That's not it. I just won't be bought.'

'And I'm not trying to buy.'

'You damn well are. You've got so used to people cowering in obeisance every time you give an order that you can't handle being refused.' My contrition had evaporated. The quarrel was going way past our usual civilised disagreements into an ugly exchange of insults. I wondered what I was doing in that place with all those chattering people whose heads were beginning to turn in our direction.

'And you think it's your duty to keep refusing me so I don't get a swollen head, is that it?' He was glaring down his nose now, trying to intimidate me into agreeing with him.

'Something like that.'

'Typical.' He threw his head back in a roar of laughter.

Jewellery flashed as more heads turned in our direction: spiky-lashed eyes took in his angry mirth, then raked my face for an answer. I felt a mortifying warmth rise up my neck and cheeks and hissed, 'Please stop this. Please.'.

But he went on roaring his amusement and several people standing nearby started to laugh too, thinking there was something funny going on which they didn't want to appear to miss. I stood like a clod, holding my plastic bag and wishing the sisal carpeting underfoot would open up and swallow me. As the laughter swelled, the gallery's black walls seemed to squeeze closer, the gaudy paintings to throb and sizzle, the spotlit carvings to stare at me with uncomprehending eyes. What was I doing there, the butt of an in-joke between this man I hardly knew and the guffawing society he moved in?

I said, 'I'm leaving,' and tried to slink away with my purchase, but his hand shot out and detained me. 'Not so fast. The issue isn't resolved yet.'

'I don't care about the bloody issue! Let me go.'

'Please don't, old girl. We'll call it quits, right?' He was chuckling, all anger evaporated. Reflected spotlights jiggled on the shiny baldness which he had made no attempt to cover. 'I concede I was getting heavy there. But so were you. We don't want to spoil a good thing with mutual pomposities, do we?'

I shook my head, unable to answer. His sudden change of mood had taken me by surprise; and it would happen often as his hopes fluctuated during the desperate fight to stay alive. I learnt to cope better but could not armour myself against a growing sense of betrayal. He was using me as he always used people – as combination sounding board and sparring partner – but how could I object now? One does not abandon a best friend in trouble. Whatever the provocation.

'Forgiven?' he asked with a winning smile.

'Forgiven,' I said, and put a clammy hand over his. Thus we proceeded round the exhibition once more, Angus nodding at his many acquaintances and I giving them inscrutable smiles that would keep them guessing as to the exact nature of our relationship.

Rolling home in the Bentley afterwards with him dozing against his cushions beside me, I sat guessing too. Just how rich was he? And besides this luxurious car and his gentleman's clothes and his rooms at the Club, what did he do with his money? He had established trust funds for his children long ago and Hannah was proudly self-supporting. What happened to all the rest? I remembered the story he had told me of the Johannesburg millionaire who, trusting neither cash nor governments nor chancy investments, had provided for his children with separate piles of gold bars in a Swiss bank, each pile bearing a child's name written on a piece of paper. Was Angus that rich? And was it money-hunger that drove him – or was there something else?

The carved ebony head from Ghana sits on my desk now, its heavy-lidded eyes and pursed lips presiding over my struggle to get Angus down on paper. It is not an easy undertaking. To say he was larger than life is to use a feeble cliché. He was a furnace, devouring people whole but also capable of bestowing grace and strength on those he valued, as a furnace turns out blown glass and toughened steel. He gave me enduring friendship and a family to make up for the one I lacked; only towards the end of his life did I learn of his many generous gifts to others. The good was tangled with the bad in the complex byways of his nature; the charm with the cruelty, the intelligence with the calculation, the Renaissance breadth of talent with the poor white's cunning.

Our social whirl continued that week with a reception at the Michelangelo for a retiring chairman, a gala performance of Aïda at the Civic Theatre to benefit Hospice, and a private dinner party in Illovo.

'What's the occasion for the dinner?'

We were standing on the Club steps late on Saturday afternoon, elevated by their sandstone elegance above the desolation of soiled newsprint, beer cartons, plastic bags, flattened cardboard boxes, rotten fruit and other detritus abandoned by the pavement vendors whom we had watched from the bay window in the dining room packing up an hour before.

'Bob Snerton and I serve together on several boards of directors. Incestuous business, the cross-holdings in this town. I suspect that he needs my support on an awkward clause at a forthcoming board meeting and hopes to cozen me with libations of fine wine and his stick-like wife's nouvelle cuisine.'

'Why go if it's so obvious?'

Angus shrugged. 'Politics. Bob has scratched my back more than once.'

I wondered if he had been involved in one of Angus's deals. 'Was I asked too?'

'By reputation rather than by name. Word seems to have got round that I've been seen squiring a woman young enough to be my daughter, and Bob asked with a smirk if I wanted to bring a partner. I told him yes. Please come. I shall die of boredom if you don't. The Snertons' bunfights are so correct.'

'I'm not at your beck and call. Yet.'

'You're being stiff-necked again. Please come.'

I stood considering. Meals with my friends tended to be home-made pasta and olive bread and salads with trendy ingredients – rocket, radicchio, sprouts, sundried tomatoes, chunks of goat cheese, toasted seeds, lentils. Being mostly academics, they live in old suburbs where dining rooms long ago gave way to open-plan kitchens with children's drawings on the walls, dog hairs on the chairs and junk shop china in different patterns. It would be diverting to experience a formal dinner party for a change, so I agreed to go.

The Snerton pile in Illovo was a Deep South mansion with two-storey columns and impressive security: armed guard, Rottweilers, radio alarm and a steel gate that slid into a three-metre perimeter wall topped with five strands of live electric wires. The combination must have had a magnetic effect on the ungodly because Bob had been hijacked twice at the gate before the armed guard was hired.

'Once more unto the fray,' Angus said as we swept up the drive between banks of floodlit tropical plants.

'Is this part of the quest for zero defect?' I asked him. 'Or will they all be safely married?'

His face was in shadow as he answered. 'Married, I expect. The top executive requires a willing spouse.'

'You seem to have managed well enough without one.'

There was a glimmer of a smile. 'I have the Club, whose ministrations beat Hannah's on every score.'

'Except warmth and affection.'

'Conceded. I do miss her at times.'

I did too now.

Behind the columns, everything matched: the pictures with the decor, the swagged brocade curtains with the tasselled brocade sofas, the crystal chandeliers with the glittering monogrammed glassware, the women in silk and diamonds with the distinguished-looking executives in dinner jackets. Bob Snerton was a big bluff red-faced man with a goatee. When he introduced me to his wife, Moira, I understood why Angus had called her stick-like. The bony frame under her couturier sheath looked as though it was nourished on black coffee which had induced a high state of stress; the hands wrapped round the stem of her martini glass were trembling.

I soon lost Angus in the pre-dinner hour devoted to mingling, business gossip and cocktails. Enthroned on a bar stool, he was beguiling a small group of women, turning from one to the other with a comment here and a compliment there. I never saw him look as good as he did that night holding court in a new dinner jacket cut to flatter his leaner body, a slick of silver beginning to show in place of his lost hair. He made the other men in the room seem subdued and colourless by comparison; and their envy showed on their faces, fighting with conjecture... How does Quain do it? Has he really licked the Big C?

I had my first daiquiri and an animated conversation with a stockbroker, then tucked myself into a corner to watch the action. The lone black couple stood in a circle of whites eager to show that they had never entertained a racist thought. Moira Snerton fluttered between the hired waiters, the bar and the door that led to the dining room. During one of her disappearances, I saw Bob edge a busty blonde into a corner and remembered Mother saying, 'Men like something they can grab hold of.' Quelling my irritation that her disdainful ghost should continue to haunt me, I thought, There's more to Moira's anxiety than meets the eye. She must rattle like a skeleton in bed – if she gets it at all.

'Penny for your thoughts?' Angus stood behind me.

I blushed. 'You don't want to know.'

'Sex? Scandal? Don't blame you. There are enough intrigues in this room to fill the gossip columns for a month. That beefy fellow over there, for example…' He regaled me with the story of a first wife who had been humiliated for years after she had been surprised in bed with the tanned hunk who ran the pool-cleaning service. The husband had made her wear a device which allowed him to check on her whereabouts at all times until she had resorted to a bottle of sleeping tablets.

'Did she die?'

'Mercifully, yes. Now he's married again, he makes his new wife wear the thing too. That's her over there.' He indicated a woebegone young blonde wearing a diamond collar.

'Poor kid.'

'Poor, hell. Silly little bitch got suckered by his wealth. This town's full of unwary females with no damn common sense.'

'How can you be so unsympathetic?'

His expression hardened. 'Had to fight my own way up, learn to fend for myself. Like you did. No time for those who allow themselves to get caught up in disasters in spite of all the warning signs. The bugger's a known sadist. She should have been more careful.'

I felt chilled, and was relieved when we went into dinner to be seated at the far end of the long table. Angus in his brash social environment was a different person to the thoughtful, perspicacious man I lunched with at the Club; he had perfected his chameleon skills to the point where they operated subconsciously.

My relief was short-lived, since my neighbour on the left owned a brewery and his conversation ran to alcohol percentages and the proud boast, when he heard I was a writer, that he never had time to read books. Upon which he turned away to discourse on the growing of hops with the woman on his other side. The chair to my right remained empty during the first course, which gave me time to contemplate the array of roses and sterling silver, the porcelain nosegays holding the place cards and the starched napkin on my side plate tortured into the shape of a water-lily. A question began to fester in my head: What am I doing here?

The first course – and all those that followed – consisted of tiny edibles in jewel-like sauces arranged like paintings which Moira Snerton must have been slaving over for hours; hence her air of exhausted anxiety. Not a bean or a snow pea was out of place; not a morsel remained au naturel. The julienne carrots were of an exact length, marshalled in neat bundles tied with spring onion leaves. The radishes looked like roses. The thumb-sized lamb noisettes were piped with blobs of pâté. The potatoes were mashed and squeezed out in identical twirls. You hesitated to disturb the composition and when you did, it was consumed in seconds. Most of the guests must have risen hungry from the table.

I was wondering how many would raid the fridge for last night's leftovers after they got home when a voice bellowed from the door. 'Apologies, all.'

'Jem!' The cry went up in several voices as people turned to greet a man whose face I recognised from the business pages of the newspapers – a supermarket mogul, I thought, or was it coal mines?

'Unavoidably delayed. Matters of state. You know how it is.' He threw a wave at his fat glum wife who was sitting between Bob and Angus, then worked the table, pumping hands and dispensing kisses. In time he pulled out the empty chair next to mine and sat down braying at his hostess, 'Truly sorry, Moira. Hate to disrupt a good party.'

There were admiring murmurs round the table. I was to learn as the evening progressed that Jem Lowing elicited a Greek chorus wherever he went, and that he and Angus were old enemies. Watching him as he joked with the people sitting beyond him, I thought that he looked like an intelligent gorilla: low forehead under a thatch of dark hair, beetling eyebrows, small bright eyes, heavy jaw.

As he speared his last tiny mouthful of the third course, he turned to me and said, 'So, I hear you're the famous Faith. When are the nuptials?'

'What nuptials?'

'With Quain, of course.'

I said, 'I've no plans to marry anyone. Least of all Angus.'

Fork poised, he grinned through shreds of masticated basil. 'That wasn't my impression. You've looked more than pally in the photographs I've seen.'

'We've been friends for years.'

'Just good friends?' With a knowing wink.

'Just friends. It is possible, you know.'

'Not with Quain.' He shot Angus a hostile look.

'Why do you say that?'

The gorilla eyes glittered. 'The man's a low-class bully. Take care you don't get caught with your pants down.'

I pushed my chair back. 'You're talking about a friend. Excuse me.'

'Leaving already?'

'Hardly.'

Heads were beginning to turn; I seemed to have developed a genius for attracting unwelcome attention. I stalked out with flaming cheeks and found a door in the hallway labelled 'Powder Room'. Moira Snerton had thought of everything. Besides the embroidered guest towels and bowl of potpourri and jar of scented soaps, it was supplied with a pile of English *House & Garden* magazines which kept me occupied until I could sidle back to my chair under cover of the rising level of hilarity over the fourth course.

Jem Lowing did not speak to me again and the evening dragged on without incident. Angus and I left early and were waiting under the columned portico for the Bentley when he said, 'I was wrong about Snerton's motives. He wanted to make mischief tonight.'

'What do you mean?'

'Asking Lowing and me to the same meal, and then seating you next to him. We haven't spoken for more than five years.'

'Why not?'

'My firm picked up discrepancies during an audit on his company, Impex Incorporated, and the Receiver made him forfeit his ill-gotten gains.'

'You're one to talk about ill-gotten gains.'

'Ah, but I'm too careful to get caught.'

'Yet you're implacable with others?'

'Quain & Associates has a reputation to maintain.'

Now he sounded pompous as well as smug. 'As financial policemen? That's like the pot calling the kettle black.'

'As a solid, reliable firm of unimpeachable integrity. Ask anyone in this town.'

'But you said…'

'Unimpeachable, do you hear?' He was glaring at me. 'My private dealings are a separate matter: mine and mine alone. Damn sorry I mentioned them now.'

I flared, 'Damn sorry I listened, and even more that I came. This has not been an enjoyable evening. The food was pretentious. The people were boring. The house is unspeakable. And as for your Mr Lowing…'

'Not mine. No time for the bugger at all, nor he for me, as you will have gathered.' Angus had heard the Bentley rolling up the drive and turned his head to watch it glide towards us. I wondered if he had even heard my outburst. 'We also caught him diddling his pension fund. Cheating his own employees. That's what I call unspeakable. He only avoided prosecution by swearing it was a clerical error and doubling the amount he was ordered to pay back. I made sure that little lot cost him his membership of the Club. As a consequence, he hates my guts.'

'Hardly surprising.'

The Bentley was drawing up and Angus took my arm, appearing to forget that we were on the verge of yet another argument. 'What did he tell you about me anyway?'

With more than usual relish – Angus was being impossible that night, alternately charming and bloody-minded – I reported, 'That you are a low-class bully. And to take care I don't get caught with my pants down.'

His roar of laughter rang out over the floodlit garden and set the Rottweilers barking. The guard charged out of the gate-house with a drawn submachine gun and swung it in menacing arcs. A second guard ran out of the shadows yelling into a walkie-talkie, then seeing that the unwonted noise came from one of the dinner guests, gestured at the first and disappeared again.

When he had stopped laughing Angus said, 'The first part of what Lowing said is true. The second is indicative of his proclivity for smutty bullshit. Hard as hell on his wife too, I hear.'

As we settled into the back seat and Praise closed the doors, I had a moment of revelation. Even mortally ill, Angus enjoyed the egg dance that his life had become. I turned to where his head lay against the back-rest cushion in his corner. 'You like being mysterious and all-knowing, don't you?'

'"A riddle wrapped in a mystery inside an enigma",' he quoted. 'Churchill talking about Russia in 1939.'

'They should call you the conundrum of Diagonal Street.'

It wasn't meant as a compliment, but I think it pleased him more than anything else I said during those weeks.

One of the last big functions we attended together was a luncheon hosted by a Japanese company at the Sandton Towers where I tasted raw fish for the first time – a leap of faith that rewarded me with a fresh and delicate sea taste. I continued to be amazed at how well he looked: spruce and full of energy. Losing the extra weight suited him; he was Marlon Brando as Mark Anthony, all zestful fury, rather than the aging Caesar he had been playing. People buzzed round him to utter their congratulations on his recovery.

I heard one man, eyeing me, ask if there was an announcement pending.

'Not that I know of,' Angus boomed, 'unless you mean the one at Amalgamated Couplings?'

Every pair of ears in his vicinity pricked up and there was a flurry of murmured comment.

'Amalgamated, eh?'

'Must be a rights issue.'

'Cautionary announcement, perhaps?'

'The share price has moved up ten in the past two weeks.'

During the next half hour I saw several men drift towards the doorway and hunch over their cellphones in the lobby outside. Angus noticed them too and bent to say in my ear, 'Avoid any man who acts on a rumour he overhears at a party. He's not worth the paper he's written on.'

'I intend to avoid them all.'

'Don't be like that. Executives are a very select group, you know. It has its share of wankers, but there aren't any won't-works or clock-punching civil serpents.' He almost spat the last two words. 'These are achievers. I haven't spotted the right candidate for your hand yet, but it's not for lack of trying.'

I said, 'Please stop the silly quest, Angus. I want to enjoy these parties, not worry about impressing people.'

He gave me his carborundum look: an abrasive blue glare intensified by the navy polka-dot silk tie he was wearing. 'Come off it, old girl. Time marches on and boyfriends don't grow on trees.'

To quell my rising annoyance, I told myself that he was definitely better if he was starting to boss me around again. And added a rider: If – when – he's recovered, I hope he keeps me on as an occasional partner. The giddy round of socialising had given my life an unexpected new dimension; I was having more fun than I'd had in years and (in contrast to Angus) putting on weight. Since the beginning of our friendship he had nagged me about being too thin and made jokes about feeding me decent lunches to fatten me up. But – biltong and chocolate excepted – eating had never been important to me. Now that I was dabbling my own snout in the trough, however, I was beginning to realise how seductive the high life and its splendid food and drink can be.

I said, 'Don't think that I don't appreciate what you're trying to do, Angus. But you can't run my affairs for me. I refuse to be organised.'

He stood jiggling his watch chain. 'You should know by now that when I set my mind to something, I don't let go. What I expect from you in return for favours rendered…' the glare intensified '…is a modicum of willingness to fall in with a scheme that you know is in your best interests.'

King Quain in all his power and glory had spoken, and he expected agreement. Questions banged about in my head… Why does he keep on doing this? If it's to put me in his debt, what favour does he expect from me in return? Is he still the friend I thought I knew, or a tyrant who kept his God complex on a leash until the death-threat of cancer let it loose? I had observed similar behaviour in married acquaintances: the male need to dominate and the female instinct to keep the peace by giving in just enough to keep him crowing on top of his dung-heap as she sneaks round while he's not looking.

But this is all wrong, I told myself, returning his glare. I'm not married to him. I don't have to do what he says and I don't want to be a damn loose end in his life. I want to go back to being simply his friend.

I was opening my mouth to blurt these things when he said, 'Put a bung in it, Faith. We're bidden to lunch in a moment and you need a serene mind for your first acquaintance with Japanese food. You can give me both barrels going home in the car.'

Of course my ire had dissipated by then under the soothing influence of sashimi and tempura and shabu-shabu and a lot of warm sake. If this was the high life, I wanted more of it – even if I had to put up with Angus's machinations.

11

Angus was away the following weekend, whisked off by Praise in the Bentley to one of the destinations he never spoke about. Prunella phoned me on Thursday to crow.

'Mr Quain said to tell you that he won't be at home this Saturday, and will you please contact the Club secretary, Mr Barkin, who will make arrangements for someone to supervise your work in the attics.' Her tone insinuated that she wasn't in the least surprised they didn't trust me on my own.

To provoke her, I said, 'Where could Mr Quain have gone?'

'I am not at liberty to say, Mizz Dobermann.' Stiff propriety tinged with triumph.

'Could he have gone to Cape Town to visit an elderly relative? Or to England to see his ex-wife and children? Or – surprise, surprise – to a health farm?'

There was a long pause while she tried to figure out whether I was being insulting or not, then she repeated, 'I am not at liberty to say. Those are his standing instructions.'

I tried a direct assault. 'Do you know where he goes, Prunella?'

Another, longer, pause. 'No. But of course I have a list of phone numbers where I can contact him if there's an emergency.'

At last, a chink in his armour. 'And have you worked out from the area codes where these places could be?'

Longest pause of all as she debated whether to tell the truth. 'I'm – I'm not at liberty to say.'

So she knew his whereabouts and was probably sweating under the black bouffant curls. I felt a pang of sympathy for her, an ageing private secretary dependent on an ailing boss for her status and livelihood.

I said, 'Well, at least I know who to contact if there should be an emergency,' and rang off.

Who else would be likely to have this list? I wondered. And the answer came at once: Mr Barkin, the Club secretary. I phoned and made an appointment to see him in his office on Saturday.

The Club office was behind the hall porter's desk and as usual Mr Barkin was hunched over his computer pecking at the keys. He was one of those polite, clever, self-effacing men who make good personal assistants to the rich and powerful. He wore a black cloth jacket and lived in the Club's shadows, ever willing and solicitous, his face the colour of skim milk intensifying to purple smudges round deep-sunk eyes, his thinning hair slick with hair gel. I had the feeling that he was a fame junkie, feeding off the crumbs of glory scattered by the more distinguished members.

Angus called him Barkin Mad. 'Never leaves the Club unless he absolutely has to. Terrified of the streets. Verges on agoraphobic, poor bastard,' he'd said. 'But he's a bloody good organiser. Keeps a beady eye on everything that opens and shuts in this place. Not a pin drops without Barkin knowing about it.'

I remembered how Hannah had called Angus a 'poor old thing' and had to suppress a smile. Now that I had met her, I could see signs of their marriage in the common words and phrases they used and the glances they had shared when struck by the same thing. I hoped devoutly that there was nothing of Kurt still lurking in me.

That Saturday, Mr Barkin had arranged for the housekeeper to sit with me for as long as I needed her. I said, 'Thanks. How much should I pay her?'

'Mr Quain has already done so. Miss Dobermann...' He gulped more breath, then ventured, 'Would you think it forward of me to offer my services – next week, perhaps? The history of our membership interests me very much. Very much indeed.'

The last time I remembered someone talking about being forward was during my Georgette Heyer period, a teenage holiday spent with my nose in a succession of historical romances. To hear the phrase being used in the 1990s was curiously touching. And if he was as efficient as Angus said he was, he'd know his way around the attics.

I said, 'I'd really value your help. How about this afternoon?'

'I'll come up later, then.' He showed a timid row of teeth. 'Barkin is willin'.'

He looked expectant, so I managed a weak smile to show that I caught the reference. Behind his head next to a framed photograph of the Queen Mother I saw a list of telephone numbers taped to the wall; if Angus's contact numbers weren't there, they could be in the formidable Rolodex to one side of the computer.

That morning I concentrated on a pair of tin trunks full of documents relating to the early days of the Club: menus and housekeeping bills and laundry lists and wine delivery slips, all the minutiae of daily living that illuminate social history. But I found it hard to keep my mind on the past. As I sifted through spattered notebooks and wads of brittle paper, I kept thinking about the new Angus who had risen like a choleric phoenix from the steady glow of our long friendship. Had I, in my need for a fulfilling relationship, blinded myself to his less attractive traits? Or had he concealed his real self from me all these years with malicious intent, leading me up a garden path sited to disclose only as much as was necessary to get what he wanted from me?

Either way I was the sucker, I reasoned, and fully justified in tracking down other information he had concealed from me, such as where he went when he disappeared. It was hard to believe that he came from a poor white family though it would explain a lot. He'd have had to graft long and hard to fight his way up to where he was now, and there would have been palms to grease and favours to repay.

It was fitting that he had started off working for a ships' chandler, because I saw now that Angus was a trader in the Hanseatic tradition, captain of his own ship, bartering and haggling his way through life in a series of treaties and trade-offs. How appropriate that he had made it to the top in Johannesburg, a city where southern Africa's trade routes converge and commerce is king. And where the mining camp ethos still rules: tough guys make it, sissies get dirt kicked in their faces and women are rated according to their entertainment value.

Thoughts of a dry brain in a dry season ⁓. appropriate for that dusty attic.

After helping me sort through documents all afternoon, Mr Barkin invited me down to the office for a chat about the Club's history. He had been delving into the archives in his spare time and was making notes about the more colourful members over the years. While I sat trying to think of a way to scan the list of telephone numbers taped to the wall, he told me with relish of the mining magnate Sir Gerald Wotherspoon who had ridden his horse up the steps and through a side door into the dining room on the day the Treaty of Versailles was signed in 1919, for a celebratory repast of Brown Windsor soup, roast sirloin, trifle and port.

'You can still see the hoof-marks on the parquet. Yes. I can show you,' Mr Barkin was saying when the hall porter called him to sign in a reciprocal member, leaving me alone in the office.

Angus's contact telephone numbers were on the list, as I had guessed. Under 'Quain – emergency' there were several numbers, though I only had time to memorise the top one before Mr Barkin came back. I looked it up in the directory as soon as I got home; 013 was the code for Nelspruit in Mpumalanga. One of the places Angus went to when he disappeared was in or near the town where his lawyer Leo Greyling lived.

I had thought it odd at the time that a businessman of Angus's stature should have his affairs handled by a country attorney. Now I was convinced that Angus had chosen the son of his oldest friend because he had secrets to hide. And why the other numbers?

Full of corrosive new thoughts, I resolved to tackle him about them as soon as he returned. But it wasn't easy to get through to him now that he was feeling so much better.

According to Prunella when I phoned on Monday, he was once again, 'In conference, sorree. And he'll be busy the whole week with quarterly board meetings, management reviews and Institute affairs. I'd try again on Friday or even next week, Mizz Dobermann.'

In other words, stop pestering him. I wondered if he had instructed her to give me the brush-off; it was quite likely, judging by his attitude at the Japanese lunch. It's interesting how people who try to do you an unasked-for favour get annoyed when you reject it, as if it's your fault they've put themselves out for nothing.

I said, 'It must be a major challenge to work for such a busy, important man,' and rang off.

He was not available at the Club that evening or the next. 'He is out, Madam,' Boniface told me.

'Do you know where he's gone?'

'Just out, Madam.'

By Wednesday my curiosity about the Nelspruit number had grown like a monstrous mushroom to push all other thoughts out of my head. Instead of working, I was either poring over a map or pacing my study in a frenzy of speculation. It was like getting involved in a good thriller: I couldn't put it down until I knew the ending.

An even greater mystery to me was how I could have become so bound up in Angus's affairs. He and I had had a blithe and undemanding friendship for fifteen years, but since he had told me about his illness, the still pond of my life had been stirred to muddy troubled water. And now that he was feeling better, he would most likely drop me as his party companion and revert to the Saturday lunches designed to provide him with company on an otherwise dull day.

I'd been used with the utmost cynicism, yet here I was asking for more punishment.

On Wednesday evening he answered the phone with his most pompous, 'Good day to you. Quain here.'

'It's me. How are you?'

'Fine. On top of the world. Never better,' he boomed. Then waited to hear what I had to say.

'Are we having lunch as usual on Saturday?'

'Can't see why not. Unless you have other plans?'

He knew very well that I never had other plans. His voice had the false heartiness of a parent who doesn't want to hurt a child's feelings. This was a brush-off.

In a sudden rage I said, 'Don't bother. I'll buy my own Saturday lunches from now on.'

He was blustering, 'What's all this now? Faith?' when I slammed the receiver down.

Though I waited a good fifteen minutes by the phone in case he called back to insist that I come as usual or demand an explanation – perversely, I would have welcomed even mocking laughter at my bad temper – the damn thing squatted there on my desk without making a peep. I sat swivelling my typing chair from side to side, trying to soothe my rampaging feelings. But the flat had fallen silent, its clear spaces oppressive, its spareness an offensive stripping down of warm-blooded detail to a skeletal nothingness that epitomised my life.

I had burnt my boats and lost my only real friend. 'Fat-head,' Mother would have said, dripping scorn in her affected county accent that meant nothing to South Africans. 'Where is your common sense, child?'

'It's just reasserted itself!' I wanted to shout back at her now. 'I've been used! I've been had! But I'm fighting back.'

'What for?' I could almost hear her long-drawn-out vowels. 'A lonely, friendless old age like I had after your father died? I don't understand you, Faith. Never did. You were a selfish, ungrateful little madam who went your own sweet way regardless of anyone else. No wonder nobody wanted you after Kurt left.'

To banish her carping shade, I stormed into the kitchen and grabbed a wineglass and a bottle of well-chilled rosé and dropped John Williams playing the *Concierto de Aranjuez* into the CD player and turned it up to full volume. Then I went out through the French doors to sit on my twee fretwork balcony and get sozzled on pink plonk.

Midway through next morning, the sound of a car on the gravel drive woke me from a doze at my desk. I had tried to quell the hangover with aspirin followed by a pot of black coffee and a session in front of the computer inputting research notes, but sleep had overwhelmed me. Now the knocker on the front door was giving an impatient rat-a-tat that could only mean one person. I shook my head to clear it and hurried downstairs.

Angus was standing outside the door, trim and forceful in his blazer, its double row of brass buttons gleaming. He was holding a large bouquet of red tulips done up in cellophane with a red satin bow and saying, 'Peace offering. I knew I'd have to bring it in person to soothe the savage breast.'

I stood looking at him, not sure how to respond. If I started apologising for slamming the phone down, it would mean that I condoned his actions and was ready to be a doormat in return for favours rendered. If I slammed the door in his face, I would be cancelling fifteen years of my life.

He solved the problem by saying, 'Don't look so stricken, old girl. I'm sorry for being a bit offhand and neglecting you these past few weeks, but I've been pushed for time. I hope you're sorry for behaving so abominably on the phone last night. We're quits, right? Pax?'

'Angus, you have to realise that…'

'Pax first,' he insisted, 'then we'll get on to the details. It would grieve me very much to lose you. Whatever my perceived drawbacks now, I've been a good friend all these years, have I not?'

'You've been a good friend.'

He shoved the crackling bouquet at me. 'Then take these bloody flowers and let me get off to work. Praise and I will fetch you tonight for dinner at eight. Agreed?'

What mortal could resist a contrite card-sharp's smile? So I agreed and said 'Pax,' and he stalked across the gravel to the waiting Bentley looking every inch the battleship commander, and was gone.

Dinner was at the Linger Longer and he had pulled out all the stops: a table for two in a candlelit private room scented with bowls of roses and freesias, a subdued saxophone on the soundtrack and Louis Roederer Cristal champagne in a silver ice bucket. 'You need a change from Moët,' he pontificated as the waiter poured with finicky care. 'Develop your palate a bit. Compare the French champagnes with our Cap Classique sparklers.'

'I'm hardly likely to have many opportunities.' Striving to ignore the fact that the champagne would cost at least five – if not ten – times what the waiter would be earning that night.

'That's not the point. I'm saying, Gather your rosebuds while ye may. You have to learn to reach out and grab opportunities, or you lose them. That's the basic difference between us. I'm a reacher and grabber. You're a ponderer who likes to weigh up the odds before you make a move, by which time the opportunity may have vanished. I've made it my mission this evening to do some plain speaking in an effort to convert you. If you don't change your spots soon, you'll never land a mate and I'll have failed.'

Keeping a lockgrip on my irritation level, I said, 'I thought this dinner was the other half of your peace offering?'

'That as well.' He picked up his glass. 'To friendship. And thank you.'

His eyes were blue and candid; the shifting candlelight glossed over their gaping lower eyelids and the knotted capillaries in his cheeks and the thinning chins. That is how I like to remember Angus now: at the peak of his power and glory and charm, with a glass of fine champagne in his hand.

I raised mine and said, 'Thank you. I'm sorry...' then stopped, determined not to apologise. 'I would welcome plain speaking. I've been bobbing along on the surface of this friendship for too long, just enjoying it. But the parameters have changed since your illness.'

'Ex-illness, I hope. The tumours have receded, my hair's begun to grow again...' he ran his hand over the silver down on his head '...and I'm officially in remission. Too bloody tough even for cancer. The doctors can't believe it.'

By his jubilant relief, I saw that this was the real reason for the celebration: it was more to give thanks for being restored to life than to Faith, his faithful guard dog, always available when he needed her. But how could I object to that? Anyone would be over the moon to be relieved of a death sentence. And now was the time to strike if I wanted to learn some of his secrets, while he was basking in the joy of deliverance and before he reconstructed his usual defences.

'Tell me,' I murmured, 'why you went to Nelspruit last weekend?'

'Who said I went there?' A sudden sharpness, head back and looking down his nose.

'I found out. Never mind how.' I kept my hand curved round the stem of my champagne flute. It would have to sound casual. 'Angus, since the day you told me about the Big C, you've been dropping hints about other sides to your life. Do you want me to know where you go and what you're doing when you disappear, or not? I'll respect your wishes if you don't, but of course I've been tantalised. I'm a history sleuth, remember?'

He gave me a long considering look, then said, 'Explain your motivation before I decide. Is it common-or-garden curiosity or is there a higher reason? It all depends, you see. I must know.'

At that moment the door opened and the waiter came in bearing a plate with a fan of smoked duck slices and a tiny salad, which he laid with reverence in front of me. We sat in silence while the same ritual was performed for Angus and the waiter retreated with a closing click.

'Ah, this looks good. Shall we postpone the revelations till after the meal?'

'Absolutely,' I said, then remembered with a blush someone fulminating about the habit of saying 'absolutely' all the time, and added, 'Motion carried.'

'Let's tuck in, then. One advantage of a fright like I've had is that you learn to appreciate life's little comforts all over again.' Sighing with pleasure, he picked up his fork.

But he gave up after the tournedos chasseur and before the crème caramel, though I managed to do full justice to the meal. When coffee and hand-made chocolates had been brought on a silver tray and the waiter had withdrawn, we sat for a while in companionable silence sipping our coffee as the candles burned lower.

Then Angus said, 'Well? Do you have your answer ready?'

I had been wondering what to say as we ate and sipped and chatted about trivia that would not interfere with our enjoyment of the meal. The reason for his secretiveness, I decided, was that he didn't want people to know where he came from. In the business circles he moved in, most men were private school and university educated, backed by extensive old boy networks: Bishops, St Johns, Hilton, Michaelhouse, UCT, Stellenbosch, Wits, Oxbridge, Harvard, Wharton and other business schools. As a loner from the wrong side of the tracks, he had had to create his own network of interlocking favours and obligations, building his image year by year and suppressing early connections that could damage the aura of success. Was there an embarrassing elderly mother tucked away in Nelspruit, I wondered, or a sister with lank hair and too many kids, paid to keep her mouth shut? Such secret compartments he would not be inclined to expose.

On the other hand, he was vain about his achievements. If I could appeal to the pride of the self-made, offer this man who had recently experienced the terror of mortality a chance of being celebrated outside his own circle, he would be tempted. To vault from obscurity to wealth and fame is a fantasy most people treasure, and the stories of those who make it are the stuff of business literature as well as blockbuster novels.

So I said, 'Digging around in the Club's attics has given me a taste for the hidden Joburg: the wheels of big business and the men who make them turn.'

'You mean the hamsters.'

'Not at all. I mean the essential cogs like you: the real power behind the company thrones.' I hoped I wasn't laying it on too thick.

He said, 'Go on.'

'When I've finished my current book in a few weeks' time I'd like to research and write about this aspect of corporate Joburg, beginning in the old mining days and ending in the present. The title would be something like *Johannesburg Magnates : The Men Who Made Our City Prosper*. It'd make a great saga.'

'And?'

'And since you're the one I know first-hand, I'd like to start by researching the life and times of Angus Quain.'

He made a brusque gesture of dismissal. 'No way. I don't intend to bare my soul or my origins to anyone.'

'I'm not asking you to bare anything. I want to write about success in business, with a Joburg focus. What qualities does one need to get to the top? How did you get there? What are the sacrifices and rewards? What's different about commercial achievements in this city? People love to read about success, specially when it's a rags to riches story like yours.'

'Bollocks.' He was glowering.

'They do. Why do you think soap operas are so popular?'

'You could hardly call Joburg business the stuff of soap opera.'

'No? What about…' and I reeled off some of the stories he'd told me about the people we'd met during the past few weeks.

'Those are just the gossip-makers. Different kettle of fish to your proposed subjects. The men with the real power in this town keep their heads down.'

'Exactly. As Hannah said of Benjamin, they move in mysterious ways. They're not democratically elected, yet in some areas they wield more power over us than the government. That's why I want to write about them.'

He muttered, 'You've got a lot of brass, planning to take on the financial establishment.'

'Not take on. Just write about from a historical perspective. Powerful men are interesting, and you could give me the key to the world they inhabit.'

He gave me another considering look before responding. 'I can't work out whether you're trying to flatter me or genuinely interested. Which is it?'

'Genuine interest, of course. Your revelations sparked it.'

'So this is all my fault?'

'I've found a lot of useful material in the Club attics too.' He looked unconvinced and I hurried on, 'A book like the one I've outlined would be a natural follow-on from my social history of the early mine compounds. It would look at the bosses whose decisions affected the workers' lives.'

'Laying us open to even more criticism from the unions? It won't wash.'

'See it from the other angle,' I urged. 'You're respected in the business environment. By agreeing to be interviewed for a book like this, you could make an important contribution towards a better understanding of what motivates and drives successful people.'

He responded with a faint smile. 'Respected for the time being. All glory is fleeting.'

His reservation gave me the chance I needed. 'Glory may be fleeting but a good book isn't. You have an eye trained for discrepancies and an inside track on information I need. If you agree to speak to me, others will. And if I back up the interviews with careful research, it could be a corporate bestseller.'

He was quiet for a long time, then said, 'Haven't let my left hand know what my right is doing for decades.'

But he was taken by my request, I could see. Who wouldn't like to have their opinions solicited and their achievements written up for posterity? I'd need to be open with him, though. I said, 'It would have to be objective: provable facts, honest assessments.'

'What makes you think I'd blab on others?'

'The power it would give you over them.'

'Ah, Faith.' It was a rueful sigh. 'You understand me far too well.'

'So the answer is yes?'

'The answer is a qualified maybe. You've hit on the only reason I'd consider this proposition of yours: it would give me a chance to crack the whip over my less-than-distinguished colleagues. Always fancied the role of ringmaster.'

I didn't want him thinking he'd have control over my choice of subjects, or that he'd be my only source. I said quickly, 'You'd have first crack, at least.'

'It's a seductive idea.'

This was the moment to go for the jugular. I said, 'It goes without saying that the people I interview will be asked to verify biographical data, though there'll be no veto over my commentary. I realise that there are…' I wanted to say 'shady areas in everyone's life' but it sounded judgmental so I changed it to, '…personal matters that people may not want to make public, and I'll respect their right to privacy.'

'No sneak disclosures? Accusations of malfeasance?'

'As far as your story is concerned, we could gloss over the problematic share deals…'

He raised a sardonic eyebrow. 'Glad to hear it.'

'…but you'd have to be more open about other aspects of your life. You'll probably hate the whole process.'

'More than likely.'

He sat with his shoulders slumped and his head bowed, looking tired. The room smelled of hot wax and coffee and the flowers which had begun to droop in the warmth.

I reached out and took his hand. 'Time to go. Thanks for the magnificent dinner. I hope you'll consider my request because I think you could make or break the book I've outlined.'

His head came up then, the once plump jowls slack, the heavy bags under his eyes rimmed with candlelight. 'You're a bloody schemer like me. I never realised it until now. You want to use me and I always thought it was the other way round.' The blue gaze held regret and a private pain I had not seen before. 'It's my nature. I'm a solitary beast at heart, a predator in many ways. I even prey on those I love. There are many days when I don't like what I see in the mirror.'

I thought, Oh God, here comes the confession.

But I had mistaken his purpose, as so often happened. With a rumble of amusement at having caught me, he added, 'And other days when I think I'm quite a handsome fellow with a vast reserve of tolerance for fools and a soft spot for cozening historians.'

He was agreeing, though I'd have to get it signed and sealed in case he tried to wriggle out in the morning. I reached for the notebook in my evening bag. 'Can I have it in writing? When can we start? Tomorrow?'

Total capitulation was not his style, though. He held up a warning hand and said, 'There are conditions. I rely on your undertaking as a friend to suppress anything that could embarrass me or my family. Don't care what you say about others, just go easy on the Quains, right?'

I nodded. 'It's rank favouritism, but I agree.'

'And while I don't expect to come out looking as pure as the driven snow, I'd like to be envied for my natural brilliance as much as for my bank account.' A gust of laughter sent the guttering candle flames into a fandango. 'Who would have thought that I was nurturing a biographer all these years? Go to it with your sharpest quill, old girl. What have I got to lose?'

12

Next morning I telephoned *The Star* and asked to speak to the librarian, one of my most reliable sources when it came to tracking down details of recent events.

'Marge, it's Faith. How are you?'

'Fair to bloody. I've been run off my feet from the moment I came in this morning.'

'Is there a crisis? I didn't hear anything on the news.'

'No crisis, just cadet journalists. There seems to be a plague of them this month, all needing their bums wiped and their bruised egos restored after the subs have cut their slaved-over prose to shreds.'

'You encourage them to run to you for help.'

'Someone has to, poor little twerps.'

Marge was blonde and calm and looked too wholesome to be working in the city – a mature dairymaid with a cow's ruminant brown eyes and heavy shanks and ponderous way of moving. She had run the library for fifteen years and could put her hand on any file you wanted in less than a minute.

After a few more pleasantries I said, 'I need some info about a businessman.'

'Local? Recent? Prominent?' Her voice crisped as she shifted from social to search mode.

'Local and prominent. It's Angus Quain. He started working in Joburg in the fifties, I think.'

'You're just in time, then. We're about to have a major clean-out of the fifties and sixties files which will go into the morgue to make room for the rest of the nineties. At the moment we're having to fight our way past the shelves.'

The morgue is the newspaper archive to which old files are consigned; a limbo from which it is difficult for an outsider to make requisitions. For events pre-dating the fifties, I went to the Johannesburg Public Library across the road which houses bound volumes of *The Star* going back to its founding in 1887.

'What would be the best time to come in?'

'Lunch hour,' she said. 'Sandwich and coffee and mutual commiseration time for the cadets, and pub and peanut time for the old hacks. I sometimes wonder whether the Press could function at all if it weren't for pubs. I'll have the Quain files waiting.'

The *Star* building is on Sauer Street, a few blocks from the Club. I parked in the basement garage I used for my visits to Angus, stowed my handbag and parking ticket out of sight in the cubbyhole, locked it, slipped the Crooklok over my steering wheel and locked it in place, looked around for lurkers in the shadows and seeing none, got out, locked the door and set off past the pay booth, up the concrete ramp and along the street with my notebook and pen in one hand and my car keys hidden in the other. You can't be too careful in that part of town these days, even in broad daylight. Or in any part of town, for that matter. When I get home it takes five keys to get out of my car and into my flat. Today's million-dollar question has to be: Is our quality of life improving or getting worse?

When I reached the library after threading through the almost empty newsroom, Marge was bent over a dejected girl explaining the vital importance of the first paragraph in a news report. Behind her were two parallel rows of desks facing each other where people sat reading and marking and clipping sections out of newspapers. I dumped my notebook and keys on one of the research desks near the windows and turned to look out at the red brick edifice of the Stock Exchange with its full-height glass atrium. Angus's stamping ground.

'Go to it, Faith,' he'd said the night before, and I intended to.

When she had finished her patient explanation and shooed the girl off, Marge brought three fat cardboard folders on Angus with his name written in the top left corner of the cover. The dates on the first one read: '1957 – 1969'. Inside, the cuttings were attached to tabbed strips of brown kraft paper glued down the left-hand side of each flap of the folder, one cutting to a tab and laid down like fish scales in calendar order so that each new one went on top of the previous cutting, leaving only its headline visible. Many of the cuttings bore traces of the red or orange pencil outlines that had marked them for particular files, with Angus's name highlighted too. The older ones in the file in front of me had gone brown and brittle with age.

Marge said, 'Is that all you want?'

I looked down at the shaggy drifts of newsprint. 'Wading through this lot is going to take hours. I didn't realise there'd be so much on him.'

'This is just the personal stuff. There'll be cross-references to his company file and any mentions in general articles. Pre-1975 folders are beige; the more recent ones green.'

'Are they all *Star* cuttings?'

'No, we file stuff from associated publications if the subject is important enough. Which yours is. How well do you know Angus Quain?'

'Reasonably well. He's a good friend.'

She said drily, 'The photo I saw in last month's *Style* made the pair of you look more than just good friends. Anything up? Are you checking on his matrimonial credentials? If so, I can tell you that he's divorced and eligible, if a bit long in the tooth.'

I gave what I hoped was a convincing denial, adding, 'I'm not that desperate. One husband was enough to last me a lifetime.'

'Why the Miss Marple number on Quain, then?' Marge may have been slow-moving, but her mind was like a switchblade.

'I'm not only interested in Angus, though I'm starting with him because I know him best.' I put on a confiding smile. 'My new book's going to be a study of Joburg business leaders from the early mining days to the present. I've just discovered a treasure trove of background material and it's the kind of thing that should sell well. People love reading about tycoons.'

'Rather you than me. He looks a tough nut.' And she went back to graze through the mess of newsprint on her desk, raising her head every now and again to give me a quizzical look.

I lifted the row of cuttings down the left side of the open folder to find the first, taking care not to tear them. Under the headline 'New Appointments' there was a studio photograph of Angus looking like a young hawk: thin hard face, hair brushed back and a look of rapt determination about the eyes. The caption read: 'Mr Angus Quain CA of Randall Eksteen has been appointed an alternate director to the board of Swazi Asbestos Holdings Limited.'

Before going on, I made some notes. 'Born – ? 1931. Started work just after the war – probably the beginning of 1946 if he wrote JC at the end of 1945. Age at the time – ? 15. Night school for Matric – 2 or 3 years? Articled, then Board exams – 7 years.' He must have qualified at the age of twenty-five or so, probably in 1956. A year later he had been appointed an alternate director; not bad going. He would have had four years in hand to fulfill his dream, according to Hannah, of being a Top Man at thirty.

They must have married at about the time of this first directorship, I thought, sitting back in my chair. I'd have been about eight when their eldest daughter was born. Had I been a daughter substitute to Angus? It had never felt that way; our discussions and arguments had been those of equals. He had managed to conceal his lack of academic background and I had managed to ignore the discrepancies of age and wealth between us. Looking back, it had been an unlikely friendship – and the fact that it had flourished under the toffee-nosed aegis of the

Johannesburg Club was a thought to be savoured. He was no more a gentleman than I was.

I turned back to the file in front of me and began to work through the cuttings, which detailed a remarkable career. The headlines ranged from: 'Quain to join board of Maxicor', 'Quain succeeds McFarlane' and 'Quain – next head of Randall Eksteen?' to 'Joburg man overlooked for top job', 'Quain quits!' and 'Quain forms breakaway firm'. Later headlines showed him becoming more involved in liberation politics, as befitted an elder statesman trying to steer the South African business community through the rocky shoals of threatened nationalisation. 'Quain appeals for meaningful dialogue'. 'Top JHB businessmen on secret visit to ANC'. 'Quain says radical changes needed'. 'Accelerate affirmative action, urges Quain'. 'Mixed economy predicted – Quain'. There was a profile headed 'Business Personality of the Week' and illustrated by a cartoon that had captured to a T his down-the-nose look; the cartoonist had dressed him in a Roman toga and given him a fiddle in one hand and a sjambok in the other with which he was lashing two grovelling slaves called Failure and Doubt.

The accompanying photographs of Angus lost their initial air of keen ambition as he grew older and acquired honours and titles: general manager of Randall Eksteen, directorships, deputy chairman of the National Council of Chartered Accountants, chief adviser to the Inner City Forum, patron of the Transvaal Arts Society and a number of charities, managing director of Quain & Associates, member of The Business Initiative, regular TV panellist.

His temples greyed as his hair thinned and receded; the cut of his suits became ever more artful as his neck began to bulge over his shirt collars and his watch chain tightened across his waistcoats. There was a photograph of him donating a computer to Wits University, and another of him among a group of businessmen standing in a respectful semicircle round President Mandela, whose jazzy silk shirt made their tailoring look stuffy and un-African. In the later photographs Angus had begun to acquire a self-deprecating air as if saying: I'd be the last person to boast about my achievements, but the publicity fellow insisted.

Publicity fellow. I flipped backwards, noting the dates on the cuttings. Interesting point here. Photographs and short pieces about him had appeared in the papers with clockwork regularity over the years, never more than a few months apart. Mostly they sounded as though they had been taken verbatim from press releases: 'The appointment is announced of Mr Angus Quain to...' and, 'In a speech to the Johannesburg Chamber of Commerce yesterday, Mr Angus Quain said...' He must have a personal publicist.

'Make sure my name appears in print – preferably the business media – at least six times a year,' I could hear him saying. 'Don't care how you do it, or how much it costs. Just keep me in the public eye and make me sound and look good.'

There was commentary too, of course. Business analysts were generally loud in their praise of companies with which he was associated: they throve and made good profits; their shares soared in the good years and stayed steady in the bad; their price/earnings ratios were attractive, their gearing admirable. As the apartheid era waned, his companies put out high-minded mission statements and stressed their social responsibility programmes. In the most recent cutting (complete with colour photograph of a dignified portrait in oils that had been commissioned for the company boardroom) he proclaimed his earnest desire to make a meaningful contribution towards the New South Africa.

One journalist was less impressed. In a profile on Angus when he broke away from Randall Eksteen with several colleagues to found his own firm, Mitch Kincaid of *The Star* had written that he was a hard taskmaster and quoted a young accountant who said, 'We're all dead scared of the Big Q. He doesn't tolerate fools or people who can't make informed decisions at the snap of a finger. New boys will need reflexes like a rattlesnake to survive at Quain & Associates.' The young accountant had not been named and I wondered if Angus had conducted a witch hunt afterwards.

In a later piece called *GUNFIGHT AT THE BIG Q CORRAL* Kincaid had commented on a hostile takeover with which Angus had been associated: 'Everything the Big Q touches seems to turn to gold. Could it be that his legendary luck has to do with certain blocks of shares tucked away from scrutiny in the impenetrable labyrinths of the share registrars' computers? It is high time that directors are required by law to disclose all beneficial shareholdings.'

When the law was passed a few years later, Kincaid had written: 'And about time too. Now we need another law for the nominee holding companies that have popped up everywhere like poisonous toadstools, aided and abetted by the firms of accountants that specialise in what is known – oh so circumspectly – as "tax avoidance". Perhaps King Quain would care to comment?'

So at least one man was on to Angus. I had met Mitch Kincaid, one of those sour nicotine-stained old-school journalists who type with two jabbing forefingers and boast about having no formal education. He had been railing against corporate fat cats at a university cocktail party, egged on by an audience of academics who would nevertheless go on bended knees to beg the same fat cats for travel expenses next time they were invited to an overseas conference. But Kincaid had taken early retirement a few years back and left Joburg to go sailing on the Mediterranean, where people said he had bought a pair of charter yachts that plied the Greek islands.

I wondered whether Angus or his cronies had had anything to do with his purchases; retired journalists can seldom afford more than a sailing dinghy.

Having gone through all three files with no further revelations, I heaved them back on to the reception desk and went across to Marge. 'Do you have Mitch Kincaid's current address?'

She shook her head. 'Personnel might know, or one of his former colleagues on the business pages. It's doubtful, though. He was a loner and didn't have many friends. Maybe the pensions people have it on file?'

'I'll try them. Thanks for your help.'

'Find anything enlightening?'

I looked down to clip my pen to the cover of my notebook. 'Quite a lot of stuff I didn't know about the early years.'

'Careful, Faith,' she said, leaning forward and dropping her voice. 'Big business is tricky terrain. You don't want to alienate the rich and powerful. They have limitless resources.'

'Alienate?' I gave a big false laugh. 'No fear. I want to sell books, not commit commercial suicide.'

'I repeat, be careful. Remember what Scott Fitzgerald wrote? "Let me tell you about the very rich. They are different from you and me." Mitch was going round quoting it before he left. He told me on his last day that he had conceded to the fat cats. "I had no choice. Their claws were out and their eyes were dagger slits," were his exact words.'

I felt her dubious gaze on my back all the way to the library door.

In the lift to the personnel department to try and track down Mitch Kincaid, I thought: Angus has three dimensions that are new to me – share-tampering Gus, Big Q the boss man and King Quain, a title as envious as it was mocking. How many more are there?

13

*T*he next dimension surfaced during the following week when I managed to pin Angus down to a series of preliminary interviews with a tape recorder. For four evenings he granted me the hour between six and seven to put my questions about his role and colleagues in the Joburg business world and record his answers over drinks in his sitting room. And during those sessions on busy weekdays at a later hour than my usual visits, I began to encounter Angus the club man: a jovial, hail-fellow member of the exclusive brotherhood that still largely controls our country's commercial pulse rate.

As he escorted me across the chequered marble of the hall and along the stately passages, we encountered men I recognised because their faces appeared often in the media: some who controlled the destinies of corporations and mines and banks, others who were leaders in their professions – lawyers, medical men, educators, engineers and accountants like him. No psychologists, though. 'Never feel comfortable with headshrinkers,' he said by way of explanation as we stood waiting for the lift on the second evening. 'Something about their eyes.'

'Oh rubbish, Angus. They're professionals like you and me.' He had my father's distrust of newfangled disciplines. While he appreciated the value of computers he refused to learn how to use them except by proxy, when he stood behind The Prune to dictate an urgent letter.

'Do you know any?'

'Psychologists? One.' I had been helped through my post-Kurt depression by a kind woman who had given me the emotional tools to fight my way back to equilibrium.

'You've never mentioned it before.'

'You never asked.'

He was silent for a while, then said, 'Did you consult him?'

'Her. Yes, after Kurt left.'

'Wasn't it difficult, telling a stranger your intimate thoughts?'

'At first, but it gets easier. Being able to unburden yourself is a great relief.'

'Unburden. "For who would fardels bear?" The idea appeals, though not the method. I can't see myself on a couch.'

I had to stifle a smile. My psychologist had taught me the trick I was using on him: how to extract information by camouflaging my questions. At that evening hour, with a whisky in his hand and his defences down, Angus enjoyed pontificating about his achievements and the talents and foibles of his competitors. Without the red herring of possible marriage-worthiness to limit his assessments, he could range more freely and I heard tales of mergers, share coups, boardroom battles, hostile bids, and men so rich and powerful that the Governor of the Bank of England asked to meet them during official visits to the Minister of Finance.

Curious about the Club's membership, which appeared to rank the scabby old drunk Monty Steyn on the same level as its distinguished achievers, I asked Angus to tell me about the men I didn't recognise in the passages. Most were businessmen and a surprising number of them ran small concerns, working out of nondescript offices buying and selling, importing and exporting – trading on world markets light years removed from the rickety stalls and pack donkeys and oxwagons used by their pioneer grandfathers. He called them jet-set smouses.

'That's a supercilious remark.'

'Not meant to be. I admire people who can make a profit buying and selling. It's the key to independence for anyone without specific training.'

'Like today's street vendors.' I had struggled through ankle-deep debris on the pavement outside the Club.

'Crime is another avenue, of course. Jumped-up cities like Joburg seem to spawn entrepreneurs and criminals in equal numbers, often with interlinked interests. Synergy, it's called. "The potential ability of individual organisations or groups to be more successful or productive as a result of a merger."'

'Do you admire the successful criminals too?'

He gave me a hard look. 'Don't push your luck.'

Of the few men we passed whose occupations or interests were obscure, he grumbled, 'God knows how they got into the Club. Undue influence somewhere.'

It became clear that besides the creature comforts it offered, he valued the brotherhood he had found in the Club. He was popular too; members would stop him for a chat or to ask about a particular share or to discuss company crises I read about in the papers next day. As he stood expounding, I saw yet another Angus: the fourth new dimension, a dominant male. Gone was the gallant companion with whom I had lunched for fifteen years. During Club encounters he was a bull elephant: greeting other members of the herd with a thump on the back, trumpeting opinions, throwing up clouds of dogmatic dust as they sparred.

All participants in this ritual ignored me, even my host. I could have been an egret perched on his thick hide, unnoticed and superfluous until we walked through the door into his sitting room.

On the third evening, irritated at having to turn down an invitation to join a group of colleagues, he let me know that it was a major concession to allow me into the Club during his social hour, adding, 'Usually spend it in the pub.'

'I thought you didn't like male-bonding rituals?'

'Do I detect a note of cynicism?'

'You do. You poured scorn on stag parties only a few weeks ago. What's the difference between them and happy hour in the members' bar?'

'Vast. One of the reasons I joined the Club in the first place was to get to know my colleagues. After work is a better time than business lunches; fellows are more relaxed, more amenable, more inclined to let their guard down. I'd say that more business gets done in the pub at this hour than over lunch at any of the expensive restaurants. A hell of a lot of members drop in on their way home.'

'So I've noticed.' I'd stood in the entrance hall often enough watching the revolving door spin as the bull elephants congregated at their twilight watering hole. 'Probably to minimise the time they're forced to spend with their lady wives.'

His black eyebrows knotted. 'You're too sharp by half tonight.'

'You called them lady wives first.'

'I was being facetious. My comment stands.' Through observation I was learning about bull elephant behaviour. 'Sharp' is a useful word for able women because it keeps them at a distance. I said, 'Couldn't you have called me clever instead of sharp?'

'Don't have to; you know you are.' The black frown intensified. 'I hope I'm doing the right thing, co-operating with you on this book. I get the feeling sometimes during our conversations that you're mocking everything I stand for.'

'That's not so.'

I tried to look indignant, but he was partly right. I found it hard to take his imperious after-work persona seriously; it was as though he had been wound up during the day to a pitch of self-importance that took time to unwind into the convivial and charming Angus I knew. Much of what he said during these sessions contradicted what he had been saying for years on Saturdays. Comparing the Angus I thought I'd known and the new Anguses that seemed to be appearing from nowhere like brass rubbings under a lump of cobbler's wax, I began for the first time to realise how complex men are.

This sounds naïve, but apart from Father – who'd been old and tetchy – and Kurt, I'd never got to know a man on such an intimate level. Watching Angus now, I found myself wondering whether Kurt had had more *gemütlich* facets than the one I'd found impossible to live with.

The thing is, when you're brought up as the only child of a strong-willed mother, you absorb her opinions like tainted breast milk. Wrapped up in her spiritual life, my mother had been sour about all men except the murmuring priest whom she hadn't considered a man anyway. No matter how hard I'd rebelled against her, the acquired sourness had remained – and been reinforced by the passionate feminists I had encountered at university, who had preferred fulminating against their perceived enemies to negotiating an understanding with them. Time and a wider acquaintance with men had mitigated the sourness but left a residual wariness. Though I soon learnt in the great school of life after university that it is dangerous to categorise people, the experience with Kurt had left me sceptical of men's motives.

Hence the prickles. But driving home that evening after listening to Angus talk about the extensive private philanthropies of an economist reputed to be as hard as nails, I realised that my mind had been made up on the subject of men far too early. I had come to see them either as successful dominators like Angus or abject failures like my father; nothing in between. The blame for the collapse of our marriage, I admitted at last, had been as much mine as Kurt's.

I'm the female version of a misogynist, I thought. Though to be fair, I was not so much a man-hater as a man-distruster. And resolved to be more sympathetic at my last taping session with Angus the following evening.

It was different from the start. As he came across the entrance hall to meet me, I thought he looked stern. Then I saw his eyes go over my shoulder and heard him booming at someone behind me, 'Vuyo! Haven't seen you for a while.'

'I've been in America, standing in for the Minister of Health.' The voice was deep and resonant.

'Ah.' Angus walked straight past me, hand stretched out. 'They've found you a place on the…'

'If you even mention the words gravy and train, I will have you strung up by the thumbs, brother.' The voice had dropped another octave.

Angus said with a short laugh, 'Wouldn't dream of it. Good to see you.'

'And you.'

I turned to look at the arrival. He was an imposing black man in a modish double-breasted suit set off by a dazzling tie depicting the new South African flag. After a three-way handshake, they stood chatting while I waited. A good three minutes later, Angus remembered what he had come down for and turned to beckon me to join them.

'This is Dr Vuyo Mkhize, our latest member. Vuyo, this is my friend Faith Dobermann, the historian. She wrote that book on the early mine compounds, *Working Life at the Shaft-head*.'

106

I said, 'How do you do, sir.'

Ironic bloodshot eyes regarded me, then he enquired, 'Do you call me sir out of respect for my government connections or my profession? Or to curry favour?'

'Respect for your profession, of course, doctor. I'm not fond of curry.'

He gave an appreciative nod. 'In that case, I'm pleased to meet you, Miss Dobermann. I enjoyed your book and commend you on your choice of subject. Few historians have bothered with the humble lives of our country's workers.'

'Thank you. The subject was well-documented, which made my research easier.'

'Indeed.' The bloodshot eyes moved to Angus, then returned to me. 'I might add that it's a surprise finding a woman here at the sacred hour of six. The Club wives have usually been shooed home and the girlfriends and dinner guests have not yet arrived.'

Angus roared and clapped him on the back. Conscious of my new resolve to be less critical of male rituals, I put on a neutral expression and said nothing.

'May I invite you both to a drink in the lounge?' the doctor said. 'I need to bounce some ideas around, and it would suit me to have a woman's point of view as well as Quain's more, shall we say, corporate eagle vision.'

Angus said, 'Of course, old chap.'

'Miss Dobermann?'

'I'd enjoy that.'

Angus's agreement had been enthusiastic and I wondered how important the doctor was in the business constellation. Over an excellent bottle of Klein Constantia Sauvignon Blanc, I soon learned. He was the managing director of a pharmaceutical company who had been asked to head a commission looking into the best way to establish links between the practitioners of traditional medicine and the South African medical profession. 'We need to gather our San shamans, our sangomas and inyangas into a single regulatory body, and to conduct systematic research into their age-old remedies and expertise. It is time for the rainbow people to work together in all respects, no?'

Angus nodded. 'I fully concur.'

I said, 'You're including the remedies used by the pioneer farmers' wives, I presume?' I had come across many of them during some research into early farming customs.

'Those too. We are conscious of our responsibility to all communities, unlike the previous government. The farmers' wives learnt their own lessons from veld plants. I am the beneficiary of one of them, in fact.' And he went on to tell us of the day his washerwoman mother had been shown by her employer how to use the broad fleshy leaves of the pig's ear cotyledon, warmed in hot water, to relieve his earache as a small boy.

'So the previous government's supporters weren't all bad?'

The jocular remark had slipped out, lubricated by Angus's second glass of wine, but it made the doctor's hands tense round his glass. 'Don't you believe it, Quain. That woman was as mean as cat shit. She wouldn't have spent a cent on medicine for the sick child of a labour tenant's wife who had worked for her for fifteen years. Leaves cost nothing.'

Angus had been put in his place with hardly a hiccup in the doctor's well-informed and probing conversation. When we parted to go our separate ways, he to a meeting and Angus and I to our final tape-recording session, I was asked, 'Would you consider writing a history of traditional medicine, Miss Dobermann? White people see witchdoctors as mountebanks – you know? – whereas they play an important role in black society, akin to psychologists.'

'My next book is already planned,' I explained, 'but the subject would certainly interest me.'

'Please contact me if you'd like to take the idea further. Sala kahle,' he said and walked away.

'You made a hit with Vuyo,' Angus said as we went up in the lift. It didn't seem to please him much.

'I liked him.'

'He's very powerful. Hope I made a hit too.'

It was the first time I had heard Angus sounding uncertain. 'Why? Is he important to you?'

'Yes. He's a sangoma himself. Went through the full two-year training after completing his medical degree. Didn't you notice the thin strip of goatskin round his wrist?'

'I don't see the connection.'

Angus rumbled, 'I may be in remission but I'm not counting on staying there. May need his services one of these days.'

'Are you serious?' I stood staring at the end product of forty years in business, the last fifteen of which he had spent at the pinnacle of his profession.

'Indeed I am. "There are more things in heaven and earth, Horatio, Than are dreamt of in your philosophy." Didn't I tell you about the sangoma who resuscitated my friend Tom after his leg was sliced off above the knee, and kept him alive till I could get medical help?'

I was speechless for a moment, then managed to say, 'How awful. What happened?'

The lift jerked to a stop on the third floor and he slid open the gate, ushering me out. 'No time now to go into it.'

I walked out ahead of him saying over my shoulder, 'You can't drop tantalising remarks like that and not enlarge on them.'

'I bloody can.' The gate clattered shut behind us and his hand on my elbow propelled me towards his rooms. 'Pressed for time tonight. I'm dining at seven-thirty with a Malaysian delegation.'

'Malaysian? That's unusual, isn't it?'

'Their biggest conglomerate and a leading royal are considering investing in one of our supermarket chains. Quain & Associates are preparing a report for them. I have to be there.'

'Which makes this evening's interview a nuisance.' As I put the small tape recorder I use for interviews down on the coffee table, I felt my resolve to be less critical of men slipping. Angus had a way of dangling comments he knew would interest me, then pleading off explanations till another day.

'An impediment, shall we say?' He headed for the drinks tray that Boniface had laid out for us. 'Let's get started straight away. Whisky for you?'

'Just something soft tonight, if there's a hurry. I've transcribed our talks so far and prepared a further list of questions based on...'

'You'll let me have a copy, won't you? I'd like to check that I haven't let any sabre-toothed tigers out of the bag.'

He stood pouring the drinks with his back to me so I couldn't see his expression. Would he be annoyed if I resisted the request? The transcriptions I'd made were an amalgam of his words and my observations and notes, some of which were conjecture. If he detected a negative tone, he could call the whole thing off.

I said, 'I'll let you have a rough draft of our discussions as soon as I've cobbled one together. Don't expect it for a while, though. I haven't finished the current book yet.'

He turned round with my glass in his hand, ice clinking. 'Are you evading my request?'

His expression was at its most forbidding that night. He was on his home ground, of course, enfolded by the mighty stone walls of his club. At the press of a button he could summon a squad of servants, a posse of fellow members, a secretary, a three-course meal, a complete change of bed linen and probably a call-girl too, if he wished. I felt a tremor of misgiving. Was that why he was hurrying me – not because of a business dinner, but because there was a woman waiting? Despite our years of Saturday lunches, I knew nothing about his sexual proclivities and he only knew the bare outlines of my relationship with Kurt.

We're a strange pair of friends, I thought, and smiled up at him. 'Evasion is my middle name. Yours too. We're verbal athletes, both of us, adept at discussing issues and skirting facts.'

The attempt at lightness went down like a lead balloon. 'On what grounds do you base that accusation, ingrate? I've been the soul of helpfulness these past few evenings, given of my time, reached into the recesses of my memory, supplied what you asked for. And now I'm being taxed with being evasive. It's too much.'

I felt my anticipated pleasure ebbing away. To conduct an interview with him in this black mood would be pointless. I picked up the tape recorder and said, 'I'd better go. This isn't working.'

'You will not leave until you've satisfied me that I'm not walking into a trap here.' He stood over me, glowering down. 'Your guarantee not to print anything that would embarrass me or my family holds, I presume?'

'Of course.' Offended, I rose to face him. 'Do you think I'd renege on a promise?'

'I'm not sure what you'd do, given a good juicy tip-off. The way the media behave…'

'I am not the media.' What had got into him? I'd heard him fulminating about many things, but never at me. Not like this.

'…the way they behave, you can't blame me for not trusting the transition from my words to your page. Did you see *Business Day* this morning?'

'No. I've been slaving at my computer. Intended to read the papers this evening when I get home. What are you talking about?'

'Rank betrayal. Yesterday evening I spoke about Sonny Prinsloo's confidential share purchases to bolster his takeover of Westridge Investments, remember?'

'Vaguely. You were rabbiting on about hostile bids and white knights.'

'This morning it's all over the front page: chapter and verse. Everything I told you.'

I couldn't believe what I was hearing. 'And you think I went running off to blab to some journalist?'

'Don't know what to think. The proof's there in black and white.'

'You're paranoid.' My fury rose to match his. 'I've given you my word not to pass on anything you tell me without your express permission.'

'Why the coincidence, then?'

'Angus, you're not the only guardian of secrets in this town.' I could hardly force the words past the rage that was squeezing my throat closed. 'Other people must have known. Other people must have told. I'm telling you that I didn't. And I'm appalled you should think I would.'

As I turned away his hand came down on my arm. 'Scout's honour? I've got a hell of a lot riding on Prinsloo's takeover.'

'My honour. Take it or leave it.'

He stood scrutinising me, questioning the core of our long friendship. I saw a man who had worked hard to alleviate solitude, who had joined the Club and created a network of business and social friendships, but who, at the end of the day, had to retreat to his rooms and face his fears alone. Having recently had to face the prospect of his own mortality, he had begun to question everything.

This is not personal, I told myself, and strove to believe it as I made him sit down, poured two whiskies and tried to emulate my psychologist when I first went to her in despair. Angus in the throes of a mood change was not easily mollified; he clung to his anger and was terse with his answers until I said, 'No offence intended, but are you in a fit state to take on the Malaysian delegation this evening?'

'Probably not, but I can't duck out.'

'You'll just have to wing it then.'

With the merest upward movement of the corners of his mouth to acknowledge the play on words, he said, 'Timely advice. Thanks, old girl. Been feeling low today.'

It was a fulsome apology, for Angus.

14

*S*everal nights later I sat with a pot of Earl Grey tea and some chocolate digestives – potent comforters on a winter evening – watching Angus give one of his vintage TV performances. He had been asked to join a panel of financial experts to discuss the recommendations of the latest tax commission, a serial event in our country where the discrepancy between the haves and the have-nots gapes ever wider in defiance of affirmative action. I have noticed that one of the post-apartheid disillusionments for my lefty friends is the difficulty of parting once-fervent radicals – let alone the bourgeoisie – from their excess money.

Looking relaxed and wearing what he called his Van Gogh tie, hand-woven silk in swirling blues specially chosen to throw up the blue of his eyes on the TV screen, Angus was holding forth about the necessity for tax incentives. 'A lower tax on manufacturers means that business becomes more lucrative, therefore more profits are ploughed back and business expands, which results in more jobs and larger tax revenues. As Robert Browning put it, "Less is more", don't you see?'

'No, I don't.' A black banker known for his uncompromising rectitude wagged an angry finger. 'And I find the pronouncements of an English poet totally irrelevant to this debate. What I see is the flaw in your argument: profits in white hands are not necessarily ploughed back. They have an uncanny way of melting overseas, never to be seen again. Tax the fat cats until they scream, I say, or we'll never level the playing fields.'

Angus swivelled towards him. 'Ephraim, my friend, you're incorrigible. That's killing the goose that lays the golden…'

'Don't patronise me, Quain.' He spoke as though he had a mouthful of rusty nails.

'Heaven forfend.' Angus raised his eyes to the studio ceiling, playing to the cameras. 'I'd never hear the end of it.'

I thought, He's stolen my expression. Typical. And realised at that moment another thing about him: as well as his chameleon traits which enabled him to blend into situations while he gauged their usefulness to him, he was a borrower with a prodigious memory. His credo, 'Everything of the best' would logically include the gleanings of other minds and previous conversations.

Several members of the panel were smiling. The banker glowered. A woman executive said, 'If we're going to indulge ourselves, could I bring up the matter of higher taxation on married women? I have to pay seventeen thousand rands per annum more than my husband does. It's iniquitous.'

Angus sobered at once. 'Madam, I couldn't agree with you more. That is one area I feel the tax commission should attend to as rapidly as possible, and I'm sure they will.'

I watched him notching up his charm quotient as he spoke to her and thought, She's important to him. An influential client, perhaps? Are his methods of operating as transparent to others as they have become to me, or am I being hypercritical?

It was strange to be analysing rather than simply enjoying Angus. My professional skills were reaching into our friendship like the tendrils of a plant parasite intent on sucking sustenance from its host.

After a while I turned the TV sound off so I could watch his body language: the abrupt nod of agreement, the adjusting of cuffs while others spoke, the impatient fingers tapping the arm of his chair, the forward body lunge at the beginning of a vehement statement, and his chins collapsing over his collar as he sat back having made a point. It was a masterful performance. Among the six experts on the panel only the banker resisted his blandishments, sitting back in his chair with a look of deep scepticism as the programme ended and the credits rolled over Angus regaling the others with an anecdote.

There had been a moment when I'd felt a twinge of alarm, in a long shot of the whole panel when someone else was talking and I saw him reach under his jacket to ease his waistband. Was the cancer in remission as he had been assuring me, or was he managing to hide his symptoms better? And then I thought, It must be in remission. He looks so well and vigorous.

The phone rang half an hour later. 'Did you see me on the box? How did I do?'

'You're very impressive in front of a camera.'

'Some damn expensive coaching in TV techniques gave me a good start. Natural ability took over after that. Though I must say that I never expected to be holding forth to the nation in my declining years.' His voice kept fading; he must be calling from his car.

'Scarcely declining.'

'Golden, then? Must say it's gratifying that in our youth-obsessed era, there are still people who value the wisdom that comes with experience.'

Because he sounded so smug, I couldn't resist a dry, 'If only they knew, Gus.'

'Steady on now. State secrets, what?' It came out on a sharply rising note.

'You know I'm the soul of discretion.' It was hard not to be irked when he said things like that.

There was a pause while he adjusted to genial mode again. 'Feel like going out on the tiles tonight? I'm aware that it's nine-thirty, but I'm on a high after the programme and feel like celebrating.'

Ulterior motive or peace offering to make up for his ill-humour at our last encounter? I said, 'What are you suggesting? I've had my supper and was about to get into bed with the new biography of Olive Schreiner.'

'I'll be a far better companion than Olive Schreiner.'

'Maybe, but you'll have to offer a major temptation to induce me to go out now. The weather forecast is predicting a cold front and snow on the Berg.'

Angus knew how to cajole. 'If it's temptation you want, how about a taste of Joburg low-life?'

'What kind of low-life?' I imagined Rockey Street or the Radium Beer Hall in Orange Grove, beloved haven of Real Men.

'I'm not telling you until we get there. Think of it as research into what you so cogently call "picking over the details" of my life.'

Through the window I saw by the street light that a wind had got up and was tugging at the dead leaves still clinging to the pin oak in the garden. 'And I'm not going unless I know where to.'

'I thought you were curious about my disappearances? This is one of the places I frequent. A bolt-hole when the pomp and circumstance of big business gets to me.'

'You've always wallowed in your executive perks.' An acid riposte; I really didn't want to go out into the cold.

'I do enjoy them. Biggest bloody ego in town, everybody says so.' There was a familiar rumble of amusement. 'But a fellow needs light relief too. I'd go round the bend if I couldn't get off the treadmill sometimes. You're speaking to a tally clerk from the Cape Town docks, remember? Slumming is in my blood.'

The remark was irresistible. If it is not yet apparent, I admit to terminal quizziness. 'Curiosity killed the cat,' Mother used to warn when I asked too many questions, implying that being pushy as well as curious would get me worse than nowhere, but of course she was wrong. Being pushy gets you everywhere. How subtly we are conditioned by manner-obsessed parents to behaviour that suppresses rather than encourages survival instincts.

I said, 'You win. I can be ready in ten minutes.'

'That's my Faith. Knew you'd come. Praise and I are already on our way.'

'What shall I wear?'

'The less conspicuous, the better,' he said, and rang off.

My wardrobe was thin on slumming outfits but I did my best, and was waiting on the veranda trousered and booted and wrapped in a black cloak when a car rolled up the gravel drive. Not the Bentley, but a mud-spattered Land Rover Discovery that I had never seen before.

Praise got out to open the door for me and I saw that he had shed his uniform for dark jeans and a leather jacket and a baseball cap. Curiouser and curiouser. I climbed up next to Angus murmuring, 'Interesting vehicle. Thanks, Praise.'

'You're welcome, Madam.' That reserved voice again. I wondered whether his casual clothes were a disguise.

'This thing's excellent on dirt roads,' Angus was saying, 'and less likely to be a target than the Bentley in the part of town we're going to. The doors seize up and the alarm system goes berserk if anyone lays a finger on it.'

He had abandoned his TV raiment for a tweed sports coat with an open-necked shirt and a cravat and grey flannels – the uniform my father had worn when he went out to the cinema or down to the bowling club for a spot in the evening. Though they were nearly a generation apart there were many similarities between them: turns of phrase and wartime memories and old-fashioned courtesies like getting up when a woman came into the room.

Over the years of our friendship I had wondered whether Angus's attraction for me was that of a father figure, but decided that it was not so. Humour and charm and a shrewd intelligence coupled with unusual energy were his greatest assets; the ease that came with a powerful position was far less important, I had told myself. Now, with my new cynicism and my historian's hat on, I saw this for the self-deception it was. Without his top-executive aura and the beguiling ambience of wealth, Angus would be considered over the hill by the pack of ambitious CAs and MBAs ravening at his heels.

'If you don't have a damn firm grip on the tiller, they write you off the day you hit sixty,' he had said once. 'Arrogant young fools. Tom Wolfe was right to mock that generation for imagining they're masters of the universe. They think they can change the world with their computer projections and business school formulae. There's no humility at all in the young today. They haven't had to struggle through a major stock market crash or a depression or a world war, which means that they're completely ignorant of the fact that we live in a random bloody universe with no rules.'

Our destination was neither Rockey Street nor Orange Grove. Praise drove us down Market Street and under the overhead motorway towards Jeppe: once-smart Jeppestown in the early days, but now a jumble of commercial buildings and small factories jammed between tired old houses and nondescript shops with bleary windows. I had only ever been to Jeppe to find a recommended upholsterer or wholesale warehouse, and once to replace some liberated hubcaps. It was not as deserted as the city centre at night – there were desultory youths playing pool in flyblown cafés and lounging on the pavements – but it didn't look like a place anyone over eighteen with more than two rands in his pocket would go to for a good time, and I said so.

'Appearances are deceptive.'

'Tell me what sort of low-life we're headed for. Are we going to an all-night roadhouse for bunny chow or fish and chips wrapped in newspaper?' I guessed. 'A gambling den wreathed in dagga fumes? An illegal casino? A new shebeen with a township jazz ensemble playing smoky saxophones?'

'Wait. You'll see,' was all he would say.

'Go on, give me a clue. Is it sizzling protest theatre in a basement lit by paraffin lamps? An action bar with women wrestling in jelly?' I was beginning to feel a giddy hilarity.

'No need for clues. We're there.'

The Land Rover nosed its blunt way through open gates into a factory yard full of parked cars. It was very dark. Two bulky shadows detached themselves from an archway and came towards us. Praise rolled down his window and muttered something, and an arm the size of a small baobab waved us into an empty space. Angus leant towards me and breathed in my ear, 'The bouncers. Nobody messes with Hennie and George. They're both black belts and carry 9-mills.'

He was lapping it up like a schoolboy let off the leash. Hilarity waned. I said, 'Don't tell me you're after cheap thrills on the wrong side of the law?'

He was patting the inner pocket of his jacket, checking that his wallet was there. 'Thrills, yes. Cheap, no. Lawful? Never asked.'

'Are we safe?'

'As houses.'

'You promise?'

I saw him lick his thumb and make a double gesture across the left side of his chest. 'Cross my heart, all the way up to heaven.'

Childhood rituals remain oddly reassuring; perhaps innocent beliefs abide in all of us. So I got out when Praise opened the door. It was the first time I saw him smile, a brief gleam of teeth. He said, 'May I go now, Mr Quain?'

'Of course. Back in two hours?'

'Sure thing, sir.'

'Why is Praise dressed like that?' I said. 'Where is he going?'

'All will be revealed.' Angus took my arm and steered me between parked cars towards a doorway in the blank wall of a brick building.

116

The heavy studded door was made of wooden railway sleepers: jarrah or teak probably, dragged by working elephants out of the jungles of Burma and brought to South Africa in sailing ships, my father used to explain – always – when we saw them piled in railway sidings after being replaced with concrete sleepers. Once a good raconteur, he became repetitive in old age.

As Angus reached out to knock, his signet ring glinted and I thought, I hope we don't get mugged. What the hell am I doing in the wilds of Jeppe so late at night? The bouncers had melted into the darkness along with Praise. The parked cars crouched like giant armour-plated insects behind us, blank headlights goggling. The gloom was so pregnant with menace that I half expected a hatch to snap open and a stubbled Mexican face lit from below to demand 'Oo are you?' over the barrel of a pistol.

I pulled my cloak up round my neck and said, 'Shades of Clint Eastwood.'

'Button up, will you, Faith? You have to remember that you're an observer tonight, not an arbiter.' He sounded annoyed.

A gust of antarctic wind rustled a pile of waste paper. The square of sky above the yard had the tarnished copper glow of street lighting reflected on the layer of smog that clamps down on Joburg in winter, the result of temperature inversion and composed of coal smoke, mine dump dust and the sulphurous emissions of too many unregulated factory stacks.

Angus knocked again and there was a sliding back of several bolts before it swung into a dimly-lit space, held by a silhouette that leant forward to peer at us, then brayed, 'Yo, Gus. Welcome. And your lady friend too. Come in.'

As my eyes adjusted to stygian walls and the feeble luminance of a bowl of artificial white arum lilies, each with a tiny bulb for a stamen, I saw that she was big and black and old. Ugly too, in the way the French call *jolie-laide* – beautiful-ugly: bold-nosed and full-lipped with the broad face, knowing eyes and ample figure of the clay fertility goddesses they dig up in ancient tombs. I had always thought the shape to be an idealised earth mother, a folk memory, yet here she was in the all-too-solid flesh and a flamboyant robe of kente cloth with a matching doek swirled round her head. The proprietary claw she clamped on Angus's arm bore a hectic glitter of rings.

He covered it with a fond hand and said, 'Hullo, Nesta. This is my friend Faith Dobermann.' Then turning to me, 'Faith, I'd like to introduce the owner of the classiest strip joint in town, the Midnite Club. This is Mama Nesta Ngcobo-Patterson. A legend in her time.'

Glossy lips demurred. 'Only in limited circles. I am glad to meet you, Faith. You're the first woman Gus has brought here in – what is it now, boy?' Her voice was a mellow foghorn. 'Fifteen, eighteen years?'

Boy? Angus? Habitué of a strip joint and almost certainly a brothel too? Was this the answer to my recent speculation about his sexual proclivities? It was hard to believe. Rich men can pick and choose women as they please, and he had ample opportunity in the social circles he moved in. Had he developed a hankering for bought women during his days on the docks, perhaps, and never been able to shake it off? Or did he – the mind boggled – have kinky tastes?

He was saying, 'Sixteen years, I think. Bingo Watson brought me here, and he's been dead for ten.'

In the dimness, I sensed her eyes inspecting me from top to toe. 'You are single, Faith?'

I nodded, speechless.

'Why don't you make an honest man of him, then? We all need somebody to warm our backs in bed at night when we get older.' The suggestion was punctuated with a belly laugh.

'But he's just a friend,' I managed to blurt. 'We...'

'...don't want to ruin a good thing.' Angus's voice boomed round the confined space. 'Stop meddling and let us through, woman. We need sustenance and entertainment. Bring on the dancing girls.'

She leaned forward to murmur in my ear, 'A pity. Even under that black shroud you are wearing, I can see you have a body that needs loving.'

What could I say? She was right.

'Come, we're wasting time.' Angus hustled me towards a second door in the far wall, saying, 'Have you kept me the corner table?'

A complicitous smile dissolved the broad face hanging in the dark space like a paper lantern. 'Of course. Go on through, Gus. I'll see you in a while.'

I had never been to a strip joint and thought of prostitutes as they appeared in grainy TV exposés, beaten-down women sitting on shabby settees telling pathetic stories of exploitation and customers who assaulted and raped. So I was unprepared for the professional-looking warehouse theatre with its haze of cigarette smoke and raucous male audience seated at tables laden with drinks; for the two naked girls taking a languorous bubble bath on stage under a revolving spotlight that bathed the see-thru jacuzzi and their wet bodies in alternating washes of colour; for the jarring thump-thump-thump of disco music; and for the dais to one side where more girls sat on stools at a well-lit bar, angled to face the customers.

They were confident hussies in the full range of honey shades from palest cream to rich dark brown, dressed in transparent blouses or low-cut bodysuits and clinging miniskirts. Several had the cropped hair and skinny bodies of siren schoolgirls; a pair at the end had the cocky-sullen faces of whores who had been through it all. Most looked like the receptionists beloved of advertising agencies: Barbie dolls with abundant tresses and nails of a length that prohibits any meaningful finger function, bar delicate scalp scratching.

Nesta had trained them to keep their wares on display. Every few minutes each girl would re-arrange her limbs and cleavage into a different position, stroking her body with suggestive innuendo. It was as riveting a performance as that of the rainbow mermaids on stage, who were now massaging each others' breasts to a chorus of hoarse cat-calls.

Gawping, I stumbled behind Angus to a table with a red cloth and a matching red velvet banquette curving round it. Laid out on trays were bowls of chips and dips and olives and cheese straws, a platter of biscuits and pâté, bottles of sparkling wine, whisky, vodka and cane spirit, a silver ice bucket and a battalion of glasses.

After I had managed to get my breath back, I said, not bothering to hide the sarcasm, 'Are you throwing a slumber party?'

'Just the usual.' He waved me into the banquette in high good humour, then sat down at one end. 'Not a bad spread, eh? Nesta used to run a nightclub in Atlanta. Now watch this.'

He put both forefingers to his mouth and gave a loud whistle. The girls on the dais jerked their heads towards it, then abandoned their stools and surged towards him.

'Gus!'

'Howzit, man?'

'Hey, Gus! Long time no see. Where've you been?'

'Shit, you look great, hey?'

I was ignored as they draped themselves over him and cooed in his ears and stroked the silver fuzz on his head, in the midst of which he sat preening.

'Girls,' he said after a while, twisting sideways to free himself from an enthusiastic kisser with her hand on his crotch, 'girls, hold off a moment while I introduce my friend Faith.'

A dozen pairs of eyes swivelled towards me under thickets of mascara, took in my stunned demeanour and funereal attire, and dismissing them – in an average five seconds – turned back to vamping Angus. I sat po-faced, growing more and more angry with him for bringing me to this place to flaunt his trashy girls. 'Out on the tiles', indeed. This was a raw male boast: see how charming and virile I am, even to girls young enough to be my granddaughters. I wondered if he hired them in twos and threes, or even half-dozens. I tried to imagine him disporting nude in a foam bath with them, and failed. I clenched my teeth in an effort to steel myself against the embarrassment of being the only woman not for sale in the whole howling place, and failed at that too. It was one of the truly appalling moments of my life.

When they had finished cooing and unwound themselves and begun plundering the dishes and bottles on the table, he shifted closer to me, adjusting his cravat.

'A fellow can always count on a good welcome at the Midnite Club. What are you drinking?'

'Nothing.'

'Whisky? Wine? Cane for the pain? Name your poison.'

'Vitriol might be appropriate.'

His roar of delight blasted a hole in the smoke billowing round us. 'You don't seem to be enjoying this. Why not? I said we'd be slumming.'

'You didn't say we'd be whoring. Take me home.'

'But the fun's only just begun. Hasn't it, girls?' He roared again and fondled the nearest behind. 'Tell Faith about the fun.'

'I don't want to hear. I don't want to *be* here.' How dare any man do this to me?

I felt his hand on mine, patting it as he had Nesta's. 'It's just a bit of sport, old girl. Not serious.'

'You're a disgusting old goat. I'm going.' I shuffled away from him towards the other end of the banquette, a lump in my throat the size of a pumpkin, intending to get up and flee, even if it meant braving the perilous Jeppe streets until I found a taxi.

But his hand grabbed mine and his sudden rage lashed me to stillness. 'What gives you the right to be so damn snooty? Where's your sense of bloody humour? This is my joke, can't you see? I don't come here to fornicate. I come to unwind and forget about affairs of state.'

'You could have fooled me.'

'I obviously did. But it was unintentional. I thought you'd see straight away that it was a lark.'

'A strip joint, a lark? I can't believe that your idea of fun is demeaning and exploiting women.'

'Bollocks. These girls are here of their own free will and they're earning a packet. Nesta keeps a clean house and strict control; she mans the door herself, as you saw, and doesn't allow drugs or any sleazy stuff like S & M or live sex on stage. If anyone steps over the line, the bouncers heave them out fast. This place is a damn sight safer than most shopping centres and a hell of a lot more fun.'

'Boys will be boys, eh?'

His voice went up. 'I feel more at home and more welcome here than anywhere else in this benighted city. I'm accepted for who I am, just plain Gus, not what I am.'

The girls were emptying the plates and bottles with the swift efficiency of those who are all too aware that good things never last.

I snarled, 'Don't kid yourself, just plain Gus. Largesse gets a man everywhere.'

'Are you saying that I have to buy my favours? You know damn well that's not true.'

'What's all this, then?' I jabbed my forefinger at the table. 'I know that you see yourself as a benign sugar daddy, but…'

'And you're behaving like the carping old maid you're in danger of becoming. If I were…'

One of the girls bent over the back of the banquette between us and said, 'Hey, you two, quit it, man. We suppose to be having a good time here, not a bleddy cat fight.'

I turned to her in outrage. 'Mind your own business!'

Her answer shut me up as no other remark has. 'Calm down, lady,' she said. 'Have a heart. Can't you see the old guy's just laying out bait so's he can feel like Father Christmas with a hard-on, even if he doesn't get one? I wish the other customers were such a fucking pleasure.' She flounced back to her bar stool, hooking her thumbs into lurex hot pants.

Angus started laughing and he went on so long and got so red in the face that I thought he'd have an apoplectic fit, and serve him right. But I began at last to see the funny side – this particular old guy was one of Joburg's most respected and feared business executives – and felt my face cracking at last into a spiky smile.

That evening stretched to three hours after I had been propitiated with several glasses of very good chardonnay and began, if not to enjoy, at least to appreciate the skill of the stage spectacle. After the girls in the bubble bath had run through their repertoire of rubbing and writhing and seductive sleights of hand, which included inserting strings of pearl necklaces into various orifices and pulling them out slowly to the huge delight of their audience, they were followed by a line of cancan dancers wearing lace-up boots but no panties under their frilly skirts, a soul singer, a troupe of nude acrobats and a belly dancer clanking with cheap gold chains who shed a blizzard of gauze veils to Ravel's *Bolero*. It was all part of my research, I told myself, trying not to cringe.

Nesta came and sat down with us, shooing the rest of the girls back to their bar stools. She told me of her years running the Atlanta nightclub, her marriage to an African-American and her decision to return home with their children after it failed. 'I opened this place in May 1976, the month before Soweto exploded.' Her full lips parted in a rueful smile. 'Never been known for my great timing.'

'Or your tact,' Angus cut in. 'Still calling me boy, for example. I'm sixty-bloody-four.'

'To me, you are all boys.' Her face became a complication of wrinkles. 'In some ways, I think, a man never grows up. He lacks one of the maturity genes, is my guess.'

Angus looked pained. 'Give me strength. It's time you retired to count your shekels, Mama.'

'Shekels? Aikona,' she said. 'Good South African rands, and plenty of them. I'll retire when I drop, and not a minute before. Talking of which, how's your health? Better, or just holding?' Her eyes scanned him as they had me earlier. 'You're looking thin.'

'Lost a few kilos and my hair,' he admitted, 'but otherwise fine. The chemo seems to be working and the hair's growing again.'

Her glittering hand moved over the table to cover his. 'I have been praying for you, Gus. I'm never sure if the good Lord listens to sinners like me, but if He does, He's heard of your case.'

Whatever made him pull away and drove him to his feet – denial of mortality or his aversion to being commiserated with – she had hit a raw nerve. He growled, 'If you insist on being negative, I'm going to chat to the girls.'

Nesta turned to me. 'He's always like this. Comes in and tries to run everybody's lives for them. Forever advising me to retire, and my girls to get off the game and aim higher. I don't know why I put up with this man, nyanisi. He doesn't do anything for my profits.'

He was wearing his most truculent glare. 'I spend a fortune on your over-priced drinks. Isn't that enough?'

'Never!' She reached up and gave him a gentle punch. 'Ag, you know I'm just having my bit of fun. Go on, boy. Go and tickle up the girls with your dreams and schemes.'

She was well over seventy, stately as a galleon, canny as a merchant banker and au fait with enough sexual secrets to decimate Joburg society. Yet she wielded her power with discretion; during the fifteen minutes we sat talking while Angus patrolled the bar stools trying to sell the girls on the idea of investing their spare cash in regular parcels of unit trusts, she did not mention her customers. Our conversation was about the Côte d'Ivoire which she had recently visited, her grandmother's daily life in rural Zululand and my books, two of which she had read and said she had enjoyed. To someone who had never met a strip club owner before, she was a revelation. It seemed that yet another of my glib assumptions had been wrong.

After she had sailed off to talk to other patrons, Angus sat down again and filled me in further. 'She still lives in a flat in the next-door building where the girls are housed, as do the bouncers Hennie and George. Says she'd rather spend her money on her family than on a fancy mansion in Houghton.'

'Are places like this lucrative?'

'Do giraffes have long necks? Mama Nesta is one of the richest women in the country. She's set up a trust running into millions for her three surviving children and eight grandchildren – of whom Praise is one, of course. She brought him up after his parents died. When he was twelve and starting to run with street kids, she packed him off to Waterford in Swaziland which seems to have nurtured a stubborn streak of independence. He refused to go to university after Matric, electing to work for me as a driver while he studies business management part-time. As a night-school boy myself, how could I refuse? Praise has a passion for well-engineered wheels and Nesta has promised to help him purchase a BMW dealership when he's proved himself. She doesn't believe in giving things away; they must be hard-earned, she says. That's one formidable old battle-axe.'

'And the girls?'

'I love 'em. Not literally,' he added, in case I got the wrong end of the stick again. 'I have – other fields to plough. But those girls are the salt of the earth, Faith. Tough as sewer rats, stroppy as hell, with no pretences. Nesta sets a strict limit of five years; after that, they're out of here. Most of them make enough during that time to start businesses of their own, which is where I can advise them.'

'Similar businesses? Franchises?'

That set him off into another paroxysm of laughter. When it subsided he said, 'You know, that's not a bad idea. I must mention it to Nesta. She could start a useful chain if she got the right managers into the right premises. Midnite Clubs could be even more successful than Nando's Chicken.'

Enlightenment dawned as I watched him following his train of thought. He saw himself as Toulouse Lautrec trawling the low dives of Paris; Dégas among the dancers. These girls were his Jeppe family to which he could come when he needed cheerful and undemanding company. As he had lined me up for Saturday lunches and intelligent conversation, so he had organised a lively venue for the nights when he felt lonely.

When we left, I turned back in the doorway to watch the next act coming on stage: the cancan dancers again, this time with their breasts bared too, jiggling across the stage and hoiking up their frilly skirts to tumultuous applause and whistling. Many and onerous are the ways in which people earn their bread. As we crossed the dark space towards the front door, I sent up a silent prayer of gratitude for my quiet office and biddable computer.

Praise materialised among the parked cars in the yard outside, holding the hand of a solemn child in pigtails and a dressing gown whose eyes reflected the dull copper glow from the clouds.

Angus said, 'Sorry we've been longer than usual. I hope you've had things to do?'

'Plenty. I've been talking to my sisters and reading stories to Thandi, who couldn't go to sleep.' He pushed the child forward. 'Gogo Nesta's first great-grandchild. She's pretty, nè? Clever, too. Gogo has already started her at Roedean.'

Angus bent to lay his hand on her shoulder and said, 'Sakubona, Thandi,' and went on for a while as the child nodded, shyly polite. He'll make a fond grand-

123

father, I thought. If he lives.

Praise's baseball cap made a jaunty silhouette against the windscreen as we drove home. He must know the other places where Angus went when he disappeared. But how could I extract the information from him without trespassing on his loyalties?

The mud-spattered Land Rover bore a hefty cargo of secrets.

15

*A*ngus went overseas a few days later –
'Only for a couple of weeks,' he said at our Saturday lunch, 'on essential business.
I'll be able to see Hannah and the girls too.'

It's a farewell visit while he's still feeling up to it, I thought in alarm. How much
is he hiding from me about the cancer? He hid so much from everyone that mere
shadows on X-rays could well be squirrelled away along with other unpleasant truths
he didn't wish to impart. I began to reach across the table. 'Are you quite sure you're
well enough? What do the doctors say?'

'Told you already. I'm fine. Strong as a bloody ox.' He ignored my outstretched
hand and raised both blazered arms to flex invisible biceps. A young waiter
standing nearby turned away to hide his smile. 'The quacks say that as long as I
fly first class and don't schedule too many meetings and promise to rest every afternoon, I can do what I like in moderation.'

'Flying first class shouldn't be too much of a strain. I've never had the pleasure.'

'Envy will get you nowhere, old girl.' His self-satisfied chuckle rolled round the
almost-empty dining room as he dropped his arms and adjusted his shirt cuffs.
It seemed that I was lunching with the Big Q that day.

'It's not envy so much as irritation. I can't stand the smug look on the faces of
first-class passengers as they vanish behind their curtains while I'm being shoe-
horned into the sardine section.'

'I'll treat you some day.'

'Aikona.' I had begun to use Mama Nesta's useful word too. 'Remember what
I said about bribes?'

'Call it a reward, then. Depending on what my personal biographer comes up
with.' There was no mistaking the caveat. 'If I'm – if this trip is successful, there
could be more revelations.'

'Such as the other fields you plough?'

He regarded me across the table's winter centrepiece of fruit in a silver bowl: Star King apples and naartjies and the last grapes from cold storage. 'Did I say that?'

'You did.'

'Moment of weakness. That's the trouble with health setbacks,' he grumbled. 'Your mind is preoccupied with questions of mortality and you make mistakes. I've had too many unguarded moments recently.'

'Regretting the interviews with the tape recorder?'

'Some.' He slumped back in his chair, pushing his plate away; his appetite had still not recovered from the chemotherapy. Though his colour was good that day, his eyes seemed less vivid; the tired blue of old jeans.

'I'll drop the sleuthing if you like and stick to exploring the Club attics.' My fingers were crossed under the table. 'Though it would be a shame.'

'God preserve us from...' He stopped.

'Quizzy females?' I prompted.

But he had fallen into a brown study and didn't answer. The waiters were moving round the room laying the tables for dinner, snapping open clean table cloths, folding starched napkins into fans, chinking cutlery, placing wineglasses just so: sherry, white wine, red wine, champagne flute. How many people live like this nowadays? I thought. How I enjoy these ceremonious meals.

I waggled my fingers at him and said, 'Cooee. Are you there, Angus? We're supposed to be having a conversation. God preserve you from...?'

'I was just wondering whether I believe in the God I invoke. Do you, Faith? Believe?'

I didn't know what to say. I hadn't believed in God since I was thirteen and Mother – the source of the embarrassing 'Cooee' that slips out sometimes – had packed me off to preparation classes for confirmation in the Anglican Church, an institution that gave her far more pleasure than her marriage ever did. The priest was bored and boring; after two dreary lessons I disliked him so much that I refused to return. Thwarted of her ceremony, Mother washed her hands of my spiritual welfare in a memorable outburst and I never set foot in a church again.

But how can you tell a man only a few steps away from death that you don't believe in either God or an afterlife? It would be like saying to a nun, 'I don't believe in the ideal to which you've devoted your whole life.' I didn't want to lie to him, but I also didn't want to betray my beliefs for the mess of pottage I had just consumed: glazed gammon with roast sweet potatoes, creamed spinach, petits pois and two glasses of Hamilton Russell pinot noir.

He was insisting, 'Do you? I want to know.'

'I...' What mattered most in this moral dilemma: our long friendship or my self-esteem?

He gave a sombre nod and said, 'You don't. I thought so.'

'I'm not sure.' There was no choice but the truth. 'My mother put me off organised religion when I was a teenager and Kurt was a lapsed Catholic, which completed the process. But if you ask me what I believe deep down, it's that the universe can't just have evolved. So there must be a controlling intelligence, even if it isn't particularly interested in the human specks that populate our planet.'

'Is that a yea or a nay? I have a vested interest in these matters now.'

'It's a maybe, and that's all I can honestly offer. Please don't dump your spiritual doubts on me as well as using me as a confessional, Angus.'

'Why not? We must have thrashed out every subject under the sun except religion at this table during the past fifteen years. Why the delicate avoidance in our society of chit-chat about God and death, do you think? And then there's that crucial question: Are we free and responsible for our own acts, or is everything pre-ordained? Do I keep fighting, or do I accept my karma and submit to cruel fate?'

He had gone existentialist on me. I floundered, 'This is hardly the place for philosophical debate.'

'It's got bugger all to do with philosophy. It's my bloody life that's at stake!'

Only then did I realise the extent of the angry fear he had managed to hide even from me, who thought I knew him.

This time I managed to grab his hand and hold it. 'I know. But you know too, Angus. You said during our dinner at the Linger Longer that you're a reacher and grabber by instinct. You're also a fighter. You've battled your way up from poverty to a place your father could never imagine.'

His hand bucked in my grasp. 'So what? You're evading the issue. I asked a simple question.'

'And I was about to say, So there's only one answer: you keep fighting as you've always done. Submitting to cruel fate isn't your style.'

'I'm losing some of my impetus.' Gravel in his voice as it dropped. 'Following in the old man's footsteps after all. He got his railway job back when the War came and thousands of able-bodied men joined up and the poor whites were needed again. Nine years later he lost the fingers on his right hand in a coupling accident and they slung him out with a disability pension only a gnat could live on. I tried to get him to sue, but he wouldn't. Said he was too old and tired. Started to drink and ran off with the floozy – and you know the rest.'

Pleased that I had managed to divert Angus's attention from himself, I let his hand go. 'What happened to your mother?'

'She had to have someone to bully after Dad and I left, so she offered her bachelor brother Ernie a home. He was a shoe salesman who never understood how money works. Kept his nose to the grindstone all his life, slaving for other people. Anything left of his wages at the end of the month went straight into the building society. "A penny saved is a penny gained," he used to say. And there the pennies sat earning a miserable interest with no growth at all. Zero!' Angus's flushed cheeks matched the wine in his glass. 'The pathetic worn savings book Uncle Ernie carried round in his pocket was symbolic of the way of thinking that kept people like my family in their places.'

'Didn't keep you down, though.'

'I thought – knew – I was worth more.'

'Is that what you call your drive to succeed?'

'Got to call it something. Life force is too general. Naked ambition sounds too bald. And it wasn't just greed.' His eyes were far away, in Cape Town before the war. 'It was sheer bloody-minded rage against the system, now I come to think of it. I had to show people that even railwaymen's sons can make it.'

'Inverted snobbery.'

He snapped back into the present. 'That's one thing you can't call me, a snob.'

'Not a social or an intellectual snob maybe, but an achievement snob. You like people to know that you made it on your own.'

'Doesn't everyone?' he shot back. 'Don't you, Miss Smartypants Historian?'

It was another of his talents, the ability to throw opponents on to the defensive with a sharp riposte. I countered, 'We'd all like to, but most of us are willing to admit to the help we've had from others. You seem to want everyone to think you're entirely self-made. But that's not true, is it?'

His cannonade of laughter made the waiters' heads turn. We were the last two guests in the dining room. I noticed with sadness that his belly no longer shook.

'Scalpels out, is it?' he said, subsiding at last and reaching for his glass to raise it to me. 'Ready to go for the jugular? Happy hunting while I'm away, Faith. I think you're in the same position as I am now, which is the reason why I'll continue to fight the good fight. There's no alternative.' I got the card-sharp's smile then, full volume. 'See you when I get back. I'll expect a preliminary report.'

I thought, Now's the time to ask, and ventured, 'Will you let me have access to some of your papers while you're away?'

His black eyebrows knotted. 'What do you mean by papers?'

'Oh, just relevant facts about your career.' I tried to make it sound airy and non-invasive. 'Material I'm not likely to find in the newspaper files: press releases and articles about you in company magazines, for example.'

'No prying into personal stuff?'

'Of course not.'

'I suppose I could ask Prunella to let you have the publicity files. But that's all, do you hear?' I was skewered by a truculent blue glare. 'No bloody prying.'

'No prying,' I promised. 'Though I don't guarantee a whitewash either.'

'Not asking for that. Nothing worse than cheap paint. Make it good quality washable PVA and you've got a deal.'

'Let's shake on it.' I reached across the table. His hand was cold: the silky-smooth cold of reptile skin.

My chameleon friend.

16

❧

*M*iss Smartypants Historian. Had it been an insult or a compliment? As Angus's health declined, there were many times when I couldn't tell. In the space of ten minutes he could say, 'I revel in clever women,' bark, 'I can't stand bloody interfering women!' and accuse me of being a carping old maid. In one breath he would compare me favourably with Hannah, calling us 'two of the most important women in my life'; in the next, he'd accuse me of being holier-than-thou or too proud and prickly, then in an eye-blink produce a winning smile and ask to be forgiven.

Though his mood changes could be ascribed to the death sentence hanging over him, I found the unexpected flashes of hostility hard to deal with. The remark about his mother had been illuminating: 'She had to have someone to bully after Dad and I left.' It explained his impulse to dominate his family and employees and why his marriage had foundered, given Hannah's strong need to be her own person. But it didn't explain why his attitude to me should have become so volatile. Our steady and undemanding friendship had metamorphosed into a strange contest in which I was alternately the supporter and the opponent.

I needed someone to talk to about the problem. But who? Because I worked alone so much, sometimes all day and into the night when a chapter was going well, I made a point of meeting friends for lunch or a night out several times a week. Like most singles, I socialised mainly in a network of others in similar situations: separated, widowed, divorced, solitary live-alones, or those in difficult partnerships from which they needed to escape once in a while. Some of the single men were gay but most were the kind of particular bachelor who has everything under control and shrinks from the idea of commitment to a lesser mortal. We all talked hard and partied late, but involvements beyond a brief fling were considered messy.

My friendship with Angus had been the antithesis of all this, its security buttressed by the gracious old Club building in which we met to enjoy each other's company. And now it was falling apart.

After a lot of thought I telephoned Lauren, a clinical psychologist friend, and asked her to have lunch with me at a Village Walk café near her rooms. Although she dressed and spoke like the born-to-shop wives of the stressed executives she counselled, Lauren was shrewd and amusing and understood the corporate world in which Angus moved.

'So, what's up?' she said when our small talk had petered out over the seafood salad. 'If you've got me here on my own, you want advice.'

'How do you know?'

Her silver hoop earrings jiggled when she laughed. 'Don't act so surprised. I can see something's bugging you.'

This was embarrassing. 'I knew I should have made an appointment instead of luring you to lunch. It's just – appointments are so formal and I'm not, well, I'm not...'

'So be my guest and spit it out. Aunty Lauren's a great listener. What are friends for, I ask?'

'It's...' I stopped. Though my friends knew that I had regular lunches with an older man, I'd never told them who he was. Discretion had been one of the cornerstones of our singular friendship, and here I was about to destroy the edifice by plucking it out.

'You don't have to say who.' Lauren's hand, clinking with rings, reached out to pat mine in a gesture she must use many times a day. And it worked.

I said, 'I have a friend who's battling cancer and I can't understand what's happening to him. To us. Our whole – well, relationship, though that's not the right word since sex isn't involved – everything between us has changed. He blows hot and cold. One moment he's firing off insults, and the next he's offering to buy a convertible to help me find a mate to replace him. It's bizarre! I don't know where I am with him any more.'

'Where is the cancer?'

'It started in the colon. They operated and he's had two sessions of chemo and says he's in remission, but I'm not so sure. He's lost a lot of weight.'

'Serious, then.' She was playing a tattoo on the table with pink-lacquered nails. 'If he thinks he's in danger of dying, it's no surprise that he's in a state of fluctuating emotions.'

'It's much more than a state.' I couldn't finish my salad and pushed the plate away, leaning towards her as I tried to explain my confusion. 'It's a profound shift in personality that's undermining everything I believed about him. He's changed into someone far more complex and threatening than the man I thought I knew, and he seems to want to spill out all the personal stuff we never spoke about. It's as though he's taken some sort of truth drug. Do you know what I'm talking about?'

'Sure,' she shrugged. 'Dying people need to get all the shit they feel bad about off their chests.'

'Even if the act of confession damages their good name?'

'Even then.' She paused, looking at me as she licked her middle finger to smooth each of her pencilled eyebrows, then said, 'You're uncomfortable with what you call personal stuff. Why? What's the big deal?'

'It isn't – wasn't – that sort of friendship.'

'Explain.'

How could I explain our decade and a half of Saturday lunches? Saturday is the essential breathing space of the week: unstructured and elastic, a time to breakfast late and catch up with odd jobs, shopping, friends, repairs and other neglected tasks. My regular lunch with Angus had grown from a pleasant interlude on a scrappy day into something far more valuable: an affirmation that I could enjoy good conversation and light-hearted intimacy with an interesting, admirable man, uncomplicated on either side by confused emotions.

I said, 'I've always thought of our meals together as a meeting of minds. We ate and talked and argued and laughed, then went our separate ways. It seemed to be enough for both of us. For fifteen years I've thought of him as my best friend.'

'Molto civilised. And now?'

'He's acting like one of those characters in science fiction films that keep changing shape…'

'Morphing. Amazing technique.'

'…and I'm being torn apart. I've changed too. That's what's so upsetting. Half of me wants to know more about this fascinating stranger, and the other half wants everything to stay the way it was.'

In the silence after I had spoken, Lauren took out a black enamel compact, checked her front teeth, dabbed at her shiny nose, refurbished her pink lipstick and ran her fingers through her streaked blonde curls to fluff them up. I sat wondering who she was trying to impress. One of the men in the café? I looked round; only women. The waiter came with our ordered cheesecake and double espressos. She clicked the compact shut and put it back in her bag.

'Faith.' She leant on her elbows over her steaming cup, ready to pronounce. 'I hear two things. One: you don't like change, which is a very rigid attitude for someone your age. You should loosen up, doll. Two: deep down inside, you believe that if you could only restore the old relationship, you could stop your friend dying. That's like trying to hold back the tide. Logically, you know it's not possible.'

I hadn't told her the worst part yet. Fiddling with the breadcrumbs on my side plate so I wouldn't have to look at her, I confessed, 'The worst of it is, I'm starting to enjoy the drama. I'm like a junkie, wanting more and more as it drives us further and further apart. It's so damn compulsive that it's given me a great idea for my next book. I'm making capital out of his tragedy, for God's sake. I don't understand my conduct either.'

'Quite normal.'

'Betraying your best friend, normal?'

'Who says it's betraying? You're planning to hang on to the good memories by immortalising him in a book. That sounds totally understandable to me. I should be so lucky.' The hoop earrings jiggled again as she picked up her fork to attack the cheesecake.

It was so trite that I was speechless for a moment, then managed to force out, 'You're trivialising what I'm trying to say. This is a crisis for me, Lauren.'

'You intellectuals. Experts at making mountains out of simple little molehills.' She was grinning at me with white flecks of cottage cheese on her glossy lips. 'It's a crisis only because you're busy turning it into one. You've got to learn to deal with problems step by step. Like, A: are you fond of this guy?'

'Of course. We're old friends.'

'B: do you want to keep his friendship?'

'You know I do.'

'Then C: put up with the shit. That's the best advice I can give you. Deal with it. If he's dying, he'll move through various stages after his initial disbelief and anger. It sounds to me like he's in anger at the moment and taking some of it out on you. But he'll get past that, I guarantee. You've just got to stop feeling guilty for acting like a normal person who's upset at losing someone they care for on the one hand, and damn relieved it's not you on the other. Nobody's perfect, okay? You don't have to be a good girl all the time.'

The last sentence stayed with me long after we had finished our lunch and the parting, 'Take it easy, now,' from Lauren. I watched her walk away down the pavement, hair bouncing, short skirt flickering about gym-toned legs, and reminded myself (yet again) not to make hasty judgments based on appearances. She had been briskly sympathetic and given me excellent advice. No one had ever said to me, 'You don't have to be a good girl all the time.' And I had, it was true, got rather set in my ways – though I thought I'd begun to loosen up during my debut as Angus's social partner.

I went into a florist to send Lauren flowers by way of thanks, then decided to drive home by a different route for a change.

It was one of those still, warm winter days between cold fronts when the afternoon sun settles like gold dust, blurring ugliness as it highlights curved gables and graceful railings and the last redness of autumn leaves. Enjoying the drive and the slanting sunlight, I detoured to one of my favourite vantage points: Brixton

Ridge with its soaring radio transmission tower, its view to the east of playing fields and the city skyline, and to the north and west of houses and gardens crowding up to the stony ridges that gave the Witwatersrand its name.

On such gilded afternoons, Johannesburg from certain angles is beautiful. You wouldn't think this glinting metropolis barely a century old was already decaying at the core, with empty offices like missing teeth because so many businesses have moved out to the satellite suburban towns, choking them too with snarling traffic.

I parked my car at the edge of the road and sat there – with the doors locked, of course, and my mace canister in my lap – until the sun went down in a snaggle of red cloud and the city skyline turned purple.

17

My publishers were pressing for the manuscript I'd been working on. With Angus away, I had time to finish it in an orgy of typing and proof-reading and endless mugs of coffee that gave me a caffeine high but got the job done. I delivered the manuscript on a Friday with the emancipated feeling that a snake must get when it shrugs off its papery skin to emerge in new radiance. Now I could concentrate on my research into the lives of the businessmen who had moulded Johannesburg in their own images over the years.

Next morning I headed for the Club where my Saturday sessions in the attics had become a regular event with Mr Barkin in enthusiastic attendance. I was not invited to call him anything but Mr Barkin, while he called me Miss D. (According to Angus, nobody knew his first name and there was some doubt as to whether he had ever been young).

He had a mind like a filing cabinet – crammed with facts and figures neatly organised in the correct compartments but without the ability to make useful cross-references. He was able to tell me the date each item had been stored away by comparing the chalked marks on them with the ledger in which they had been noted, and often added an anecdote about their owners. Ask him to relate the artefacts or their owners to social trends and historical events during their time of tenure, however, and he was lost.

I had encouraged him to expand on his character notes and he had taken to the idea with gusto. Every member since the Club's founding in 1904 was now listed on his computer, and he spent his spare time combing the archives and old newsletters so he could construct a potted biography for each.

'It's become my hobby, you know? Very rewarding. Very.' A diffident smile illuminated the deep-sunk eyes.

I became fond of Mr Barkin for all his nervous ways and whiffs of the Vicks spray he used to try and subdue the allergy that made him sneeze when dust was disturbed. We gossiped together over tea which he ordered from the kitchen at regular intervals. Boniface brought the trays up if he was on duty, stern with reproach at our meddling in the Club's past. He could not understand why I should want to unpack the creased old clothes, mould-spotted linen and sunken shoes that had been squashed together for so long that they parted with reluctance.

'Why do you take out these things, Madam?' he asked one afternoon. 'Why not leave them sleeping?'

'Because I want to know what men wore in those days,' I explained. 'What fabrics were involved, how their clothes fastened, whether they wore soft or stiffened collars. Things like that.'

'But why, when there are books to tell you? I have seen them in the library.' His face was as stiff as the venerable leather portmanteau I was busy unpacking.

'I intend to write my own book, Boniface, that's why. A social history of Joburg businessmen, many of whom belonged to the Club during the early days.'

'Social history, what is that?'

'The story of the things people used and what they wore and what they did at work and what their homes were like. Wouldn't you like to know how your people lived in the old days?' Historians are striving to recapture the long-ignored data relating to workers' lives, as I had in my book on the early mine compounds, and I thought that the idea would appeal to him.

But he said with disgust, 'Nobody wants to know about such low things,' and stalked away.

When he was out of earshot, Mr Barkin confided, 'Boniface is the ultimate conservative. That's what makes him so acceptable to our members.'

Mr Barkin seemed to enjoy dropping caustic remarks about the Club and its membership, secure in the knowledge that he had a discreet audience in me. I had soon realised that his enthusiasm for our task was partly due to loneliness. His terror of the streets meant that he seldom left the Club and because he was always there, he was at everyone's beck and call, a perpetual servant with no private life. 'Old Barkin' the members called him with patronising condescension, though most of them were far older. 'Ask Old Barkin, he'll know,' they said, ignoring the hall porter and jabbing their fingers on the bell at the front desk to bring him scurrying out of the office with his painfully bright smile hovering above the black cloth jacket.

'Boniface is well named,' I said. 'Does he ever unbend?'

'Never. He indicates his approval or disapproval by slight alterations in his expression, and that's about as much as you can expect.'

'Imperturbable as Jeeves. The ideal club servant,' I agreed, meaning Mr Barkin as well.

'Too right,' he sighed, fielding the implication. 'We're like reliable robots, programmed to please and soothe and flatter. Ego-stroking is an important aspect of club service. Maybe that's what clubs are for, yes?' He peered up at me from his kneeling position by the portmanteau. 'Ego-stroking.'

I had a mental picture of Angus. 'It's more than that. There's the sense of belonging to an exclusive group – the brotherhood – as well as the perks on offer. The Joburg Club offers superb creature comforts, thanks to your talent for organisation.' No harm in giving his ego a stroke too.

'You're not bad at flattery yourself, Miss D,' he said, looking pleased. 'Not at all bad.'

It was a fortnight after my lunch with Angus, who was expected back on the following Monday or Tuesday. Mr Barkin and I were unpacking various containers in one of the middle attics, he listing their musty contents on a clipboard pad while I made annotated pencil sketches of any unusual garments or accessories. As we struggled to close the lid of a cabin trunk on its repacked contents, which seemed to have swelled to twice their original size, I heard someone outside in the passage.

'We're not finished with our tea yet, Boniface,' I called out, assuming he had forgiven me for rootling through his gentlemen's past lives and come back to fetch the tray.

'That's not Boniface,' Mr Barkin said, then stopped with his head cocked, listening.

There were dragging footsteps: a person shuffling along the linoleum. 'Who is it, then? The Club ghost?' I joked.

But Mr Barkin didn't answer. He dropped his clipboard and hurried towards the door saying, 'Sir! Sir! Are you alone?'

The footsteps stopped and a voice mumbled something. Mr Barkin disappeared.

'Who is it?' I repeated, rising to my feet and letting the trunk lid bounce up again.

'Just...' Mr Barkin's face came round the door, wreathed in apology, '...just a member gone astray. If you don't mind waiting a few minutes, I'll get him back to his room and we can carry on.'

Gone astray. Odd choice of words, I thought. And there had been real alarm in his 'Sir! Sir! Are you alone?' Why shouldn't a member be alone up here in the attics? Curiosity won over the note of warning in Mr Barkin's voice and I put my drawing block down and went to the door and peered into the passage.

He was standing with his arm round the shoulders of a bent old man in a dressing gown that exposed skinny legs ending in trodden-down leather slippers. The old man's face was hidden by long grey dreadlocks. Mr Barkin was saying, 'Come on, Stanley. Let's go back to your room,' and urging him towards the stairway next to the lift. The old man began to shuffle along obediently, head nodding and slippers dragging. 'There's a good man,' Mr Barkin encouraged. 'Let's go back downstairs and find Philomena. She'll take care of you. There's a good man.'

I watched them negotiate the top few steps and went back to my drawing block wondering about this new category of club member. When Mr Barkin came back, breathless and frowning, I said, 'Who was that?'

'You saw him?'

I nodded. 'Couldn't help taking a peep.'

'Sorry it had to happen. His bedroom door was left unlocked and...' He gave an uncomfortable shrug. 'Stanley's presence here isn't common knowledge. I'll catch it if anyone finds out that you saw him. I'll really catch it.'

'A Club mystery?'

'Not at all. No. No mystery. Just...'

'A skeleton tumbling out of the cupboard? This begs for further investigation.'

His face grew alarmed. 'Please, Miss D, I must ask you not to say anything to anyone about this confidential matter. My job could be in jeopardy. Yes. In jeopardy.'

I'm an expert at putting on the screws when I need to. 'Tell me who he is, then. And why he's here.'

'You didn't recognise him?'

'Didn't see his face. Should I have?'

Mr Barkin sat down on the lid of the too-full trunk. 'You would have, a few years ago. That's Stanley Linklater. Remember? One of the first big industrialists to make overtures to the ANC. A great man in his time. Great man.'

I remembered the newspaper archive files on Angus and a photograph of businessmen standing in a semicircle round President Mandela. Stanley Linklater had been one of them: a chain store millionaire famed for his ascetic way of life who was said to have enraged his family by devoting the bulk of his fortune to a charitable trust that built new schools and clinics in poor rural areas. Among the press cuttings had been Mitch Kincaid's sour piece about various firms' efforts to improve their corporate images, headed 'Public Relations Coups of the Decade'. He hadn't replied to my letter yet, and I wondered why.

I said, 'What's wrong with Mr Linklater?'

'Can't you guess? Alzheimer's, poor chap. Hit him in his early sixties. After the initial diagnosis was made, he was heaped with honours and retired. When his behaviour deteriorated last year, his family wanted to put him in a home. The rich know how to get rid of their embarrassments. Oh yes.' Mr Barkin was bristling like a threatened dog.

138

'I'm sure it wasn't a case of getting rid of him. Alzheimer's patients need specialised nursing.'

'He could have been nursed at home! He deserved it. He was a great man; not mean like the newspapers said, just careful how he spent his money. He'd worked damned hard for it, he said, and expected value in return. Sweat equity, he called it. Sweat equity. Always tipped me and the Club staff very generously, saying we were workers too.'

'And as a final service, you found him a room here to end his days among his gentlemen's comforts?'

Mr Barkin's answer was a surprise. 'Not me. No. It was Mr Quain's idea. He said that he didn't see why Stanley should be bundled into a loonybin while his family made free with their pickings. So I was asked to try and fix him up, and I did: with a suite on the third floor plus a roster of day and night nurses. Keepers, really, I have to admit. He's getting very naughty and tries to escape all the time. It's a shame, you know? All that money and his mind's gone. Completely gone.'

'Don't the other Club members object?'

'Only the residents know about him, and they're sworn to silence. He won't be here much longer anyhow; poor old Stanley is going downhill fast. Has to be fed mush and his nappies changed and doesn't know if it's night or day any more. The doctors say his kidneys are failing. It's not long now. Not long.'

'Poor old Stanley, is it? No more Mr Linklater?'

'He doesn't recognise his surname any more.'

Musing over the story as we unpacked a valise containing several wing-collar shirts, a box of pearl studs, a white cummerbund and a set of tails reeking of mothballs, I said, 'Does the Club have other secrets besides Stanley? Unusual residents? Locked rooms into which no one dare go?'

Mr Barkin hunched his shoulders and bent his head closer to his clipboard. 'I really couldn't say.'

I'd never seen anyone look so cagey. 'So there *are* secrets. Let me guess... One of the residents is a member of the British royal family ... illegitimate, perhaps? A ducal black sheep banished to the colonies? Or – I know! You're harbouring Lord Lucan.'

'The Club would never...' he blurted, then firmed his lips. 'You won't catch me that way.'

'Hmmm.' I struck a thinking pose, forefinger on forehead. 'Maybe it's hidden treasure. There's a bagful of uncut diamonds in your safe which has been there since 1910, waiting to be claimed. Or could it be a hank of Cecil Rhodes's hair, preserved in a locket? No? Then how about a cache of gold artefacts stolen from the Mapungubwe dig by an amateur archaeologist who left them to the Club in

139

his will, only you can't sell them because they were nicked?'

His pained expression at my conjectures only encouraged me to wilder guesses.

'Perhaps it's a member who murdered his wife and now lives in one of the servants' rooms, protected by the Club's code of honour? Every night he sneaks into the kitchen to dine on leftovers followed by a glass of vintage port and a cigar from that enormous humidor in the library.'

He blurted, 'This is no joking matter, Miss D! You know I'm not at liberty to discuss members' affairs.'

'But you told me about Stanley.'

'Your seeing Stanley was an unfortunate accident. Most unfortunate.' He put his clipboard down and kneaded his hands. 'The Club is an old and respected institution. Of course it has secrets: some noble, some tragic, some regrettable, some frankly distasteful. I can tell you that. But you must see that I can't disclose them to an outsider.'

'I'm not a complete outsider.' I waved round the attic with its dim dangling light bulbs and dusty trunks and shrouded furniture. 'I was given permission to investigate and write about all this, so I have a vested interest now.'

'You're a woman,' he said with an air of clinching his argument and picked up his clipboard again.

Checkmate. But I wasn't going to be thwarted of promising new revelations. After a few more minutes of careful unfolding and sketching, I ventured, 'The corporate success stories I'm researching are much of a muchness: all hard work and dull grind before the triumphs happen. Surely you can tell me about some intriguing members who weren't or aren't businessmen, and therefore don't fall into the category I'm writing about? I wouldn't blab. I'm very discreet, as you know.'

His answer was sharp. 'As I don't know, Miss D. Journalists are not renowned for their ability to keep their pens still when they come across classified information.'

I leant over the open valise and put my hand on his shirt sleeve. 'I'm not a journalist or a sensation-seeker. I'm a historian and your friend, I hope. We should be able to talk in confidence.'

The look that came over his face then made me sorry I'd said it. He was a lonely, timid man and the emotion I saw was longing coupled with the knowledge that I could never be a real friend, whatever I said. His voice when he spoke was hoarse, his eyes pleading. 'You may call it talking in confidence. They'd call it disloyalty. My job hangs by the thinnest of threads. Believe me, the thinnest.'

My exploding laughter made him pull his arm away, offended. When I had managed to stop, I said, 'Don't you believe it, Mr Barkin. The Club couldn't function without a man of your integrity and dedication to run it.' I wasn't trying to flatter him now; it was true. The members relied without shame on his willingness to please and to work long hours that few employees would countenance.

'You are too kind.'

'Observant, rather. They depend on you. This job is yours as long as you're prepared to put up with the condescension.'

I didn't deserve the slow, sweet smile he gave me then. 'Thank you for that. I'll bear it in mind next time one of the members looks down his nose to give me an order. Yes.'

Angus looked down his nose sometimes. In reflex apology I said, 'I'm sorry I asked you for something which makes you feel uncomfortable, because I value the time we've spent together. You've given me background material I wouldn't have dug out in a hundred years.'

'But not enough gossip, eh?' His head was cocked to one side, comb marks furrowing his hair.

'You know what women are.' Irony never went amiss with Mr Barkin.

'If…' He hesitated, then went on with a brave effort, '…if I disclose information I've put together about certain members, will you keep it under your hat? Not use it to the Club's detriment or tell anyone it came from me?'

'Not without your express permission. I promise.'

He accepted my qualification with a jerky nod. 'Very well, then. I'd hate these footnotes to Joburg's history to go to waste if I never develop them myself. You are probably the best person to tell anyway, being in the trade, so to speak.'

And for the next half hour I was regaled with Mr Barkin's quirky gleanings from the Club's archives: tales of hunters and gentlemen crooks; ladies' men who used to bribe the hall porter with ten-pound notes to look the other way while they sneaked women up the stairs; balloonists, batty scientists, exiles from the Indian Army and the British weather; a diamond digger who made and spent three fortunes, then died a beggar in a Doornfontein doss-house; a gold prospector who blew off his hand and shattered half the windows on the third floor while experimenting with a mixture of ammonium nitrate and diesoline in his bathroom; Monty Steyn who kept himself permanently drunk with cheap sherry.

'And then there's our resident celebrity in hiding,' he ended, in full flow now.

'Who is that?' I had put down my drawing block so he wouldn't think I was making notes of what he said, but of course I was storing mental notes.

'The White Spectre. Does the name ring a bell?'

It did but I couldn't remember why.

Mr Barkin whispered, 'He was one of the mercenaries who fought alongside Colonel Bob Denard and Mad Mike Hoare.'

Now I remembered. He'd been dubbed the White Spectre after a photographer had snapped him in a shadowy rebel doorway: a mad smile under a bristle of short white hair, eyes squinting along the barrel of a rocket launcher aimed at a tank. The photograph won a Pulitzer Prize and the White Spectre's subsequent notoriety earned headlines all over the world. He was one of the violent adventurers Africa seems to attract, only he hadn't gone exploring or empire-building or crashing about mutilating the bush in a 4 x 4; he had offered his military skills to whichever dictator bid the highest.

I said, 'You mean to tell me that awful man is living here in the middle of Joburg?'

'I do.'

'But I'm sure I read somewhere that the White Spectre was executed by trigger-happy guerrillas.'

'He's by no means dead. He lives in Room 14 on the third floor, just round the corner from Mr Quain.'

'In this bastion of respectability?'

'Indeed, yes. Mr Doig – that's his real name, Rex Doig – has been a member in good standing since the mid-sixties, and once a member, always a member. Unless you do something unspeakable.'

'I'd put mercenary activity in that category.'

Mr Barkin pursed his lips. 'That's debatable. War is a time-honoured gentleman's occupation – except for Hitler and his ilk, of course. Members do draw the line at genocide.'

The bleak sarcasm was a surprise; it was the sort of remark Angus would make, not this ever-willing man who seemed to revere everything the Club stood for. Speech habits must be contagious, I thought, or Mr Barkin has unplumbed depths.

I said, 'Biafra and Ruanda both involved genocide.'

'Mr Doig was hors de combat before Ruanda blew up. He's crippled with arthritis now.'

'Poetic justice.'

'Unnatural wear and tear, rather. He was a soldier of fortune for something like thirty years, you know. Started as a big game hunter and safari guide in Kenya, and when the wealthy tourists went elsewhere after the Mau Mau uprising, he joined the Foreign Legion and fought with them at Dien Bien Phu and in Algeria. After his term was up, he worked his way south on the mercenary trail from Biafra to the Congo to Angola, with pit stops in Chad and Somalia and Sudan and the Comores. Busy fellow, he was. Very busy.'

'And now he's immobilised.'

There was a thin smile. 'Stuck in a wheelchair for his sins. Never leaves the room now, which is why you haven't seen him. It's a shrine, of course. A shrine.'

'To what?'

'Guns. Classic English hunting rifles, mainly. He's been collecting for decades, often buying them for peanuts from looters and scavengers of colonial relics. They line his walls from floor to ceiling; the pair of matched 1910 Purdys over his bed is irreplaceable.'

'And the Club allows it? Isn't an arsenal like that dangerous?'

'Not with the White Spectre on guard.'

'But you said he has arthritis.'

'In his neck and spine and leg joints, though his hands for some reason are still mobile. He spends all day sitting in his wheelchair facing the door with his favourite elephant gun across his knees. People have to give a special knock to be admitted, or they face the business end of a twelve-bore.'

'It's one way to deter unwelcome visitors.'

'Doesn't happen often, as you can imagine. Mr Doig has a personal manservant who attends to his daily needs, so contacts between him and the staff or other members are rare. Very rare.'

'That must be a relief for Boniface.'

Mr Barkin leaned closer. 'Between you and me, I suspect he wears a bulletproof vest on the occasions he's summoned to the room. Boniface has expressed a strong desire to meet his Maker with a priest's blessing and holy water on his brow, not a bullet through it.'

'Very sensible.'

'Nevertheless, Mr Doig is treated with the usual consideration. There were objections to his armoury from some of the younger members at first, but when it was pointed out that he was unlikely to last long, they subsided. He's a crabby old loner and no trouble except for the gun-pointing. I'm assured by the manservant that the cartridges are blanks but haven't had the courage to check.'

'Don't blame you. I bet everyone tiptoes past that door, though.'

Mr Barkin began to snicker, a high hollow whistling noise that could have been bazooka trajectories. When he stopped at last he said, 'Mr Doig only has to cough and everyone within ten metres freezes. We're not the bravest club staff in town.'

'You're the best, though, I hear.'

He accepted the compliment with a gracious nod. 'Thank you. We're very conscious of our duty to our paymasters. It is written that those who lose the Great Game of finance are bound to serve those who win.'

'What do you mean?'

'Every day in this building I am reminded of that enigmatic utterance by St Matthew: "Unto every one that hath shall be given, and he shall have abundance; but from him that hath not shall be taken away even that which he hath." It's always seemed so patently unjust. Un-Christian, even.'

'As unjust as old mercenaries dying tamely in their beds,' I agreed. Then trying my luck, added, 'Is there any chance of an interview with the old man?'

'None at all.' His answer was swift and decisive. 'I wouldn't dare ask Mr Doig if someone could interview him. Specially not a woman. He has an ugly temper and an even uglier vocabulary.'

I thought, When the members of this club aren't treating women like lepers, they're trying to hoist us on to pedestals. And said, 'Strong language doesn't offend me. My father swore like a trooper when my mother wasn't around. I'm sure I could give the White Spectre a hell of a lot better than he gave me.'

'Perhaps you could, Miss D. But you're not even going to try. We have an agreement, remember?'

We had an agreement that I wouldn't blab, but didn't preclude my following up on his stories. I didn't want to upset Mr Barkin after his interesting revelations, though, so I nodded and dropped the subject.

The Club's celebrity in hiding could go on to the back burner till my book on Joburg businessmen was finished – then perhaps I could write a history of mercenaries in Africa to follow Dr Mkhize's suggestion about traditional healers. My books often lead into each other in this serendipitous way.

I thought about the Club's secrets on the way home in the car and wondered how many more lurked behind the imposing sandstone facade, undetected even by Mr Barkin's sensitive antennae. Angus had been a loyal friend to Stanley Linklater, as he had to me. Would our friendship survive if I uncovered the less savoury aspects of his past?

And I thought, apropos Stanley and Rex Doig, Mutual support is one of the admirable qualities of this Club: members stick together like barnacles if they feel one of them is under threat.

Men have clubs and old-boy networks. Women have – what? Fragmented lives divided between their families and their work and their friendships, and if they're lucky, a pragmatic shrink like Lauren to run to in emergencies.

The following Monday, as if on cue, I received a flimsy Greek air letter postmarked Khios. In a scrawl of black felt-tipped pen Mitch Kincaid had written:

Dear Faith D
Of course I remember you – the tall thin snotty one with the dirty laugh.
Unfortunately I can't help. As you have guessed, my lips have been expensively sealed. Will risk one hint, though: look for the nigger in the woodpile.
And my best to the Big Q, damn his ice-blue eyes.
Sin Bad the Sailor

18

*I*t was time to venture into the lion's den of Quain & Associates and do some digging. I gave my line of attack some careful thought and phoned Prunella.

Underwhelmed as ever by my overtures, she fluted, 'Oh hullo, Mizz Dobermann. You do know that Mr Quain is away?' Translation: Didn't he tell you he was flying to London? Everyone else knows.

It was hard not to be riled. I fluted back, 'Of course. He told me to contact you for additional information while he was gone. "The indispensable Prunella will lay her hand on anything you need," he said.' Translation: You are his paid minion. Don't mess with me, his friend.

'Information about what?' Suspicion gave her voice a strong vibrato. 'He didn't say anything to me.'

'His business career. I need copies of his press releases and any magazine articles featuring him.'

There was a long pause, then, 'What do you want them for?'

'I'm writing a profile on him for my new book and need more biographical details. Dates of his appointments to various jobs, awards, outstanding achievements, that sort of thing.'

Another, longer, pause. The Prune was not the world's fastest thinker and I was putting her on the spot most dreaded by secretaries: where does useful publicity end and confidential begin? Finally she said, 'Writing what, exactly? He didn't...'

'Stop bleating about what he didn't do. Just fish out his publicity file for me, will you? I'll come and fetch it this afternoon.'

'But I'm not at liberty to hand over the MD's files just like that!'

'Then phone for his permission.' I hoped that Angus would remember giving it. 'Can you get through to him right away? I'm in a hurry.'

'I'll try,' she said, glissading from doubt to obstruction as only a secretary can.

'He's in the London office today at an important meeting which can't be interrupted, so it'll have to be by fax. Not a thing goes out the door of this office until I have spoken to or had a personal fax from him.'

'The sooner, the better.'

'Patience, Mizz Dobermann,' she snarled. 'I'm bound to go through the proper channels.'

'Use plenty of lubricant, then.'

'What do you mean?'

'Make it slippy.'

As I rang off I heard her mutter an indelicate word. Despite the enamelled exterior Prunella had a cracking point, it seemed.

A talking lift whisked me in seconds up to the four-storey domain of Quain & Associates. 'You are now on floor…' pregnant pause '…eighteen,' a sepulchral American voice announced. 'Have a nice day.'

Floor eighteen was the holy of holies where the partners' offices were, all blonde wood and deep-piled Wilton and original paintings. Each vista ended in a narrow shelf sporting an ikebana arrangement. I wondered if the partners had had a member of staff trained in the art of adorning tortured twigs with as few flowers as possible to save on florist bills.

Alerted by the security intercom, Prunella was waiting in the foyer poised for combat. That morning she was wearing stilettos and a pin-striped power dress straight out of the previous month's issue of *Cosmo*; I had paged through it in my dentist's waiting room. Her massive rolled-gold shell earrings – 'Make a statement with important costume jewellery!' – only just cleared her padded shoulders.

'Ah, Mizz Dobermann,' she cooed through a slash of carmine lipstick with fissured edges, the only visible sign of her age. 'With Mr Quain's approval, I have made copies of the contents of the file you requested. Here they are.' She handed me a large white envelope.

So he had remembered. I said, 'Is that all?' It was far too thin for several decades' worth of publicity.

'That's all I could find in the file. Sorree.'

'Are you sure?'

She tilted her raven beehive. 'That's the lot, I'm afraid. Mr Quain said to tell you happy hunting.'

I was being fobbed off, whether by her or Angus or someone else in the firm I couldn't tell yet. I said in my brisk researcher's voice, 'That can't be the lot. I'll have to check his filing cabinet myself. I presume it's in his office?' And set off down the passage towards his eyrie in the north-east corner of the building.

'Members of the public aren't allowed down there!' Her indignant voice rose over the dulcet hum of expensive air-conditioning.

I kept going, throwing back over my shoulder, 'I'm not a member of the public, I'm a friend.'

Angus had given me a guided tour of his newly redecorated suite a few months before. There was a vast office with panoramic city views, two large oil paintings of the bushveld and important furniture, a secretary's anteroom, a conference room with shelves of matching law and accountancy books, and an adjoining washroom where the decorator had run amok with imported wallpaper, silk blinds and gold taps. 'Luxurious privacy is the ultimate perk,' he'd said with complacent pride.

'You can't go down there. Stop.' I heard Prunella teetering after me as fast as she could, her stilettos pecking at the Wilton. 'Stop!'

'Won't be a minute. I need to check the files.'

'It's not allowed. Security! Help!' she shrilled.

Thanks to my advantage in years and heel height the space between us was widening, though I saw the security cameras mounted high on the passage walls swivel to follow us. Doors began to open. From one of them a narrow face peered out above a shirt of oatmeal linen; large mild eyes, a winsome expression and a blow-dried grey mane completed the effect of well-bred horseflesh. He gave a surprised whinny when he recognised me and said, 'Faith, isn't it? What are you doing here?'

Cameron Greenacre was one of the senior partners. I'd sat next to him at a charity dinner in aid of battered wives and been bored silly with cricket talk. He always reminded me of my father's favourite joke: A horse walks into a bar and the barman says, 'Why the long face?'

I produced a harassed smile and said, 'Escaping from this officious employee of yours. She's trying to prevent me from going to Angus's office to collect some information he promised me.'

The winsome expression snapped to alert mode. 'You can't just waltz in here, my dear, and expect to be let into someone's private…'

Prunella came up panting, 'Stop her, Mr Greenacre. She's trespassing.'

I tried stamping my foot but it only made a dent in the thick pile, so I was obliged to raise my voice instead. 'That's nonsense! Angus has given me a mandate to write a personal profile and I need copies of his press releases. He's authorised access, which Prunella will confirm, but she refuses to let me check the files.'

'You can't go rifling through a fellow's private papers!' Cameron looked shocked.

'I'm not asking for private papers, only material on public record.' I leaned a little closer to confide, 'We historians do like to get our facts right.'

'But I *gave* her the copies she asked for.' Prunella was breathless with outrage.

I wagged the envelope. 'This lot can't be all Angus's press releases over the years.'

'That's all I found in the file.' But her eyes were evasive.

'Let me go with you and satisfy myself. You too, Cameron,' I urged. 'You can stand by as referee.'

There were tense seconds when I thought the gamble wouldn't succeed. Then Cameron said, 'Rightyo,' and we trooped on down the passage to the hushed click of closing doors.

Sure enough, there were four files marked PERSONAL PUBLICITY in the filing cabinet to the left of Angus's desk. The Prune had only given me copies of the papers in the last and most recent file. When I pointed this out, she snapped, 'You didn't say you wanted them going back *so* far,' and snatched up the files to copy them.

Cameron watched her stalk away across the Wilton, haunches rolling under the pinstripes, and murmured, 'Fine woman, Prunella. Very well turned out and conscientious. Don't make 'em like that any more.' He dragged his eyes away and returned with some reluctance to the problem of my alien presence. 'Would you like a cup of coffee while the copies are being run off?'

'I'd love a cup. Thanks.'

'Come along to my office, then.' He led the way back down the passage. I couldn't have managed it better if I'd tried.

His office was a smaller version of Angus's with a less serendipitous view over mine dumps to the south, and I recalled that he was only number four in the Quain & Associates hierarchy. We sat making desultory conversation until coffee arrived in an elegant white porcelain pot with matching cups and home-made biscuits. No doubt there was an executive dining room nearby where a cordon bleu cook toiled over preparations for a gourmet lunch. Partners don't stint on their creature comforts.

He said, with a whinny of pleasure this time, 'I do enjoy my mid-morning cup of coffee. Perhaps you'd pour? Then I'd like to know exactly what you're up to.'

I had rehearsed this bit so it came out pat as I reached for the coffee pot. 'Actually, I'm trying to kill two birds with one stone. I've started research for a new book about influential Johannesburg businessmen – a historical overview which will include Angus. At the same time, I'll be putting together a profile on him.'

'Writing a biography, you mean?' Cameron was agog. A full-length biography went way past the usual level of executive grandeur.

'Nothing as posh as that.' I passed him his cup. 'Since Angus became unwell, he has been concerned that his career should be properly assessed. I volunteered to write an appraisal that could serve as a press release if – if he goes.'

'If he goes?' The long jaw worked from side to side in alarm. 'Has he had another setback we don't know about?'

'No. Just trying to be realistic.'

148

'Ah. It's a precaution, then.' Cameron helped himself to a spoon of sugar. 'Forgive my rather intrusive questions. Thing is, the firm keeps a PR company on retainer and I'd have expected Angus to use those chaps rather than an outsider.'

So I'd been right about his having a publicist. Couldn't let him usurp me, though. I said, 'You can hardly call me an outsider.'

Cameron squirmed, 'Sorry. I meant, you know, someone outside the firm.'

My acceptance of the apology was gracious. 'Since I was putting him in my book anyway, I'm the obvious choice.'

'It's just like him, to use a lady historian to try and influence his obituaries.'

I had to smile. That was just like Angus. As calling me a 'lady historian' was just like Cameron.

He went on, 'So he commissioned you?'

'No, as I said, I volunteered. A tribute from a friend.'

'It's so sudden, all this. He's seemed much better recently.'

'Remission is the operative word.'

'So you don't think the cancer's cured?'

He was pumping me instead of the other way round. I said sharply, 'What I think is irrelevant. If this is a formal inquisition, please remember that I am his friend, not his wife. Or mistress, if that's what you're getting at.'

Cameron turned bright pink and began blustering, 'Of course not. I wouldn't presume to...'

'Everybody does.' My coffee cup was rattling in my hands. 'It's impossible to have a straightforward friendship these days without people unloading their own emotional baggage all over it. Angus and I have Saturday lunches and sometimes go out together, that's all.'

'I'm not trying to pry, I assure you,' Cameron said, so embarrassed at my unseemly outburst in his male sanctuary that he had to get up and walk around. 'I have to satisfy myself that your motives in coming here are above-board. You must understand.'

Oh, I did. I had him in a corner, trapped by his gentlemen's code into giving me whatever further assistance I needed for fear of offending the lady historian again.

I bestowed a forgiving smile. 'I'll try. And could you pass this message on to the other partners? If sheer willpower counts, he'll beat the illness.'

'And if he doesn't?'

Did either of us want the truth? Probably not, but it was time to face it anyway. I said, 'His doctors won't commit themselves, but I've talked to medical friends and they say that the prognosis for advanced bowel cancer is not good.'

Cameron's appalled look was not tinged with the calculation I saw on other faces as to who Angus's successor would be. He was a true friend, then, like me.

149

I was sorry I hadn't been straight with him. Courtliness unmixed with conde-scension is an almost extinct quality.

I stood up to go and collect my copies. 'Thanks for your help and the coffee.'

'Thank you for the chat, my dear.'

As he ushered me to the door, one nicely manicured hoof hovering the requi-site distance behind my back, I asked as an afterthought, 'Which PR company does the press releases for Quain & Associates? I should speak to them too.'

'Saxe Brown. The man who usually handles our account is Frank Saxe, though he's been out of action for two months with a slipped disc. You could try his part-ner, Rory St Clair Brown.'

Brown. The nigger in the woodpile? I wondered as the talking lift whisked me down again to the real world at ground level.

'You are now on floor…' pregnant pause '…zero,' the sepulchral voice an-nounced. 'Have a nice day.'

Reading through those press releases was an education. I started in the present and worked backwards.

'Always client-driven, we are currently re-examining our role in the context of the New South Africa and its Southern African neighbours,' ran the most recent *pronunciamento*. 'Our divisions include: accounting and auditing; corporate gov-ernance services; tax affairs; management consultancy; specialised advice relating to the financing of mergers, acquisitions, etc; and multi-disciplinary, value-added services for our clients.'

Now that professional strictures had fallen away, Quain & Associates weren't shy about punting themselves. Further down I read: 'Mr Angus Quain, Manag-ing Director and Founding Partner, was recently awarded the President's Medal for Meritorious Service to South Africa, in recognition of his successful broker-age of several trade agreements with Malaysia.'

Perhaps that was one of his getaway places: Malaysia, England, Nelspruit … and where else?

As I read on backwards, wading through superlative after transcendent su-perlative, I decided that my next port of call would have to be the headquarters of Saxe Brown, authors of the purple prose.

19

*B*efore I could make the appointment with Saxe Brown, Angus returned from England with his eldest daughter. I was bidden to meet her at the Club a few days later when he had recovered from the flight, and was shocked to find him in a wheelchair.

I stood in the doorway of his sitting room, gathering my wits before I went in. The daughter was an unmistakable Quain. The gawky schoolgirl of the photograph had grown into a tall dark-haired woman with his imperious way of holding his head; she stood by his desk with an open book in her hand, reading aloud from it.

It was Angus who spotted me first, calling out with a summoning wave, 'Ah, there you are, Faith. Come and meet Indigo.'

She stopped reading and turned to examine me as I walked towards him, self-conscious as a teenager on her first date. I had dressed with care that morning in my plainest skirt and pullover and cameo brooch, wanting to create the impression of a sober lunchtime companion.

I said in a too-loud voice, 'What are you doing in a wheelchair? I thought you said that you were as strong as an ox?'

'Oxen have their off days.' He shrugged. 'I seem to have developed a spot of back trouble from sitting in the same position for too long during the plane trips, and my quacks have decreed wheels for a few days. So I brought a pusher back with me.'

Oh God, it's got into his spine, I thought.

'Pushover, you mean,' she said. 'You get around fine by yourself, Da. Seem to enjoy buzzing about in that thing, actually.'

Da! Yet another persona beside Gus and the Big Q and King Quain and Angus the jovial clubman. How many more were lurking under the skin of the chameleon?

151

'You're not begrudging your old man the pleasure of your company, under the circumstances?' He was giving her the winning smile I knew so well.

'I do feel rather whisked away from my work. But I'm not begrudging, of course not. I wanted to see the new, improved South Africa after all the guff that's been written about it.' She put her book down on the desk and came over to me with appraising eyes and her hand out saying, 'I'm Indigo, the eldest.'

I said, 'How do you do?' then thought, That sounds much too stiff.

'Em and I have heard a lot about you.'

At her circumspect tone, I swung back to Angus. 'What have you been saying about me?'

'Oh, this and that.' He looked cagey.

'What, exactly?' I demanded.

My trust in him had been further eroded while he was away by the news that Amalgamated Couplings had shot up another eight rands on the Stock Exchange before a shock announcement that the company had been forced into liquidation. The financial press was seething with speculation about insider trading. I'd wondered whether he and Jumbo and Hugh had sold their shares in time, and how they and their nominees expected to weather the inevitable scrutiny of share dealings. Jem Lowing's words kept coming back to me: 'The man's a low-class bully. Take care you don't get caught with your pants down.'

'I've been telling them about our regular lunches,' Angus was saying, 'and about your work and your books. Boasting about my friend the writer. Did you know that Indigo is an editor? Poetry, critical essays, highbrow stuff way above my head. She works for...' He named a well-known publisher.

'I'm impressed.'

'Don't be,' Indigo said. 'They pay peanuts and expect unstinting devotion. But I enjoy working with writers, so I've persisted. Like all editors, I hope some of their talent rubs off on me so I can write my own books some day.'

'It's easier than it's made out to be, I assure you.'

There was an awkward pause, then Angus said, 'I tried to get Emerald to come out as well, but she's too pregnant to fly. She...'

Indigo cut in, 'They're ridiculous names, I know. Our dear mother wanted us to be vivid and develop strong personalities. As if mere names could help.' Her habitual mode, I soon learnt, was guarded sarcasm. 'Luckily Benjamin was born a boy or he'd have had to struggle through life as Saffron.'

'Your mother's intentions were pure.'

'But Indigo! Makes you think of dyed cloth.'

'Bollocks. It's an excellent name. Suits you.' He glared up at her. 'One thing I can't stand about offspring is the way they continually heap blame on their parents. When does it end?'

152

Her answering glare was identical; there'd be fireworks soon.

I said quickly, 'You didn't tell me one of your daughters was pregnant, Angus.'

'Nearly eight months,' he growled. 'Our first grandchild.'

From the suddenly stricken look on Indigo's face, she and I were having the same thought: He's wondering if he'll live to see the baby. She forced a smile and went towards him saying, 'Let's ring for tea. Boniface, is it? Such a dignified man. Reminds me of our gardener – what was his name again? Something biblical.'

Angus's face cleared as he chuckled. 'Jehosaphat. How could you forget? You called him Jumping Jehosaphat and he used to give you rides in the wheelbarrow. Remember...' They began to reminisce and the bad moment passed.

Indigo's initial wariness – it couldn't have been easy to be presented with her father's irregular woman companion – eased a little over the teacups. When Angus got involved in a long conversation on the telephone, she and I discovered a shared interest in the problems of being single professionals. 'Da has been trying to fix me up with eligible men by remote control for years,' she confided. 'He's a control freak. Likes people to do his bidding.'

'"Never fear, Quain is here"? Don't I know it. He's started on me now. Says I'm a loose end and he wants to marry me off before he...' I broke off, feeling stupidly tactless.

She said with an exact replica of her father's carborundum look, 'You don't have to pretend. We all know the score. Mum asked me to tell you that his London doctors aren't optimistic.'

I shook my head, trying to dispel her words.

'It's why I came. This could be my last chance to be with him. And after what Mum told us, I wanted to meet you too. We'd always thought that the mysterious Faith he talked about was his...'

'Mistress?' The bleak word forced its way past the lump in my throat. 'Hardly. Our friendship has been confined to Saturday lunches for fifteen years. I've been the person he's used as a salve on dull weekends. Only in the past few months has he even hinted at the other dimensions to his life. He's a complex and secretive man, your father.'

'And a skater on thin financial ice too, though I trust not in the same league as Robert Maxwell?'

'He doesn't – he's not...'

'Don't try and deny it. I know he's confided in you.'

I wondered how she knew. And said, feeling my way with care, 'He seemed to want to get things off his chest after the cancer was diagnosed, and I was available to dump on. How do you know?'

'Circumstantial evidence and informed guesses. Da's close with everyone, not only you. That's one of the reasons why Mum left him. She couldn't stand the secrets and the power-mongering, she said. But he's been a good father to us in his way. Doesn't consider Em and me to be lesser mortals because we're female, which is unusual for a man of his generation.'

She'd been lucky; my father had never ceased to remind me of my inferior status. Maybe Angus's appreciation of women was one of the qualities that had drawn me to him? I said, 'He likes women, which is unusual for a South African male.'

'Too well?'

'I'm not qualified to answer that one.' I thought of the contrast between his clubs: the stately all-male one he lived in and Mama Nesta's rootin' tootin' girlie haven – both ends of the spectrum.

'Diplomat. What are you hiding?'

'Nothing of importance.' When she opened her mouth to argue, I went on, 'I'm not privy to his sexual secrets, and if I was, I wouldn't tell. What I do know is that he has a vast social network and women seem to like him too.'

'You don't have to tell me about the charm level. I grew up watching people fall before his scythe. He'd also carry on ad nauseam about his so-called life force and how we should try to emulate it. As if we could.' Vehemence forced colour into her pale English cheeks. 'You've no idea how hard it is for a shy person to grow up in the shadow of ambitious, confident parents. It's why I buried myself in books, of course.'

Well-off people who moan about minor hardships always get up my nose. I said in my prickliest voice, 'You should try having parents like mine were.'

That cast a pall over our conversation for a while. Then she said, 'Ouch. We're doing exactly what Da complained about in his offspring: blaming our parents. I didn't mean to make invidious comparisons, really. Could we start again?'

'If you'll allow me to make a request before we change the subject.'

'Go on.'

'I wish you'd tell Angus that you think he's been a good father, because he thinks otherwise. He said to me once, "Fathers are not to be depended upon. I'm the living proof," and I know it bothers him.'

'I'll make a point of it.' She hesitated. 'If we're being formal, I'd like to thank you for the friendship you've given him all these years. He sets great store by your Saturday lunches.'

'My participation has been partly selfish,' I had to admit. 'He's all I've had by way of a family.'

'And by way of repayment you're threatening to dig around in his past and write about him?'

The sudden thrust was unexpected and I saw that this was the source of her initial reserve. My answer would have to be a good one. If his family objected, he would withdraw his approval of my planned book without a qualm.

I said, choosing my words, 'It's not only Angus. I've begun researching a book about the men who've wielded the real power in this town over the years. And your father doesn't seem averse to being immortalised in print after he's gone – quite the contrary. I think he's been trying to plant the idea in my mind for years. Why else would he have gone on cultivating a rather boring historian?'

'That sounds like a typical Quain ploy.' We both turned to watch his eloquent gestures as he laid down the law to the person at the other end of the telephone line. 'But not true, I think. When she came home, Mum said he told her that you'd been his mental tonic, and she realised what he meant when she met you. So of course I wanted to see for myself.'

'And?'

Her answering look was direct. 'It's the sort of friendship I could do with. I don't ever seem to meet the kind of single men I'd want to spend the rest of my life confronting over breakfast. Em reckons I'll be on the shelf for good because I'm so choosy.'

'Don't tell me.' My emphatic answer was part recognition, part relief. This was a friendship I could do with too.

Ten minutes later Angus interrupted our mutual commiseration about the dearth of intelligent, sensitive, amusing men to call her to the telephone, and buzzed across the room to me. I'd been worrying about his reaction to my foray into Quain & Associates, but all he said was, 'That was a bold move, to invade my inner sanctum while I was away.'

'You don't mind?'

'Prunella did. And Cameron warned me in his elliptical way to beware of inquisitive females poking their noses into my past. "She's not quite one of us, old boy," he said.'

'And I thought I'd persuaded him otherwise.'

'Oh, he likes you. He just doesn't trust you. If it's any consolation, I can tell you that it's a matter of principle for Cameron, not to trust women. Mainly because they terrify him. This is what being sent to an elite all-boys boarding school does for you. Thank God I was thrown in with girls from Class One. Exchanging ink balls and squashed sandwiches from an early age demystifies the other sex, you know?'

'Angus,' I said, 'I'm well aware of your predilection for girls. What I want to know is whether you mind my invading your office. It was rather going beyond the bounds.'

He patted my hand. 'No reason to mind. The press releases are a matter of public record. And we have an agreement, do we not? You will stick to the conditions?'

'Of course. You want an honest assessment, and you'd like to be envied for your brilliance and acumen as much as for your bank account.'

155

'That's about it. And my right of veto?'

'As agreed, over anything that could embarrass your family.'

'Cross your heart, all the way up to heaven?'

'Cross my heart.'

Neither of us mentioned the obvious flaw in his conditions: that the right of veto would be able to be exercised only as long as he was alive. Thereafter he'd have to trust me to be fair to him. That gift of trust was the greatest compliment he ever paid me – specially as he knew my trust in him was faltering.

Angus was lunching with his partners at the office as he was due to go into the oncology clinic next day for another battery of tests. Having installed him in the Bentley with Praise's help, Indigo and I lunched together in the Club dining room. We sat at his usual table in the bay window, an islet of feminine solidarity in a sea of dark suits and business conversations, talking about our different lives. It was comforting – a plus to set against the frightening minus of Angus's illness – to have acquired what felt like a sister in the course of a few hours. My proxy family was growing.

The bad news, Angus told me when I phoned two days later to hear the results of his tests, was that the oncologist had decided a third course of chemotherapy was necessary.

'Bloody remission didn't last long.' His voice was spilled gravel. 'I feel buggered by lunchtime, even in this invalid's contraption.'

I could imagine him banging the wheelchair's arm in frustration. 'What did the latest scan show?'

'More shadows, they say. Secondaries.'

'When are you scheduled for the chemo?'

'Next Wednesday. Told them I needed time to be with my daughter before she flies home on Tuesday. "Not too much time, Mr Quain," they said, wagging their forefingers as if I were a schoolboy playing hookey ... which I'm half inclined to do. I don't know if it's worth submitting to another onslaught of nauseating drips that stink like hell and leave me feeling like death warmed up.'

'Of course it is.' I tried to sound encouraging, but it came out shrill. 'You've got to keep fighting.'

'It's farting against thunder, and we both know it. What's the use of dragging out this dismal process? May as well get it over and done with.' He sounded drained. 'Fact is, I'm running out of steam, old girl. The life force is flickering.'

'Don't give me that defeatist talk.'

'Defeatist?' he bellowed. 'Dammit, Faith, where's the percentage in going on with repeated chemotherapy when the prognosis is so poor?'

'Because chemo treatment is getting better all the time.'

'They just like to be seen to be doing something – anything – and I'm putting myself through unnecessary torture. It's not bloody worth it.'

I was babbling now. 'But you've got to keep going. It's the only option. Your family's rooting for you. I'm rooting for you. The whole business community is…'

'You're not going to say the whole business community's rooting for me? Bullshit. They're rubbing their hands at the prospect of my imminent demise. It'll let a good many of them off some nasty hooks … unless I decide to pull the temple down with me as I go. That's an option.'

'You wouldn't.'

'I have considered a final grand gesture.'

I said again, 'You wouldn't. You may be a reacher and grabber, as you once said. You may be a stubborn old bastard. But you're not a despoiler.'

He was silent for a while, then said, 'You've got more faith in me than most. Can't think why.'

'I'm your friend. Your old pally blue.'

'And you and my daughter are going to bully me into having this unspeakable treatment even though we all know it probably won't work?'

'It's the only option.'

'You sound like a stuck needle on a bloody gramophone,' he grumbled. 'God help me.'

'We'll all help you.'

'Thanks. With God and my family and my pally blue on my side, how can I lose?' The sarcasm was savage.

'Don't, Angus.'

Another silence, then he rumbled, 'Still, there are compensations. I haven't told you the good news yet: Benjamin is coming. With the help of the British Embassy, Hannah managed to locate him at a Buddhist temple on a remote crag in the Himalayas. He's flying Air India from Bombay on Saturday so he can see Indigo before she leaves.'

Angus was intent on his daughter having a good time despite his backlog of work, so Praise and I were on constant call the following week. We took her on an excursion to Sun City and the Pilanesberg game reserve and round town on the tourist circuit. In the evenings when Angus felt restored after an afternoon sleep, he wined and dined her. Though he tried to insist that I come too, I declined so they could talk. It could well be the last time they'd have together.

The mechanics of a wheelchair took getting used to, as did the sight of Angus sitting in it like a furious tethered Caesar. He hated being pushed about and fussed over, but he would have hated even more not being able to squire his daughter to his favourite restaurants. On Saturday morning, he ordered Indigo and me into the Bentley and we set off on a round of shops and boutiques.

This anxious-to-please father was yet another new Angus. He would have show-ered both daughters with gifts but she teased him out of what she called 'com-mitting unnecessary extravagances'.

'Give Em's baby some unit trusts to help with his or her education instead,' she suggested as he swept us into Read's in Rosebank to tempt her with silver and antique jewellery. Being in the wheelchair didn't inhibit his compulsion to bend others to his will.

'I'll do that anyway. What about this rather nice diamond and opal ring?' he pleaded, hovering over the black velvet tray that had been placed in his lap.

'When would I wear it? I'm a hardworking editor.'

'Go on,' he urged, 'let me buy a bauble for you. I'd like to make up for lost time.'

She looked at the ring, then at him. 'You could tempt me, but not for that rea-son.'

'Why not?'

She squatted down by the wheelchair. 'The father-shaped hole will always be there in our lives. But we understand what happened between you and Mum; we know it was inevitable. You tried to compensate. You don't owe us anything.'

'I do,' he said, one of the sudden mood switches plunging him into sadness. 'I owe so many so much. You can't repay all the debts you incur as an avid young man. They mount up like thunderclouds while you're not looking, until suddenly there's a clap of lightning and the whole damn lot piss down on your head.'

'What are you saying?' She shook his arm in distress.

'I've been taking stock. Dr Johnson had it exactly. He said, "When a man knows he is to be hanged in a fortnight, it concentrates his mind wonderfully." I'm only beginning to realise now, at the brink, what I've thrown away in pursuit of suc-cess.'

His head was bowed over the velvet tray of beautiful jewellery. Until that mo-ment I had tried to convince myself that Angus would fight his dread disease and win. He was used to winning; he had schemed and slaved and charmed his way up from a railway shack to the pinnacle of the business world where he was fêted, envied and fawned on. Now I saw that the illness was sapping his will and be-ginning to detach him from the concerns that had always driven him.

'Nonsense,' Indigo was saying in Hannah's brisk voice, using the wheelchair's arm to help herself stand again. 'You're just undergoing capitalist's remorse ... a common affliction of the affluent, Em's William says. He's a raving socialist. Odd for a farmer.'

I saw Angus force himself to look up. 'Don't I know it. He spent two very long hours explaining his principles last time I stayed with them.'

'Em thought you were discussing the farm's future.'

158

'Among other things. I'm sure William could be persuaded to look the other way for once if you found something for her from an unregenerate old capitalist.' He held the tray out to Indigo and turned to me. 'What about you, old girl? You're to choose a bauble too. I won't countenance a refusal,' he added as I shook my head. 'We've taken up your working time all week. This is our thank you.'

I must admit that they didn't have to prevail on me very hard. There was an exquisite moonstone necklace that would look wonderful with my grey silk. Trying it on in front of the jeweller's mirror, I wondered if my days of swanning about the corporate social network with Angus were over. And had he dropped the quest for zero defect? He hadn't mentioned my being a loose end or buying a convertible since his return from England.

'That shimmery necklace suits your colouring.' Indigo had come up behind me.

'Thanks. It's lovely. But I feel bad about…'

'Thula, now,' she said, using the Zulu word for 'be quiet'. 'It's from Mum and me as well as old Moneybags in the wheelchair.'

'You remember your Zulu?'

'A little. Coming home has brought back a flood of things I thought I'd forgotten. Da insisted that our nanny should speak only Zulu to us, and we were quite fluent until we went to school and lost it. She was a plump, comely woman from Uncle Tom's farm. I love that word, don't you? Comely. People never use it any more.'

Tom Greyling, I thought, as I bent my head to unclip the necklace. Another clue to Angus's past.

She went on, 'We used to drive down there for weekends and us kids would run wild in the bush with Leo. Have you met him?'

I nodded, remembering the lanky lawyer who had knocked over his chair when I came into the room.

'What did you think of him?'

'Reticent. Nice. A bit clumsy. There wasn't time to form a proper opinion. We met briefly when he came to see Angus before his second course of chemo.'

'I'd love to know how Leo turned out. He was an unusual boy: independent and self-contained in a way city boys never are. After the melodrama of the divorce and his mother's dreadful death, living with Uncle Tom and Brendan can't have been easy.' She paused and before I could ask the questions burning on my tongue, held up the brooch in her hand. 'Do you like what I've chosen? It's art nouveau, my favourite period. I've been looking for something elegant to tart up my work jackets.'

Later, in a diamond-cutting workshop while his daughter was poring over a display of diamonds having the nuances of the four Cs – carat, cut, colour and clarity – explained to her, Angus tugged at my sleeve to get me to kneel down and complained, 'The girls are hard to spoil. Unacquisitive, like their mother. Will you watch Indigo for me? Keep an eye out for anything she seems to like, and I'll send Praise round to buy it before she leaves.'

'Sneaky,' I said with approval. I'd have loved to have had a father who called me hard to spoil with such obvious pride.

'That's me. Sneaky and underhand. She's a great girl, eh?'

'Hardly a girl. Indigo's only nine years younger than I am.'

'You're not unalike.' He looked surprised, as though he had only just thought of it. 'Perhaps that's why I was attracted to you in the first place. Birds of a feather, what?'

Now he was calling me a daughter substitute. I said, piqued, 'Thanks very much, Grandpa.'

'That's a bloody sharp reply to what was meant as a compliment,' he grumbled. 'As I've said to you more than once, I revel in bright women.'

'Not to mention Mama Nesta's bar girls.'

'Variety is the spice of life, what?'

But the jaunty words were at odds with his pale exhausted face on which the eye bags sagged ever lower and the once-substantial chins were as translucent as the little geckos that patrolled my pressed-steel ceilings at night, feeding on the insects attracted to the light. He had lost more weight in England and was trotting out pompous platitudes, both bad signs.

Benjamin flew in from India on Sunday morning, to be met by his sister and Praise who whisked him from the airport to a family lunch at the Club. I was bidden that evening for drinks.

Introducing him, Angus said, 'This is our son Benjamin who has nobly torn himself away from the hippy trail to attend his father's sickbed.'

An angular young man unfolded himself from a heap of cushions on the floor and shambled towards me, his long tangled blond hair at odds with a loose Indian kurta and baggy trousers of rough creamy cotton.

'Cool,' he said, and shook my hand.

Indigo said with sisterly severity, 'Can't you manage a more civilised greeting?'

'Namaste. Blessings be upon you, oh Faith.' He put his hands together under his chin and bent his head.

'And upon you, Benjamin-ji.' I copied the gesture and he grinned and went back to loll on his cushions.

'Forgive the happy wanderer. He seems to have abandoned his English roots to embrace the arcane sub-culture of the ashram.' Angus gave him a fond glare.

'Won't eat eggs or meat, among other things. Boniface is beside himself and predicting imminent starvation.'

'Westerners don't starve, Da. We're far too worldly.'

Angus had an air of determined gaiety that evening despite a restless shifting in the wheelchair which kept tilting his successive glasses of whisky and soda. Several times I noticed his hand dropping to ease his belt. His daughter noticed too – we exchanged glances – but Benjamin seemed unaware of the tension and talked on about the months he had spent singing his way across Europe and the Middle East and then setting off across the Indian subcontinent armed with his English innocence, mosquito repellent and a twelve-string guitar.

His only real crises had been encounters with a band of Turkish pickpockets, a severe case of Delhi belly and a predatory Australian girl who had suggested marriage after she heard of his trust fund and been difficult to shake off.

As we laughed and chatted that night, all of us were trying to ignore a more devastating crisis. Angus had begun to look like death.

20

Rory St Clair Brown had a masterful jaw and glacier eyes. I met him in the health bar of his sports club on Sunday afternoon – the only time he had available – towelling his blond curls dry with one hand while he gulped at the glass of carrot juice held in the other.

Raising his voice to make it heard over the disco beat thumping out of a nearby loudspeaker, he said, 'Pleased to meet you, Faith. Sit right down.' I was waved into the empty chair on the other side of a wrought-iron table. 'Fancy some carrot juice?'

'No thanks.' I abhor orange vegetables.

'Herb tea?'

I shook my head.

'Coffee?' He spoke as though offering a pesticide.

'Yes please.'

'I beg yours?' He leaned forward, cupping part of the towel behind his ear.

I shouted, 'Yes please!'

'Bran muffin? Whole-wheat crunchie? Health bread sandwich?' They would absorb some of the poisonous caffeine, his expression said.

I couldn't help it. I said in my most carrying voice, 'No thanks, but I'd like cream and sugar and a doughnut, if there is one.'

He shuddered visibly as he turned to call the waitress, giving me time for a more detailed inspection. He had a sunbed tan and hillocks of muscle competing under a skimpy vest. A squash racquet leaned against one furred knee. His feet were shod in serious socks and a complicated arrangement of neoprene, nylon and rubber, laced like an Edwardian corset.

Turning back to me, he exposed two rows of perfect teeth and said, still towelling with a vigorous hand, 'Sorry I couldn't see you at the office. Crucial deadlines, you know? Never a dull moment in Pee Arr.'

Mesmerised, I found myself murmuring, 'I'm sure there isn't. Aren't.'

'What was that?'

'I'm sure there isn't a dull moment!'

He looked gratified. 'As a matter of fact, I only got back this morning from a new car launch that we organised in a game reserve. And tomorrow there are two company presentations. Busy, busy, eh?'

'Thanks for agreeing to see me at such incredibly short notice.'

The sarcasm was lost on him. 'No problem. One of our oldest clients, Quain. Longest-standing, I mean.' He gave me a manly grin to show that he was aware how sensitive people could be about age. It made me feel about ninety-four. 'If he calls, we jump. So. What do you want to hear?'

A waitress came bouncing towards us in a pink T-shirt over a matching striped leotard and plonked down a tray bearing a crisp sugary doughnut and a cup of coffee, some of which slopped into its saucer. 'These okay for you, ma'am?'

'They look fine.'

'Anything more?'

'Could you possibly ask someone to turn down the sound system? I can't hear what Mr Brown is saying.'

She rolled her eyes as if to say, What's this unfit geriatric doing here? 'It's the step class, they need a fast hard beat. I can mute the loudspeaker in here, though, if you want.'

'I want. Thanks.'

I creamed and sugared and stirred as he put his towel down to sign the chit she presented, pleased to have a few moments in which to go over my plan of attack. When he'd asked the hunk to speak to me, Angus would have said, 'Brief Faith on my publicity campaign, will you?' or something equally terse. But I needed to get beyond the feverish wording of the Saxe Brown press releases to the real motivation behind them.

The waitress said, 'Ta, Ror. I'll just turn the sound down for the lady, okay?'

We both watched her bounce over to the chair under the loudspeaker, spring up on to it and adjust the knob. Her leotard narrowed at the back to a thin strip between muscular buttocks encased in flesh-coloured lycra. Transfixed by the sight, the hunk took another long slurp of carrot juice.

When she had rejoined the passing parade of co-ordinated gym wear in the corridor outside the health bar, I said into the blessed silence, pen poised over my notebook, 'Ready now? Question number one. How long has your firm been doing press releases for Mr Quain?'

He returned my opening serve with a nifty volley. 'I can see you've got a list of questions there. Give it to me and I'll fax my answers back.'

'No time, sorree.' I'd learnt a thing or two from Prunella.

A shadow flitted across the tanned visage. 'Will you be long? I have another appointment in…' he consulted the impressive-looking stop watch/heart monitor on his wrist '…approximately twenty minutes.'

No doubt with your personal trainer, I thought. Nothing makes me more acerbic than to be surrounded by perfect human specimens, all preening themselves on their glowing health. The level of narcissism required to maintain a body beautiful must be staggering, not to mention the expenditure on vitamins, organic health food, gym subscriptions, trendy tracksuits, nips, tucks, liposuction and breast implants. Fatties and skinny malinkies unite, is my motto.

I said, 'I'll make it quick, then. How long has your firm been doing press releases for Mr Quain?'

'Ten years or so.' Having relinquished the towel, his fingers were toyi-toying on his knee. 'Before that they were handled by Quain & Associates' publicity department, a bunch of complete amateurs with no personal media contacts. We told Quain we could get double the exposure for half the cost.'

'And did you?'

Confident flash of incisors. 'Sure thing. Media liaison is Saxe Brown's forte. The contract guaranteed at least two mentions a month for Quain and four for the firm as a whole. Half to be in financial publications.'

'Were you to cover a specific angle, or angles?'

'For Quain, personal achievements, rumours about upcoming mergers and takeovers he was involved with, informed insider stuff. The usual. For the firm and the other associates, general glory-snatching.'

So this was how Angus helped to spread the word when he needed to manipulate shares. I said, 'Is that what you call media liaison? Planting information?'

Jaw thrust forward, eyes narrowed, he said, 'You making allegations here? Am I talking to a member of the alternative press, by any chance?'

'No. Maybe if I was, I'd be less surprised.'

He gulped the last of his carrot juice and the empty glass clattered on the table. 'What are you trying to get at? I thought we were discussing Quain's press releases as per his instructions, not the philosophy of Pee Arr. I must tell you frankly that I can't stand people who take the moral high ground when it comes to publicity. Specially when they don't know a damn thing about the way it works.'

'Which is?'

'Do I need to spell it out? Businesses need to inform people about what they're doing and how well they're doing it. Newspapers need news and views to fill their pages. Pee Arr people like me are the go-betweens. That's all.'

'But you admit to slanting the news and views you provide to suit your clients?'

He sat looking at me, then said, 'You're kidding, right?'

'I'm not. I'm asking.'

'Jesus, some people can be naive.' Scorn radiated from every chiselled plane of his face. 'That's the way the world goes round, Faith. Everybody knows it, most of all the media guys. They know that it's up to them to sort the facts from the – shall we say – fancy embroidery. And you know what? They hardly ever do. Nine times out of ten a well-written, properly spelled, persuasive press release goes into print just as it's received, without comment. Editors only question the controversial stuff and the obvious puffs. Otherwise it's a little trim here and there, then off to paste-up. Specially with under-staffed publications like the suburban knock and drops. They don't have the resources or the manpower...'

'Person power, you mean.'

'A feminist too, is it?'

I wanted to smack his self-satisfied face. Instead I did the next best thing: picked up the fried doughnut and looking straight at him, took a large bite. He flinched. I gulped down the doughy lump and took another. He flinched again. I felt like Albert Finney in *Tom Jones*, only it wasn't foreplay. It was eco-torture.

'Don't you mind about...?' he managed to croak.

I shook my head and took another bite.

With a mighty effort he tore his eyes away and looked at the multiple chronometer again. 'Listen, sorry, I've gotta go. If you don't believe what I'm saying, check Quain's press releases against what appeared in print. Ciao for now.' He snatched up the damp towel and the squash racquet, scraped his chair back and fled.

Leaving me to luxuriate in my small triumph and finish my doughnut in peace.

21

*I*t was to be a busy and instructive week after my time off doing the tourist sights.

On Monday morning the papers carried news of a shock report by a task group on South African business ethics. 'Ethical standards decreased as we went up the corporate ladder,' it thundered. A corporate governance expert said, 'Our ethics in this country are shot and we all have a responsibility to do something about it.'

So Angus and his cohorts are not unique, I thought, and sent out feelers to research acquaintances who would know how to get hold of a copy of the report. My new book was taking on a dimension I had not anticipated; the reasons why businesses flourished and fortunes were made would have to be researched with as much care as the lives of the men who built them up. Which led to the question: Is it even possible to create a business empire without making certain – as Angus had put it – accommodations?

After breakfast I sat down at the computer to plan a more detailed outline for my publisher, who had sounded keen when I approached him but wanted chapter and verse so he could sound out the market before committing himself.

I forgot to put on the answering machine as I usually did during working hours, so when the phone rang I picked up the receiver and barked my number, hoping to frighten the ringer off.

No such luck. He said, 'Is that Faith Dobermann?'

'Yes.'

'Do you have a moment to spare?'

'No, I'm busy. Who is this, please?'

Ignoring my query, he said, 'Could I just ask you a few questions? It won't take a moment.'

The voice was familiar: well-spoken in a somewhat stagy way. Had I met this man before or was it one of those car radio voices you get to know by default while driving? Except for the news and occasional music programmes I don't listen to the radio at home, being averse to the creeping pox of chat shows.

I said, 'You've got a nerve. If you don't tell me who you are, I'm putting the phone down.'

There was silence at the other end, then with clipped reluctance he identified himself. 'Brian Lapidus, Vanguard Trust.'

'Do I know you?'

'I should hope so. I was the speaker before the Minister of Finance at the Carlton luncheon, and Angus Quain introduced us afterwards.'

'I don't remember.' Over the past few social months Angus had introduced me to dozens of important men whose features had blurred into one master face: wine-flushed, well-fed and pleased with itself under a receding hairline. However familiar the voice may have seemed, the name rang no bells.

'Listen,' he said, exasperated by my amnesia, 'I have some pressing questions that require answers.' He paused, then dangled his bait. 'In return, I'm offering information that could be to your advantage.' He made it sound like one of those ads lawyers put in the newspapers to let people know they've been left a modest legacy.

'No, I won't listen. I'm far too busy.' The receiver was on its way down when he said something that arrested it in mid-air.

'Hear me out, please! You're writing a book about white-collar fraud, yes?'

I sat astonished. As far as I knew only Angus, Marge and my publisher were aware of the subject matter of my new book – and until this morning's news it was intended to centre on the lives of Joburg businessmen, not their possible predilection for fraud.

'Faith, are you there? Can you hear me? I said...'

'I heard what you said.' My voice felt faint, as though it were coming from the next room.

'And? Am I right?'

His questions needled me into answering, 'Only in a partial sense.'

'Ah. So I'm partly right. That's a start.' He cleared his throat. 'It doesn't change my initial proposition. I have information that would be of great interest to someone writing about corporate wrongdoing in this city.'

'In return for answers to unspecified questions? You must be joking.' And I had the satisfaction of slamming the phone down. Basking in the afterglow as I turned back to my keyboard, I once more forgot to put on the answering machine.

The phone rang again ten minutes later, just long enough for me to have relaxed into thinking it was someone else calling. The same voice said in a rapid stutter, 'Please listen to me. It's of vital importance to someone's c-career. Please.'

Resisting the impulse to say, 'Down on your knees, boy,' I demurred. 'Why should I?'

'Meet me, and I'll tell you. There are things you should know before starting your book.'

'I've started. Two chapters are with the publisher already.' That should put the wind up him. He had no way of knowing it wasn't true.

There was a sharp exclamation and he blurted, 'I must warn you…' then collected himself and said, 'I urge you, *urge* you, not to proceed without speaking to me. It's extremely important. Vital. I don't know how to put it more strongly. This has to do with…' his voice dropped at least an octave '…executives at the highest level.'

All I could think then was, Is this Mitch Kincaid's nigger in the woodpile, or one of the fat cats who bribed him? Can't pass up the opportunity of being offered a yacht or two. I said, 'Assuming I agree, do you have a venue in mind for a meeting?'

'It would have to be private. I can't risk…' He broke off, then asked, 'Could I come and see you?'

'No.'

'Would you meet me in a hotel suite?'

'Not without a bodyguard.' This was fun.

'A restaurant would be too public.' He made a couple more suggestions, rejecting them before I had time to answer, then said with the same clipped reluctance he'd shown when giving his name, 'It'll have to be my office. One-fifteen suit you? I'll send the staff out to lunch.' He named a building a few blocks away from my flat.

'Shall I wear a headscarf and a false nose and dark glasses so no one can identify me?'

'This is no joke. Believe me.' He rang off.

I pulled a sweater over my jeans and walked there. The building was one of the new monstrosities built on the bones of the Edwardian mansions flattened to make way for them. A venerable jacaranda tree stood guard at the entrance, its winter foliage yellow and feathery against klinker brick and mirror glass. A bank of stepped concrete blocks held pockets of soil planted with lush ivy and philodendrons.

The Vanguard offices took up the whole of the first floor: expensive modern furniture in kiaat and black leather, slate tiles, meaningless abstract paintings in the Kurt mould and giant ceramic pots holding spindly yuccas and more philodendrons. Why such carnivorous-looking plants should be so popular in the halls of commerce beats me. I never sit too near them in case one of those sinister air roots reaches out unnoticed and wraps itself round my throat.

There was nobody in the reception area. Beyond it was a series of glass-walled offices that looked as though they had been abandoned as suddenly as the Marie Celeste: computer screens crawling with coloured patterns, pens thrown down, papers in disarray. I followed the only sound – telephone keys being punched – along a passage to an open door, knocked, and heard a phone receiver cradled and the familiar voice say, 'Come in.'

The man who swivelled and rose from his executive chair was younger than I had expected – early forties, I guessed – with a ginger brush cut, round glasses, a pale freckled serious face, pin-striped shirt and baggy trousers held up with red braces. He was one of those lean, peppy, aggressive men you expect to be in advertising, though I knew he wasn't because I had done my homework before coming. The stockbroker who helps me act on Angus's tips had informed me that he was the financial brain behind the new Vanguard Unit Trusts.

'They're the most successful on the market, with the slickest promotion material,' he had said. Then added, 'If you're thinking of investing on the strength of last year's growth, be sure to cover yourself. It was an unusual year and these smart boys can get carried away by their successes.'

'Would you advise me against Vanguard?'

He backtracked as he always did, nervous of being held to account if his recommendations turned out to be ill-judged. 'I'm not saying that. Just hedge your bets. It makes sense to hedge high-risk investments.'

Brian Lapidus stuck out his hand and said, 'Hullo, Faith. Thanks for coming.'

Our hands connected. 'Mr Lapidus. I couldn't resist your bait.'

'Brian, please. It was the only way to get you here. Sit down.' He waved towards a pair of chrome and suède dining chairs on opposite sides of a small table with an inlaid chessboard. 'I find direct eyeballing best for difficult confrontations.'

I sat. 'Is that what you're expecting?'

'You weren't exactly forthcoming on the phone. I'd have preferred not to make physical contact.' He turned his chair round so he could straddle it with his hands on the backrest, facing me across the table. 'But here we are. So tell me what your book's about. We have an hour or so before the staff gets back.'

His prominent eyes were fixed on my face; his fingers drummed on the backrest; one knee was jiggling. This was an anxious man, for all his apparent confidence.

I said, 'No, you first.'

He blurted, 'I need to know who you're writing about.'

'That's bald enough.' I let him sweat for a bit longer, then said, 'We could do this in the form of twenty questions, if you like. I ask one and then you ask one. The winner is the person who manages to winkle the most information out of the other.'

He grinned with a boy's suddenness. 'Okay. Fire away.'

'First question: Where did you get your accent?'

The good humour vanished. 'Why do you ask that?'

'I want to know.'

'I prefer to try and forget. That's not a fair question.'

'And I'm learning fast that nothing is fair in business. Answer me if you want me to answer you.'

He sat frowning, trying to read my intention on my face. I looked back at him with a half smile I know to be infuriating. At last he said, forcing the words out, 'My mother made me go to elocution lessons.'

'Why?'

'We were poor. I was clever. She was ambitious for me, working nights as a hotel receptionist so I could have elocution lessons to improve my accent, which was supposed to help me make my way up in the world. All they did was make me a misfit. It's not often that people spot it as quickly as you have.'

'I had mother trouble too, though her modus was sabotage.'

We sat regarding each other, one skin stripped off. He said, 'Now my turn. What exactly is this book of yours about?'

'I'm beginning to wonder myself.'

'Explain.'

'I'll try. It's had an unusual genesis. As I was finishing my previous book, two instigating factors came together. One is Angus Quain's illness – I expect you know he's fighting cancer?'

He nodded.

'The second was my discovery of the attics at the Joburg Club, which are crammed with relics that go back to the early days of the city and made me wonder about the men who used them. I decided to write a study of the lesser-known businessmen who've changed the face of Joburg history – the powers behind the company thrones. But you seem to know that too?'

'Barkin told me.'

So that was where he had got his information. I hadn't thought that Mr Barkin was a gossip but realised with a pang of pity that titbits of information must be the common currency of a life as a Club servant.

Seeing my expression, Brian said, 'I wheedled it out of him but I know he didn't give me the whole story. Which is why I phoned you. I think you're on to something else.'

'What brings you to this conclusion? I haven't…'

'That's four questions already, while I've only asked two.'

'Answer it, and you can have two in succession.' I was beginning to enjoy the verbal duel, a pleasant change from my monologues on the computer.

'Logic tells me that if a historian of your calibre investigates the tycoon class, you'll soon begin to realise that many of them got dirty hands – to put it mildly – in the quest for fame and fortune. Plus, white-collar fraud and business ethics are in the news at the moment. You can't fail to put two and two together.'

Exactly what I'd been thinking that morning, and an eerie echo of the conversation I'd had with Angus after the advent of Jumbo and Hugh. 'Are you telling me that most businessmen are crooked?'

He shook his bristly head. 'Oh no, you don't. My two questions next… I presume you're starting with Quain. Have you decided on your other present-day subjects? And if so, who are they?'

Apprehension showed in the hunched shoulders; he believed I was on to something because of the Quain connection. Was it common knowledge that Angus indulged in questionable financial transactions, and if so, why would it make Brian Lapidus so nervous? It was my turn to apply logic. Unit trusts meant substantial amounts of other people's money that could be at risk – perhaps invested in companies with hidden problems, vulnerable to disclosure by a nosy researcher.

'Well?' Every tendon in his neck showed. This would be a big scandal, not just fingers in the till. Did he have flexible ethics like the unnamed executives in the shock report, or had he got caught in one of their subtle scams – been conned into buying overrated stock, perhaps? This wasn't 'someone's' career at risk, I realised; it was his. If he could avert a looming scandal long enough to sell the stock before its value plummeted, he could preserve his reputation.

But I wasn't going to let him off the hook until I'd found out who was giving him the collywobbles. I said, 'I haven't decided yet between…' and named five business leaders whom I had either met at Angus's side or knew to be connected with him.

The hunched shoulders relaxed. I had not named the one Brian feared. So I went on, 'And then there are…' and named more names until I reached one that made him flinch: Jem Lowing, the man who'd sat next to me at the Snerton dinner and Angus had called 'that swine'. I'd made it my business to find out later that he was managing director of Impex Incorporated, an import/export business with strong ties to Europe, the Far East and Australasia. I tried not to look triumphant as I breathed, 'Bull's-eye.'

For the first time Brian looked disconcerted. 'You're just guessing.'

'Better still – deducing. Now my questions. What is he up to, and how much are you in for?'

It came out sounding more sympathetic than I'd intended. I found myself liking this sharp, impatient man who worried at things like a bull terrier and asked leading questions. Was this how financial deals were made, with a stark trading of assets and information… you scratch my back and I'll scratch yours, as Angus was fond of saying? The range of opportunities for enriching yourself must be vast, specially if backed up by the clause in the old boys' code that prohibits tales from being told out of school. When, I wondered, was I going to be offered my yacht?

He said, 'I've obviously made a mistake about your sphere of interest. It doesn't intersect with mine. Should have kept my lip buttoned.' He pushed himself away from the back of the chair. 'Like some coffee before you go?'

'Not so fast.' I put out my hand to stop him getting up. 'And no need for regrets. You've only confirmed something that started to niggle at me when I read this morning's news. I go back to one of my previous questions: how many of our top businessmen are not as honest as they should be?'

'On a scale of one to ten?'

I nodded.

He sat jiggling his knee, trying to decide how much he could trust me. When he spoke, his words were bitten off as short as chewed fingernails.

'It's hard to say. I started in this business with an MBA, high ideals and a straightforward goal: to work my arse off and make enough money to retire a rich man before I reached forty. Then I'd buy a wine farm in the Cape, find a nubile wife and spend the rest of my days as a gentleman farmer renowned for his fine wines which would include a sparkler to put Veuve Clicquot in the shade. Ambitions, ha!'

The sudden bark made me jump. His freckles stood out against a wash of angry pink.

'That was before I entered the chancy world of high finance. There is nothing straightforward or logical about dealing in shares as my partners and I do. The buggers behave like yo-yos sometimes, shooting up or down for no apparent reason. Or there'll be an earthquake in Japan or an out-of-control trader like Leeson in Singapore or unpredictable circumstances that send the markets into a tailspin, leaving the so-called experts like us with egg on our faces. Then there are the cunning bastards like Jem Lowing who conceal their company's problems and dump their shares in dribs and drabs so nobody notices, catching all the poor suckers who believed the rosy predictions in their annual reports.'

'Like you.' I slipped in an extra question. 'What is the extent of Vanguard's involvement?'

'Thirty million or so.' He waved his hand round the office. 'Enough to sink us if we can't unload our shareholding before the shit hits the fan. And feeling as I have since I found the rumours to be true, I'd put the dishonesty level in business at four or five on a scale of one to ten. Though that's a clearly prejudiced assessment at this moment in time.' He pulled a face at the cliché. 'Don't quote me.'

'What are you doing about your shares?'

'We're trying to unload them, but it's not something you can do in a hurry. A parcel here, another there, nothing too big or the price will start moving and the financial journalists will sit up and take notice.'

'Which they haven't yet?'

'Not yet, but it's coming. The rumours are bound to reach them soon. I phoned you this morning to find out if you'd heard.'

'You overestimate my contacts. I work solo. Always have done.'

'You've been seen around a lot recently. I thought you may have heard whispers in high places, that sort of thing.'

'I've been partnering Angus as a favour. He's an old friend.' I glared at Brian, defying him to draw any other conclusion.

'He hasn't mentioned Lowing?'

'Only that they're old enemies.'

'There's a connection, you see. That's another reason why I phoned.'

'What connection? What are you talking about?'

'Jem Lowing is married to the daughter of a Joburg Club resident, old Doig, and I thought you may have witnessed clandestine meetings.'

I remembered the glum wife at the far end of the Snertons' dinner table. 'Rex Doig? The mercenary?'

'The so-called White Spectre.' Anger faded to mockery. 'Journalists have a way of putting a gloss on evil by giving villains catchy nicknames. Doig is a black-hearted sod who killed and burned and robbed his way through half of Africa, but instead of being tried for his crimes, he ends up in club cuckooland: the last redoubt of the gentleman.'

'Whom you despise along with journalists?'

'They're not the issue here. It just makes me sick when ill-gotten gains are used to subvert common justice.' He banged his fist on the table. 'I can cope with greed and the lust for power and status; you have to, in this town. Evil is different. We have to stop it succeeding, or we're all sunk.'

He was glaring at me now. A moralist, I thought, in this day and age. It was a pleasant surprise.

I said, 'Mr Barkin and Angus have told me about Doig but I've never seen him. Except for the odd occasion when he needs something his manservant can't supply, no-one at the Club ever does. He's reputed to sit with an elephant gun across his lap to keep visitors at bay.'

'Loaded with dumdums, no doubt?'

I shook my head. 'Blanks, substituted by the manservant on the orders of the Club's management committee. Can't have the venerable plaster chipped, what?'

The tense fist on the table relaxed as he smiled.

I went on, 'The elephant gun is only one of a unique collection of classic firearms hanging in the room, Mr Barkin says. Mostly war loot. But he didn't mention that Mrs Lowing is the White Spectre's daughter.'

Brian leaned forward. If this was what he meant by eyeballing, I thought, I'm enjoying it. 'Not many people know. She loathes her father and sees him only under protest. He'd wanted a son and abandoned her mother when a daughter was born, leaving them to fend for themselves. The kid grew up to marry Lowing and when her father came home old and ill and found out who his son-in-law was, he put the screws on her: be nice to me, and I'll leave you my gun collection when I die. Lowing pressured her into it. Fancies himself as a hunter; thick as thieves with the old man, who of course gives him guest status so he can still visit the Club even though his membership was terminated. So you see why I thought you may have inside information.'

'It was a hell of a long shot.'

He shrugged. 'Worth trying. I'm desperate.'

'What were you going to trade for my valuable insight? I'm curious.'

'Some choice examples of high-level fraud. It would have been a worthwhile trade if you'd been able to reassure me.'

He wasn't going to get off that lightly. 'But you said you were offering information that could be to my advantage. Did you mean financial advantage? An insider's tip to puff up my share portfolio?'

The round glasses glittered. 'You play the market? Not a usual diversion for a writer.'

'I have an excellent financial adviser.' I wanted to show the expert that I knew what I was talking about. 'My measly inheritance went into blue chips and the modest profits from my books go into rand hedge stocks, with ten percent of the total for speculation and another ten in cash, invested on call.'

He threw back his head and laughed.

'What's so funny?'

'I thought I was dealing with a financial innocent.' There was growing respect on his face. 'I also kept a warning in reserve in case you were reluctant. News is about to break that will be an unpleasant surprise for Quain. How is his health?'

'Not good. He's due to go into the clinic on Wednesday for more chemotherapy.' My arms were getting goose-bumps. The last thing Angus needed as he faced the renewed onslaught on his body was more stress. 'What's the warning?'

'Big trouble coming for an old colleague of his. There could be complications if they're still doing business together. It's...' He named a man I didn't know, then said, 'If you can think of a way of warning Quain, you should do so. The Office for Serious Economic Offences is involved.'

'I'll pass the message on.'

'Don't say it came from me. I'd rather not get involved. And one more thing.' He leaned towards me again. 'Threatened executives can be dangerous. Be careful with your revelations.'

We'd come to the melodramatic bit. I said, 'Ta for the advice, but I was expecting to be offered a yacht.'

He didn't laugh as I'd expected. He frowned and said, 'Mitch Kincaid got too close. He'd kept some hefty insurance up his sleeve, though – documents in a bank vault – so they were forced to buy him off. That's all I'm able to say.' The soft clipped voice was back, his expression grim. 'There's big money involved, Faith. And I mean seriously big, not tiddlers like us.'

I shivered. If Vanguard was a tiddler, who was the whale? Angus had called himself a Southern Right whale once but he had been talking about his personal wealth. 'Seriously big' money in Brian's estimation could only mean one of the conglomerates that dominated the Stock Exchange. Or – the thought hit me with nauseating force – drug barons, said to be moving into our newly respectable banking system to launder their dirty money.

'So.' He sat up, pushing himself away from the chair back again. 'How about some of that coffee?'

I quelled my dismaying speculations and checked my watch. 'Won't your staff be coming back soon?'

'It doesn't matter if we're seen together now that I know you have no connection with Lowing.'

I have to say that my reaction then was as uncharacteristic as my long-ago acceptance of Angus's first invitation to lunch. There is a lot to be said for impulse. I said, 'In that case, I'd love a cup of coffee. And I declare myself the winner.'

'What of?'

'Our game of twenty questions. I think I got more out of you than you got out of me.'

'I wouldn't say that. Your information allows me to believe that the rumours haven't spread too far yet. We should be able to unload our bundle in time. Enough to survive, anyway.' His face crumpled into complicated wrinkles when he smiled; he must be older than I'd first thought. 'Thanks very much for coming. Sorry there's no yacht on offer.'

'Not even a tiny luxury cruise?'

What he said then was to haunt me later. 'If you knew the guys involved, you wouldn't joke about it.'

We talked on over our coffee and I found an original, curious mind under the spiky ginger brush cut. Leaving by the lift after I'd run the gauntlet of curious faces watching me from the glass-walled offices, I thought, Can't see a man like that leaving the cut and thrust of commerce to devote himself to a pastoral life of tending vines and sipping preciously at vintages. However nubile the wife.

Angus was out when I phoned the Club to pass on Brian's warning. 'He has taken the young people out to dinner and a show, Madam,' the hall porter said. 'They will be late back. Call in the morning, please.'

'Could you put a message under his door that I phoned? It's quite urgent.'

'Very well, Madam. It will be done.'

'I'm sure it will. Thanks.' I thought of Angus being wheeled through his door at the end of an exhausting evening and having a message marked 'Urgent' thrust upon him. 'On second thoughts, don't mark the message 'Urgent'. Just say I phoned.'

'Very well, Madam.'

I had to smile at the tone of masculine forbearance in his voice as I put the phone down. At all levels of Club service, women were a cross to be borne.

22

*N*ext morning the main headline of *The Star* screamed across four columns: *FIFTY MILLION RAND FOREX SCAM! Business Day*'s lead story was a more sober: *EXCHANGE CONTROL FRAUD – TOP ACCOUNTANT HELD*. The person arrested was not named. My warning to Angus would be too late.

When I phoned the Club, hoping to catch him before he left for work, it was Indigo who answered. 'Hullo? Is that you, Mum?'

'No, it's Faith.' I felt a cold clutch at my heart. 'What's wrong?'

'Da's had a bad turn. He collapsed over his breakfast tray and the doctor's insisting on complete bed rest. I asked the switchboard to try and get through to Mum in England.'

Collapsed. The cancer or the prospect of imminent arrest? I managed to croak, 'Is it serious? How is he?'

'White as a sheet but sleeping at last. And now I'm in a real quandary. I'm booked to fly home tomorrow, as you know, but with him falling ill like this and calling for his lawyer…'

'Leo Greyling?'

'Yes. Before Da would let the doctor give him something to make him sleep, he asked me to send for Leo who has promised to drive up from Nelspruit as soon as he can get away.' Her voice faltered, then went on, 'It sounds so final to summon a lawyer. And the worst thing is, I promised to be back at work on Thursday to complete an urgent job.'

'I'll hold the fort.'

She went on as though she hadn't heard. 'He seems to be rambling as well. Keeps muttering about elephants. It sounds like, "Softly, Jumbo, softly".'

Jumbo Urquhart and Hugh Softley. I said, hoping it didn't sound too breathless, 'Can I come and see him?'

'No point now. The doctor says he'll be out cold until this afternoon and must stay in bed for the next few days. So we've cancelled the chemotherapy and arranged for nursing sisters to come, rather than move him to the clinic.'

'Good idea. He'll be far more comfortable at the Club.' How could I strengthen my request without alarming her? 'Look, I really do need to speak to him about something that's cropped up. Could you let me know as soon as he's able to have visitors?'

Her voice sharpened. 'Can't it wait? I really don't want him bothered.'

I was being fobbed off, but it was vital to get through to him before more damage was done. 'It's urgent. He'll be anxious to know...'

'About what? Tell me and I'll pass it on.'

'Confidential, sorry. Please ring me when he wakes up.'

'Very well.'

The sharpness was still there in her abrupt assent. I thought, Bloody interfering daughter. I should be with him. I said, 'It's important. I wouldn't ask otherwise.'

'I've *said* I'll let you know.'

Irritated, I shot back, 'I'm not begging for favours. I need to see Angus on a vital matter that concerns some business associates.'

'Calm down, Faith. I'm not stopping you from seeing him. Just saying that he's under sedation and...'

'Protecting him from a meddlesome female.' I tried to make a joke of it to defuse the tension between us. The last thing I wanted was to alienate a new friend.

Her response was a strained laugh. 'Sorry. I didn't mean to be snappy. I'm just so worried about him and what would be the best thing to do – go or stay.'

'Remember what I said: I'll be here to hold the fort.'

'Thanks. If he has you and Benj around, at least I won't feel I'm abandoning him. Poor Da, he's been so good to me this week.' She rang off.

I sat teetering on my typist's chair, thinking back to the conversation I'd had with Angus only a few months ago. Were he and Jumbo and Hugh involved in illegal foreign exchange transactions as well as – what had he called it? – 'creative dealing' on the stock market? Tax evasion was on the rise world-wide, my research sources had told me. A whole new financial advice industry had sprung up to help rich men protect their money by whisking it into offshore havens and investing it in a world-wide spread of funds to burgeon unfettered by the taxes mundane salary-earners had to pay.

I'd have to learn more about forex regulations and how they were flouted. Marge would know.

'*Star* library,' she said at the other end of the phone. 'Palms read, bums wiped and editors pacified. Can I help you?'

The anarchic sense of humour cultivated by journalists must be catching. I said, 'Hullo Marge, it's Faith again. Got a moment? I want to pick your brains.'

'Pick away, but be gentle, will you? I have raging toothache and nobody can find the codeine stash.'

'You need oil of cloves. My mother swore by it.'

'I need a good dentist. Mine's emigrated to Houston. They're like swallows, our medical specialists: flock overseas for the high-paying jobs but come winging home every summer for the sunshine and the social buzz at Plett or Hermanus.'

The acid comment was unusual. Marge was a cheerful soul who looked for the best in people. I said, 'You must be in severe pain to sound so jaundiced.'

'Just short on temper this morning, but the little grey cells are still operative. How can I help you?'

'What do you know about foreign exchange fiddles? I need any extra information you can give me about your lead story this morning.'

'Aha. As soon as I saw the headline, I wondered if you'd call.'

Damn and blast. I'd been indiscreet in contacting her again. I managed to croak, 'Why me?'

'Two and two together, my dear Watson. Your sudden appearance on Angus Quain's arm in the social pages, followed by the investigation into his past for your wheeler-dealer book, and now his old firm Randall Eksteen getting involved in a forex scam. QED.'

I closed my eyes thinking, She'd make a mean detective. I hadn't given her the shadow of a hint that Angus could be associated with illegal financial activities. Nor could I let that shrewd mind behind the cow eyes think it now.

I manufactured a laugh and said, 'This is nothing to do with Angus. Heaven forbid. He'd take enormous umbrage if he thought anyone had connected him with a crook in his old firm.'

'Crook? The man's only being held on suspicion. Nothing proved yet, unless you know more than I do?'

Her tone was wary; I'd have to go into denial mode. 'Sorry, don't know anything about today's scandal but I've heard of some lulus recently.'

'Who from?' Still dubious.

'My source would only speak to me in strict confidence, so I can't give details.' I lowered my voice. 'But something that keeps cropping up during my preliminary research is the huge variety of ways in which money has left South Africa illegally during the past few decades. The financial guys reckon that there's well over eighty billion rands in funk money out there. I'm telling you, the more the plot thickens, the more fascinated I get.'

'It's nauseating, if you ask me. Remember that old song, *Ain't We Got Fun*? "The rich get richer and the poor get children." It was dead right.' She spoke with the irritable envy of those who have no spare cash to tuck away in tax havens. 'But don't let's get on to the population explosion. I'll be plunged in ecological gloom for the rest of the day. What do you want to know about this morning's drama?'

'Specifically, have the forex people uncovered a new leak or has the money gone out via one of the traditional exits? The report doesn't say.'

She said, 'It's one of the global unit trusts, I believe. Not sure how the scheme works, but it involves buying here and selling elsewhere and depositing the difference in secret accounts after it's been laundered through travel agencies. That any help?'

Angus had told me that Jumbo ran the country's biggest travel agency chain; if he were involved with the arrested man, Angus was vulnerable. Struggling to sound casual, I said, 'So it's nothing new.'

'You've heard of this one?'

'Oh, yes. It's a favourite route.' I hoped the assurance rang true; I wasn't used to bending the truth with friends. 'And while we're on the subject, I'd be interested in any more background stuff you come across relating to forex fiddles. Happy to pay for it.'

'In what? Nice portable foreign bank notes? Don't be a twit. I wouldn't dream of charging for something that's part of my job.'

She sounded miffed and I thought, Oh hell, now she's offended. I put on a now-let's-be-practical voice and said, 'I pay students for research material and my publisher covers the cost, so there's no reason why I shouldn't pay a newspaper librarian too. Nothing worse than people who expect professionals to give up their time for nothing.'

'I'm not giving up my time. It's part of my job,' she insisted. 'I love being asked to track things down. Making quantum leaps between known facts and memory tickles – you know, those feather-brushes at the edge of your consciousness, something read or heard long ago that suddenly connects with a great flash.' Her laugh was mocking. 'We librarians do have our moments.'

'How do you handle the public perception that being a librarian is all filing and catalogues and admonishing people to speak in whispers? I'm always being told that historians are dry as dust and irrelevant to boot, and it drives me crazy. It's such a put-down.'

'I always say, Maybe in ordinary libraries, but not on a newspaper like ours.' Her humour was restored. 'There's never a dull moment here. Journalists are unbelievably demanding, and you should hear some of the weird things people come in and ask for. I've started a file of my own now called *Strange – But True*. It's filling up fast with odd news items like wolf children and flesh-eating viruses and old women found chained up in cow sheds because they disgraced the family forty years ago. If you hang on a sec I'll read you some of the headlines.'

I hung on, of course. Her news-gatherer's instinct had been alerted by my interest in Angus and I owed it to him not to let her catch the faintest whiff of impropriety where he was concerned. I wondered why he had asked for Leo to come: was it to do with his will or financial problems or...

Marge's voice broke into my anxious speculations. 'Here we are. The most bizarre items have to do with death. *MUMMY FOUND ON COUCH. PIG KILLS CRIPPLED TEENAGER. SON KILLS MOM OVER NOODLES. TRUNK WAS A TOMB FOR BABIES.* And listen to this one: *WOMAN'S TOES WIRED FOR SHOCK.* It seems that her lover wound wire round her big toes while she was sleeping and connected them to a wall plug, then turned it on.'

She went on for several minutes, breaking off into a long moo of laughter at one point, which allowed me to cut in. 'I'd love to see that file. Perhaps next time I come in? This book is going to take months of research.'

'Sure. I'll keep it aside for you.' I heard someone calling her, then she said, 'Sorry, got to go. Good to talk to you, Faith. And...' Her voice dropped again. '...remember what I said last time.'

'About the rich?'

'And powerful. Mitch Kincaid got too involved when he was investigating some iffy financial deal last year. He told me it would sink him.'

She was giving me the same warning as Brian Lapidus had. I forced a laugh and said, 'Both yachts?'

'I'm serious. He was forced to leave the country. I'd hate the same thing to happen to you.' She spoke close to the mouthpiece.

'Dire warning noted and thanks for your help, Marge.' I kept the tone humorous. 'But I must point out that I'm writing a simple history, not digging for dirt.'

'You could find more than you bargained for. The Joburg business world is no place for sissies.'

'Don't worry, I won't allow anyone to kick sand in my face. Hope the toothache goes away soon.'

As I put the phone down, wondering just how much she did know, I heard her breathe, 'I mean it. Be careful. Money is power.'

A sentiment worthy of Angus.

Indigo phoned in the late afternoon to say that he had woken and was asking for me. I found him enthroned in the mahogany bed, eyes closed, pale sunken face lustrous with sweat, the fuzz of hair clinging like grey seaweed left behind by the tide.

She got up from the chair by his bed and came whispering to where I stood in the doorway. 'He's dozing again. I'm sitting with him until the night nurse comes on duty. The doctor says he's exhausted but that his vital signs appear to be fine.'

181

'What happened this morning?'

'When I arrived after breakfast Boniface was hovering outside the door, having called the doctor to examine him. It seems that he rang the bell at eight gasping for help.'

'Poor Angus.'

I looked round the comfortable male lair with its military chest and dumb valet, its tobacconist's aura and serried photographs of the family and business triumphs. He had lived here for so many years that the carpet was worn and the velvet curtains had faded from maroon to a mellow plum. The morning edition of *Business Day* lay folded on his bedside table with half the main headline showing: ... *TOP ACCOUNTANT HELD*. No wonder he had had a shock.

'Can you think what could be bothering him?' Indigo spoke near my shoulder. 'You probably know him better than I do. I felt so helpless this morning when he lay there muttering about elephants. Does he go to game reserves often?'

'I don't know.' I turned to face her. 'All I can tell you is that he slips away sometimes for a week or two. Praise would know where he goes. Perhaps you should ask him?'

'I don't want to pry. Just ... why elephants? He's always seemed such a city man. When we used to go and stay with Uncle Tom on the farm, Da would sit on the stoep or perhaps stroll round the garden or the dam, but we could never get him to come out in the Jeep with us. He disliked being bounced around the veld, he'd say.'

'Let's sit down and have a drink, and you can tell me about Uncle Tom,' I murmured, gliding into the sitting room to ring the bell for Boniface. I had her to myself that afternoon as Praise had driven Benjamin across town to the Eastgate mall.

'They've gone to shop for warm clothes. Benj's feet are like ice blocks in their sandals,' she was saying, 'and I want to make sure he's decently dressed before I go. Da will be mortified if he keeps wandering into the Club looking like a hippy.'

'So you've decided to go?'

'Tomorrow. The doctor says that Da's not in immediate danger.'

'Sensible decision. What is Benj going to do?'

She sat looking at me, trying to decide how much she could say to an outsider. I prodded, 'Angus worries a lot about him.'

'That doesn't surprise me.' She spoke in hesitant bursts. 'Benj and he are fond of each other in principle but they have incessant arguments. Da calls him a rolling stone, and it's true. Benj never stays anywhere for more than a few days. He's very ... unfocused is the best way to put it. Of the three of us, he suffered most from not having a father around. So on top of being irritated by him, Da feels guilty too.'

The silence that follows a confession fell between us. The Quains were a contradictory family. I recalled Hannah saying, 'There were five of us revolving round the house... all with monumental egos, all very different. There had to be a big bang at some stage and when it happened, Angus and I decided that we were better apart than together.' Yet they had an obvious affection for each other that I envied.

Indigo lunged forward in her chair just as Angus did when he wanted something. 'Benj isn't very reliable. I only feel justified in going because you're here and can keep us informed.'

I said, aware how stiff it sounded and not caring, 'I'm here because I'm Angus's friend and he is mine. Your family relationships are not my concern. And just for the record, Hannah has already asked for regular reports on his condition and she gets them every week.'

'Now I've offended you.'

This daughter is so like Angus, I thought. Even in apology the Quain eyes looked directly at you and the Quain chin went up as if to take the next punch square on. I said in my most astringent voice, 'Misperceived my role, rather.'

'I didn't mean to. We're all so grateful to you for being his...' She stopped, uncertain what word to use.

I felt a laugh exploding for the first time in days. I couldn't help it; she looked so embarrassed. Anomalous Faith – imperious Angus. Nobody knew what to make of our irregular friendship that had flourished for fifteen years well outside the boundaries people set in their minds for explaining older men who enjoyed the company of younger women, and vice versa.

Why is it so difficult to believe in friendships that bridge chasms of age and sex? One of the happiest relationships I know is that of a successful woman advocate in her sixties who has been married for two decades to a much younger man who clearly enjoys her mature and confident sexuality as much as he luxuriates in their beautiful home, stable of sleek cars and elegant social life. They supply needs in each other that the most logical matchmaker would never have suspected; their contentment is an inspiration to anyone who feels intimidated by conventional norms.

'His friend,' I said when I had sobered up. 'Finish and klaar. Do you remember that useful South African phrase?'

'Of course I do.' Her face was pink. 'It means that I've put my big foot in it. I don't know how to apologise.'

'Don't even try.' It was my turn to be candid. 'Nobody but Hannah has ever understood Angus and me. She saw at once how our needs have interlocked. That's the only way I can explain it. But now it looks as though the relationship, to quote King George V's doctors, is drawing peacefully to its close.'

183

'Does that mean you think there's no hope?'

There were tears in her eyes and I had to look away to answer, or I'd have started too. In a low voice so Angus couldn't hear if he was awake, I said, 'I wouldn't say so to him. Like all of you, I urge him to keep fighting. But one must be realistic. He's beginning to look awful.'

At that moment, saving further distress, Boniface knocked on the open door and came in, his face even more funereal than usual. 'Apologies for the late coming. How is Mr Quain now, please?'

Indigo said, 'A little better, thanks, though still dozing. Is it too early to ask you to bring us a drink?' She turned to me. 'I think we both need one.'

I agreed as Boniface said gravely, 'Never too early, Madam.'

He served drinks at all hours in the Club. You passed him proceeding – there was no other word for it – up the stairs and along the passages with clinking tray and impassive expression, the perfect butler. 'And why not?' Angus had said once. 'It's a fellow's prerogative to drink when he wants to in the privacy of his club.' Mr Barkin had confided during one of our attic Saturdays that there was an elderly naval man on the third floor who couldn't face the day without several large pink gins for breakfast, and that Stanley Linklater was slipped a tot of brandy in his night-time baby's bottle of milk to help him sleep.

'I'm hoping we'll get a member like the Queen Mother one day, yes indeed,' Mr Barkin had gone on. 'I read in a magazine that she enjoys a glass or two of French champagne in the evenings, then sends the rest of the bottle down to the servants. I wouldn't mind being below stairs in that household.' Below stairs? I had thought. The members certainly know how to keep him in his place.

Indigo was saying, 'Wine or stronger? I usually have wine.'

'Wine for me too. Thanks.'

She said to Boniface, 'Could we have another bottle of that delicious chardonnay we had last night, please?'

'Very well, Madam.'

When he had bowed and stalked away beyond earshot, she said, 'Being in this club is like going back in a time machine to a country house before the First World War. Quite disconcerting. I didn't know people still lived this way.'

'Johannesburg Club members do. And there are still rambling homes on the bigger farms with fleets of house servants and gardeners, just like the old days, though the numbers are dwindling as wages rise.'

She picked up the lead as I hoped she would. 'Uncle Tom never lived like that. He's very down-to-earth and egalitarian. Hates being waited on.'

'I've never met him.'

An odd expression appeared on her face. 'What do you know about Uncle Tom?'

'Only the crumbs Angus dropped on the day I met Leo: that the two of them started their first jobs together after the war, working for a Cape Town ships' chandler, and that they had both come up the hard way. "We were two wild boyos," he said.'

She hooted, clapping her hand over her mouth so as not to wake him in the next room. 'That's putting it mildly. Did he tell you they got drunk one day and drove a crane off its rails so that it toppled off the quay? And that Uncle Tom lost his leg as a result?'

'He told me about the leg and how a sangoma had kept Tom alive while he ran to call an ambulance.'

Indigo chuckled. 'The saga of Uncle Tom's leg. They both used to tell it, with actions and a lot of laughter, as a kind of party piece round the braai fire on the farm. Da managed to jump free of the crane but Uncle Tom wasn't so lucky; as he fell, one of its steel cables sliced his leg off above the knee.

'He had a whole routine about how he watched it sink under a harbour oil slick, never to be seen again, with curious seals nuzzling at the cloud of blood billowing from the raw end. Gone to feed the crabs, he said. He was half frozen and in shock, of course. Da and a watching sailor dived in and fished him out, and among the crowd of dock workers that ran to help was a sangoma who stopped the gushing blood by wrapping his sweat rag tightly round the stump and chanting something over and over in Xhosa.

'It sounded like a spell, Da said, and it worked. The ambulance medics couldn't believe their eyes when they got to the scene, expecting to find a man bleeding to death, and there was Uncle Tom propped up against a bollard smoking a joint which the sangoma had rolled for him to take his mind off the pain.'

'Sounds horrific.'

'Da never forgave himself. It's why he's always been so protective of Uncle Tom. When nobody in Cape Town would have anything to do with him after his wife's suicide, Da persuaded him to come north with Brendan and Leo and helped them buy the farm.'

I thought, Brendan must be Leo's brother. That's some act of friendship, to help buy a farm. 'Is Tom a good farmer?'

She looked surprised. 'He's not a farmer, he's a painter. Da opens his exhibitions every year. These are all Uncle Tom's.' She gestured at the paintings on the walls. 'It's his lover Brendan who's the farmer. After all the fuss over the suicide and the inquest, Brendan became a recluse. He's gifted at growing things, though, hence the farm. They're exporting avocados and bananas to Europe now.'

It was so unexpected that I felt my mouth falling open. Tom Greyling was gay. I looked up at the graceful painting of the male nude and thought, Is that the reason for the mysterious disappearances? Is Angus gay too?

There was a knock and Boniface came in with a tray. 'Your wine, Madams. I

185

have put an extra glass for Mr Quain, in case he wakes up.'

On cue, Angus called in a groggy voice from the bedroom, 'That you, Bonny?'

'Yes, sir.'

'Could you find my daughter for me?'

Indigo got up and went to the door. 'I'm here, and so is Faith. Would you like some wine?'

'Spot of medicinal Chivas would be more appropriate, don't you think?'

'Da, you've been told to cut down on the whisky.'

'Bugger the quacks. Ask Bonny to fetch me a double tot of Chivas, no ice, and send Faith in, will you? I want to ask her to do something for me.'

Indigo made a sign to me not to move and said to her father, 'Are you sure you're well enough for visitors?'

'Faith counts as family, dammit. And don't you start trying to manage me. I may be down but I'm not out yet. One thing I can't stand is bloody bossy women telling me what to do.'

Where I would have bristled, she shrugged. 'It was just a suggestion, and you're an old curmudgeon who won't admit he's ill.' She turned to the hovering Boniface. 'Would you bring a double Chivas for my father, please?'

'In one quick moment, Madam.' He disappeared, looking relieved.

Angus called out, 'I'm not an invalid yet! Perfectly capable of running my life. Just give me a hand with these recalcitrant pillows, will you?'

Indigo gave me a conspirator's smile and said, 'Coming? We'd better make the paterfamilias comfortable before he works himself into a state.'

Standing on either side of the bed, we heaved him into a sitting position, plumped up the pillows, settled him back against them and smoothed the rumpled sheets. He sat there glaring at us, looking much better than he had when I arrived: a watercolour wash of colour in his cheeks and no longer sweating.

'See what a family man has to put up with, Faith?' he grumbled. 'Hag-ridden, that's what I am. Thank God Benj has come to redress the balance.'

'Am I included among the hags?' I sat down on the chair by the bed thinking, Is this a gay man speaking? Would a gay man enjoy the company of Mama Nesta's girls? The answer had to be yes.

'Of course you're included! Haven't I just said so? Trouble with hags is, they make themselves indispensable. It's a ploy for keeping us at their mercy.'

'Oh, nonsense.' Indigo picked up the water jug on his bedside table and went into the bathroom to fill it. 'You are being disagreeable.'

'Not so!' he called but his eyes were on me, asking for something.

'What is it, Angus?'

He said in a low voice, 'I have a commission for you. Remember Urquhart and Softley?'

186

My urgent information was too late; he knew the score already. I said, 'How could I forget? Jumbo and Hugh. Apropos whom, what happened when Amalgamated Couplings went insolvent? Did you achieve your target?'

He gave me a warning look and jerked his head towards the bathroom: his daughter was not to know. Then said, looking smug, 'We made a bundle. Now I need you to give them a message. Soon as possible. It's not something we can discuss over the phone.'

The matter must be really serious, then. I said, 'You haven't forgotten the last time they were here, when you roared at them to get out?'

'Of course not. But our mutual interests supersede personal animosity. It's a good business principle. The message is: Close the stable door at once. Got that?'

'Got it. And I had a message for you, though I see it's too late. I was asked to let you know that an old colleague of yours is running into...'

A black frown warned me that this too was *verboten* in Indigo's hearing. He was flicking through the desk diary by his bed as she came back with the full jug, saying, 'The addresses you need are in here: Astra Travel and Figgis & Softley.' He added with venom, 'I'd hang up that whingeing little bastard by the balls if I could.'

'Hardly a fitting sentiment for a sickbed,' Indigo murmured.

'This isn't a sickbed, just a temporary horizontal setback. Feeling much better now. Should be up and about by the morning. Ask Praise to be on call by eight and book a table for our farewell lunch tomorrow, will you? You're invited of course, old girl,' he tossed at me. 'And tell Prunella...'

He was still issuing orders when I left armed with the addresses. 'Tell those thundering idiots I'll pull the plug if they don't jump!' was his parting shot.

Indigo walked with me to the lift. 'He's playing commander-in-chief again. I can go home with an easy conscience.'

We reached the lift and I pressed the ivory Down button. 'It doesn't make sense to stay, with your commitments.'

'To be honest, I'm no dutiful daughter. Da's very demanding and free with advice. I can't decide whether it's rampant boss behaviour or the daddy-knows-best attitude so many men of his generation still have. It's as though they're intent on ignoring the advances women have made over the past four decades. I don't know how you put up with it.'

'I'm not his daughter. I'm his friend and debating partner. Big difference.' I tried not to sound too facetious; I'd had a far worse problem with my father.

She put her hand on my arm. 'He's lucky to have you, specially now. If he goes soon...'

'Angus will be okay for a while yet, believe me. He's got resilience and energy and he knows how to roll with the punches and bounce up fighting again.'

'You've been studying him?'

'For years, without realising it.' Often wondering whether he had lovers; never whether they were male. Was I just unobservant or blinded by his glamour?

With a return of the carborundum look, she took her hand away saying, 'I'd be nervous of having a friend like you, always analysing and making mental notes. Please don't put me in your book.'

'You don't qualify, not being a businessman.'

'That's something to be thankful for.'

I said, 'Pax?' and pressed the Down button again.

'Pax.' As if it had needed a second reminder to move, the lift jerked to life and began creaking upwards. She went on, 'I don't think Benj will stay around for long. He never does. So please keep in touch with me as well as Mum, will you?'

'I don't let go of friends easily.'

Her smile for the first time had some of Hannah's warmth. 'I'm glad.'

The lift shuddered to a stop and I pushed open the concertina gate. 'Thanks. See you tomorrow.'

Driving home through the threatening city darkness I wondered, between speculations as to Angus's sexual orientation, how high the stakes were in the financial drama that had blown up: millions or billions?

23

The nerve centre of the Astra Travel Agency chain ('Twenty-two busy busy busy branches country-wide!') was the penthouse level of a Sandton office tower. I walked into a space the size of a small hangar crammed with desks, filing cabinets, snaking cables and clickety-clacking computer terminals manned by travel consultants in perky Black Watch tartan uniforms. At the perimeter of the chaos, blinds were drawn across the windows to exclude the winter sunshine while neon lights glared overhead and central heating vents pumped out hot stale air at waist level, optimum height for feet to freeze as noses redden with recirculated viruses. It was a vision of the future that awaits us when the machines take over and we become their acolytes.

'Kin ah help yew?' The receptionist at the main desk lowered her photo romance as she struggled to raise barbed wire eyelashes.

'I've come to see Mr Urquhart.'

'Got an appointment?' The barbed wire rose higher then fell again as she assessed my make-up, hairstyle, clothes, sex appeal and social status, all in a single expert sweep.

'Yes. Ten thirty.' I tried to return the look but failed, being unskilled at visual insult.

She gave a thin smile and said, 'Ah'll see if he's available. Take a seat, hey?'

'I'd rather stand. I'm in a hurry.'

'Suit yourself. Ah'll jiss go and see.' And she vanished.

Nobody else paid me any attention. The travel consultants went on clickety-clacking. The air grew staler. After ten minutes I felt a headache seeping up the back of my neck and thought, I'd leave in a huff right now if it wasn't that I've promised Angus to…

'Are you the lady for Mr Urquhart?' The voice came from somewhere near my elbow, uttered by a wan girl with a mouse's bright apprehensive eyes.

'Yes.'

'This way, then.' She scuttled off, feeling her way through the maze of desks as though she were still not quite sure which path led to the trapdoor with the piece of cheese behind it. I followed some distance behind to give her time to retrace her steps at dead ends. When at last we reached a door marked CHAIRMAN at the far end of the hangar, she turned to me in triumphant relief and squeaked, 'Here we are. Mr Urquhart.'

The chairman's office was in a corner position with glimpses of a view through the vertical blinds at the windows, though the persistent stuffiness showed that they were seldom opened. Patches of sweat had ballooned and waned under Jumbo's armpits all day, staining his shirt in concentric yellowish rings. He was jabbing data into his own desk terminal when I was shown in, eyes screwed up against the smoke from the cigarette dangling at his lips.

The mouse gave a nervous cough and said, 'This lady says she's Miss Dobermann and she rang earlier.'

'Aye – Faith, if I remember rightly?' He broke off to reach across the desk, tusks bared, to shake my hand. 'Sit ye down while I finish what I'm doing. It'll only take a wee moment. There's a major tourism conference coming up and I want to confirm the bookings for our overseas VIPs pairsonally.' He thundered at the mouse, 'Coffee, Darlene!' and she flattened herself against the door before slinking out.

I sat looking round the office which had been done out recently – you could still smell the glue – with new wallpaper, carpeting and upholstery in matching Black Watch tartan. The blinds were alternate strips of navy and dark green plastic. Hung on the walls were travel posters featuring Scottish scenery, display boxes of salmon flies and a clan map with a border of very purple thistles. On the coffee table next to a heaped ashtray was a miniature Loch Ness monster with cairngorm eyes.

As the jabbing continued, I got up and went to one of the windows, pushing aside the dangling plastic strips to look at the view. You could see half the northern suburbs from up there: houses nestled in what town planners call The Greater Johannesburg Forest – the garden trees that have been cajoled to grow, in defiance of nature and water restrictions, in what was once dry grassland. Beyond were the receding blue ridges of the Magaliesberg where I sometimes went walking with friends who belonged to the Mountain Club.

Haven't been for months now, I thought, turning to go and sit down as I heard Darlene come in with the coffee. I'd have to pull my old life together when Angus was gone. From the look of him the previous evening, it wouldn't be long. I'd make changes too … force myself to get out and socialise, as I'd become accustomed with Angus. I had the wardrobe for it now. Have clothes, will party. It was a pity the quest for zero defect had fizzled out. Despite my denials, I'd nurtured a flicker of hope that Angus would conjure up a soul-mate. If he had to go and die on me, the least he could do was find me a replacement.

'White or black?' Darlene held the milk jug poised. 'Lady? I asked if you...'

I snapped back into the over-heated present. 'White, please. No sugar.' The coffee mugs featured different views of Edinburgh Castle.

'Sweet enough, eh?' Jumbo stubbed out his cigarette and lumbered over from his desk to sit on the opposite tartan couch, mopping his forehead and neck. When he too was armed with coffee ('White, two sugars – no need to stir, for God's sake!') and Darlene had fled, he grumbled, 'That lassie's pathetic. Can't find a secretary who knows how to behave and speak the Queen's English these days. Let alone spell it.'

'You can if you pay enough.'

'Ah. A labour activist, are we?' he said, looking pleased at having placed me.

'Just a believer in fair and equal wages.'

Alarm replaced pleasure. 'Ye're not representing one of the trade unions?'

His huge scarred lock forward's ears had begun to flush red from the bottom up, an awesome sight. I couldn't keep my eyes off the rising tide which exactly matched the Royal Stewart tie he wore, loosened at the knot. Those radiant flaps would have been a real asset in a rugby scrum with the light failing.

To put him out of his misery, I said, 'No, I've come because Angus Quain asked me to give you a message.'

My reward was another display of tusks as relief replaced alarm. Jumbo was one of those people who bare their teeth clear up to the gums so you can see the roots when they smile. 'Had me worried for a wee moment there. Those union people seem to be toyi-toying their way in everywhere nowadays. Fire away, then. How is Gus, poor fellow? He didn't seem too keen on me last time we met.'

'He's not well.'

Jumbo fished a crumpled packet out of his shirt pocket and tapped out another cigarette. 'Cancer spreading?' He seemed oblivious of the irony.

'I can't say.' Angus would be furious if I went about dispensing bulletins on his condition. 'He asked me to tell you to close the stable door at once. He also said that he'd pull the plug if you don't jump to it. Whatever that means.'

'Surprised he didn't telephone.' Showing no reaction to the message, Jumbo picked up the Loch Ness monster and depressed its tail, which made its jaws gape and belch a blue flame with which he lit the cigarette, saying between drags, 'Neat little souvenir, eh? Amuses the kiddies no end.'

'I'm sure.' Leave kiddies gambolling alone in the tartan office for five minutes and the whole place would be in toxic flames. I went on, 'Angus felt I should deliver the message in person after yesterday morning's news.'

'What?' The monster crash-landed on the coffee table so hard that one of its cairngorm eyes fell out.

'*FIFTY MILLION RAND FOREX SCAM. TOP ACCOUNTANT HELD*,' I quoted. 'Surely you saw the headlines?'

'God almighty,' he muttered, 'so that's it.'

I wasn't sure how to respond. His face had gone livid behind the smoke spiralling up from the cigarette wilting in his clutch – whether with fear, rage or in a fury of doubt, I couldn't tell. After waiting a full minute out of respect for his anguish, I ventured, 'Angus asked me to give the same message to Hugh, but his office doesn't know where he is this morning.'

'What?' he trumpeted. 'Both of us? It's not safe, man! If the forex people make the connection…' He stopped and glared at me. 'What do ye know about these matters?'

'Nothing. I'm merely a messenger.' I lowered my eyes to reinforce the point.

'I thought the two of ye were – what did Gus say? – "Friends for many years"?'

'That doesn't mean I'm privy to his financial affairs.'

'Not privy, is it? I doubt that. I doubt it very much. Ye're no fool, that I know.' He took a lingering pull at the cigarette and shifted his great sweaty bulk forward. 'Tell me what's going on.' He had bloodshot eyes from the chain-smoking, alert with distrust now.

I shrugged and said, 'Your guess is as good as mine. Angus doesn't discuss his business with me. I simply volunteered to deliver his messages this morning,' and got up to go.

'Aye, he's tight,' Jumbo muttered, then as I bent to pick up my bag, 'Aren't ye going to have yer coffee? Darlene will think she's failed again.'

'You drink it, in that case. I don't have time. There's still Hugh Softley to track down.' I headed for the door, looking forward to fresh air.

His parting words rose above the clickety-clacking in the outer hangar where Darlene cowered next to a wallscape of Loch Lomond, waiting to conduct me back to the starting point. 'He'll be in Sandton City – Dunhill's or A & D Spitz, probably. Bugger haunts those shops. Likes people to know he's a man of means.'

The laugh that followed was nasty, brutish and short.

When Darlene and I managed to locate the main desk again, the receptionist had reappeared and was blowing on wet cerise nails behind a copy of *Playboy*.

'Can you find your way out from here okay, lady?'

'Yes.' The lifts could be seen through the glass entrance doors. I added, 'Thanks for your help.'

Darlene bit her lower lip. 'Mr Urquhart says I'm not much good at directions. Or anything, really.'

'He could be wrong.'

The apprehensive eyes generated a single flash of profound sarcasm. 'Him? Never.' And she scurried away.

The word 'mall' once meant a level, shaded walk; a place for strolling under the trees, taking the air and greeting friends as carriages rattled past. Now it means a vast concrete bunker sprawled at the edge of a city, surrounded by a sea of tarmac and tarted up inside with lavish decor, hanging plants and artful lighting designed to avert claustrophobia. The mugger and hijack situation being what it is these days, Joburg shoppers only feel safe in malls with armed security guards manning the entrances and patrolling the car parks. Even then several cars a day get stolen, though the more cunning hijacker has learnt to lie in wait at entrance gates in the quiet streets of posh suburbs for a better class of vehicle.

I found Hugh Softley, as predicted, in Alfred Dunhill's sleek modern shoplet in the heart of Sandton City. He stood in front of a rack of vivid silk ties with an assistant hovering at his elbow. I watched from the doorway, not wanting to interrupt. Having selected four and handed them to the assistant, he prowled past a rail of blazers, fingered a pile of cashmere sweaters, pored over a glass showcase of watches and lighters, tried on a panama hat, tried out an ebony walking stick and admired a display of fine inlaid humidors before moving towards the till. I was riveted, never having watched someone contemplate spending several months' salary in ten minutes.

'Does the madam require anything?' a hushed voice said in my ear.

'No thanks. The madam is waiting to speak to your customer over there, when he's finished.'

'Oh, Mr *Softley*,' the voice breathed. 'One of our best customers.'

I wondered how many fraudulent transactions were required to finance his outlay on elegant gentlemen's accessories. Hugh Softley would not have an office that looked like a Scottish stand at a trade exhibition, I thought. It would be ultramodern and in the finest materials: suède, raw silk, chrome and rosewood, Caucasian kelims, cocktail bar stocked with exotic liqueurs. He wouldn't have a meek flustered secretary who called me 'lady'; he'd have a willowy blonde with legs up to her armpits, redolent of French perfume.

Is he gay too? I wondered, watching him unfold his wallet with precise fingers. And my thoughts went back to Angus raging against his increasing disability in the mahogany bed. Was that why we had got along so well all these years – because the question of sex never came into the equation? I remembered Hannah's veiled look when she said, 'How well do you know him?' and him saying, 'I have other fields to plough.' I thought of the magnificent black male nude in his newest painting, and wondered.

Hugh Softley was coming towards me, dark head down as he tucked his wallet into his inside pocket. I said, 'Hugh. Just a minute.'

He looked up in alarm, then relaxed to a tense vigilance as he saw it was me. 'Mizz Faith Dobermann. What a surprise.'

'I've been looking for you. There's a message from Angus.'

'Yes?' His close-set eyes were the colour of Stroh rum, expressionless as he waited to hear what I had to say. There was no gold chain bracelet showing today on the wrist of the hand holding the shopping bag … perhaps he kept it up his creamy silk sleeve during working hours, along with his other secrets.

The mall was almost empty that morning, its pleasant quietness enfolding the passing footsteps on the marble floors, the click of a sweeper's broom, the muted ting of a cash register, the escalators trundling nearby.

'And?' he prompted.

'He says to close the stable door at once.'

Not a muscle moved either in the taut face or under the immaculate tailored suit with a sheen of mohair in its fine weave. He stood there looking at me, trying to calculate how much I knew.

Unnerved, I added, 'After yesterday's headlines, Angus didn't want to contact you by phone. He also asked me to say that he'd pull the plug if you and Jumbo didn't jump to it.'

After a moment Hugh said, 'I'd know it was a message from Quain just by the language.' The rum-coloured eyes scanned my appearance then looked away. Not in Hugh Softley's league, they implied, for which I was grateful. 'You can tell your boyfriend that he needn't worry because I'm not a fool. The door was locked and bolted yesterday.'

'He's not my boyfriend!'

'What, then?' The eyes were back on my face, mocking the childish heat of my answer.

'Just friend. Is that so hard to comprehend?'

'What's hard to comprehend is that he has friends at all. Quain is more devious than a knot of eels.' His hand tightened on the loops of the Dunhill bag. 'Call the book off, Faith.'

I was shaken. How did he know about the book? This was my third warning about a project initiated out of friendship and intended as a simple social history. With numb lips I said, 'What do you mean?'

'The book you're concocting to gild the Quain lily. Drop it, is my advice. Applying gilt would be like painting a whore.'

It was his baroque conceit that made me flare, 'Angus called you an unmitigated shit and a whingeing bastard, so the feeling's mutual.' I turned to go.

Not soon enough to avoid the words that followed me down the escalator. 'Being a bastard has its advantages. We have nothing to lose by being unmitigated shits.'

194

When I got back to my car in the rooftop parking lot, the Crooklok had jammed in the sauna-box heat and the key got stuck. Having to call a locksmith to come at huge expense to release your steering wheel is bad enough; when the plastic seat burns your thighs and the security guards laugh behind their hands as you drive away fuming an hour later, the rest of the day is a write-off.

Angus had been right, I realised. My old banger was ready for the scrap-heap and it was time for a new car with an alarm and an electronic locking system. The planned book would have to be a bestseller or I'd be in hock for the next four years, paying the damn thing off.

A mixture of colourful business tycoons and some juicy examples of white-collar fraud should do the trick. I could weave in a number of the elements that make for a successful soap opera: wealth, intrigue, dominating personalities, twisted talents, villains and fools. And there was also an assassin, the White Spectre with his collection of beautiful, deadly rifles.

24

Angus had rebounded overnight. He buzzed into the Club dining room for the farewell lunch in a blazer and flannels and a white open-necked shirt set off by a paisley cravat in deep blues and reds. Carefully chosen, all of them. Angus understood the importance of appearances. He stopped several times on his way to the table to talk to acquaintances, fiddling with the wheelchair controls as he spoke so that it moved back and forth on restless wheels.

The lunch was a long and cheerful repast that ended with brave smiles. I didn't have a chance to report on my meetings with Jumbo and Hugh, except to lean closer to Angus in a quiet moment and say, 'The messages were delivered, as requested.'

His answer was a brief, 'We'll talk tomorrow.'

I didn't go with them to the airport. Benjamin would provide moral support, Praise would drive him home in the Bentley and Boniface would cosset him out of the wheelchair and into bed with a double tot of Chivas. He wouldn't need me that night.

And I needed time alone to think about my meetings with Jumbo and Hugh. Both had suspected my motives. Jumbo had been afraid of the consequences of his mysterious deal with the other two, and scathing about Hugh. In contrast, Hugh had seemed in control of the situation and had warned me off Angus, whom he appeared to loathe.

Where did this leave me? Had I been wrong about my friend all these years: seen him in the rosy glow of a relationship that had been all-important to me – however limited on his side – rather than as the predator he appeared to others? Had I, sceptical Faith, discreet scholar, proponent of calm decisions and creative silences, allowed myself to be seduced not by the man himself but by his aura of power and wealth and his genius-level instinct for people's weaknesses?

We are all snobs of some kind. I don't mean the caricature social snob that Mother was, but snobs trapped in our own sources of pride. Intellectual snobs are the curse of academic campuses – and dangerous too since their poison can blight tenuous opinions that would flourish in a more encouraging atmosphere. With Angus, I had met achievement snobs at the crest of their careers; in Brian Lapidus, I had found a less established version. Among my friends, I numbered health and fitness snobs, decor snobs who sniggered at lounge suites, and food snobs who wouldn't be caught dead without their spattered copy of Elizabeth David and bottle of balsamic vinegar.

It was my snobbery I was examining here, not Angus. I had to face the fact that I was a meeting-of-rare-minds snob who for fifteen years had thought she was engaged in a special friendship but in truth had been gulled by a charming scoundrel.

Who phoned me the next morning and barked, 'Can you make it to the Club by eleven-thirty? Tom and Leo will be here for lunch and we need to talk beforehand.'

'Won't I be in the way?'

'Of course not. Need you. Don't be late.'

The phone clicked off. I had been summoned and my work would have to be put aside yet again. I felt a niggle of rebellion; the lapdog digging her paws in. He was demanding more and more of my time – I forgot that I had offered it – and what was I getting in return? He hadn't even managed to conjure up an eligible man to replace him when he…

I pushed the treacherous thought away. I'd need to toughen up to face the truth of what Angus really was, and the terrible yawning pit he would leave when he went out of my life forever.

The Club was always quiet at mid-morning; the lounge and bars empty, the lift still, the grand staircase and stately passages deserted. I had to knock on Angus's door twice before he called in a sleepy voice from the bedroom, 'That you, Faith? Come through.'

He was lying against a small mountain of pillows in shirt and trousers and socks, his shoes paired on the Persian rug, his body slumped, the ebullient mood of the previous day gone. The wheelchair squatted at the foot of the bed, testimony to his growing debility.

'Hope I didn't wake you?' Knowing that I had.

His face was pale and grumpy with an unhealthy sheen and a ready lie on his lips. 'No, just resting. Quack's told me to take it easy when I can. Carries on like an old hen since that turn the other morning.'

The dining chair with the worn black leather seat was standing where Indigo had left it. I sat down saying, 'How are you?'

He groused, 'Everyone asks me the same questions. "How are you?" "Better today?" Or even worse, "How are we feeling?" I expected a more original opening gambit from you.'

He had these aggressive needling moods sometimes, when he launched sudden attacks giving you no time to marshal defences.

I sat back and folded my arms. 'Such as?'

'Oh, something buoyant and witty. Different, anyway. I get so bloody tired of being reminded I'm ill.'

'It's difficult to avoid the obvious.'

'Takes a hell of a lot of getting used to.'

'I'm sure it does.'

But my mollifying words were flung back at me. 'You're sure? Nobody could be as sure as I was, poor fool. Except for the night I spent in hospital after having my tonsils out when I was six, I've never had a moment's worry about my health. At my last check-up the specialist told me my cholesterol level and blood pressure were good for my age. Prostate and lungs fine, all organs functioning as required. Somewhat overweight, he said, but otherwise a clean bill of health. Now I'm told I have a fatal disease but if I'm a good boy and take my medicine and look after myself, there's a chance I could get better. A slim chance, but at least something to hang on to. God damn it, I can't stand being patronised!'

He lay glowering up at me, lower eyelids sagging, beads of sweat standing out on his forehead. He's in pain, I thought. Aren't they giving him enough medication? Yet I would only feed the anger with commiseration.

I resisted the impulse to reach for his hand and said instead, 'Having been a patron yourself for so long, it must be a bugger having to submit to being patronised. Lèse-majesté and all that.'

The glower intensified. 'Think you can make things better by throwing French words at me?'

'Would Zulu words be better? Arabic? Latin? I could go down to that absurdly baronial library and fish out some dictionaries and regale you with…'

'No need.' He turned his face towards the window. 'Sorry, old girl. I'm being the curmudgeon Indigo so dislikes. This business of being an invalid gets the better of me sometimes.'

'And you're in pain,' I slipped in.

He lay looking out at the Joburg cityscape of peeling tin roofs and new concrete and tall cranes swinging round the skeletons of the glass skyscrapers that have been replacing the old mining town buildings with unseemly haste. 'Must admit it seems a bit worse this morning.'

'Are you on sufficient medication?'

'Pills have been fine until now. Quack says there are stronger drops when…

198

if,' he corrected, 'if I need them. Plus something called a syringe driver. Goes in under the skin. Delivers a constant trickle of painkiller and a tranquilliser called Serenase.'

Angus's once florid and leisurely way of speaking had become staccato with increasing illness, as if he were intent on punching out what he wanted to say as fast as possible in the time left to him.

He surged on, 'The word reminds me of that science fiction film, *Soylent Green*. Remember? World overpopulated, starving masses, anarchy. Useless people, the old and the sick, cajoled into ending their lives in a death chamber. Had a raised bed surrounded by a film screen showing glorious scenery set to soaring music. Humane suicide, you thought. Wouldn't mind going out in a blur of Beethoven when my time comes... Until you saw the bodies being recycled into protein gunk to feed the masses.'

He was lying there adding horror to the horror he faced. With a foretaste of dread, I said, 'No, I don't remember. It sounds like something dreamed up by Orson Welles.'

'Wasn't him. Can't remember who. Back in the mists of time now. But it's a dire word, eh? Serenase. Essence of mother superior. Tranquillised to the eyeballs so I can't think straight any more.' His voice dropped to a mumble. 'Godawful prospect. I'm terrified of losing my mind at the end and turning into a witless hulk. Really afraid sometimes.'

His eyes were asking for reassurance, and I had none to give.

'Angus...' What could I say? He didn't need soothing fibs. 'Angus, I'll be here for you, I promise, if your family can't be.'

'They won't. Too far away. Too busy. The split-up was too final. Children don't forgive a parent who abandons or doesn't love them.'

'But your children know...'

'...that I'm concerned, but love?' His head moved about on the damp pillow as if it couldn't find a comfortable position. 'What's love? Not sure I know myself any more. There are too many damn variations. Too many fugues and laments.'

He wants to tell me about being gay, I thought, and felt a quickening of anxiety. What should one answer? 'I didn't realise'? 'That's nice. Some of my best friends are gay'? 'Bully for you'?

But he didn't. He demanded, 'Promise you won't pity me at the end? Look down at my mouldering remains and think, That was a man, once? Alas, poor bloody Yorick?'

One of the nursing sisters had warned me he would get morbid, and to coax him out of it if I could. I reined in my conjectures and said, 'I promise, no pitying looks. I shall be as stony-eyed as a basilisk.'

The attempt at black humour foundered in a pit of silence. Angus lay glaring up at me from the depths of his need; my friend, begging in vain for comfort. I had not yet learnt the art of good cheer at the bedside, though it would develop as his condition grew worse into a fragile hilarity always on the brink of tears.

His sudden crack of laughter was a fist punching through mica. 'Haven't heard that word in years! "Wyn byt soos 'n slang en spoeg soos 'n basilisk." Bible text that used to appear on the board outside the Jesus Saves Church when I was a kid. "Wine bites like a snake and spits like a basilisk."'

I grumbled, sour with released tension, 'About time something amused you. I wasn't expecting undiluted gloom this morning.'

'Good reasons for it. Hardly slept last night. Hated seeing my girl go. Flew into a rage with Benjamin on the way back. Drives me to drink, the way he wafts about the world. It's pathetic.'

'I find him interesting.'

'He was. Such a bright, keen little kid. Loved engines – what he called their beat and music. Had a travelling library that went everywhere with him in a school suitcase: books about cars, trains, aeroplanes, computers, robots. We had high hopes for him. He's got the brains for engineering but no bloody application whatso-ever.'

'Maybe that's part of his problem,' I ventured. 'He wants to do things his way, not yours.' I remembered Hannah telling me how determined her son was not to get trapped in the corporate world as his father had been, and Indigo saying, 'Benj and Da are fond of each other in principle but they argue incessantly.'

'Goes without saying.' He made an irritable gesture of dismissal. 'I was the same. Full of scorn for my parents' pinched little lives. Hell-bent on reaching the top of my profession, whatever it cost. Trouble is, Benj seems to be hell-bent on plumb-ing the depths. Have guitar, will travel. Gurus and ashrams and macrobiotic food. Today's kids take it for bloody granted that they can do their own thing regard-less. Ambition and zeal have become dirty words. It's such a damn waste.'

'Now you do sound like a curmudgeon.'

'Things on my mind.'

'What things?'

'In the small hours last night, I decided on no more chemotherapy. It's in the lap of the gods now. More chemo won't help. I have to be realistic. Don't want to prolong the agony.'

'But…'

'If this is the end game, I want to play it with finesse. And I'll need all the sup-port you can give me.' He paused, seeming to gather his breath, then said, 'Lying here waiting for you, I've been thinking about the meals we've had together over the years. Mere fractions of our lives but quality time, yes?'

Again I nodded, mesmerised. His need to justify our friendship, to give it provenance and substance, was much more flattering than a simple compliment. He valued me as I valued him. It had been a special friendship after all.

'So. There we have it.' The slack folds of skin under his chin slid about as he spoke. 'You may reach the pinnacle you've been aiming for but you can't rely on staying up there. Fate's a funny thing. Tricky as the Cape Town harbour mouth in a howling south-easter. The Lord giveth and He fucking taketh away.'

I grabbed for his hand then. 'Angus, you don't have to submit to cruel fate. You can keep fighting.'

'I'm too tired,' he said, and he looked it: livid, limp and drained. 'Life force ebbing away.'

'You've been overdoing things. You'll bounce back. You always do.' I heard the insistent, illogical denial in my voice but couldn't stop. 'Just try one more session of chemo. It could do the trick. Tumours sometimes disappear.'

'No. I'm done now. And I'll thank you not to keep harping on about the wonders of chemo. My decision is final.'

The carborundum look was a shadow of its former self but just as effective. This was a command that a friend could not ignore. After a moment I said, 'Agreed. I'll button my lip on the chemo if you'll tell me what you'd like me to harp on about instead.'

As if it had been bracing for a refusal, his hand relaxed in mine. 'To start with, a full report on Urquhart and Softley's reactions to my message. Don't trust those two. Snakes in the grass.'

There was no heat in his words. He's detaching, I thought.

But I was wrong. He went on with a sly upward glance, 'After which, we could discuss the quest for zero defect. You're a loose end I don't intend to leave untied. Specially not in that clanking heap of junk you call a car.'

The fact that I'd been cursing it the day before was none of his business. 'Don't start on my car again.'

'I bloody will. That thing is unsafe. How about a Honda Ballade? It'd suit your style. More than willing to provide a loan.'

'Now you're harping on the unacceptable,' I warned, removing my hand to stress the point. 'I've told you: no bribes for me.'

'As opposed to bribes for others?'

'I didn't mean to imply…'

'You did. And touché.' Astonished, I saw his eyes were watery. 'It's ironic. Only begin to treasure things when you're in danger of losing them … like the good opinion of friends and colleagues. I've been a remiss and selfish man. Reaping what I've sown now.'

'Rubbish,' I said. 'Bunkum. Tommyrot. Codswallop. Poppycock. Twaddle. Self-pity doesn't become you.'

The verbal parade earned me a wan smile. We had enjoyed tossing words at each other during our lunchtime conversations. 'You've left out claptrap, bosh and piffle.'

Laughter exploded. 'Piffle! I haven't heard that in years. Mother used to fire it at poor old Dad when she disagreed with something he said. "Piffle, Henry!" she'd bellow. "Absolute piffle!"'

'Woman of good sense, like her daughter. I've missed that laugh of yours in recent weeks.'

His eyes still looked shiny so I rattled on. 'She despised fools and had a thing about the exact word. I must have caught it from her.' It was years since I had remembered Mother with any pleasure. Are all daughters hard on their mothers, or is it just me? Being the only child of a proud, disappointed woman wasn't easy.

As if tuning into my thoughts, Angus muttered, 'Lot to be said for daughters.'

To keep the diversion going, I described my meetings with the two men the day before, embroidering on Jumbo's tartan office with its flame-throwing Loch Ness monster and the sight of Hugh agonising over his choice of silk ties.

Angus was looking more himself by the time I finished. 'Thanks, old girl. Appreciate your help there, knowing that it cost you a morning's work. Had to make sure those two knew the score.'

'Which is? I hope you're going to enlighten me.'

'Any reason why I should?'

Down as he was, he'd lost none of his mental acuity. My answer would have to strike the right note or I'd never get to the bottom of the Jumbo/Hugh connection.

I said, 'Background for my book, of course. I'm well into the research now with the help of two Wits Business School students. They're combing various libraries according to a schedule I've drawn up, starting with the Randlords.'

'Don't see that my private affairs have any bearing on your book.' He was truculent again. 'They're not for publication.'

'I wouldn't dream of trespassing on your private affairs. It's the mechanics of being a tycoon that I'm interested in … the ways in which dishonest businessmen enrich themselves. To quote your own words: All the schemes and fiddles.'

'I'm hardly a tycoon.'

'How would you characterise yourself, then?'

I thought I knew what he would say: something along the lines of, 'A success in my field but nowhere near the stature of the mining magnates.' But he surprised me, turning his head to look towards the gallery of photographs of his business triumphs and saying, 'A jumped-up harbour rat who made good.'

After a moment I said, 'Is that it?'

'What else do you want me to say? That's what I am. These trappings I've surrounded myself with,' he lifted his hand in a weary gesture, 'mean nothing now. Local boy makes good, but what for?'

His renewed anger was savage. I made a mental note to contact the oncologist and ask if he was treating Angus for depression. I didn't care if it was contrary to medical ethics. Hannah would back me.

I said, 'Bit late to come to that conclusion.'

'No fool like an ambitious fool.'

'Now you're talking piffle.'

'Depends on your perspective.' There were deep grooves between the black eyebrows that seemed to have grown wilder and wirier as he grew paler and sicker. 'Sorry now that I let you talk me into your book. Not sure it's a good idea.'

The about-turn was a shock. He had seemed amenable, even flattered when I first spoke of the book; I'd begun to think that he may have engineered it from the beginning. I said, 'There was no coercion, Angus. You agreed to talk to me and made your own conditions.'

'Big mistake. Shouldn't let people into your secrets.'

'Do you really mean that?'

He lifted his chin in the haughty way I had seen him use on minions, evading my question with another. 'What has all this beavering of yours uncovered?'

I took a deep breath and let it out slowly. 'Apart from what you've told me, nothing much. Your PR releases are corporate flimflam designed to obscure rather than illuminate. It amazes me that important people find it necessary to pay others to blow their trumpets so badly.'

'Balls to that. Saxe Brown are professionals. The best. Who said you could raid my office anyway?'

'I asked your permission, remember? And my problems weren't only with your PR files. I had a meeting with Rory St Clair Brown at his health club, and he...'

'Poncey faggot. Can't stand the bugger. Frank Saxe is all right, though.'

I thought, That doesn't sound like the sort of comment a gay man would make. Is he or isn't he? How can I ask? In my experience, gay people let you know their orientation to avoid awkward misunderstandings; but Angus had never dropped the slightest hint. On the other hand, he was of a generation whose gay men were forced to stay in the closet if they wanted to get ahead in the golf-playing, conspicuously wived and jut-jawed male domain of business.

The imminent lunch provided an excuse to change the subject again. I said, 'Since the idea of the book seems to be upsetting you this morning, let's talk about something else. Indigo says that Tom is a painter. Why didn't you ever tell me?'

His answer was a growling, 'Tom values his privacy as much as I value mine. More, in fact.'

'So I should stop poking my nose where it doesn't belong?' It was more challenge than question. He had summoned me to be present – insisted that I come – yet seemed annoyed by everything I said.

'Didn't say that. But you're confusing me, Faith. You've always been the soul of discretion. Never seemed to want to pry. That's why I've enjoyed our friendship. You made no demands.'

'Nor did you.'

He ignored my interjection and thundered on. 'Everybody else in my life has wanted something. Even Hannah, for all her tact. She wanted me to be a good father at a distance, and I tried. Didn't succeed, of course. Not with Benj, anyway.' His cheeks had flushed in angry red blotches. 'You never seemed to want anything besides lunch and a good argument. Until now. Now you're taking great bites out of my life in a feeding frenzy. There's blood in the water. I feel defenceless. I feel taken advantage of while I'm down. I feel betrayed.'

It was as though he had rammed his fist into my stomach. I gasped, 'But you've been encouraging me.'

'Weakness! False pride!'

With the shards of my new book falling round me, I stuttered, 'I – I – I never meant to pry. You seemed so keen to tell.' Then clamped my mouth shut or I would have sobbed aloud.

'Christ!' he shouted. 'There's nothing worse than emotional females. First Indigo last night, and now you. Even my bedroom's not sacrosanct any more. Even my…'

'Drop dead, Angus.' Rising in fury from the chair, I realised what I had said and sank back babbling, 'I didn't mean that. You know I didn't. Forgive me.'

He turned his head away. There was a long silence. I sat straining forward, hands clenched in sweaty remorse. His shoulders began to tremble. I thought, I've cursed a dying man. I am anathema, the lowest of the low.

Then I saw that he was laughing. He turned back, shaking with laughter. 'Only you,' he wheezed when he could catch his breath, 'only you, oh faithful friend, could tell a man on his last legs to drop dead.'

'I'm sorry. I'm so dreadfully sorry. It was unforgivable.' I didn't know where to look.

'It was bloody funny. And I was being a self-pitying fool. You were right about that.' He lay wiping his eyes and heaving with return bouts of laughter. 'Let's start this conversation again, right? You knock at the door, and I'll say, "That you, Faith? Come through." And we'll begin again.'

Avoiding his face, I mumbled, 'It's nearly time for lunch. I'd better go.'

'Oh no, you don't. You're joining us for a specific reason. Attendance is obligatory.'

'But I don't know them. I'll feel out of place.' Having violated the friendship I most valued, I couldn't wriggle out of the arrangement fast enough. I needed to go home and lick my wounds.

He reached for my hands, imprisoning them in a grip that had lost its plumpness and become almost as bony as mine. 'You've already met Leo.'

'Please let me go, Angus. I'm not in the mood for sparkling conversation. Please let me go,' I begged.

'Aikona. You owe me now, and I'm very much in the mood. Atmosphere cleared. Cobwebs swept away. I'll order a bottle of French bubbly for lunch to celebrate. Go next door and ring for Bonny while I make myself decent, won't you?'

'How can you do this, after what I've just said?' I felt a rising nausea.

'I have magic powers of revival.' His smile radiated self-mockery. 'We'll make two wrongs add up to a right. I'll banish the black dog that's been sitting on my shoulder if you'll stop apologising.'

'But...'

'And then you can escort me downstairs to the lounge to wait for Tom and Leo.'

'I'll come down with you, of course, but I can't stay.'

'You can and will. I'll tell you more about them while we wait. Right?'

'Right,' I sighed as he pushed my hands away and levered himself up on to one elbow. I felt as limp and drained as he had looked when I came in. With the colour back in his cheeks and orders booming once more from his lips, Angus was rising like a phoenix from his bed and preparing to take command again.

Perhaps he did have magic powers.

25

Angus's powers of recuperation were astonishing – aided, no doubt, by the painkillers. Ten minutes later he was buzzing along the passage in his wheelchair towards the lift, spruce and jaunty in a linen jacket I had not seen before, his face redolent of Old Spice and wreathed in a sardonic smile, his confused lapdog Faith trotting along beside him.

As with the previous mood swings, this one had caught me unprepared. Once I learnt to accept his rage and conflict and need to lash out as manifestations of his anger at dying rather than at me, I could handle them better. The person who helped me most to come to terms with his behaviour was the Hospice sister who paid him regular visits from this time on, Beverley Grant. She was kind, staunch and unflappable and worked with his oncologist to keep him as pain-free to the end as could be managed. She made the two of us laugh with her droll stories about her days as a theatre sister and the foul jokes surgeons told each other to keep themselves going through long operations. And she propped me up when I faltered in courage as he grew thinner and greyer.

But all that was still to come. The day of Tom and Leo's visit I was in turmoil, embarrassed by my faux pas, uncertain of Angus's intentions and not sure whether I would be able to continue with the projected book. All of which must account for the frankness of the conversation I would have with Leo, on a level of intimacy I'd never considered possible with a stranger. Reticence was a handicap we both suffered and strove to hide … which Angus, busy hauling at his loose ends in order to tie them together, was too preoccupied to notice.

As we descended from the third floor that morning, he was saying, 'Tom's my oldest friend. And the most battered by circumstances. I've helped him out many times. Felt bound to. I was luckier than he was. Richer, for one thing. Less scrupulous, for another.'

The lift creaked slowly downwards in its wrought-iron cage towards the entrance hall; a sealed capsule for two, ideal for revelations. I prompted, 'What do you mean, battered by circumstances?'

'He's had a hell of a life. Grew up poor. Lost his leg. Made a disastrous marriage. Then after it fell apart, ended up on trial for murder. Lottie was a neurotic wimp when he married her. He had no way of knowing she'd go off her head when he left. Silly cow drank the weedkiller he'd bought for the garden.'

The lift stopped with a jarring thump and I leaned forward to slide the concertina gate open. 'How can you be so unsympathetic? It must have been agony to realise her husband was gay. The ultimate rejection.'

'Gay. Gay?' Angus rolled the word round his mouth. 'Effete word, I always think. Most of the queers I know scorn it. Older generation, of course.'

'Queer is a horrible word.' I held the gate back so he could buzz out ahead of me.

'You prefer faggot? Homo? Poofter?' He looked up at me over his shoulder, broadcasting the words so they echoed round the entrance hall, causing startled looks and stumbles in a phalanx of sleek young executives headed for the dining room.

'Prefer isn't the word I'd choose in this context.'

'Don't be prim.' He shot a look at the upset he had caused and said in an even more carrying voice, 'Queers don't mind being called queer. It's what they call themselves. Far more exclusive club than this one. Membership strictly limited.'

Jaws were dropping as one of the stumblers recognised him and muttered to the others. I wondered how fast it would take the news to flash through Joburg boardrooms: King Quain's gay. But he couldn't be; he'd said, 'Most of the queers I know...' On the other hand, it wasn't necessarily an exclusive phrase.

I bent down and said close to his ear, 'Why are you doing this? You're shocking the up-and-comings.' It was the phrase he often used for young executives.

'Intended to. Think they're God's gift to the world at that age. And I've seen what havoc they cause in the lives of men who don't fit the mould. Done it myself. One of the many sins ambition generates.' He buzzed across the chequered marble towards the lounge, commanding me to follow with an imperious wave. 'We'll wait in here for Tom and Leo. Usually deserted by now in the stampede for lunch.'

He was right. It was empty except for the waiter removing used glasses and ashtrays from the side tables scattered among the armchairs. Smoking was permitted in the lounge although not, after an acrimonious fight between the Club's cigar smokers and its growing body of health and fitness devotees, in the dining room. The spectres of high cholesterol, ulcers, nervous breakdowns and other manifestations of corporate stress haunted the Club's upwardly mobile achievers as enlarged prostates, strokes, cirrhosed livers, general debility and domination by bossy wives threatened its older members. I had seen naked fear on the face of a recently retired managing director as his wife laid down the law that would govern their domestic future.

I was thinking of the tragedy that shadowed the wealth and power stalking the Club passages, when Angus swivelled round beside a group of armchairs and stopped. 'Here we are.'

'Will they know where to find us?'

'Always meet here for a drink. They're thirsty after the long drive.' Raising his voice, he called to the waiter, 'Harrison! Bring the makings for gin and tonic, will you please? Four glasses, plenty of ice.'

'Yes sir, Mr Quain.' The waiter was gone with a cheerful beam and a clinking of glasses.

'Damn good service in this club,' Angus said. 'Mostly Barkin's doing. He's good at staff training. And Bonny keeps them in order below stairs.'

I thought, That phrase again – below stairs. It must have fallen into disuse in England half a century ago, yet I've heard it twice during the past month. How is it that we continue to chug along the worst ruts of our colonial past – the rigid schooling, the social castes, the restrictive male uniform of suit and tie – while ignoring our manifest African assets?

Angus was saying, 'Tom's the most generous, hospitable fellow I've ever met. Bloody talented too. It was partly my fault that he lost his leg.'

I wrenched my thoughts back to the lounge. 'So you said. And Leo?'

'Poor little chap was only ten when his mother died. Found her screaming and frothing and called the ambulance, but too late. Tom was living with Brendan by then. Whole situation was damn tough for a kid but he took it on the chin. Left Cape Town with the two of them after the acquittal. I helped Tom buy a farm the other side of Nelspruit. Tremendous culture shock after the Cape, of course.'

I nodded. Capetonians think the boondocks start just north of the Hex River. 'How did Leo manage?'

'Mother's agonising death left its scars. Came to terms with his father and Brendan, though. Bright boy, did well at school. Went on to university to study law, then returned to a Nelspruit practice. Lives on his own now, visits the farm at weekends. Never seems to have met the right woman.'

It was only then that I realised what was going on. Angus was trying to set me up with Leo, tying two of his loose ends in a single knot.

'Oh no.' I started to get up, fishing in my pocket for my car keys. 'The quest for zero defect stops right here. I am not available for matchmaking to a man with appalling memories of his parents' marriage. This is beyond a joke.'

Angus made a grab for my hand. 'Just consider the idea. He's perfect for you. Clever, sensitive, good in an argument, kind. Reclusive too, I have to admit. But every bit as fine and generous a man as his father.'

'And scarred. What are you wishing on me? I refuse to be a panacea for anyone's wounds.' I sat on the edge of my seat, tethered by his grip. 'Let me go. I won't be dangled like bait.'

'You're scarred too, don't forget.' Compassion in his eyes, gravel in his voice. 'You're wary of men. For a long time I've known that you're using me – using our companionable lunches together – to avoid more significant friendships.'

I sank back, pulling my hand away. 'What utter rubbish. I have men friends.' It came out in a whisper.

'Nobody close. Be honest. You're stuck in a pleasant groove with a man old enough to be your father…'

'I am not!'

'…and who is about to leave you in the lurch. Can you blame me for trying to find a successor?'

I sat with a whirling head, unable to answer. Was I wary of men? Had my failed marriage to Kurt scarred me too? I'd never seen it that way. I'd seen myself as a self-reliant, independent woman with an interesting career and an enviable lifestyle. Yet Angus was implying that I was some kind of hermit crab who retreated from meaningful relationships, afraid to wave even a tentative claw in case the gesture was misinterpreted.

'Can you blame me?' he repeated. 'I've known Leo since he was a baby, and you for fifteen years. Your qualities are well matched. I guarantee you'd make a good partnership.'

I found my voice and croaked, 'But you can't organise people's lives like that.'

'Why not?' Eyebrows knotted, splotches of anger on his emergent cheekbones, knuckles whitening on the wheelchair's arm. 'Why the hell not? Business partnerships are arranged according to mutual need. Why not marriages, eh? Maybe they'd last better if we went into them using our brains as well as our hearts.'

'It's not so simple, Angus.'

'Balls. You and I have both suffered from ill-considered unions. We should be open to better ways of making a choice, dammit.'

He was working up to one of his truculent moods and I saw with relief that the waiter was advancing with a tray bearing gin, flasks of tonic water, a plate of thin lemon slices, a silver ice bucket and glasses. Perhaps I could slip away while Angus busied himself with a drink. I needed to consider this new persona I had been presented with: a neurotic wimp in the mould of poor suicidal Lottie, and who feared getting too close to a man in case he rejected her like Kurt had.

Angus disengaged his glare and looked up and said, 'Ah, Harrison. Put the tray on the table, will you? I'll pour for the madam.'

'You will not,' I said, shuffling forward in the chair. 'The madam is leaving.

No offence intended but I'd rather arrange my own liaisons.'

'The thing is, you never do, old girl. You just smile vaguely at any man who ventures towards you showing interest, and turn away.' He gave me an effulgent smile. 'Trust me. I have found you the ideal partner. All you have to do is show some enthusiasm and bat your eyelashes at him.'

'For God's sake,' I hissed, 'you're pushing this thing too far. I'm going. Thanks for the kind thought, but...'

'Quainers!'

It was too late. Booming from the doorway came a voice that could only belong to Tom Greyling, and standing behind him was the future that had been plotted for me: Leo, a tall serious awkward small-town lawyer.

Tom was a big man with an odd thrust of the right leg when he walked. His broad humorous face and burly arms had a deep farmer's tan that ended just inside his open khaki collar; a matching pallor where his forehead met thick grey hair showed the line of an absent hat. I had never met a man who looked less gay or painterly. The only physical hints of his profession were the traces of paint rimming his fingernails, and his watchful eyes that lingered on details – the blue shadow in the fold of a napkin, the slow curve at the neck of a wine bottle.

The lunch was, as always, delicious: grilled Cape salmon, new potatoes and spring vegetables followed by creamy trifle and a cheese board. When Tom turned down French champagne on the grounds that South African bubbly was good enough for a loyal farmer, Angus ordered a bottle of fine yeasty Pongracz for us and a weak whisky and soda for himself. After the initial pleasantries, Leo lapsed into silence and ate with an absent air. Unable to extricate myself from the situation, I savoured my food and listened to the shorthand of old friends exchanging man-talk.

Angus spoke of the forthcoming cricket season, a niggling problem with the Bentley's radiator, interest rates, the general state of business and an odd story he had heard in the pub one evening. 'Steve Worksop – remember him? – told us about a chap who can't shake off a ritual he started during his schooldays. Every night he takes a running jump at the bed with a full glass of water. Object: to land on his back without spilling a drop. The long-suffering wife has to be careful not to go to bed first.'

When they had stopped laughing, Tom talked farming and the price of diesoline and the drought in Mpumalanga. I learnt that the avocado crop was down and the bananas showing worrying signs of Panama disease, and when the conversation turned to politics as South African encounters inevitably do, that the newly elected provincial council was doing a good job.

'Much to the surprise of the white diehards who expected chaos when the blacks took over,' Tom said. 'There's no worse bigot than a white farmer intent on hanging on to land his forefathers grabbed a hundred years ago. But the mindset is changing, thank God. The younger generation is far more pragmatic and the potential for tourism is vast.'

'Sell many of your paintings to tourists?'

'Some. The Yanks want the Big Five, Brits go for elephants and steam trains, Germans like lowveld scenery and the Aussies seem to have a mystical affinity with warthogs. Maybe they're most comfortable with nature's oddities?' His guffaw made heads turn to appraise the noisy interloper in the murmuring dining room. 'Japanese visitors, on the other hand, like tribal portraits: bearded old chiefs and women in beads.'

'And the male nudes?'

Tom reached for another roll; he had done a healthy man's justice to the meal where Angus had only picked at it. 'City fodder. They've been a sellout at the Joburg and Cape Town exhibitions, and my agent in New York is screaming for more.'

'I see you have a new black model.'

'Gibson Twala, our best avocado sorter. Beautiful body, good bone structure, skin the colour of draught Guinness. I have to fight Brendan tooth and nail for his services.' Busy buttering his roll, he chuckled and added, 'As a sitter, of course. He's superb in repose. Face like the young Cassius Clay.'

Angus said, 'Occasional lewd thoughts, though?'

I saw Leo look down and fiddle with the stem of his wine glass.

'Not made of stone. But it's all in the mind, boet. Getting past the rough and tumble now.' Tom glanced at his son and changed the subject. 'Where's Benj? We expected him to be here today.'

'Coming later. He's down at the Market Theatre jamming – that the right word? Some new rock group that plays ethnic music. Seems to have hooked into his African roots again. Great relief. Thought we'd lost him to Buddha and the ashrams.'

'And what of your health, Angus, man? Tell me. Is it better or holding?'

'Just holding. End-game, maybe.'

Tom's big callused hand reached out. 'That's a bugger.'

'Had a good innings.'

'Better than most.'

'Knocked a few sixes in our time, eh?'

'Bloody sure.'

'Last ball shaved my stumps. Next one could finish me.'

This was getting morbid. I said, 'Time for coffee in the lounge, don't you think?'

Angus's head snapped up. 'You go through with Leo. Tom and I have things to discuss.'

Leo looked disconcerted. I started to object.

'Get along with you. Modicum of tact needed here, what?' Angus glared at me with tired scheming eyes. 'We'll join you in a while.'

He had me cornered. I said, not trying to hide the sarcasm, 'Your wish is my command, Quainers,' and got up motioning Leo to follow me, which he did with an unflattering reluctance. We helped ourselves to coffee and headed for two chairs in the corner, out of earshot of the lone members who sat with their port and newspapers. These club easies must have been chosen for their somnolent qualities, I thought, settling back into a brown leather embrace and preparing to sit out the next half hour until Angus came to the rescue.

Leo stood looking down at me, cup in hand, his lanky body exhibiting signs of mild panic at being trapped with a strange female. When he spoke, it was an abrupt, 'I could do with a zizz myself.'

A zizz. I laughed. 'Haven't heard that word since school.'

'It's the best time, after a big lunch.' He looked round the lounge with its dark panelling and heavy furniture and banked proteas in the fireplace, the winter fire having been snuffed out according to Club ritual on the first of September. 'But to my mind, a zizz belongs in deckchairs under a tree. Bees humming, coucals burbling, sprinklers chip-chipping on the lawn and a distant clatter of dishes being washed by someone else.'

He could be agreeable when he stopped being so serious. I said, 'Sit down, won't you? I feel uneasy with people who hover.'

'No more uneasy than I do at the moment.' He abandoned his cup and saucer on a nearby table and sat in the chair next to mine. 'Can't think why I helped myself to coffee, which I dislike. Far prefer rooibos tea.'

'The Club would never stoop to serving such a common beverage.'

His face cracked a slight smile. 'The accommodation and meals are good, though. Dad and I look forward to coming up to Joburg to be cosseted in city comfort.'

He was keeping up the conversation with visible effort. I returned the serve with, 'You're both members, then?'

'Yes. Angus arranged it years ago.'

'Angus the All-powerful.'

He sat looking at me as though trying to puzzle something out, then said, 'Do you get the impression that we were shooed away for a reason?'

'How perceptive of you.'

'Meaning?'

Now that he was leaning towards me, I saw that his tan did not end inside his collar as Tom's did. Leo had a most unlawyerly muscular brown leanness and complicated crow's feet round his eyes.

I said, 'Forgive the cynicism; it's not aimed at you. Meaning, Angus has set us up. He's got it into his head that we're loose ends in his life and he's trying to tie us neatly together. In a word, matchmake.'

'So that's it.' He looked amused.

'I begged him to desist but he won't listen. I've become a problem, you see. He thinks I'm dependent on his friendship, so he's been trying to arrange for someone younger to take his place when he goes. It's so damn arrogant, I could spit.'

'You don't see it as an act of thoughtful friendship?'

'Condescending patronage, rather. He invented excuses to parade me round the Joburg social circuit in the hopes that I would attract a more congenial husband than my first, but no luck so far.' The words were clattering out like hailstones on a tin roof. 'I'd have stopped it earlier if I'd been aware of his motives.' Liar.

Leo looked down at his hands. 'What happened to your husband, if I may ask?'

'He left years ago. To my great relief.'

'And now?'

I put down my empty cup and turned to Leo, anxious to emphasise how contented I was. 'I have a fulfilling career, a good lifestyle and my own resources, which include sensible investments. The last thing I need is Angus meddling in my affairs. He has this irresistible urge to control people, you know?'

'I know.' His sudden smile was confiding. 'He's been trying to organise my life since I was a kid. Wanted me to be an accountant. Said he'd pull strings to get me into whichever top firm I chose, and that I'd never regret it because most of the captains of industry are accountants and I'd be rich and successful like him one day.'

'Sounds familiar. So you chose law to get him off your back.' I found myself liking this man, as Angus had said I would.

'Him and my father and Brendan. All so concerned that I'd be marked for life by my mother's tragedy and wanting to make it up to me. It didn't occur to them that it was too late. Aren't all parents the same?' I watched the smile fade and his eyes fill with an old anger. 'They act out of pure selfishness and do exactly as they wish without considering the effect on their children, then spend years trying to exculpate themselves by being over-solicitous. It's a vicious circle, bound to repeat itself. I've sworn off having children. Too afraid of the damage I'd do them.'

I thought, He has scars that will never heal because they've been inflicted by a betrayal of trust. As mine were.

'You understand what I'm saying.' When I nodded, he said, 'The classic defence is to toughen up and build a shell. Takes time, though.'

The hermit crab image flashed into my mind. 'Time and persistence. I've managed to put my life together the way I like it. It's not perfect. I am lonely sometimes. But it's mine and I'm proud of it. This is what Angus can't understand. He's like all self-made men, so chuffed with their careers and achievements that they can't conceive of other people's quiet satisfactions.'

'That's it exactly. Now I know why you're a writer. You put things so well.' He leaned closer over the worn leather arm of his chair, his face intent. 'With me, it's wildlife photography. I spend all my free time in the bush with my cameras. The necessary precision of shutter speed and aperture please me in the same way as the practice of law. Pedantic and solitary, that's me.'

'Sounds like an accountant.'

We both laughed. I said, 'You must have inherited your father's genes if you're good at photography.'

'Maybe.' He shrugged. 'Though I prefer to think it's a combination of hard work and close observation. I'm beginning to win prizes and sell my portfolios to magazines now, so it's become more than a hobby.'

'Will you give up law?'

'Not until I can make a decent living with my photos. I like the things a good income can buy, much as I hate to admit it. Angus would say, "I told you so." Old fraud.'

I pounced. 'Why do you say that?'

'Because he's a lot softer than he cares to admit. Generous to a fault.'

'He says the same of your father.'

'Angus's generosity has far exceeded the normal bounds of friendship. He supported Dad all the way: stood up for him when nobody else would talk to him, paid for his defence by senior counsel during the trial, then helped him and Brendan buy the farm.'

'Angus says it's because Tom losing his leg was partly his fault.'

'It's more than that. He's loyal to the point of obsession where his family and friends are concerned. As soon as I qualified he asked me to draw up his will and handle his private affairs, which is why I've come up today. He wants to add some codicils.'

'Do you handle his financial affairs too?'

Leo looked surprised. 'Don't have the know-how. Dexter handles the financial side.'

'Dexter?'

'Schoombie, of course. From his Sunday family.'

It came like a thunderbolt out of a clear sky. Angus didn't only have me as his Saturday friend – he had a Sunday family too, called Schoombie. Another fragment of his mystery whereabouts revealed. Why had I never thought to question what he did or where he went on Sundays?

'Oh.' Leo was looking at me in consternation. 'You don't know about the Sunday family. Forgive me. Put my foot in it. I thought Angus confided in you.'

'So did I.'

The lounge was silent, its other occupants sleeping. I wondered how many more revelations there would be, aware at the same time that Angus was under no obligation to tell me anything about his private concerns. I had no rights over him; none but a friend's. What kind of conceit had made me imagine that I understood him – a man whose life was a labyrinth of secrets?

'I'm sorry. That was ham-fisted.' Leo looked wretched.

'The damage is done. Better tell me the rest.'

He shook his head. 'You know I'm bound to discretion as his attorney.'

'Lawyer's talk.' I could feel my lip curl. 'Too late anyway.'

'Please understand, Faith. It's not within my brief to disclose further details.' He was pleading now.

'Bull.' Rage at having been deceived was replacing my initial shock. 'We're not talking about an ordinary client here. We're talking about a man you've known all your life as an honorary uncle, and I know as a friend who has given me permission to write about his life and achievements.' Angus had mentioned my projected book over lunch with a deprecating remark about having made it into the tycoon class. 'If you don't explain the Sunday family, I'll make it my business to find out from someone else. Which could do Angus far more damage than your telling me.'

Leo sat hesitating, clearly unused to angry females making unorthodox demands. Was he as bush-happy and solitary as he'd suggested or did he have girlfriends? A game rangerette, perhaps, all sunglasses and short shorts and blonde hair tucked into khaki bush hat. Or would she be a bored young farmer's wife who slipped into town for lunch and a quickie with him at a motel? He'd be quite a catch in Nelspruit – or anywhere, I admitted. Presentable, well-educated, not bad looking, and nice. Angus had said I would like him and I did. Liking sympathetic men has always been easy for me; it's loving that I don't seem to be able to generate.

Thoughts of a dry brain in a dry season... I'd imagined I knew Angus quite well but the past few months had shown me how wrong I was. My life had turned into a poker game played against an expert in which I held cards that changed faces faster than I could calculate their worth: king to queen, queen to ace, jack to joker.

I burst out, 'What I want is a straight flush: just one good hand dealt off the top of the pack with no fancy tricks. Please tell me the rest. You know that it will go no further because I'm as much of a loner as you are, and just as loyal as Angus.'

He didn't reply at once but let his mouth curve upwards a little as he sat looking at me. Then he said, 'You play poker?'

'Sometimes, with a mathematician friend who does a running calculation of the odds.'

'Does he win more often?'

'No, she doesn't. I do. I'm a better psychologist.'

'Touché.' He sat back in his chair, crossing one long leg over the other. 'Which I suspect was the intention. People assume mathematicians to be male.'

'Lawyers too, though I'm told that more women than men are graduating from law school now.'

'So they are. My senior partners are in a froth at the moment over a choice they have to make between two candidates for articled clerk: a black woman with a *cum laude* degree and a judge's son with an exceptional gift for oratory but so-so marks.'

It was a diversionary tactic, typical of lawyers. I said, 'You won't shake me off that easily, Leo. I won the hand. Your penance for being the loser is to explain Angus's Sunday family.'

But my blandishments had gone too far and lost me the small advantage I'd gained. He shook his head and firmed his lips to a straight line again. 'No, I can't. You'll have to ask him yourself.'

'I will if you don't tell me.'

'I've said enough.' He would not be swayed, though I kept trying until there was a buzzing from the doorway and Angus came rolling towards us saying, 'Tom's gone to make a phone call. Have you two had an interesting talk?'

'Argumentative.' I got up, feeling for my car keys. 'I'm off home now. Thanks for the lunch.'

The anticipation on his face gave way to disappointment. 'You didn't even try.'

Keys in hand, I stood in front of him. 'I tried, but your plan of action didn't work. Leo is the most obdurate man I have ever met, barring yourself. He is impervious to women's wiles. And this particular woman has a bone to pick with you, which I will do when your friends have gone home.'

Leo unfolded himself from the armchair. 'I made a fool of myself, Angus. Told her more than I should have.' He looked so stricken that I felt sorry for him.

'About what?'

'Dexter.'

Angus fidgeted with the wheelchair controls, making the rubber wheels squeak backwards and forwards on the parquet. 'Bloody clumsy of you.'

I watched a deep blush redden Leo's neck and face under his tan. 'Sorry. Slipped out.'

Angus's eyes flicked up at me. 'And? Shocked by the revelation?'

'Betrayed, rather.' I wasn't going to make this easy for him. 'I don't know enough to be shocked. Leo wouldn't tell me any more. I shall expect a full disclosure.'

'What if I don't choose to tell? This book of yours,' he raised his hand off the

216

controls to make a shaky fist, 'this effing book has changed everything. Can't open my mouth these days without worrying what's going to end up in print.'

'But you've been egging me on.'

'Not to delve into my innermost secrets!' His glare would have blistered paint.

'I'm not delving, I'm researching. We agreed on the limits at the start of the book. You have a veto. You're the one who decides how much you want to reveal.' I felt a rising fury. 'The problem is, you keep changing the rules. One week you're ladling out confidences and dragging me round town as your social partner and off to your favourite...' seeing the way his eyes shifted to Leo, I changed the word to '...nightclub, and the next week you're telling me to back off. I don't know where I'm supposed to draw the line.'

He sat looking up at me for a long moment, then said in a voice that faltered in a way I had never heard before, 'Doubt is not your sole prerogative. I don't know whether I'm Arthur or bloody Martha any more.'

It was said in despair, and shut me up at once. I kept forgetting that this wasn't Angus Quain the managing director speaking, but a mortally ill man at the pinnacle of his career who was about to lose everything.

Contrite, I bent and covered the hand curled into a fist and said, 'You're Arthur, you're the king, and don't let anyone tell you otherwise.'

His eyes were wells of blue-black ink. 'Keep saying it, old girl.'

'I will. Just make sure you have a proper rest after you've finished your consultation with Leo.' I patted the fist and stood up again. 'Would you like me to come in tomorrow?'

'Please. Mid-morning would suit. And simmer down in the meantime, eh? Not as bad as it seems.'

'I'll work on the heat controls. Till tomorrow, then. Goodbye, Leo. I'm sorry we blew it. I enjoyed our talk.'

'Despite the revelation?'

He stood looking chastened and regretful. Our brief moments of mutual insight would be soured for him by his lapse of discretion. He'd be slower to confide in the next woman he met, perhaps spend the long drive home trying to understand what had gone wrong and working on strengthening his shell.

I said, 'Despite the revelation. Please say goodbye to Tom for me. I hope you have a pleasant journey home.'

'Thanks. My apologies again.'

'You weren't to know. There are too many secrets anyway. I just wish...'

The words congealed in my throat and I turned and hurried away. Mother taught me that men don't like tears.

26

*N*ext morning, Joburg wore veils of fine dust blown by an icy September wind howling across the highveld from the Malutis. Dust whirled off the bone-dry farms and the ochre mine dumps and the dun walls of the slimes dams, their hardened mud eroded into badlands; whirled up to boil in the air like clouds of poison gas and sheet against the tall buildings and sift down through cracks and holes and the rattling windows of shacks and houses. Joburg streets are choking misery when the dust winds blow; people cough and wheeze, noses clog, eyes smart, car engines stutter. Even the beggars who usher drivers into empty parking spaces and the artful dodgers who hang round traffic lights on busy street corners to snatch things through open car windows huddle dispirited in doorways.

My usual garage had FULL signs up. I parked in the underground municipal garage, hurried up the steps avoiding puddles of stale urine and plodded head down along gritty pavements towards the Club. When I pushed through the double set of doors gasping for clean air, Mr Barkin was standing just inside gazing out. He said, 'Foul day, Miss D.'

'Awful.'

I struggled out of my coat and would have shaken it out if he hadn't confiscated it to hand to the hall porter saying, 'Please see to Madam's coat, will you?'

'Very well, sir.' Holding it at arms' length, the hall porter stalked across the half acre of black and white marble and gave it to the menial polishing the brass plates of the library doors, with an air of banishing the unclean object from his domain as fast as possible. Misogyny filters down at the Club.

Mr Barkin rejoined his hands behind his back. 'Mr Quain has another visitor this morning.'

'Who?' We knew each other well enough by then for me to ask what would otherwise be considered an indelicate question. The members of the Club's man-

218

agement committee were very hot on the proprieties. When I'd queried some facts relating to my research, a quivering moustache had intimated that women allowed in on sufferance should not poke and pry.

'I don't know. A different face,' Mr Barkin said, leaving me to wonder as I creaked up in the lift what he meant by different. Female? Low-class? Non-corporate? Foreign? Angus had eclectic tastes.

When I tapped on the door of his suite and walked through to his call of 'Come in!' the different face looked up from the screen of a laptop computer on the desk. At first I thought it was Leo, only more tanned; then I realised the visitor was coloured.

South Africans at both ends of the spectrum are experts at sorting out the tanned from the coloured, though the skin may be the same shade. It is a matter of eye shape and slant, facial bone structure, tightness of hair curl, and of course accent. While assessments like this may be suppressed today in the light of our new rainbow nationhood, the reflex is still there.

Shamed by my automatic categorising, I said a falsely bright, 'Good morning, all.'

Angus looked up from his wheelchair next to the visitor. 'Thought it would be you.'

'I hope I'm not too early.'

'Prompt, as always.' He gave me a bland smile and said, 'This is Dexter Schoombie.'

Of course.

'Hullo.' I blundered forward and stuck out my hand. 'I'm Faith Dobermann, Angus's friend.'

'The famous writer? He often talks about you.' Dexter got up out of his seat to shake, saying, 'Pleased to meet you,' then hovered there looking uncertain as to whether he should sit in my company.

'Hardly famous.' Typical, was all I could think. Angus dropped my name to him but didn't bother to mention him to me.

'Sit, sit, both of you.' Angus waved an impatient hand. 'Would you mind ordering tea, old girl? We have business to complete. Ten minutes should do it. Then we can talk.'

I went across to the bell to ring for Boniface, subsided on to the sofa and picked up the new *Financial Mail* on the side table, needing something to hide behind while I considered this new facet of Angus's life.

Dexter Schoombie, Leo had said, from the Sunday family. Was he the grown-up version of the small boy sitting on the old woman's lap in the photograph in Angus's bedroom? If so, what was the relationship? Protégé? Nephew? Had Angus's poor white family been try-for-whites who had managed to slip across the racial border because they were paler than the rest, leaving darker brothers and sisters behind? Or could this man be a son conceived in his rackety youth on the Cape Town docks? Leo had also said of Angus, 'He's intensely loyal to his family and friends.' So loyal that he would support and later come to rely on an illegitimate child? Dexter looked about forty-five, which would make him the right age.

Boniface came and went and came back again bearing a tea tray with a platter of sandwiches cut in delicate triangles nestling in sliced lettuce – cucumber, anchovy paste, egg mayonnaise and gentleman's relish, judging by the colour of the fillings. The Club chefs made exquisite sandwiches, which are one of the few useful relics of the colonial era.

The two men were still hunched over the computer screen, muttering together. 'Shall I pour and bring your cups to you?' I offered.

'Help yourself. Won't be a minute,' Angus threw over his shoulder.

I poured and nibbled and flicked over the pages of the *Financial Mail*, not reading a word as I tried to puzzle things out. Dexter Schoombie handled Angus's financial affairs; therefore he was probably an accountant or a financial consultant. Where Brian Lapidus had looked trendy with his brush cut, round glasses and red braces, Dexter was Everyman in a hand-knitted pullover and grey flannels. His ears stuck out above a neck too small for its shirt collar. I thought, If I passed him on the street I wouldn't notice him. Is that why Angus uses him, not just because he's loyal but because he's circumspect and hugs the side creeks of the financial shark waters?

Talking of which, I had yet to return a call from Brian who had left a terse message on my answering machine saying, 'Please phone me ASAP.' What was it this time? I wondered. More information on Jem Lowing? The offer of a yacht at last? And if such an offer were made, would I refuse it with as high-minded distaste as I had refused Angus's attempts to help me buy a new car … or would I accept with alacrity and dump the book, emulating Mitch Kincaid?

'You look pensive. What's the problem?' Angus had buzzed across the room and come to rest in front of me.

'Oh, nothing interesting.' I dropped the magazine next to the tea tray, knocking over my empty cup.

'From your expression, I'd guess a dreamboat of some sort.'

He had these moments of acute, almost telepathic perception; he must have been born with extra antennae. But I didn't want him to know he'd hit a nerve. So I said in a teasing voice, 'Dreamboat! That's a word from the fifties. Shades of Doris Day and Dean Martin.'

The ruse worked. He looked up over his shoulder at the younger man who had come up behind him. 'Don't let her take you in. She was just born then.'

'You don't say?' When Dexter spoke, the Adam's apple in his thin neck jiggled up and down. 'I remember them, just. Ouma went every week to the Gem bioscope in Woodstock, sometimes twice if there were good fillums on, and she always took me with.'

Angus banged his hand on the arm of the wheelchair. 'The old Gem! Haunt of my youth. I was a Roy Rogers fan but your Ouma loved the glamour of the big Hollywood musicals. Dorothy Lamour and Esther Williams were her favourites.'

'Rock Hudson too. She was crazy about him.'

'As all the girls were then. Poppie...' Angus broke off and said, 'Sit down where I can see you without having to twist my head off. We need to explain who you are and the role you play in my life. Faith has appointed herself my official biographer, you see. If I don't come clean, she's liable to start digging around in the compost heap and uncovering maggots best hidden.'

Maggots, I thought, another hint at covert secrets. Angus was beginning to play me like a trout fisherman dangling illicit juicy bait.

Dexter sat down and turned towards me, hands side by side on his knees. 'If you're pouring, Miss, I take my tea strong and sweet.'

'Faith, please. Same as usual, Angus?'

He nodded. He had been drinking weak black tea with lemon and honey for some time now, claiming that it tasted better than with milk and sugar. But I knew it was because his stomach was beginning to reject certain foods – and he could slip whisky into his black tea when he thought no one was looking.

'Sandwiches?'

I handed plates and platter and napkins to each in turn, playing the social game that has made English tea such an abiding ceremony. Conversational cracks are gracefully papered over by the pouring of the hot aromatic liquid, the passing of food and sugar bowl, the clink of silver teaspoons and comments about the weather.

Angus opened the batting with, 'Bloody awful wind, eh? If this drought goes on much longer, the whole damn country will blow away.'

'The situation is bad in North West province,' Dexter offered. 'I was there only laaast week...' he dragged the word out Cape-style '...and they told me that half the boreholes have dried up. The windmills are pumping fresh air.'

'It's El Nino again,' I contributed, and watched Dexter as we went on exchanging banalities. He was a slight man with an air of contained humour and a quick smile, head cocked to one side, that soon faded. He turned full brown eyes alternately on us, looking at Angus with respect and me with apprehension. What was he expecting, I wondered, an inquisition?

Angus broached the subject by turning to me with an abrupt, 'So. You want to know about my Sunday family?'

'It would seem appropriate. Unexpected revelations have a way of festering.'

'Meant to tell you one day. Never seemed to find the occasion.' It was as close to an apology as Angus would get. 'This is off the record, though. Doesn't go into the book, right?'

'Agreed.'

The glare he gave me was less truculent than usual. He's getting weaker, I thought; relinquishing his privacy bit by bit as he never would have if he were still fit and well. I remembered my father before he died, lying paralysed by a stroke, watching with equanimity as his black nurse manoeuvred his poor shrunken old penis into the neck of the glass flask he peed into. Father who had been so modest that I had never seen him in his underpants – who had been a paternal racist like all his contemporaries, belittling the intelligence and capabilities of black women – relying in his last days on their kindness and expertise, his modesty evaporated by dependence. I dreaded the time when Angus would dwindle to that state, though I needn't have. Modern pain control is so precise that he was able to be alert and almost pain-free until he slipped into his final coma.

'The contentious book,' he muttered now. 'You're quite sure you want to go ahead with it?'

'Quite sure. I've planned the outline, my researchers are turning up some fascinating background material and the publishers are already pressing me for a completion date. I'm really grateful to you and the Club for the inspiration.'

'Think you can flatter me into compliance?'

I shrugged. 'Flattery wouldn't have made you agree to talk to me. I knew you'd be more attracted by the chance to impart your hard-won wisdom to a new generation of aspiring businessmen.'

'Poor buggers.' He spoke the words like small explosions. 'Don't know what they're in for. The South African corporate world is an egg-dance today. Unions shouting 'Capitalists!' and demanding scrutiny of the books. Shareholders yelling for profits. Government yelling for more jobs. Taxman bunging corks in all the old loopholes. Perks have gone to hell too.'

'It must be frightful hardship,' I murmured, and was rewarded by an appreciative upward twitch of Dexter's mobile eyebrows. If he's been handling Angus's financial affairs for a while, he knows all the loopholes, I thought. He'll be a good source of information. I'll have to earn his trust, though.

If Angus had heard my comment, he ignored it. He was saying, 'I often wonder what my life would have been like if I'd stayed on the docks. Worked for my maritime tickets. Made it to port captain, maybe.'

I couldn't help the acid laugh that erupted then. 'Yo-ho-ho and a bottle of rum. Not you, somehow, Angus.'

He was not amused. 'Cut it out, old girl. Trying to give you the background that relates to Dexter. First thing you've got to understand: there's no nepotism involved in our business relationship. He's a damn fine accountant. Careful and thorough. Adept at everything I require.'

Dexter acknowledged the compliment and Angus went on, 'That's the trouble with Benj, you see. I keep comparing him to Dexter. Find him not only wanting, but totally bloody deficient. Wafts about like a lost fart. Hannah brought him up to believe that Art is Life. Or was it Life is Art? I forget. Benj thinks questing for his inner self is more important than applying his nose to the grindstone. No commercial sense whatsoever.'

'It's easy to blame a divorced spouse, isn't it?' Angus seemed to be hitting all my exposed nerves that morning.

The look he gave me was thunderous. He disliked being interrupted when making *pronunciamentos.* 'Of course it's my fault too. Partly. Not trying to evade responsibility. Wasn't around enough to counteract her propaganda. Then I made the mistake of restructuring their trust funds. Wanted to make them independent, give them an income from the age of twenty-one. Didn't affect the girls. Sensible females, both of 'em. But it ruined Benj. His philosophy seems to be, If you can live on Dad, why work?'

I said, 'The classic dilemma of the wealthy: how to bestow a share of your fortune on your offspring without spoiling them. At least us peasants are spared that problem.' From the corner of my eye, I saw Dexter cover a smile with his hand.

Angus roared, 'I was a peasant too, you forget! I've worked bloody hard all my life. Studied. Sweated. Laboured without stinting. So why am I saddled with a layabout for a son?'

His chin had shot out Quain-style, sinews straining where there had once been jowls, a thick pulse beating in his neck. Alarmed, I thought, I mustn't work him up. This isn't my old bantering companion but a very sick man who bears a load of guilt about his son, among his other burdens.

I said in a gentler voice, 'Hang on, you can't judge kids like that. Some of them take longer to mature than others. Benj strikes me as a nice bright talented boy.'

'Boy is the right word. Mishmash of woolly ideas in his head and no application. He's twenty-four and can't stick to anything. First he tries art college. Then he gets carried off by hippies to India. Now, if you please, it's African music. For the past week he's been talking non-stop about the magical sound of mbiras. Not to mention wooden xylophones and paraffin tin guitars and pennywhistles. It's unconscionable.'

'But if that's where his talent lies...'

'If only he did show some talent, instead of sponging his life away. We've done a bad job there, his mother and I.' He banged the arm of his wheelchair with his free hand. 'Total failure.'

And King Quain wasn't used to failure. I said, 'Easy on. I thought we were discussing Dexter?'

'We are. That so-called boy is the reason why Dexter's here today. I want to protect the trust funds against squandering on outlandish causes. Not worried about the girls and Hannah, but Benjamin scares me shitless. Or should I say shiftless?'

If I didn't divert him, he'd be off for another ten minutes on the untrustworthiness of modern youth. I said, 'Let's get back to the Cape Town docks.'

Angus grumbled, 'Can't stand layabouts,' and lapsed into silence. Dexter looked up at the ceiling, then studied each of the paintings on the wall behind me. I sat perched on the sofa, afraid that Angus would try and wriggle out of the explanation he had promised.

To break the impasse, I reverted to hostess mode and reached for the teapot. 'More tea, anyone?'

'Nay, thanks all the same.' Dexter leant forward to put his empty cup and saucer on the tray.

Angus conceded, 'I'll have another cup. Oil the wheels, what?'

There was silence while I poured and he sipped and reflected. When he spoke again, his tone was calmer.

'Thing is, nobody knows who Dexter's father was. His mother was a packer at the ships' chandlers where Tom and I worked. Ravishing little flirt of sixteen or so: good body, fine legs, lively way about her. Tom and I were just out of school. Wanted to sow a few wild oats to prove that we were men at last. Took bets on who could get Poppie Schoombie into bed first. Sorry, Dexter.' He looked across at the man sitting very still in his chair. 'Faith will find out if I don't tell her. But I can vouch for her discretion.'

Dexter cleared his throat and said, 'It's okay, Oom. You just go ahead. It's okay.'

Oom. Yet another appellation for Angus – a title this time, the term of respect used by Afrikaans children for male adults.

'We took bets,' Angus repeated, 'and Tom won. He was the first. Had a lot to prove, as it turned out. Then I was given a chance. Two of us alternated after that.' He sent Dexter another apologetic look. 'She liked a good time: going out, parties, presents, nice clothes, attention. The Schoombie family was dirt poor, much poorer than ours. Lived in a District Six shack. Seven kids, drunk father, often no food on the table. Tom and I gave Poppie another kind of life to aspire to.'

I remembered a couplet my father had often quoted: 'Two men look out from their prison bars; one sees mud, the other sees stars.' Poppie had been the kind who saw stars.

'Soon we weren't the only ones. Then she told us she was pregnant. "I doesn't know who the faaather is," she said when we asked. "Maybe you. Maybe one of the other guys. But you started me off, so you got to help me, ja?"'

Angus had slipped into Dexter's Cape accent, and he did it so well that my doubts about his claim to come from a poor white family were dispelled. There were many areas in those pre-apartheid days where people of all races lived, united by their common poverty. He and Poppie and Tom were from the same stratum, ambitious kids kicking off the bottom as hard as they could to try and rise up in the world. He would understand Poppie's dilemma only too well.

'She wouldn't have an abortion. Tom and I paid her expenses. Gave what we could for child support. When Poppie left and didn't come back, Ouma Schoombie brought Dexter up. She was a widow by then, hardworking and tough as nails. Couldn't control Poppie but kept the other kids on a tight rein. Made sure they went to school and got proper training and good jobs. "No more Poppies in this family," she'd say, fixing the kids with a look that would have cut through steel. "You stay clean and decent, you hear?"'

'Shame, Ouma.' Dexter shook his head. 'She used to give us kids hell. She'd klap you across the face for the smallest thing: not saying please, picking your nose, too much rubbing out in your homework book.'

'Salt of the earth, Ouma Schoombie.' Angus was in full spate. 'Tom and I kept contact. Dexter was good at maths in school, so I arranged articles after his Matric. It was a long struggle because his schooling hadn't been too hot…'

'You can say that again. Sixty kids in the claaasses and half the teachers drunk by the afternoon session. But there were some real good ones too. Saints at the chalkface, nè?' Dexter hesitated, then said, 'Though we were lucky compared to some.'

Angus gave me an eloquent look that said: See what I mean about Benjamin's deficiencies? He went on, 'Dexter gained his CA in the end, as we expected. Works as a financial consultant to NGOs now.'

'And married with four kids of my own. We live in Yeoville so they can go to Sacred Heart.' Dexter spread his hands palm-up, clowning. 'Big advaaantages for the kids. Decent facilities, and the teachers all saints and no drunks, you know?'

I laughed in the edgy way white South Africans do now, trying to imply that of course we never supported the apartheid school system.

Dexter went on, 'Oom has established a whole lot of bursaries at Sacred Heart for township kids…'

'…which is also not for publication, right?' Angus cut in. 'They're in Dexter's name. He administers them and keeps an eye on the recipients.'

To make sure they're not slacking like that layabout Benjamin does, I thought, beginning to feel sorry for him. Being Angus's son can't ever have been easy. How much more convenient to be his possible son, for whom Angus could claim kudos without the drawback of feeling responsible for character defects.

'I've a standing invitation to Sunday lunch at Dexter's home to enjoy his wife's Malay cooking. So you see, it's nothing sinister,' Angus concluded. 'A bloody good meal and a bit of family life.'

And they all owe you, came the realisation. However pure his initial motives, Angus's code of just rewards for good performance meant that he ended up using the people he'd helped ... though he would have been appalled if this were pointed out to him. Glancing at the man sitting in the chair on my right, I thought, Angus may believe that he chose Dexter to handle his financial affairs because he's 'family' and therefore trustworthy, but the real reason is much more potent: a grateful man is a biddable man.

A minute later he was standing up saying, 'Is that all you need me for, Oom? I must be going now.'

'I hoped you'd stay for lunch.'

'Shame, I can't,' he said, 'but thanks all the same, eh? There's work to do on that comparative graph you asked for, and I'm flying to Durban for a meeting tomorrow.'

'But you will give my matter urgent attention as soon as you get back?' Angus fussed.

'Of course. Didn't I say I would?'

The slight asperity in Dexter's answer was the only hint he gave of the difficult path he trod as Angus's protégé. When I followed him to the desk where he went to pack his laptop into a black leather briefcase, he turned to me and shook hands again. 'Enjoyed the chat. I was glad to meet the famous writer at last.'

'And I to discover that the Sunday family isn't the threat I feared it was.'

'Not us,' he said, looking hard at me and dropping his voice. 'There's others, though.'

'Who?'

He shook his head. 'Can't say. Just watch out, you hear? Some of the maggots Oom's talking about are getting ready to hatch, and they not butterflies.'

He closed the briefcase locks with a double click and was gone before I could ask him what he meant.

I looked at Angus, pale and ill in his wheelchair, half his bulk gone, and thought, Maggots or not, you're still my friend. So who's perfect?

How extensive was Dexter's involvement in his financial affairs? I wondered as I braved the buffeting wind on the way back to the parking garage. The younger man could be a plain and simple guardian who kept an informed eye on his wealth and investments. More likely, he'd be adept at the stratagems of accountants retained by rich clients: the tucking away of foreign funds, *inter-vivos* trusts and other tax avoidance dodges. Angus was dabbling in far murkier waters with Jumbo and Hugh, however, and I couldn't decide whether Dexter was involved there or not.

He'd hinted at the maggots Angus had mentioned but gave no other clues, either then or later. His loyalty was impregnable. 'Nay, Faith,' was all he said when I phoned him the following week to ask for a list of Angus's donations. 'That's confidential.'

'I'm only asking about the good things he does,' I pleaded, 'like providing the bursaries at Sacred Heart. Not the other stuff.'

'What do you mean by that, eh?' His voice went up in alarm.

If he knows, he won't tell, I thought. The habit of gratitude is too ingrained.

'Nothing,' I said. '"For Angus is an honourable man. So are they all, all honourable men."'

'Come again?'

'It's a quote from Shakespeare.'

'Oh, him. For a moment I thought you were talking about Joburg guys.' Dexter was laughing as he put the phone down.

27

*W*hen I got home, there was a second message from Brian on my answering machine: 'I need to speak to you urgently. Please call as soon as you get in.'

I made myself some coffee, sat down at my desk and tipped my chair back before reaching for the phone. Teetering makes for more light-hearted conversation, and I needed cheering up after helping Boniface heave Angus out of his wheelchair and into bed when Dexter had gone. Angus's face had been as white as his beautiful cotton sheets and he'd fallen asleep within minutes.

'I think he needs a nurse again, Madam,' Boniface had whispered, and I'd stayed with him until one came.

The phone rang twice and Brian answered with a brisk, 'Lapidus.'

'It's me, Faith.'

'Ah. Hullo there. Been waiting for this call.'

'I've been out all morning, which is why I didn't phone back earlier.'

'No matter.' But I could hear his fingers drumming on his desk. 'Book going well?'

'In the immortal phrase, as well as can be expected. And your share-dumping?'

'Half done so far, though we're on tenterhooks about the remainder. I heard Jem Lowing's name mentioned twice this morning. If we can get rid of another quarter before the news breaks, we'll be okay. No profit but the bacon saved.'

He's quite different from the businessmen I've met through Angus, I thought. Less pomp. Is this the business school influence or his own style? I said, 'Not to mention the wine farm.'

A rasping laugh. 'The nubile wife is probably out of reach, though.'

I remembered my mother's voice saying, 'All men are the same. After a fat bank balance, their priorities are a willing blonde, preferably dumb, and a brace of sons. You score zero on every point, Faith.' And heard myself say in the same tone, 'No

228

great loss, if you ask me. Bimbos are boring.'

He clucked his tongue. 'That's a very judgmental attitude. Give me credit for some taste. In my book, nubile means good-looking and marriageable rather than bimbo.'

'Not from my perspective.'

'Which is?'

'Advancing middle age.'

'Forget it. You can't be a day over...' There was a teasing pause, then he said, '...thirty-nine?'

'You're wrong.'

'Not far. I'm an expert on women's ages.'

'You've had a lot of field experience, then?'

His reply was a terse monosyllable. 'Some.'

Indulging in conversational sword-play with a likeable man gave me no right to ask leading questions. I fortified myself with a slug of coffee and said, 'Sorry, that was out of line.'

'No need to apologise. It's a sore point at the moment because I've just been dumped. She said I was too intense.' His fingers were doing a fandango on the desk. 'Which brings me to the message on your answering machine. I have significant news, a request and a proposition. Which do you want first?'

I teetered, considering. Whatever the request and the proposition, my answers would depend on the significance of the news. 'The news, please.'

'Right. You know that your friend Quain has been sailing closer to the wind that he should have, in company with Urquhart and Softley?'

'No comment.'

'I'll take that as a yes. Also that this covert arrangement was so successful until its termination last week that certain noses were put out of joint. Belonging, I might add, to the people who donated the yachts to Mitch Kincaid. He caught them in a compromising position and they were forced to buy him off, which didn't improve their tempers.'

I said, 'You are talking in riddles. I don't think I want to hear any more.'

'You must because it affects your book.'

'I can't see how...'

He broke in, 'Just listen to me, now. This is important. The market is humming with rumours of a soon-to-be-published exposé relating to stock market and foreign exchange fraud, supposedly written by a journalist linked to Kincaid who is said to have supplied the information. To say that the yacht donors are annoyed is a gross understatement. They've got the hatchets out for Kincaid and they're also gunning for your patron and his partners. This affair is blowing up into a crisis which only you can avert.'

When I had got my breath back, I bleated, 'Why me?'

'You're the perpetrator of the offending book.'

'But my subject isn't fraud, it's…'

'Prominent Johannesburg businessmen, I know. The whole thing's been distorted in the way rumours often are. I phoned this morning to ask you or your publisher to release details of your book at once to quash the rumours, or there could be major trouble.'

'You're exaggerating.'

'No, I'm not.'

My typing chair gave an eldritch shriek as I crashed down on to my feet sending my coffee cup flying. 'It's a perfectly innocuous book that covers a period of Joburg history ending in the mid-eighties! Nothing to do with what's happening now.'

'Just so. And if you'd announce it as such, the whole rumpus will die down.'

'Hang on a sec.' I put the phone down and fetched a damp cloth from the kitchen to wipe off the coffee splashes sliding down the wall, clamping the receiver between shoulder and ear. 'Why should I? Most writers dislike talking about books in progress and I'm no exception. This furore you're describing has nothing to do with me.'

'On the contrary. You're at its epicentre, which makes you a target too.'

This was absurd. 'A target for what?'

'Preventative measures.'

'What do you mean?'

'Do I have to spell it out?' His impatience blazed down the phone line. 'If you endanger people's wealth, you threaten to negate their past efforts as well as their hopes for the future. Your book is perceived as a threat which certain individuals will go to great lengths to remove. Believe me.'

My first reaction was to tell him not to be so melodramatic. Then I remembered the warnings I'd been getting ever since I'd started researching the book.

Marge had said, 'Careful, Faith. You don't want to alienate the rich and powerful.'

Jem Lowing had said, 'Take care you don't get caught with your pants down.'

Brian himself had warned at our first meeting, 'Threatened executives can be dangerous. Be careful with your revelations. There's big money involved.'

Dexter had said less than an hour ago, 'Some of the maggots Oom's talking about are getting ready to hatch, and they not butterflies.'

Now Brian was talking of hatchets and gunning and my being a target. I seemed to have stumbled out of my staid scholarly rut into a battlefield. I heard myself moaning, 'Why is this happening to me?'

'Karma? Fate? Who can say? Just be grateful you're not Kincaid. He's cruising

230

somewhere off the Turkish coast and nobody has been able to make contact to warn him.'

'Are you suggesting that his life is in danger because he's suspected of tattling to me, despite the heavy bribe? Come on.'

'Let's not be melodramatic.' He was using the word on me now; we had similar thought processes, it seemed. 'This is Joburg, not Chicago. I'm simply telling you that you don't know the meaning of ruthless until you've been in business for a while. There's a timber merchant called Gerard Donnington-Black, for example, who'd sell his own mother for a profit.'

The line from Mitch's letter appeared in sizzling neon before my eyes: 'Look for the nigger in the woodpile.'

'Oh my God. He also warned me.'

'Who? Who warned you?' I told Brian about the letter and its cryptic injunction. When I'd finished he said, 'So you're convinced now? Will you do as I ask?'

'Under the particular circumstances...'

He burst out, 'Drop the academic bullshit, will you? Just do as I ask. For your friend Quain's sake, if not for Kincaid's.'

Chastened, I said, 'All right, then. I'll phone my publishers and ask them to put out an advance press release. Should I explain why?'

'Better not. Just tell them it's urgent and make sure the release goes out by mid-afternoon at the latest. I'll draw up a list of news editors who should be sent faxes marked URGENT – USE SOONEST. If they get the information well before deadline, it'll make the morning papers and the whole fuss could have died down by lunchtime tomorrow.'

'I can't believe this is happening.' My calm life had been thrown into confusion by a telephone call.

'You'd better. Money doesn't just talk, Faith. It bellows.'

Grasping for the saving grace of sarcasm, I said, 'How much danger am I in, would you say, on a scale of one to ten?'

His answer was precise and chilling. 'Under five, but only as long as the rumours involve a journalist. I don't think you need to hire bodyguards yet. Tomorrow might be another matter.'

'You're joking, right?'

'Don't take it for granted.'

I thought, I'm in the middle of a thriller which Angus would enjoy reading, though finding himself involved would be another matter. I said, 'What about Angus? He's in no state to be worried.'

'Quain is amply protected inside that bastion of the British Empire he lives in. You're the one who concerns me.' Brian's voice took on a different tone. 'Which brings me to the proposition.'

'Spit it out. Can't be worse than the news.'

The rasping laugh again. 'Depends on how you feel about unit trust managers with short tempers and even shorter red hair. I'm keen to see the new Chinese movie at the Rosebank Mall this evening. How about the six o'clock show followed by some Thai food at Cranks?'

The shock was absolute. Besides Angus, I had not been asked out by a lone man for several years. My first thought was, I wonder what he wants from me now? And my second, It'll have to be the academic/intellectual look for this one.

I said yes, of course. Divorcees don't look gift invitations in the mouth.

The awkwardness of a first date dissipated before our carafe of house wine was even half finished. We worked our way through a series of enjoyable arguments about foreign movies, the English used in subtitles and the hot green sauce of the shrimp curry, before moving on to the real subject of the evening.

I mopped up my remaining sauce with a piece of bread roll, burped behind my hand and said, 'Thanks, that was delicious. And just to reassure you, the press releases went out at two-thirty, duly marked URGENT. My publisher has been promised that the news will be published tomorrow.'

'I'm relieved.' His teeth were green-flecked. 'It's been a bad afternoon. Touch and go with Lowing's Impex shares until five to three, when our brokers managed to shift all but fifteen percent to an unsuspecting pension fund. Saved by the bell, we were. Everybody on the floor had heard the rumours by then except the fund's broker, who'd been at a long boozy lunch.'

'Serves him right. But what about the pensioners?'

'Won't suffer. Our Impex shares will be peanuts to that particular fund. The broker might get the chop, though.' He was starting to relax, his eyes amused and interested behind their round glasses. The sociable buzz in the restaurant seemed light years away from the *sturm und drang* of the stock market.

'Angus says it's the people who forget there are no free lunches who suffer from indigestion.' I pushed my empty plate away and reached for my wine. 'He's wrong, of course. I'll have to plunder the Rennies packet when I get home. I love curry but it doesn't like me very much.'

He reached into the pocket of the jacket hung over the back of his chair and proffered a white-wrapped lozenge. 'Have one on me.'

'You too?'

He nodded. 'Goes with the temperament. Explosive A-type personality, short on charm and no patience with fools.'

'I wouldn't call you short on charm.'

The fork he was tapping on the table clattered against his plate in mock surprise. 'May I take that as a compliment?'

It had slipped out easily, lubricated by the ambience and too much wine. I wasn't in the habit of paying compliments – my mother's talent for disapproval was hard to shake off – but it had felt good. I said, 'You may.'

'I'm flattered.'

'You should be. I don't dispense them at random.'

'Then I'm doubly flattered.'

I looked at him over the rim of my wine glass. 'When you've got over being flattered, perhaps you'd tell me more about the people who dish out yachts to nosy journalists? Howcome you know so much?'

Three fingers with chewed nails began drumming on the tablecloth. Was this his way of releasing coiled energy, or a sign of anxiety? Angus jiggled his watch chain when he grew impatient with someone.

Brian said, 'Self-preservation and good informants. In my business you have to keep your ear to the ground at all times. Millions may depend on a financial detail slipped to a trader who uses it against you. It's taken me ten years to build up a network of connections with access to the inside information I need, and I use it like a spider web. The slightest vibration and I move.'

'You make it sound very sinister.'

'Not at all. It's my control system: a necessary defence against being taken for a damaging ride. The sinister aspect is that large sums of money have their own dynamic, creating a vortex which sucks people in. It's hard to resist the allure of wealth.' The reflected flame of our table candle danced a duet on his lenses. 'I have to admit that I'm partly sucked in myself. Quain and Softley and Urquhart are even more so, though none of us is as far gone as Lowing and the guys who are threatening Kincaid. We're still gentlemen. Or at least think we are.'

'Angus says much the same.'

'You sound disapproving.'

'I am.' Even muzzy as I was with wine and exotic food and the pleasure of intelligent company, I could not still the needles of disquiet. 'I don't understand the mystique of the money god, and in particular why he is worshipped – it must be a he – to the exclusion of other desirable ends like happiness and health. Without these, what good is the wealth?'

He sat looking at me, head on one side like a quizzical parrot. 'I didn't know you were a moralist.'

It had happened again: he had used a word I'd applied to him in my mind during our meeting in his office. We had eerily similar thought processes.

I said, 'I'm not. I have my own set of obsessions which irritate my friends.'

'Such as?'

I brushed the question away. 'I wouldn't dream of boring you with my obsessions. The point I'm trying to make is, I don't understand how the acquisition of money becomes an end in itself. Surely it's what you intend to do with money that's important?'

'Of course it is. The prospect of a wine farm has been a potent spur to my efforts. But money feeds on itself, you know? I've been noticing ominous symptoms creeping on recently.'

I echoed his previous question. 'Such as?'

'It's a progression. The initial reason for heaping up money becomes less important as the heap grows. The higher it gets, the more it dominates your motives until the size of the heap becomes the goal. When it's high enough for you to relax a bit, you get nervous about tunnelling into it in case it collapses. You want to keep it heaped up and growing ever higher so people can see and appreciate your achievement.'

'You mean, so you can sit on it crowing to the wind?'

He shrugged. 'Something like that. You've got to admit it's a grand madness.'

I thought of Stanley Linklater and Angus, two rich dying men, both largely abandoned by their families and looked after by nurses and servants.

And said, not trying to hide the sarcasm, 'Madness is right. You can't take it with you, so who gets to enjoy it? Your kids, if you took enough time off to have any. And they have no incentive to keep the heap growing because they neither worked for it nor expended any energy piling it up. So they shout hallelujah for the old man's labours and dig their own tunnels, rejoicing in their good fortune. If the edifice collapses, why should they care? It's such wasted effort in the end.'

He said, 'Ouch. You sound angry. I thought we were speaking hypothetically?'

'It's hard not to get angry when I see someone I care for dying all alone on top of his heap.'

He gave a disbelieving snort. 'You could hardly call Angus Quain all alone. That man attracts disciples like bees to jam.'

'Almost alone. His family lives in England, except for a son he disdains. His business colleagues are wary of him. Apart from certain Club members, he seems to have few friends.' I thought, That I know about, anyway. I had a feeling that Angus was still holding things back from me; there'd been several other telephone numbers besides Tom's on the list of emergency contacts in Mr Barkin's office.

'Sounds about par for the course. Business nabobs at his level don't have time for mere friends.'

'He's made time for me all these years.'

'There are always exceptions. And I can understand why, in your case.' When I raised questioning eyebrows, he said, 'You're a great talker.'

'Thanks a lot.'

'I don't mean in the sense that you never stop talking. I mean that you throw out new ideas and enjoy looking at them from different angles. The noble art of debate.'

I said, repeating another of his previous questions with only a touch of mockery, 'May I take that as a compliment?'

'You may.' His knee began jiggling under the table as he picked up the thread again. 'What about Quain's partners?'

'They're trying to ease him out now that he's so ill. Without a hope of succeeding, of course.'

Angus had growled as I helped Boniface get him into bed that morning, 'My bloody partners aren't keen to have a sick man in a wheelchair cluttering up the office. Upsets the clients, they say. Never mind that it's my name at the front of the masthead.'

Brian said, 'You look so sad. Have you known him long?'

I clenched my hands under the table to keep my voice steady. 'Fifteen years. He's my best friend. And now he's dying.'

'Your best friend. That's quite a statement.'

'I mean it.' I looked at him across the small table, willing him to understand. 'I was very lonely after my divorce, with both my parents dead and no family. Angus and I began having lunch together at his club on Saturdays and it turned into a tradition. A good meal, a few glasses of wine, stimulating conversation, business gossip – you've no idea how the prospect can sustain you through a working week. I don't care what other people think about him, or what speculations they indulge in about our relationship. He's been a damn good friend to me. An anchor. It's hard to believe he won't be around much longer.'

For once Brian was sitting quite still. After a while he said, 'I hope I make a friend one day who says half as nice things about me.'

It was the reaction I needed; I'd had enough snide innuendo from Angus's business colleagues. 'I'm sure you will.'

'I'm not so sure.' He looked down at his freckled hands which had begun teasing at the remains of his roll. 'I don't make friends easily. I seem to turn women off because I bark at them and challenge their views. Can't help it. Not in my nature to sit smiling and nodding agreement. There's so little time, you know? One likes to feel that it's well used, not just frittered away.'

'Not wasted by inanities. I know what you mean.' He's very serious, I thought, then, Is it excessive ambition or just that he's never learnt how to relax?

He gave me a pinched smile. 'Sorry, that sounded much too solemn. I've had a bad patch the last few months, ever since my girlfriend told me she was leaving because I'd turned into a grim boring yuppie. She was right, of course.'

'Ah.' I'm a good listener as well as talker; had to be, with Angus.

'We'd been together four years and I'd cast her for the nubile wife, only hadn't

235

got around to telling her. It was a hell of a shock when she backed out. Takes time to re-adjust your sights.'

'Don't I know it.'

He fell silent, fracturing little bits of bread crust on his plate with his thumb-nail. I sipped the last of my wine and eavesdropped on the conversations at near-by tables.

'It'll absolutely blow your mind. Spangles all up the front, neckline down to *here*.'

'Six fucking tries and only two conversions. What's happened to his bloody kick-ing, man?'

'The movie was terrible.'

'I don't eat chillies or garlic or curry. What have you got that isn't hot or spicy?'

'This is a Thai restaurant, madam.'

'Haven't you ever seen a vibrator?' Giggle. 'There's a shop in Melville that's got amazing ones: eels, dolphins, rainbow shockers, you name it.'

'The beer's too warm.'

'I'm allergic to seafood. All I want is a T-bone, medium rare, fried onion rings and chips.'

'This is a Thai restaurant, sir.'

'There's this sale on, see? So I say to Mervyn, I reckon, "Merve, let's go and check out the sale. Maybe we can find a new lounge suite for the lounge, then we can put the old one in the family room and move the one in the family room out on to the patio." So what does he say? "No ways, doll. I need new seat covers for the Bee Em. Your lounge suite will have to wait." So I say, "Merve, excuse me my dar-ling, do you remember...?"'

'Let's get out of here.'

'It's a Wonderbra. Not bad, hey? The boss couldn't keep his eyes off them.'

'If you ask me, that last tracking shot was way off beam. Way off. Scorsese's camera work isn't what it used to be.'

'So Merve says to me...'

'Let's get out of here.' Brian was leaning across the table, tapping my arm. 'I need air.'

'Oh. Yes. Of course.'

He paid the bill and we threaded our way past the packed tables into the cool spring night and walked along the pavement towards Tyrwhitt Avenue. There were still a few hopeful vendors with their wares spread out in the square of light at the Mall entrance, and a dreadlocked Rasta selling *Homeless Talk*.

Brian said, 'Would you like coffee? There's a pavement place across the road if you think it's warm enough to sit outside. I don't feel like going home yet. Just...' He stopped and looked at me.

I stopped too. 'Just?'

'I got claustrophobic in there. Felt I'd been mawkish and embarrassing. Needed to get out. Do you understand?'

His face had the open, querying expression you see on young people when they've left the certainties of home and school and haven't yet decided which direction to take in life – when they still think they have a choice. It was as though he had stripped off the aggressive business mask he wore in the office to show me the hopeful boy beneath it who dreamed of a wine farm. The ex-girlfriend couldn't have seen him looking like this, or she'd never have called him a grim boring yuppie.

Flattered, yet conscious that these were middle-aged thoughts, I said, 'Of course I understand. And I'd love some coffee. I don't feel like going home yet either. It's too quiet sometimes.'

'Where do you live in Parktown?' We had met at the entrance to the Mall.

'One of those old houses along... '

It was after twelve when I went through the five-key ritual to get into my flat, and it didn't matter that it was too quiet. I had found a new friend in Brian, I thought. Not a replacement for Angus – nobody would ever replace Angus – but someone I could talk to and argue with and sometimes phone up to suggest that we see a movie and have supper afterwards. He was missing the girl who had jilted him, and working too hard as a consequence. I liked him and thought he liked me. It was a good basis for a friendship.

Only one thing bothered me. He hadn't responded to my questions about the people who dished out yachts to keep nosy journalists quiet. As the target of their rumours, I felt it was my right to know more. I'd have to think of a way to see Brian again soon and wheedle the information out of him ... or should I say, as a professional historian, conduct more in-depth research.

The answering machine showed that there had been two calls, but there were no messages. Only silence at the other end. There were two more during the night.

28

*T*he news reports next day generated a flood of phone calls from friends, academic colleagues and secretaries of Top Men who were keen to be in my book. I tried explaining that the selection of personalities had already been made and most of them were past history anyway, but the more persistent secretaries kept nagging.

'You're writing about Angus Quain, aren't you? And he's still alive. So why not...'

I would get a rundown on how amazing the boss was, how distinguished, how well qualified, how good at making profits for his shareholders. I was bombarded with faxes and CVs, press releases, company reports and glowing references from admiring peers, many of them reciprocated. ('You scratch my back, and I'll scratch yours.')

Among the calls were several more silent ones. When I phoned Brian and told him, his first reaction was a sharp, 'Have you reported them to the police?'

'No. Should I?'

'Not sure. Let me get some advice on this.' He rang off without saying goodbye, then called back ten minutes later. 'It's Brian. I've sorted the matter out. A private agency will monitor you and your calls for a few days. No need to contact the police. They're badly under-staffed anyway.'

'What does this mean?' The cold clutch at my heart again.

'Someone's trying to intimidate you. I don't think it's anything serious,' he went on quickly, 'just some silly bugger throwing his weight around. The news reports should soon put a stop to it.'

'Stop to what? Am I in danger?' Thinking, I'm writing a *book*, for God's sake, not an indictment. 'What's going on, Brian?'

'Listen.' His voice tense but calm. 'I told you the score. Rumour had it that you were writing an exposé. That's been officially denied but some of the ... objectors,' he hesitated before choosing the word, 'may not have got the message yet. Hence the silent calls. If they persist, the surveillance will establish the source.'

'Surveillance? Does that mean private detectives?' This was turning into a TV crime serial with hair-raising implications.

'Investigators, they call themselves. They'll be around for a few days but you probably won't notice them. And I assure you that there's no danger, Faith. These are just precautions.'

I felt a tickle of mirth starting under my rib-cage. 'This is ridiculous. I sit down in all innocence to write a book, and the next moment there are heavy breathers on the phone and private eyes dangling off the eaves.'

'Just precautions,' he said again.

The tickle grew and burst and I laughed and laughed until I heard an answering chuckle as he put the phone down. There were no more silent calls after that, though I noticed an unusual number of telephone cable repairmen working down the manholes in our street during the next few days.

The meetings with Tom and Leo and Dexter marked the beginning of Angus's final battle with cancer. His rally waned within days; soon he was too weak to sit in the wheelchair for more than a few hours at a time. Mr Barkin and Beverley Grant of Hospice arranged a roster of day and night nursing sisters skilled in pain control, and an aluminium medicine trolley stood next to the wheelchair at the foot of his bed, exuding hospital smells.

'God, I hate being an invalid!' he fumed from his throne of pillows against the carved mahogany headboard, surrounded by a radius of files, letters, reports, board papers, balance sheets, newspapers and business publications. Though he could no longer go into the office, he refused to relinquish his position as head of the firm he had founded. 'They'll have to wait until I'm completely non compos to prise my hand off the bloody tiller,' he roared, and Praise was sent to fetch Prunella every weekday morning to take dictation and transmit his orders for the day.

One sight of the Prune stepping grandly out of the Bentley and swaying up the Club steps in her power suit and black stilettos was enough for me. Thereafter I confined my bedside visits to the late afternoons and weekends. Angus was at his best when he had slept after lunch and could look forward to evening drinks with fellow members and business acquaintances who dropped by to see him according to a discreet schedule orchestrated by Mr Barkin, so there would never be more than two at once to tire him. He was eating mushy foods supplemented by Complan, glucose drips and lemon tea laced with honey, but he refused to give up his whisky.

'Only pleasure left,' he growled when Beverley tried to persuade him not to have a second double on the rocks one afternoon.

'You know that it's contra-indicated.' She was standing guard by the drinks tray Boniface had brought and set on a second trolley close to the bed where Angus could reach it.

'I don't give a stuff. More logical to hasten this fucking awful process. Wouldn't wish it on my worst enemy.' He sounded as jaundiced as he looked.

She said, 'Cancer is exacerbated – sometimes partly caused – by excessive alcohol consumption.'

'You can't win, can you?' He lay glaring up at her, furious at losing control to the women who were taking over his physical functions. 'Researchers insist that a few drinks a day are good for you. Relax tension, keep your arteries open, etcetera. Take them at their word, and you get told too much is bad for you.'

'It is. Unquestionably.'

'Bugger that. Habit of a lifetime.'

'I do understand, believe me, but…'

'Not stopping now. No point. Shut up and pour, will you?'

She did not persist though I noticed that she poured a bare tot. 'Here you are, then. Stop if it makes you nauseous.'

He took the drink from her, gulped it down with a defiant scowl and turned away, hunching his shoulder into the pillows and moving his head about until it was comfortable. His farewell mumble was muffled. 'Better than any bloody sleeping pill. Begone, dull hags.'

She pulled a commiserating face at me, picked up her medical sling bag and stood looking down at him with kind tired eyes that had seen too many people die before their time.

'I feel a failure when my patients get so angry,' she said as we left the room together after he had fallen asleep. 'The aim of Hospice is to help the dying go in dignity and peace, but it's hard to breach lifelong defences against the fear of death. People can put up a vicious fight for their prejudices. It's only when the bolshy ones like Mr Quain get so sick they can't fight any more that you're able to reach them.'

'I don't know how you keep going.' Her case load of dying patients was never less than fifteen.

'It's exhausting and there's no remission for good behaviour,' she admitted, 'but you can't imagine how rewarding this job is.'

We were walking down the passage to the lift and I noticed that the Club members who passed us gave her a wide berth, then turned to stare after her. 'Even when people go out of their way to avoid you?'

'It's the uniform. Men seem to…' She looked at me sideways, struggling not to smile. 'Men seem at the same time to fear and be attracted to uniformed women.

It must be a throw-back to the nanny and servant era: pert little frilly caps and aprons and stockings have undeniable allure. You'd be surprised how many deathbed propositions I get.'

'Propositions? You mean…?'

'The works. There's a certain sameness to them, though. The approach ranges from, "Please cuddle a dying man" to "Won't you take your bra off for me? I just want to look" to "My last wish is to spend the night with a special woman. Be a sport and climb in." They'll even do it with the wife and kids sobbing in the next room. I call it the Nightingale syndrome.'

Our laughter had the bite of grief in it. I went down in the lift with her to see if there was post for Angus, who had regular letters from Hannah and his daughters. Mr Barkin was behind the hall porter's desk riffling through the phone book with agitated fingers.

'Oh, Sister Grant!' he cried when he looked up and saw us leaving the lift. 'You're the answer to a prayer. Mr Doig has taken ill and I can't raise the Club doctor.'

Beverley's hand tightened on the strap of her medical bag. 'I could certainly check him and call emergency services if necessary. Where is he?'

'In his room on the third floor, not far from Mr Quain's suite. The manservant will take you up.' He disappeared into his office and came out with a tall, very thin black man in a white robe which, combined with a long sad face and the mass of grizzled hair standing out round his head, gave him the look of a Coptic saint. 'This is Abubaker.'

My curiosity reared up spreading its cobra hood: here was my chance to get a glimpse of the legendary White Spectre whose career I had followed up in the extensive *Star* files on mercenaries. 'Can I go too? For moral support,' I added when I saw Mr Barkin was about to refuse. 'Angus says the old man hates women. Beverley shouldn't have to face him on her own, let alone run the gauntlet of the elephant gun.'

His mouth went into a worried pucker. 'I can't give permission. You know that. Club rules.'

'And I won't let her go in there alone.' I had learnt a lot from Angus about the art of bullying underlings.

'But Abubaker…'

'…will be protecting us.'

Mr Barkin looked at the manservant who nodded and said, 'For sure, sir.'

I had a vision of a red-eyed old warrior slumped in his wheelchair with his gun swivelling towards us, and said, only half joking, 'Will we need bullet-proof vests?'

'Oh Madam, no, it's all right.' Abubaker stooped over me, his eyes glossy with tears. 'My bwana is too sick with a fever and the gun is put away.'

I thought, Hemingway could have written that line. …The gun is put away.

It is a good gun. The best. I found it smoking under Sam's body, twin barrels of hot blue steel. And his blood still pumping out of the terrible wound in his groin. The red blood soaking into the red soil of Africa...

Mr Barkin was saying, 'Very well, Miss D. You may go up. It's an emergency, after all. The management committee can't blame me.'

'I'm sure they won't.'

'You don't know them.' He was sweating seed pearls. 'Whatever goes wrong in the Club is my fault. If they find out I've told you about Mr Doig, let alone authorised you to visit his room, there could be severe repercussions. Severe repercussions. You will be discreet?'

'Discretion is my middle name, as you should know.'

I gave him what Angus calls my turd-eating smile and turned to follow Beverley towards the lift. The time-warp we walked into was the oddest event of the long weeks I spent in the Club while Angus was dying, and it had repercussions far surpassing Mr Barkin's fears.

Beverley was saying to Abubaker, 'Has your employer had a fever like this before?'

He had hurried after us on soundless leather sandals. 'With malaria, many times. After septic wounds, twice. With dengue fever and a broken arm that would not heal, once each.'

She pulled open the lift gate and motioned us in. 'You're very specific. Have you had medical training?'

'Two years, army medic. Twenty years with my bwana. Please help him, Sister. He is getting old now, like me.'

She pressed the Up button and the lift rose, complaining under our combined weight. Mr Barkin was a fretful pawn on the receding black-and-white marble floor, calling up after us, 'I'll keep trying for the doctor. It's rush hour, you know.'

Standing close to Abubaker, I saw a face scarred with tribal hatchings and desiccated by the age wrinkles of a desert man – Somali or Masai, judging by his height and thinness and long-boned grace. The name was Muslim. He smelled of spices I could not place until months later on a trip to the Middle East when I walked into a Dubai souk and was assailed by the memory of Abubaker that rose from the spices heaped in open sacks: cardamom, turmeric, cloves, star anise, cinnamon bark and the amber chunks of frankincense that are burned in fretted clay pots.

That afternoon as we groaned upwards in the lift, I stood wondering how long he had lived trapped in a white man's club so far south of his home. Were the tears from devotion or loneliness? The devotion must have been great, or the reward large, to have brought him to the alien building where he must have moved about like a shadow, because I had not seen him before.

Beverley said, 'Any other medical problems?'

He gave a sombre nod which sent tears coursing down his cheeks in dark trails. 'My bwana has the arthritis, although it is not so bad in his hands. I make for him a preparation of lion fat to rub on his hands – you know? – to keep the fingers moving easy for shooting. It is very good medicine taught to me by my father.'

I thought of Dr Mkhize's suggestion that I write about traditional healers. 'Where do you buy lion fat in Joburg?'

'Mai Mai,' he said, naming a street bazaar close to the M2 motorway. 'Though it is not the good quality, like in my country.'

'Where do you come from?' I asked in reflex politeness. Not expecting any more than an answering politeness; not expecting the elemental wail that widened his mouth to a gash of pain.

'Haaai, from nowhere,' he said, more tears slipping out. He lifted a loose white sleeve to wipe them away. 'Twenty years past, camel-drivers come to my village. They kill my wife and my children, everybody. They take our cows. They burn our huts. After one day, the bwana come with soldiers and find me lying for dead. He take me away out of that place. In the great emptiness of my heart, the bwana is my father now.'

The lift jerked to a stop and nobody moved. Beverley and I stood appalled by the revelation. 'In the great emptiness of my heart,' he had said, and I wanted to reach for the hand so near to mine and say I understood his sorrow. But how could I set my small urban sadnesses against the holocaust of his life? This is the great obstacle between black and white in Africa: our lives are so far apart, so unevenly and unjustly blessed and cursed, that there are boulders of shame and rage and agony between us which can be insurmountable.

Then he said, 'Oh, sorry. Please, my bwana is very sick,' and we hurried after him down the passage into unknown territory. Women visitors are not allowed to roam about the Club's upper floors. Until you're tried and trusted (a status that had taken me years to achieve), Boniface or one of his underlings escorts you to the door of the member you have come to see, and he is expected to see you out in person afterwards.

The door we came to did not bear a name as the other permanently occupied rooms did, but two words in harsh red capitals: KEEP OUT. Abubaker let us in with a key and an apology. 'Please not to worry what it says on the door, eh? My bwana, he think that people will come to steal his guns.'

We walked into a dim stuffy room with chinks of late afternoon light at the edges of drawn blinds, each reflected in differently angled metal gleams off the hundreds of guns mounted on the walls. Prepared for the sight of a few weapons, I was stunned by the scale of the armoury.

Beverley muttered, 'I don't believe it. A war museum in the Joburg Club?'

Par for the course, I thought. Yet another dark secret. 'Mr Barkin says they're mainly classic English hunting rifles. The old man was a mercenary and picked them up after battles or bought them from looters and pawnshops.'

'The spoils of war, then. How horrible.' She folded her arms as if to shield herself against them. 'Who was he?'

'Do you remember reading about the White Spectre? He was quite famous at one time.'

'I thought that was a Wilbur Smith character.'

'No, he was only too real. I did some checking in the *Star* library. Rex Doig, born in Yorkshire, shot for his school at Bisley, killed someone in a violent fight and was sent out to Kenya to cool his heels in the late thirties where he joined a safari company and…'

'My bwana is over here, please.' Abubaker's urgent whisper came from the far corner of the room.

We groped towards the oblong shape of a bed under a carapace of glinting arms. An old man lay on rumpled sheets fighting for each gurgling breath: fly-away white hair, staring eyes, bleached face oozing sweat, emaciated arms thrashing in the armholes of a soiled vest.

Beverley had a Pavlovian response to sick people: galvanised, she dumped her bag, turned on the bedside light and imprisoned one bony wrist. After checking his pulse against the watch pinned to her blouse and feeling his forehead, she said, 'You were right, Abubaker. It's very high. Over forty and climbing fast, I'd say. There's a danger of convulsions, so we'll have to get it down.'

She began to give orders: a bowl of lukewarm water, cloths or sponges, towels. As Abubaker moved about the room and the adjacent bathroom collecting them, I held the restless old man still while she pulled down the sheet over his naked backside and gave him an injection.

For half an hour we sponged him as he tried feebly to fight us off, mumbling curses. When he slept at last, his breathing less raucous, she repacked her bag and stood up saying to Abubaker, 'You'll need to keep a close eye on him until the doctor comes. The injection should be effective for a few hours but his temperature may start climbing again. You know what to do?'

'For sure, Sister. I use the wet cloths all night and all day but they do not work any more. That is why I go down to ask for help from Mr Barkin. My bwana, he will be very cross when he wake up because he never ask for help. Never.' His eyes were swimming in tears again. 'Not even from the Madam, his daughter.'

'Shall I ask Mr Barkin to phone her?'

'No, no, please, no. My bwana, he not like.'

Remembering the glum, fat Mrs Jem Lowing at the Snertons' dinner party, I could understand why.

'But will you be able to stay awake?' Beverley fussed. 'Perhaps we should phone for a night nurse.'

'No, no, please.' Abubaker's hands made frantic denying movements. 'There is no extra money, Sister. I will stay awake. Truly.'

Nothing venture. My cobra spread its opportunist hood and wove a fetching pattern as I suggested, 'Let me sit here for a while so Abubaker can get some sleep. I'm used to sitting with Angus, I'm not at all tired and there's no one waiting at home for me.'

'Are you sure?' Adept at making the best of difficult sick-bed situations, Beverley was more than ready to agree.

'No, no, please,' Abubaker said again. 'My bwana, he not like...' There was a pause while he tried to think how to put it with more finesse. '...he say no always.'

Particularly to women, I thought. 'If he sleeps for the next few hours and I leave before he wakes up, he needn't know I've been here.'

'No, no, no. No. No.'

The denials became less vehement as Abubaker began to realise he was up against two adamant women. I wondered if he came from a society which saw women as most of the Club members did, preferably decorative and quite worthy of affection if they behaved themselves and obeyed their lords and masters, but otherwise to be treated with caution as a different species.

It was a thought soon banished because during the course of that strange night I discovered in Abubaker the rarest of souls: a person who had suffered unimaginable hardship yet managed to retain a conviction that there is some good in everyone – even his blackhearted old employer. Abubaker, a Muslim, epitomised the Jewish belief that there are Just Men in every generation whom God has chosen to bear the suffering of their people. It was an irony compounded by the fact that the man who had been one of Africa's most violent and detested mercenaries lay in the sterterous sleep of a feverish child, secure in his city bed.

'You see, Madam,' Abubaker said, leaning towards me as we sat in two folding canvas camp chairs with the bedside light on the floor, dimmed with a wrapped towel. He appeared to want to talk rather than sleep. I thought of the great emptiness of his heart and hoped that my presence was alleviating a small fraction of it. 'My bwana, he chase people away. He sit with his gun and his face like the thunder storm, and people think he want to shoot them. But no. He is guarding his life's work. These guns,' he gestured round the glimmering walls, 'they are his children. Me too, he call his son. To me, he leave the guns when he die, so I can go back to my country and build a place to live my last days. His daughter she not need them, he say, because she got a rich husband.'

I remembered Brian telling me how the guns had been promised to the reluctant daughter, with Jem Lowing's enthusiastic approval. The old man was double-dealing his last cards like the villain he was.

'Do you know this husband?' Abubaker asked.

'I know of him.'

'He come here to talk to my bwana sometimes; a rough man under his smart suits, with clever small eyes like the elephant. He is very rich?'

Wondering how many Impex shares Lowing had been able to dispose of before Brian's spider web picked up what was happening, I said, 'I think so.'

'You see? My bwana say his daughter is all right, and so he can help me. This is not the way of a bad man.'

He was intent on preserving his benefactor's reputation and who was I to disabuse him? So I said, 'No, it doesn't seem so,' then, grabbing my chance, 'Do you look after the guns, Abubaker?'

'For sure. Each and every one, I know from the inside out because my bwana, he teach me to clean and oil them. These are the hunting guns of the English.'

Designed for grouse moors and genteel safaris with all the trimmings, I thought, not people-hunting in bloody African wars. A gun is a dealer of death at the whim of its owner; the master craftsmen who made these weapons with such pride had no control over their use. Half repelled, half intrigued, I said, 'Would you tell me about some of them?'

'That will be a good thing.' The hard grain of his face softened as he leaned towards me. 'I thank you for staying here tonight. You are very kind.'

'Not at all.' It was an embarrassed denial. I was there out of brazen curiosity, not kindness.

'Truly, I am thankful.' Then he sat back again and said, 'Do you shoot, Madam?'

'No.' Thinking, With the increase in hijackings, maybe I should learn.

'Then why you want to know about guns?'

'Because I'm a historian, a teller of stories about the past. I write books about the way people lived and the things they used in the old days. The Club management allows me to go up into the attics on Saturdays and look at the old things stored up there.'

'I have seen you.'

It gave me a small shock. I had never seen him. 'When?'

'Too many times. It is where I live, up there.'

I was being obtuse. The Club servants' rooms were on the fourth floor with the attics. How many other eyes watched me and Mr Barkin at our labours and poor Stanley Linklater shuffling to his demented finis?

I said in lame apology, 'Yes, of course.'

246

'Boniface, he say you are disturbing the spirits of dead men.'

I had suspected as much; it was an emotive issue for him. 'Boniface doesn't understand the importance of factual evidence in historical studies.'

'Ah,' was the quiet reply, and I realised how pompously academic I was being and blushed. How does one bridge the huge gaps of education and privilege? Sympathy is not enough; empathy is a feeble word for wanting to connect but not actually doing so.

In the ensuing silence, the laboured breathing from the bed recalled the steam tractors and puffing billies of my father's childhood; machines which had fascinated him as guns must have dominated the life of this sick old reprobate.

After a while Abubaker said, 'I do not think my bwana will like you to write about his guns. Maybe somebody will truly come to steal them.'

There was as much treasure trove for a historian in this room as in the attics, and besides, I never guarantee how my research material will be used. 'If I write about them, I won't say where they are. Would that be all right?'

'You make for me a promise.'

His eyes were onyx in the subdued light, polished with tears that kept threatening to spill over. I wondered if he often cried in the shadows of that grim armoury, bereft of everything but his menial job and the hope that he would outlive his benefactor. And said, 'I promise.'

'So.' He spread his hands with their pale palms upwards. 'What you want for to know, Madam?'

'Where did your bwana find the guns?'

'From all over: Biafra, Kenya, Ethiopia, Chad, Somalia, Zambia, the Congo, Angola…' He paused, then said with a quick glance at my face, 'You know they are for hunting the animals?'

I couldn't help saying, 'To start with.'

He shook his head in sad agreement. 'Haaai, is true. Many are stolen when the wars come. Bad people use them for bad things. They do not oil or use the pull-throughs after shooting and the guns rust, or maybe the ammo runs out. My bwana, he must save them, he say. They are too good for to rust and rot.'

I thought, He would have picked them up either to sell – knowing their value – or to equip his men with a greater range of weapons than the ubiquitous AK-47s.

'My bwana, he know straight if it is a good gun, even if the stock wood is rotten. See, I show you.'

Abubaker's tall skirted shadow flowed up the panoply of weapons as he reached for a double-barrelled rifle which he took down and laid with gentle ceremony in my lap. 'This one is for the elephant: the Holland & Holland .465. My bwana find it in a village, in the thatch of a burning hut. He pull it out quick, before the fire can catch it.'

As Abubaker lifted it back on to its metal cradle and reached for a second rifle, I had a vivid mental image of mercenaries storming a village with spitting weapons as women and children ran away screaming and huts blazed. Guns equalled violence and war and death. Yet ranged up the walls of this singular room, giving off the dull gleam of steel and the warmth of polished wood and the clean smell of gun oil, they were a paean to precision engineering: well-designed for their task and lethally beautiful. God help me, I felt their allure in my pacifist bones.

'Here,' Abubaker was saying as he proffered his second example, 'is the Cogswell & Harrison. See the engraving, Madam? The ducks, the pheasants ... all English birds, you know?'

'Scenes of the chase.' The mumble came from the bed where the old man lay. 'Traded in an old C-grade Purdy for that one. Damn good deal too.'

His eyes were gummed shut and I realised he didn't know I was there. I pulled away, gesturing at Abubaker: Should I go before he sees me? He signed back: No, but move to where he can't see you. I'll tell you when it's safe to slip out.

'You there, Abu?' A faltering hand reached for the black man's as I melted into the shadows.

'I am here, bwana.'

'Feeling bloody awful. Must have been that Irish stew. Mad sheep disease, maybe.' There was a weak cackle. 'Doig's Law. If a bullet doesn't get you, a fucking unknown virus will.'

'Try for to rest, bwana.'

'Bugger that. Hand over my Cogs.' Abubaker laid the gun he was still carrying down the length of the old man's skeletal body and stood watching him caress it as he crooned, 'Cogswell & Harrison side lock. Nairobi dealer. Came in a classic carriage case, leather with brass corners and green baize inside. Had a night bead too, before I took it off: warthog ivory, doesn't yellow with age like elephant ivory. Chap who bought a night sight like this and had it fitted could get into a herd of elephant in the dark and just pull the trigger. Wouldn't have to aim because his eyes would focus naturally with the swelling adjusted for his cheekbone. Game control fellows could get in there and fire away, Bang! Bang! – reload – Bang! Bang! And they'd all go down with a heart shot.'

'Bwana.' Abubaker kneeled at his side, hand on the ravaged forehead. 'You all right?'

'Cooler now. Bring water, Abu. Water.'

With a glance to check that I was well enough concealed, he padded to the bathroom for a tin mug of water and held it to the old man's lips after raising his head off the pillows. When he was lying back again, he mumbled on as though there had been no interruption. 'Couldn't make a fucking bean as a hunter in Kenya after the Mau Mau. Rich Americans went south: Tanganyika, Rhodesia, Bechuanaland. Had to sell my skills elsewhere. Bloody hot shot, I was. Bisley medal. Commendations from heads of state. "Mr Doig is awarded the Order of the Golden Hyena, Second Class, for killing all my enemies. The whole damn tribe.'"

Laughter gurgled like phlegm. 'Brenneke slugs in my shotguns, made of lead alloy. Fluted ridges at an angle, spin like rifle bullets even when you're using a smooth bore. You could take out two people with one shot, easy; slap through their rib cages. Better than swatting flies, man. Mowed the buggers down in droves.'

Another uneasy glance at me. 'Try to rest, bwana.'

But the old man went on muttering. 'It's all in the bullet. You want to kill someone and not be found out, you make your own damn cartridge. I hand-loaded some that looked like a Holland & Holland .275 but the calibre and weight were like nothing they ever put into use. Even the barrel on that rifle was engraved Holland & Holland .275. The fuckers were wonderful for thin-skinned game. Lion and buck. And men. I was a professional, and a bloody good one. Hell, Abu, when we took on those shrieking wogs in Eritrea...'

His hand moved up and down the gun by his side as the poisoned words dribbled out, his gnarled fingers rippling over its protuberances and stroking the worn wooden stock and exploring the arabesques engraved in the steel side pieces as though it were a woman.

And I realised at that moment something else about the Club ... about all clubs: that they are havens for people who believe they transcend the common herd with its bourgeois norms of marriage and family and steady employment and mundane living. Havens too for eccentrics and those with uncommon passions. This man loved guns and fighting; other Club members I had met loved with the same intensity golf, fishing, their cars, rugby, fine wines and their money. Monty Steyn wanted only to get drunk, sitting all day in the lounge slurping his cheap sherry and wreathed in smoke, shedding curses and ash when they made him get up and shuffle to meals where he sat alone and isolated because he smelled.

Angus had a broader range of interests that ran the gamut from low-class strippers to high finance, but he too behaved like a rogue elephant, a law unto himself.

As I slipped out the door of that eerie armoury while Abubaker created a diversion by moving the camp chairs about, I wondered how long my best friend had left to trumpet his delight at being alive, rich and – for the time being – independent of the herd.

It was he who taught me that though the mass oblivion of the elephant graveyard awaits us all, there are ways to make the journey towards it an exploration of interesting jungle byways rather than a drifting progress along the too-well-trampled path.

29

The Lowing scandal that broke the following week reverberated from Rotterdam to Singapore to Sydney to Rio. The main headline in my morning *Star* bellowed: *SA INDUSTRIALIST GOES BUNG WITH A BANG. Business Day's* more sober lead piece read:

> 'Johannesburg: – Impex shares were suspended on the JSE shortly after midday yesterday when chairman James Lowing was arrested at Lanseria Airport as he tried to board a private plane that had registered a flight plan for the Seychelles.
>
> Informed sources say that after the undisclosed disposal of all his shares in the failing company, he is alleged to have plundered its pension fund and diverted an estimated ninety million rands to overseas bank accounts via illegal channels. Details have not yet been released, though it is expected that the funds will be recovered.
>
> This is the second arrest of a chief executive in recent weeks for contraventions of exchange control regulations. Impex attorneys Ferreira de Waal have applied for bail. Shocked employees at the company head office confirmed that wages had not been paid since...'

I phoned Brian. 'Have you seen what they're saying about Jem Lowing in the papers?'

'Heard the news late yesterday. We made it by the skin of our teeth.' He was ebullient with relief.

'Do you know if anyone else has been implicated?'

He didn't answer straight away. As I opened my mouth to repeat the question, he said, 'Are you worried about your best friend?'

'Not particularly.' But it wasn't true and this man was also a friend now. I amended my answer to a bleak, 'Yes.'

'You needn't be. Word is that he and Lowing have been acrimonious rivals for years. The last thing they'd do would be to collude in something like this.'

'I know they loathe each other, but the prospect of mutual profit overrides personal animosity, Angus always says. He and Hugh…' I was on the verge of blabbing secrets and pulled myself up with a lame, 'One gets jumpy, you know?'

'He's ailing fast, I hear.'

'Not mentally. That's what makes it so heartbreaking.'

'I know how you feel. My mother died of cancer, fighting every inch of the way.' He paused again as if choosing his words with care, then said, 'There's nothing to worry about where Quain is concerned. That I'm aware of, at least.'

'Thanks.' I rang off before anything seriously indiscreet slipped out. My misgivings about Angus's activities must remain sub judice.

His reaction to Jem Lowing's misfortune was gleeful. 'So the bugger's finally overstepped the mark.'

There was an air of deliberate gaiety about him that Friday morning as he sat lording it among his pillows, resplendent in new paisley pyjamas. Prunella was on compassionate leave while she moved her father into a frail care facility, and he was enjoying both the freedom from office affairs – which had become increasingly burdensome though he would never have admitted it, for fear of losing his grip on the tiller – and the contemplation of his enemy's downfall.

'What do you mean, overstepped the mark?'

'He was too greedy. Others have managed it better. Me, for example. Used all the loopholes, and then some.' The wasted face had a glow of self-satisfaction.

'You're hardly lily-white when it comes to stock market and foreign exchange regulations.'

'I'm not a common crook either. Wouldn't sell my staff out, for one thing.'

'Or fiddle your tax?

He gave me a smug grin. 'Can't fault me there. Dexter's an expert on tax avoidance. Knows all the dodges.'

'Or smuggle valuables overseas?'

I'd hit a nerve there. His answer came in an irritable staccato. 'That's something else again. Had to secure the family's future. Bloody rand's behaving like a yo-yo. Got to hedge my bets.'

'You'd find some other excuse if you didn't have the family.'

'What do you mean?'

'If I've learnt anything from you, it's that people get away with what they dare.' There was an indignant rustle from the heap of papers around him. 'Daring

251

isn't everything. I've worked damn hard. Kept raising my sights. Conquered peaks whose foothills I wouldn't have aspired to as a young man.'

'Because you learnt to concentrate and target your efforts. It's classic business school strategy.' I'd been skimming through business publications as part of my research and was learning the jargon.

The black eyebrows knotted in one of his famous scowls, incongruous now on that sunken white face. 'Balls to business school strategies. Wouldn't know how to work any other way than flat out.'

'That's you, all right. Focused towards the vanishing point and going flat out all the way.'

'Not to the exclusion of the better things in life, you must agree.'

'Heaven forfend.'

His laugh was weaker now but as contagious as ever; I found myself smiling back.

He said, 'How's the book going? Feel like coming for a walk while you bring me up to date?'

Angus went for several 'walks' every day along the passages and through the lounges in his motorised wheelchair. 'Trawling for company,' he called it. 'Get sick and tired of looking at my wallpaper.' Though a remote-control TV had been installed next to the medicine trolley at the foot of his bed so he could watch the news and business programmes, he had a frustrating sense of being cut off from what was happening in the city he had come to think of as his domain. 'Nobody tells me a bloody thing any more,' he would grumble, demanding the latest rumours of his visitors. 'Give us a bit of spice and sizzle. I'm surrounded by bossy hags these days.'

In my role as attendant hag that morning, I helped the day nurse get him up and into his wheelchair in dressing gown and slippers with a rug over his knees. Then I walked beside him on a circuit of the third floor, explaining the progress on my book and wondering whether to broach the subject of Mitch Kincaid. Angus was in a jovial mood that morning and if I asked nicely, perhaps he'd expand on the ruthless men who paid people off with yachts. Had Jem Lowing been one of them? What were the maggots that Dexter had said were getting ready to hatch? Did they involve Hugh Softley and the be-tartaned Jumbo? And who could be making the silent phone calls?

The more I delved into Angus's life and career path, the more questions needed to be asked.

He interrupted me as we passed Rex Doig's door with its crudely-lettered KEEP OUT sign, saying, 'Lowing's arrest will leave the White Spectre's daughter high and dry. Hazardous business, marrying money. Never know when the stuff's going to evaporate.'

'He probably hasn't heard yet. He was very ill last night.'

Angus stopped the wheelchair and did one of his slow careful turns to look up at me. 'How do you know that?'

'I came up to his room with Beverley Grant.'

'Trollops!' he would have roared once. Now he said, muted to quizzical, 'Were you offering yourselves as living targets, pray? And why wasn't I told?'

'Haven't had a chance yet. After we left you, Mr Barkin spotted us going down in the lift and asked her to check on the old man because he had a fever and the doctor wasn't available. I volunteered to go with her.'

'Bit risky, wasn't it?'

'Not really. Abubaker was there.'

'Tall thin fellow in a white robe?' When I nodded, he said, 'Doig must be at death's door, then. Detests women. Not even the housemaids are allowed across the threshold. Room's only cleaned properly when they can get him out of it on a pretext.'

'I'm surprised the Club allows it.'

'No alternative. He's a long-standing member like that walking compost heap, Monty Steyn.'

'And therefore sacrosanct?'

'Untouchable is a better word. Both entitled to their pet idiosyncrasies. One of the good things about this Club: nobody interferes. It's why I've always felt comfortable here. Autonomy with privacy is a rare combination.'

His head was beginning to tremble with the strain of staying turned to look up at me, so I squatted down in front of the wheelchair, earning a grimace of thanks. 'You mean, anything goes as long as you pay your dues, keep yourself to yourself and don't rock the boat?'

'Club's philosophy in a nutshell. Useful credo for today's chaotic society.'

'Even if it means sheltering mass murderers like Doig?'

'Wouldn't go so far as to call him that. Cynical entrepreneur living off other people's wars, rather. Worked for gun-runners and warlords all over Central Africa, you know? Often flogged arms to both sides, then taught the jittery recruits to use them.'

'I'd call that being an accessory to mass murder.'

'I'd call it supplying a demand. How the world goes round. Wars are a major industry. You want to hear a chilling statistic? In 1985, a quarter of the world's nations were involved in wars. One quarter! That translates into big profits for arms manufacturers and vermin like Doig.'

'Your fellow member, vermin?'

He ignored the jibe, intent on developing his argument. 'Thing is, wars aren't big national productions any more. They're small, vicious and dirty. Everybody fires at everybody else – women and children too – until the ammo runs out. Then the battlefield ghouls move in, scoop up the arms and sell 'em on to the next megalomaniac who fancies a war. Poor bloody Africa. Basket case like me.'

'You're not…'

He cut in with an abrupt gesture that disallowed sympathy. 'Barkin swears there are hundreds of classic rifles in that room. Is it true?'

He needed distraction that morning, not arguments. I said, 'True's bob! You won't believe what a chilling sight it is: an armoury ranged up all four walls – even above the windows. All maintained in working order by Abubaker who cleans and oils them one by one under the old man's supervision.'

'Must be like painting the Golden Gate bridge.'

'It's a labour of love. He idolises his bwana, who he says rescued him from the scene of a massacre at his village where he lost his whole family.'

Angus muttered, 'Good God. Will the strife ever end?'

'Not until men stop idolising their weapons.' It came out tarter than I intended. Mindful of my resolve to be more understanding of male concerns, I qualified it with, 'Men like Rex Doig and the rabble who live by violence, I mean.'

He laughed. 'That was a neat side-step. Is it a sign of mellowing, old girl? Putting a bung in the verbal fire and brimstone?'

Was it? I hoped not. I'm too young to mellow yet, I thought, and said, 'Mellowing, hell. Don't expect kid gloves just because you're laid low.'

He sat looking at me for a long time then – so long that my knees began to ache from squatting and I stood up to rub them, wondering if the riposte had offended him.

'Rheumatism setting in too?' Illness hadn't diminished his flair for sneak attack.

The parry was obvious. 'You know that bending the knee has never been easy for me.'

'No, thank God.' His voice was so low that I had to strain to hear. 'You've always given as good as you got. Solid arguments. No pussyfooting. None of the sycophantic bullshit I get from others. Appreciate it, what?'

The eyes in the sombre white face had gone dark as quarry water; he looked haggard and, for the first time, old. 'I'm only sixty-four, dammit!' he had said a few months ago. Now he looked ten exhausted years older.

Before I could think of an answer, he went on, 'Been wanting to say that for a while. Never know when I'm going to lose it upstairs. Crab's spreading fast now, the quack says. Got into the bladder and spine. More pain than I can take.'

I bent to touch his hand. 'Shouldn't you ask for that…?'

'They're hooking up the syringe driver this afternoon.'

I thought, He's been waiting for the right moment to admit the retreat, and he chooses a public passage. Typical. Angus hated emotional gush, though in those last months he revelled in gossip which kept him in touch with the receding world. He went down fighting as hard as he had on the way up.

So I just squeezed his hand and stood up and said, 'Do you want to hear more about the White Spectre?'

'Can't wait.' He pushed the forward switch on the wheelchair and we proceeded with our circuit of the third floor passage. 'Give me the dirt. What were you doing in the old bastard's room last night?'

I thought of Abubaker's devoted service and remembered the argument about loyalty. 'Loyalty is using the same brand of marmalade all your life,' Angus had said. 'Loyal people are boring. They're the ones who stick around trying to be pillars of the community and volunteering for all the dull routine jobs no one else will do.' Yet he was the most loyal of friends and demanded loyalty in return.

And I said, 'Naked curiosity apart, I was watching an impending tragedy unfold.'

'Tragedy's not a word I'd associate with Doig.'

The wheelchair buzzed along beside me. Angus's face was so avid for diversion that I spun the story out.

'Not his tragedy, Abubaker's. He says that his bwana is going to leave him the guns when he dies, so he can return home and buy a place for his old age. I'm not quite sure where this nirvana is – Somalia or Northern Kenya, I think. But I hear the old man has promised the collection to his daughter as well, and Jem Lowing can't wait to get his hands on it. They must be worth a fortune now because they've been looked after and maintained by experts. If Lowing gets a jail sentence and the daughter's left without a penny, she'll need the proceeds to keep going. But what if the old man carries on living or bequeaths them to Abubaker? What then?'

'Ah. Stalemate.' Angus was intrigued.

'If women rate as low as you say in his scale of values, he may well choose Abubaker over his daughter.'

'As any true clubman would.'

I swung on him. 'How can you say that?'

'Got you.' The card-sharp's smile was back. 'I didn't say I concurred.'

Relieved to be back in argument mode, I conceded the point and we went on in silence for a while as the wheelchair buzzed past the lift cage on our second circuit of the passage. The weight was sliding down the shaft, indicating that the lift was on its way up. It must be Boniface, I thought, bringing up a tea tray or more pink gins. The Club passages were quiet at mid morning on weekdays. City noises did not penetrate the core of that sturdy old building and the only other indication of life was the whine of vacuum cleaners behind closed doors.

Angus was going on, 'Always told you I liked women. The daughters have a damn sight more spunk than our boy. Sterling women, like their mother. Benjamin is a total washout by comparison.'

'You hardly know him.'

'I know enough. Ambles through life with his guitar in one hand and a lotus flower in the other. Spouts esoteric ideas I don't begin to understand. Won't – or can't – work. What did I do to deserve such a bloody unsatisfactory son?' He was glaring again, and I wondered if the volatile moods were a result of the high doses of painkiller he was already receiving. Where I would have expected a dulling, he seemed sharper and angrier; pain and disappointment had given him an edge that drove him to question everything.

I said, 'Benjamin knows a lot about music and books and India. He seems – how can I put it? – more uncertain than confused. Maybe he just needs time to build up confidence in his own abilities. You can be quite overbearing, you know.'

'So it's my fault? That what you're saying?'

'Not at all. I'm suggesting that you go easy with him and learn to accept the fact that he's arty and has no inclination for business. Pin your hopes for a future managing director on Indigo.' I tried to soften it with a smile, but he got the message.

'Competence wins regardless of sex, you mean? With respect, that's bollocks, old girl. Business is still a man's world. Worse in England. Indigo hasn't a hope in hell of getting to the top in publishing.'

'Liz Calder did.'

'Who?'

'Never mind. We're getting off the point anyway, which is Benjamin. I think he's…'

As we rounded the corner, I heard the lift gates being slid open and two pairs of footsteps hurrying down the passage behind us. Halfway down the stretch ahead, I heard the White Spectre's door open and saw Abubaker peer out. I put my hand on the back of the wheelchair to slow it down and bent to say in Angus's ear, 'That's Abubaker. Stop when we get there so I can ask how the old man is, and you can get a squizz at the rifles on the walls.'

'We won't be sprayed with shot?' But I could see he was taken by the idea; he was pushing the forward switch to make the wheelchair speed up again.

For a moment I imagined that Abubaker had come out to watch our approach, but as we grew nearer I saw that the onyx eyes were looking past us to the sound of the footsteps, and that his face was filled with apprehension.

'What's wrong?' Angus and I had reached him first. 'Is the old man all right?'

The eyes dropped to me. 'Oh, Madam, trouble,' was all he could say before

256

the footsteps caught up with us and a large weeping woman in floral silk pushed past with a harried Mr Barkin in close pursuit. They collided in the doorway, shoving the unbraked wheelchair into the jamb and trapping Angus's slippered foot.

'Ow!'

His indignant cry was lost in the pandemonium that broke out in the White Spectre's blind-dimmed bedroom... The woman wailing as she tried to throw herself on the old man in the bed. Abubaker holding her back by one arm as he pleaded, 'No, Mrs Rita, please, no, he is very sick.' Mr Barkin making tentative grabs for the other arm, and a rising howl as the gibbering old man scrabbled to get away from her.

After I had tugged the wheelchair back to release Angus's foot, I wasn't sure what to do: comfort him or run to help Abubaker and Mr Barkin keep the hysterical woman from smothering her father. Mrs Lowing was twice his size, a vast pallid marshmallow in floral silk. She was howling, 'Please, Papa! Lend me some money for bail. Please.'

'Jesus wept,' Angus muttered, bending forward to massage his foot through the slipper.

'Are you all right? I ought to go in and help.'

'Go. Go.' He sat up flapping his hand. 'I'll survive.'

'Is it very sore?'

'A mere fleabite compared with what's gnawing at my guts. And don't take that as a play for sympathy,' he added. 'Get in there and help old Barkin while I have a look round. Not likely to get another opportunity.' He swivelled the wheelchair to face inwards; when he saw the glinting walls, I heard him breathe, 'Look at all those bloody marvellous guns. No wonder the daughter's come begging.'

'I told you there were hundreds.'

'And I thought you were exaggerating.'

'Moi?' But he was too absorbed in the sight to respond and I had to persist. 'How well do you know her?'

'Been introduced, that's all. Lowing's a bully. Poor woman's never allowed to open her mouth in company. Lucky there are no kids.' He turned to look at the display on the left wall and by the rapt expression I knew I had lost him to a *Boy's Own* dream. F C Selous on safari, perhaps: 'Bearer! Bring me my Jeffery 8-bore. There's a wounded lion in that thicket. Must get him first shot or we'll all be in deadly peril of mauling...'

So I abandoned him and joined the fray but it didn't help much. Rita Lowing was strong as well as heavy, and she was determined. She reached out for her bewildered father, who hunched further and further into the corner behind his bed as a spider does folding itself into a cranny. The long white floating hair gave him a crazy look. He was panting in hoarse shallow bursts between whimpers.

Up close, her small pink mouth was stretched to its limit as she wailed, over and over, 'Money for bail! Jem needs bail and I want the Purdys!'

Abubaker struggled to hang on to one massive arm pleading, 'No, no, Madam, no.'

Mr Barkin pawed at the other. 'It's not allowed. Please, Mrs Lowing. Members don't like a disturbance. It's not allowed.'

I put my arms round her slippery middle, planted my feet on the floor, leaned back and struggled to hold her off the old man, whose eyes were beginning to roll back in terror. It looked as though the White Spectre, Mr Barkin's celebrity in hiding, was in imminent danger of joining his many victims.

As people gathered in the doorway behind Angus – curious residents, Boniface, the hall porter, cleaning maids, members of the kitchen staff, security guards and finally two policewomen who managed to subdue Rita Lowing before leading her away sobbing – I was thinking, When there's trouble, you need the boring pillars of the community. They're what keep the roof from falling in.

The incident had turned into low farce for which Mr Barkin – as usual – shouldered the blame. At a meeting of the Club's Infringements Committee, held round Angus's bed since he was the current chairman (and reported to me later), Mr Barkin was censured and given a stern warning. Though not fired; the Club would have had to be far more embarrassed to discharge such a useful and biddable employee.

It was held that Mrs Lowing shouldn't have been allowed into the lift.

'She just pushed past me,' Mr Barkin said, kneading his hands.

'You should have resisted her.'

'I tried. She wouldn't stop. Honestly, she's like a steamroller.'

Laughter. 'Rueful, of course,' Angus told me. 'Small men might be terrors in the boardroom but most of them are afraid of large women.'

It was suggested that Club rules should be tightened up and women visitors excluded from the upper floors. 'Over my dead body,' Angus growled. The motion was dropped.

But the disturbance on the third floor didn't end there. Rex Doig died of pneumonia several days later. He had left everything he possessed to Abubaker, who at once gave the matched Purdys, the Holland & Holland elephant gun and a rare pair of Henry Atkins to Rita so that she could sell them and bail out her husband. Angus arranged for a well-known Cape gunsmith to fly up and value the rest of the armoury while Abubaker began to pack the old man's possessions and make plans to return to his homeland.

Not quickly enough. An hour after his release on bail, Jem Lowing arrived at the Club with his wife and a lawyer's demand that she be granted the right to search her father's room, 'For items of sentimental value.'

Mr Barkin felt he could not deny such a reasonable request. He escorted them up to the room where Abubaker was packing, showed them in and left, mistaking the rage in Jem Lowing's eyes for angry shame at having been arrested and jailed. There was no way Mr Barkin could have known that he had concealed a box of .404 slugs in his pocket, given him for safekeeping by Abubaker when the old man's mind had started to wander.

As the lift gate began to close behind him, Mr Barkin heard a thunderous shot. Transfixed, he did not think fast enough to get his shoe into the gap and seconds passed before he could wrestle the gate open again and yell down the open lift well to the hall porter, 'Emergency! Call the police!' As he began running down the passage towards the room he had just left, there were two more shots.

Old Barkin, the meek club servant, received a commendation for bravery from the police for his next action. Finding Rex Doig's door locked from the inside, he broke the glass in front of a nearby fire extinguisher, wrenched it off its mounting and smashed it through one of the teak panels.

He told Angus and me later in the day, still in trembling shock, 'That terrible man had blown off the back of Abubaker's head and shot his wife twice in the chest. It was slaughter. You wouldn't have recognised them. So much blood. All over the floor. All over the walls. All over the guns. Blood. Bits of flesh. Shattered bone. Abubaker's legs were still moving.'

He began to shudder so badly that he couldn't speak for several minutes. His pupils were pinpoints of horror, his eye sockets cavernous.

Angus soothed, 'It's all right, old man. You don't have to talk about it.'

'I must. Get it out of my mind, or it'll stick there like the bits of bloody flesh everywhere. And rot.' He clamped one shaking hand with the other. 'Lowing was sitting in one of the camp chairs with a shotgun butt resting on the floor and the barrels against his chin and one foot bare. As I leaned through to try and turn the key and unlock the door, he shouted, "Get away! I'm not going to jail! It's my fucking money they've taken! I made it! It's mine! Bugger the shareholders! Bugger the lot of you!" His spit was frothing like a rabid dog's. Then...'

Mr Barkin gulped and stopped again. Angus and I, for once, sat speechless.

'...then he closed his mouth over the barrel and jammed his big toe down. Bam! Blew his head off. Blood spraying everywhere. Closed my eyes. Felt it settling on my face like flies. Had to feel for the key to turn it. Got the door open.' Another long shuddering pause. 'When I opened my eyes again, his body had begun to topple out of the chair like a tree falling in slow motion. Wiped my face with my hand. Slimy stuff all over it. Blood. Brains. Little fragments of bone gritting together. That's what did it. Why I vomited. Not so much the slime as the gritting. Last straw. Still feel the vomit rise when I think of it.'

It was half an hour before he would stop talking and allow us to call Boniface to help him to bed.

All the elements for sellout newspaper editions were there: well-known businessman, fraud, scandal, murder and suicide in a toffee-nosed exclusive club. The Infringements Committee met in urgent conclave to lament the adverse publicity, but under the circumstances decided against censure this time in the light of the commendation for bravery. Though Old Barkin, they agreed, had only acted as they would have expected him to. He was well paid for it.

Lowing's actions, of course, were unspeakable. But they took comfort in the fact that he had been expelled from the Club well before the unpleasantness, which showed perspicacity and foresight.

Monty Steyn was the only one to voice the real fear in members' minds. In a fuddled voice he predicted from his corner of the lounge, 'Bloody *Sunday Times* is going to make a meal of us.'

30

*T*he sale of the White Spectre's effects took place a month later. By then the notorious rifle collection had been so well documented by news reports that it fetched four times the estimated value, despite the absence of its star items: the matched Purdys, the Holland & Holland elephant gun and the rare pair of Henry Atkins so generously given to Rita to raise Jem Lowing's bail.

Though attempts were made to trace Abubaker's relatives, nobody knew where he came from and none were found. No Doigs with a direct family connection were traced either, and the Lowings had died childless.

After a suitable interval the Johannesburg Club applied to be granted the proceeds of the sale, giving as a main reason the cost of renovating the devastated room. There was also the likelihood, it was pointed out, that in the absence of heirs, he would have left his effects to the Club as so many of its solitary members did. The judge who was to decide on the matter was taken up to the Club attics and shown the rooms full of dusty trunks and suitcases and abandoned personal possessions; with a sense of vindication, I supplied a long and detailed list of the contents I had annotated.

The judge ruled in favour of the Club and the Doig bequest was used – in a fitting irony – to upgrade and expand the security system to cope with the increasing lawlessness in the surrounding streets. To enter the hallowed portals, it has now become necessary to run a gauntlet of armed security guards, card slots and identity checkpoints that would do credit to Pretoria Central Prison, and has the older members muttering about what the world is coming to. Such is progress.

I have to say that for all its Gothic horror, the Lowing disaster perked Angus up for days, aided by the relief from pain and anxiety after Beverley Grant installed the syringe driver. He began to hold court in his living room again, seated in his favourite armchair and dressed in comfortable slacks and a sweater over an open-necked shirt. The slippers were left in the bedroom; over navy socks he wore soft hand-stitched suède shoes that Benjamin had found at a flea market.

'D'you think they'll meet with Da's approval?' He opened a brown paper bag to show me when we met in the entrance hall as I was leaving one evening.

'I'm sure they will.'

'I'm not. Can't seem to do anything right where he's concerned. He sees me as an irresponsible kid still, you know? The family rolling stone.' He closed the paper bag with a lopsided smile. 'The shoes were made by society dropouts, of course.'

'Don't tell him that.'

'No fear. They're a peace offering, not an attempt to convert him to my lifestyle.'

I had a quiet chuckle over that. Angus had always been the epitome of the corporate man, despising free spirits and won't-works who he said sponged off taxpayers like him. The biggest bone of contention between father and son was the fact that Benjamin had never had a regular job – yet Angus himself had made it possible by setting up the trust fund. The folly of encouraging dependence in their children by lavishing them with the fruits of wealth always seems to escape self-made men.

Benjamin had Hannah's straightforward manner and frizzy blond hair and downy cheeks, the sum of which made him seem younger than he was; but there was a contrasting spare boniness under his loose Indian clothes, a hard edge to the agreeable nature that surfaced when he spoke about things that were important to him. Despite his tentative way of speaking he was no pushover in an argument, even when pitted against his father. He stuck to his guns with a shrugging off of inimical views that infuriated Angus, who was used to dominating conversations. With a lifetime's experience under his belt, he knew he was better informed than an untried boy who persisted in rejecting advice.

Benjamin's passion was ethnic music. We'd have long discussions about his travels and discoveries when we found ourselves marginalised by Angus's conversations with other visitors. 'What concerns me is not only the obvious need to preserve traditional instruments and tunes and songs,' he explained once, 'but keeping them vital by incorporating them in the music we're making now.'

As well as his much-travelled Spanish guitar, he had brought a sitar with him from India. Five days after arriving in Johannesburg he had found and joined a group that played a blend of African, stringed and jazz instruments to produce what he called, electric with enthusiasm on his next visit to the Club, 'the most exciting new sound I've ever heard. Honestly, Da. It'll blow your mind.'

Angus had responded with a sour, 'I wish to keep my mind intact and free from the pernicious influence of modern music, thank you,' and Benjamin didn't mention the new sound to his father again.

Within weeks he had become lead guitar for Mazambane Market, writing parts for his sitar and taking lessons on the mbira, the penny-whistle and the wooden xylophones that gave the group their distinctive liquid percussion sound. 'They're amazing instruments,' he told me, 'the singing soul of Africa. I feel as though I've come home at last. I'm here to stay.'

'Even when Angus…?' I couldn't say the word.

'Yes.' For all his assumed coolth, he couldn't say it either. 'This is what I've been looking for, ever since I left school: a commitment to unique music. Did you know we've got a gig for next week's rock concert at the FNB Stadium? Only warm-up, but it's a start.'

Benjamin's contribution to the group must have acted as a catalyst. Within weeks music critics had begun to take notice and there was talk of more gigs and a contract to put together a CD. 'Benji Q's sitar riffs are the cherry on the top of MM's fantabulous new Afro-sound,' I read in *Star Tonight*, 'oozing style from every pore. Tusk is said to be nibbling at the bait. Could be a major breakthrough for these SA musos if Sony picks up the ball and runs with it.'

Angus deplored both the mixture of metaphors and his son's new name. 'Benji Q! It's nauseating. Sounds like a range of poofter clothing or a bloody pomade. Though I'm grateful he's not using his full name. I wouldn't know where to look at the next board meeting.'

Except on the days when he was too exhausted to get out of bed, he had kept up his attendance at board meetings even though it meant being delivered and hoisted into and out of a wheelchair by Praise. His pride was bruised every time he was lifted in the young man's arms or helped out of bed by a nurse; having made a virtue of self-reliance, being dependent was hard to bear. To see him wheeled down the Club steps in suits that now sagged off him and formal shirts whose collars stood away from his thin neck wrung my heart. Praise had ordered a custom-made padded seat for the back of the Bentley, however, that raised and held him in his former position with a safety belt, so once installed he could look like the powerful business magnate of old being chauffeured to his appointments.

A meeting would drain him for the whole day, though thanks to the syringe driver which he could activate himself when he needed more painkiller, his intervening days were comfortable. The armchair became his new refuge: a position from which he could receive visitors in dignity and properly clothed.

To Benjamin's gratification he wore the handmade shoes all the time now, extolling their virtues as though they were his own discovery.

Mr Barkin had a minor breakdown after his harrowing experience and the management committee had made him, very much against his will, take leave to recuperate. A temporary secretary was manning the office and irritating everyone with a laugh that tinkled all day like broken glass across the marble hall. Since Beverley had a heavy caseload and Prunella, trying to hang on to her job – any job – was more than willing to be poached by Angus's partners for extra work, I had been asked to orchestrate his visitors. Which meant I was spending more and more time at the Club.

I detained his doctor in the passage after one of his visits and said, 'Is it really necessary to limit visitors? Angus is looking and feeling so much better.'

'He's not better. It's the painkiller.' He was overworked and harassed.

'How long does he have?'

'One can never say. I've stopped putting time limits on the human will to survive.' Seeing my dismay, he said in a less curt voice, 'There are new secondaries in his stomach and small intestine, and it won't be long before his liver is involved. So keep the number of visitors down, eh?'

I dug in my heels. 'Visitors keep him mentally alert. I think they're important.'

'Not disputing their importance, just don't want him too exhausted to fight on, you understand?' He skewered me with a tired glare. 'Are you assuming management? What about the family?'

'They're back in England except for his son, who works odd hours. I'm a friend. With Mr Barkin away, the Hospice sister asked me to control his visitors.'

'Just a friend? Bit irregular, isn't it?'

I stuck my chin out, Quain-style. 'Not at all. I've been asked to represent the family. Tell me what's best for him and I'll do it.'

'Right.' With an abrupt nod. 'No more than two visitors at a time, and one is preferable. He should rest all afternoon and see nobody after seven-thirty.'

'It sounds like you're giving him a sentence.'

'Optimum conditions for my patient, that's all.'

'Does he have any choice in the matter? If I know Angus, he'd rather have his fill of taxing visitors and go out with a bang than fade away in solitude.'

'It's not your decision, and he'll go out with a whimper rather than a bang. Cancer's not a heart attack, Miss Dobermann.'

With the affront of a man who is not used to being questioned, the doctor went on with his orders. Regulars were to come at particular times; occasionals were to come only by appointment; those who turned up while he was occupied were to be sent away. Since Angus was to be kept as stress-free as possible, business colleagues should be warned not to discuss their problems or ask for decisions that would cause anxiety.

I interrupted him there. 'You're asking for the impossible. Angus hates being cut off from what's happening, and he loathes being managed.'

'These are the optimum conditions,' the doctor insisted. 'If the patient wishes to go against my suggestions, that's his business. Not yours.'

'Try him,' I said, turning away.

He was right about the number of visitors, though. Too many at a time left Angus exhausted; when I regulated the visits (with the help of the tinkling secretary and Prunella, who handled the requests from his business acquaintances) he could enjoy talking to one or two people without strain. As is so often the case, the people who came often were the busiest: his partner Cameron Greenacre, Dexter and Dr Mkhize, who would bring a packet of what Angus called 'his dassie droppings': brownish-green pills that looked as though someone had mixed finely chopped weeds with clay, then rolled small blobs round and smooth between the palms.

'Sangoma muti,' he'd say, dropping the packet in Angus's lap.

The first time it happened, Angus looked up from his examination of the contents and said, 'Thanks, Vuyo. Are they animal, vegetable or mineral?'

'You don't need to know. Just try them. Two before each meal and another two before you go to bed. They're good for settling the stomach and have a therapeutic effect on swollen lymph glands, though we're not sure how it works.'

Angus's answering smile was sardonic. 'You're not using me as a guinea pig? Never know what tricks you pharmaceutical types will get up to next in the quest for the lucrative health dollar.'

'Aikona. We don't need guinea pigs. After generations of use, we're confident of the formulation's efficacy. We just don't know how it's achieved because the ancestors have chosen not to reveal it to us. As yet.' Dr Mkhize raised his hand to touch his forehead in a warding-off gesture and I saw the strip of goatskin round his wrist under the cream linen cuff.

'I'll try them, then. Never say die.' Angus scrunched the paper bag closed and put it on the table at his elbow. 'Stranger things than dassie droppings have worked miracles.'

And they fell to talking about natural remedies which became an ongoing subject during subsequent visits by the doctor, who was much in demand on the corporate circuit for his urbane wit and mission-taught manners.

'Altogether P L U,' I had heard a northern suburbs socialite say of him at one of the cocktail parties. 'He likes trout fishing and shops at Sandton City and sends his children to private schools. What more can we ask of our new lords and masters? Except tax relief.' Everyone in the vicinity had snickered.

When I reported the incident, Angus growled, 'People like us? Condescending bitch. Vuyo doesn't need anyone's approval. He'll make an excellent Minister of Health one day.' I think Angus truly believed that his club would never have dreamed of excluding qualifying blacks if it hadn't been for the apartheid laws.

Tom began to drive up once a week from Nelspruit to stay at the Club, sometimes with Leo and once with Brendan, a quiet self-effacing man who said little. Tom brought trays of perfect ladyfinger bananas and export avocados which Angus could still enjoy mashed, and one afternoon when I was there, an unframed oil painting that he stood on an easel by the window. It was Cape Town harbour just before sunset: fishing boats, cranes, gulls, a tug furling the water as it got under way, and the late sun slanting across Lion's Head and the western buttress of Table Mountain.

Angus looked at it for a long time before saying, 'God, that's lovely. A feast for my rheumy eyes.'

'Old times.' There were tears on Tom's cheeks.

'Good times. Before the complications.'

'Seemed so straightforward then. Work and play and a life to look forward to.'

'Instead of back on. With regrets.'

Tom's broad brown hand clamped on Angus's frail arm. 'Fucking bad luck, boet.'

They had forgotten I was there. I put down my tea cup and crept away.

Benjamin came every day at times necessitated by practice sessions for the forthcoming CD, to be called Mazambane Mantra. Once Angus had got over his grumpy reaction to 'Benji Q', he seemed quite diverted by the muso-talk Benjamin brought with him into the sedate rooms hung about with business trophies. Soon they were discussing the music industry in South Africa and the economics of producing a CD, with Angus for once listening as his son expounded.

Such harmony would have been unthinkable a month earlier. Is he mellowing because of the illness or accepting Benjamin's difference at last? I wondered, and e-mailed Hannah about it.

Her responding message said, 'I'm glad. Benj needs his father's approval; it will steady and focus him. He's such a talented boy but diffuse, you know? Angus always called it lack of backbone but I think it was uncertainty in the shadow of two confident older sisters. Maybe he'll stop seeing Benj through the prism of complacent achievement and find the son he never knew.'

She was planning to return to Johannesburg in a few weeks' time after the birth of Em's baby, though without Indigo who was preoccupied with work. I looked forward to seeing Hannah again; our correspondence had grown intimate and I had begun to feel that I'd known her for most of my life. We are Angus's women, I thought, wallowing in self-congratulation: wife, daughters, good friend. Staunch female islands in his overwhelmingly male ocean. The Midnite Club girls are mere coracles of no importance.

So it was a tremendous shock when a woman walked through the door one day while we were having tea together, dressed to kill and saying, 'Howdy, Ango. Remember me?'

His head snapped up. 'Sonya?'

Since he was facing away from the door he had not seen her, yet he'd known her voice. I felt ice cubes sliding down my back.

'The very same.' She crossed the room – fur-trimmed jacket, broad-brimmed black hat, short skirt, long legs in black fishnet stockings, heavy gold jewellery, sizzling red lipstick – and stopped in front of him. 'Long time no see. I heard a rumour you were sick.'

He was looking up at her with the reminiscent smile and I heard him breathe, 'My elegant fowl. How are you?'

'Fine. Fine.' I felt myself assessed from beneath charcoal eyelids, then she went on, 'What's the problem, hon? Heart? Prostate? You retired yet?'

Angus seemed to glow and swell under the rain of questions instead of showing his normal irritation at being quizzed. To my amazement he said in a jokey Mafia accent, 'Cancer of da bowel, babe. And it's toiminal. I'm on da skids.'

I thought, Angus goes to Hollywood? *Ango*?

'Shame. Dat's too bad.' She took off the hat, releasing a tumble of impossibly red curls, and skimmed it with a flick of her wrist across the room to land on the sofa. Then she bent and held his shoulders and kissed him. At length.

Sonya was everything Hannah wasn't: tall, glamorous, poised. Her mouth was wide, her eyebrows plucked to slender arches, her python body and trim backside a tribute to daily workout sessions. Instead of nails rimmed with pottery clay, her hands ended in long red talons that dug into Angus's sweater. Paralysed with shock, I sat thinking, This is worse than the Midnite Club girls. It looks serious.

When she disengaged herself, Angus looked dazed. She stood up, ruffled the silver fuzz on his head and said, 'What's all this? Falling out already?'

'Chemotherapy.'

'Hell, that's a swine. How many times?' She was slithering out of her jacket now, kicking off high-heeled crocodile pumps and making herself at home.

'Two courses. Both unsuccessful. The cancer's got away now. I don't have very long.'

It was the bleak acceptance in his voice that galvanised me: I wasn't going to have anyone come in and depress him. Least of all this gold-decked minx who had thrown her jacket after her hat and was standing on stockinged feet in front of the gilt mirror, plucking a yellow silk blouse out of her waistband so it puffed over her hips, making them look even narrower.

I rose up in wrath and stormed over to her saying, 'Who are you? Who allowed you to come up here? This is a sickroom, can't you see?'

Full lips parted on a gap in her front teeth as she grinned at me in the mirror. 'Are you the nursing sister? Don't get mad. Me and Ango are old friends.'

Rage welled like lava. I barked, 'Unauthorised visits are not allowed. Doctor's orders. You'd better take your things and get out.'

Behind me, Angus said, 'Faith, calm down.'

I swung on him. 'Why should I? This woman's upsetting you.'

'No, she's not. She's…'

'…an old friend, like I said.' She had turned away from the mirror and was tapping me on the shoulder. 'Hullo-o-o? I'm Sonya. I used to do Ango's PR when I worked for Saxe Brown ten years ago. Please let me stay for a bit, Sister. Promise I won't upset him.'

Sister. And *I* was the old friend. I pointed towards the door and said, 'Out! He's only allowed certain visitors. You have to phone before you come.'

'Bossyboots.' She moved forward to stand next to me, appealing to Angus, who was looking at us in turn as though he were a keen spectator at a tennis match. 'Tell her to shut up and get off my back, Ango. Can't she go and count pills next door or fetch tea, or something? I want to talk to you. Heart to heart.'

Like a threatened puffadder, I hissed, 'I am *not* a nurse, and I won't shut up. Who do you think you are, just walking in like this? He's very ill, you know.'

'Faith,' Angus said in the hard voice I had only heard him use on minions who had stepped out of line, 'you are getting pompous and overbearing. This is my room and I'd like to talk to Sonya without being made to feel I'm playing hookey.'

'But the doctor said…'

'Bugger the doctor. Bugger this bloody disease. Bugger all the pettifogging, stupid sickroom rules. I will not be dictated to, do you hear? Nobody tells me what to do. Nobody.'

The king was back in all his power and glory, risen from the ashes of my mortally ill friend in the armchair. It was a switch as sudden and more savage than any of the mood changes that had gone before, and I couldn't handle it in front of the *ersatz* redhead who stood by my side.

'Nor me,' I heard myself say. 'I'm off. You can suit yourself.'

'Don't go like this.'

He was ordering, not asking. I snarled, 'Try and stop me, *Ango*,' and stormed out into the passage, though I lingered near the open door.

Long enough to hear him say, 'Don't mind my friend Faith. She's got so involved with my decline that she's beginning to think she owns me.'

There was a giggle. 'Fat chance, hon. Just a friend?'

'A good friend. I'm deeply indebted to her.' This crumb of comfort was followed by the sound of his hand patting the leather seat next to him and an ominous opening in the Mafia accent again: 'So, babe, tell me what-a you bin doin' all dese years?'

I heard her nestling into the leather as she said, 'Nuttin' much. Mauritius. Sardinia. St Moritz. Bali. Aspen. Da usual crap.'

'And Sidney?'

I thought he'd said 'Sydney' until she answered, 'Boring. Rich. No balls.'

'Why did you marry him?' His voice serious now.

'It seemed the right thing to do at the time. And I didn't know about the balls. You always had those.'

'Had. It's all over bar the shouting now.'

There was a rustle as she moved – closer? – saying, 'It's a helluva shame finding you like this. Always the way, though. Only the best die young.'

'I'm not dead yet.'

She hooted. 'You kidding, or what? This place is like a bleddy coffin already. Half the size of the State Theatre and twice as dead.'

His answering chuckle was the most cheerful I had heard him in weeks. 'You never minced your words.'

They both laughed then.

Numbed, I tiptoed away and drove home and made myself some tea. Then I phoned Brian and asked him to the new Peter Weir movie, followed by supper at a restaurant in Sandton Square where we could watch the strollers in the spring evening and talk. I needed to get the stench of betrayal out of my nostrils.

Two days later, Praise delivered a box of hand-made Belgian chocolates and a dozen yellow tulips in a silver vase with a note that read: 'Please come back. All is forgiven. A Q.'

I handed them back to him with a curt, 'Tell Mr Quain that I'm very busy and I don't want his damn peace offering.'

Praise was wearing reflective sunglasses and I couldn't see his eyes as he said, 'I will pass these words on, if you really want me to.'

'I do.'

'Why, Madam?'

The impertinence was too much. I snapped, 'Because your employer is impossible and I have lost my patience with him.'

As I turned to go back inside, I felt a tentative hand on my arm. 'You know that he is very sick now?'

'I know.'

'And very sad without you. He asked me to say…'

'I don't want to hear what he has to say any more.' I shook off his hand and reached for the doorknob to close the door.

'He asked me to say…' The precise voice stopped, then he said, 'Please look at me when I talk.'

It shook me, this request for common courtesy from a messenger who was only trying to do what he had been asked: deliver flowers and elicit sympathy. He would not be aware of the sarcasm expressed in Angus's note and I had no right to burden him with my jealous rage. Embarrassed, I turned back. 'Sorry. I didn't mean to be rude.'

He reached up with his free hand and took off the sunglasses. The young face was stern with reproach. 'You do this to a dying man?'

'A devious, manipulative dying man.' I didn't care that my words sounded shrill and bitter. 'I've had enough of his secrets. I've spent all the emotional capital I have to give and I can tell you that the returns aren't worth it. This minor refusal is nothing to the stunts he's pulled on me.'

'You are wrong, Madam. Among my people, the wishes of a dying man come before personal disagreements. That is all I can say.'

I thought, Unfair judgment is being passed here, and said, 'I have been a faithful friend to Mr Quain for fifteen years, much longer than you have been employed. He will agree with this. And he will also agree, if you ask him, that he has not treated me with the openness I deserve. I am not, honestly, being unreasonable.'

He was unimpressed. 'Maybe not unreasonable, but unyielding. It is always the same with you…' He checked himself.

Whites, I thought, feeling my gorge rise. This is a racial confrontation. Whatever civilised views we new South Africans may exchange in media debates, our differences will always boil down to the basic fact that black and white are opposites.

'…older people,' he said with the arrogance of youth that sees itself as clear-thinking and right in contrast with its soiled and muddled elders who have taken too many wrong turns to be relied upon any more.

I felt my cheeks begin to burn at my automatic assumption of racial conflict. He was right. Part of me was still living in the past. I said, 'But I'm not that old,' and tried to smile.

His face did not soften. 'You are too proud, though. I am not so proud. I have been driving Mr Quain since I left school, doing this boring job to show my grandmother I can earn my own way in life, as she has. From the beginning Mr Quain encouraged me to go to night school also, saying that hard work is the best teacher he knows. Now I see he is too much alone.'

'Nonsense. He's surrounded by people.'

'Not family. A dying man needs his family, is what he asked me to say.'

I closed my eyes against this new example of Angus's genius for remote control. He knew exactly how to press the emotional button that would bring me back: including me in his family. In a last weak effort to resist, I said, 'He has Benjamin, and Mrs Quain is coming soon. I heard from her yesterday.'

'But they are not every-day family like you.'

The way he phrased it had a familiar ring (no pun intended) and for a moment I tried to puzzle out why. 'They are not every-day family like you.' It was a flattering appeal. And then it hit me: Praise had not only been going to night school but had been taught the art of persuasion by a master – Angus. Had it been a deliberate passing on of skills to the next generation, this future salesman of luxury cars, or instinctive? If I was to get through the emotional minefield in which I was floundering, I realised, I'd have to figure out where the genuine feeling stopped in Angus and the calculation began.

'Madam?'

He stood in his chauffeur's uniform, correct and censorious behind the profusion of tulips, and – as usual where Angus was involved – I gave in.

'Very well, Praise, you can tell Mr Quain that I'll come in tomorrow at the usual time. But tell him also "No nonsense", do you hear?'

The firm lips relaxed a fraction. 'You sound like my teachers at Waterford.'

I said in my driest voice, 'Beware, if you can; the authoritarian personality is catching.'

He took my meaning at once. 'Thank you for the warning. But I think the danger will not last long now.'

He'll do well in business, I thought, if he manages to combine Angus's drive and charm with Mama Nesta's shrewd insight. And said, 'Thank you for coming, Praise, and for your concern.'

'The chocolates and the flowers?' He held them towards me again. 'They should not go to waste.'

'Give them to your grandmother,' I said. One has to retain some dignity when climbing down.

Angus was too unwell to get up next morning, which served as a reproach in itself. He was subdued and apologetic in his rumpled pyjamas, his sunken face far from king-like.

'Sorry. Got a bit carried away when Sonya came,' he mumbled. 'Heat of the moment, what?'

Sensing depression, I gave him immediate absolution. 'It's all right. I know I'm touchy.'

'Makes two of us.'

There was a long moment while we summed up each other's reaction, then I sighed and said, 'You'd better tell me about her. I presume you were lovers. Was she the only other field you had to plough, or was there a whole farm?'

His laugh was much weaker now and left him sweating. 'There were a few liaisons, really. Never anything serious. Didn't want commitment.'

271

'Just the odd roll in the hay?'

His answer surprised me. 'Just a bit of warmth and fun. Dinner, bed and breakfast in a nice hotel. Occasional weekend at the coast. Flitted across to Mauritius sometimes. Needed a break from the company of men. Too one-track minded, you know?'

'I always thought you were so comfortable here in the Club.'

'I was. Am. It's central, all mod cons, no household to worry about. Attentive service. But lacking in the special grace women bring to our lives.'

'You divorced your special grace,' I pointed out.

'Arrangement wasn't working. You know that. Didn't mean I'd gone off sex, though.' He shot me a glance to assess how I felt about this new candour.

'I thought...'

'I know what you thought. Encouraged it. You thought I was channelling my energies into my business affairs. Didn't want you to think you weren't attractive enough to qualify.'

'For what?' I could hardly believe my ears.

'As one of my elegant fowls. Barnyard diversions.' Was there a pink tinge on his face? 'Thing is, you were much more to me. Needed your intellectual challenge as well as your presence on Saturdays. Didn't want feathers to get in the way. Do you understand?'

It was the feather image that made me explode into laughter: gorgeous Sonya had breezed in like a bird of paradise and I had been jealous instead of realising that a landlocked, bolshy, recalcitrant ostrich beats them all when it comes to fine feathers. I laughed until the tears came and Angus had gone red and then begun to laugh too, and the day nurse came through from the living room to admonish me for disturbing her patient.

After he had shooed her away and she had gone next door in a huff to phone the doctor and complain that she was getting no co-operation from Mr Quain, who was behaving like a silly schoolboy, I heard myself spluttering, 'I have to confess that I never saw you as a sex object either.' And we both roared again.

Sonya was swept off by her textile tycoon to cruise the Caribbean and didn't come visiting again, though she must have passed the news around because two more elegant fowls fluttered in to perch briefly at the end of Angus's sickbed. Meryl had been a ballet dancer, and was furious with accusations that Angus had used her, then cast her off when she lost her looks.

'You seemed quite relieved at the time,' he chided. 'What happened to the suitor who was going to set you up with a studio in Durban and a luxury flat on the beachfront?'

'He dumped me. As you did.'

272

'Oh, no. There was never any suggestion of permanence. You also showed far more enthusiasm for my farewell diamonds than you ever showed for me.'

'They were only worth ten thousand when I pawned them. Not enough for services rendered.' And she flounced out.

Angus looked abashed. 'That one was a gold-digger, I have to admit.'

'I'm surprised at a financial guru like you not spotting it.'

'Did, but too late. Felicity, on the other hand...'

Felicity was a personnel consultant who had given him a good run for his money, he said: two years of stolen weekends until she had said her biological clock was ticking and broken it off to marry a hotelier. 'We still keep in touch,' Angus said with the reminiscent smile I was getting to know. 'Stayed there quite often on business trips, in fact. She has four kids now and a bum like an airship. Great fun, though. Bloody good mother and wife. You'll like Felicity.'

And I did, once I had managed to suppress the vulgar speculation that sprang to mind when I tried to picture Angus in bed with her. She wore a spotted grey suit that made her look like a buxom guineafowl and the blonde tresses that bounced on her shoulders did not match the fine pleating round eyes and mouth, but she cheered him up with tales of shenanigans at the weekend business conferences in which her husband's country hotel specialised.

'Musical beds, and we're always having to replace the mattresses,' she said. 'We'd advertise our conferences as aphrodisiacs if it weren't for the spouses and partners sitting fuming at home. It's not that participants spend all the time whooping it up; most of them work hard during the day. It's the nights that do the damage. Being hundreds of kilometres from home with colleagues who are eating and drinking too much seems to have a rousing effect on the libido.'

'You should know about that.'

She shot him a coy smile. 'Not any more. But it was lots of fun while it lasted. You were a lovely man, Angus.'

Felicity left soon afterwards without realising that she had had made a faux pas.

'Were.' Angus moved his head against the pile of pillows behind it, trying to find the most comfortable position. I had switched on the bedside lamp to dispel the gathering dusk and its harsh light threw his bony nose and cheekbones into cruel relief. 'I'm not a lovely man any more, am I?'

'That's a matter of opinion,' I shot back. 'You can't expect old birds to have much taste.'

His slow tired blink of acknowledgment at the play on words was my reward.

31

*T*he newspapers were buzzing with reports from all over the world of fraud and corruption, bank scams, tax evasion, bribery scandals involving government ministers and the growing financial power of drug cartels – factual evidence of greed which bore out Angus's revelations.

On top of which, my Wits Business School researchers had turned up material on a number of my proposed subjects that was beginning to nudge my book in a different direction. The trove of historical artefacts in the Club attics that had sparked my interest was fading into the background. Since Jem Lowing's spectacular burnout, I'd become fascinated by the corporate underworld. The machinations of Joburg's big-business shysters and con men were far more entertaining than the lives of the worthy captains of industry I'd set out to chronicle.

But there were two problems to face if I decided to write about corporate malfeasance: would further investigation be dangerous, and what would I do with the Angus interviews? I could hardly feature my best friend in a book about shady financial operators, however well the glove fitted. So I'd either have to dump the material or plan a second book in which he could star with his more respectable peers.

When I explained my dilemma to Brian at one of our now-regular meals together at a restaurant that specialised in African dishes, he laughed and said, 'Digging up dirt is far more fun than eulogising worthies. Go for the jugular, I say.'

'But won't it be dangerous? You were talking about hatchets and hiring private investigators last month.'

'That was last month. Now that Lowing's self-destructed, it's a whole new scene. Heavenly choirs belting out corporate anthems and haloes being polished up.'

'Convince me. I don't want to have to deal with any rough stuff from fallen angels.'

'Keep your focus on past transgressions, and you're quite safe. If you want to live dangerously and delve into some of the scams going on today, you could score a couple of yachts like Mitch Kincaid or end up with no kneecaps.' He was still smiling.

Irritated by the teasing when I needed advice, I said, 'Be serious. I'm a historian, not a seedy journalist. I want to take a long hard look at the nineties culture of greed and what led up to it, not indulge in cheap sensation-mongering.'

'Getting all hoity-toity, are we?' His eyes were vivid with mockery. 'You're beginning to sound like my sainted aunt who goes about foisting good deeds on people who don't need them. There's nothing new about the culture of greed. Behold a living example.' He picked up his fork and attacked his Moroccan couscous.

I sat watching him and toying with the serving of *bobotie* I'd ordered and now didn't feel like. He was so different from the other men I knew. Academics saw themselves as distinguished mentors and thinkers, unique in their cleverness and a cut above ordinary mortals. This unconventional, disturbing man made no claims to distinction yet you felt a solid core of honesty under the teasing talk. Where Angus was a Hanseatic captain skilled at sleight-of-hand transactions and slipping through customs barriers, Brian was a market trader in carpets with a good tight weave underlying intricate surface patterns.

I caught his eye next time he looked up and said, 'You're an enigma, you know? One moment the compleat corporate whizz kid, and the next taking the mickey out of the financial world that provides you with a living. Which is the real Brian Lapidus?'

'Do you really want to know?' Grains of couscous on his lips, serious at last. I nodded.

'I've been in what you call the financial world for nearly twenty years and I'd rather be elsewhere.'

'Why? You're good at what you do.'

'Good and disillusioned. I don't subscribe to Quain & Co's philosophy of milking the unwary.'

'Even though you've just done it yourself with the Impex shares?'

'That was different. Self-preservation.' Fork arrested, he was giving me the direct eyeball. 'Nor do I subscribe to your gloomy view of humankind. All you're seeing are the black headlines: graft, bribery, corruption, and who's got his hand in the till. Let me tell you, there are millions of good honest souls who go quietly about their lives…'

I cut in. 'Quietly and boringly.'

'From a writer's – sorry, *historian's* – point of view, I have to concede that they aren't bestseller fodder. But they do vastly outnumber the great and the greedy. The business world isn't as black as you're painting it.'

'Yet you're disillusioned?'

'Tired of wheeling and dealing. Tired of putting my reputation on the line every time I pick up the phone to call a stockbroker. Tired of being on my toes all the time. I'm obviously not made of Quain's sterner stuff.'

'I'd call you the sterner, actually. Less compromising anyway.'

'Is that a compliment?'

'I'm not sure. Yes, I think so.'

He had that effect on me: uncertainty as to where I stood. As I bent to eat at least a few forkfuls of my neglected *bobotie*, I was thinking, He'll make a tougher sparring partner than Angus. More abrasive with less of the need to play the urbane gentleman.

And he didn't convince me about the culture of greed: it seemed to be flourishing world-wide. In France within a matter of weeks, one chairman was arrested on charges of misappropriating funds, another for the alleged diversion of company money to improve his home, and a tycoon turned politician for fraud and tax evasion. *Time* magazine ran a seven-page article on government corruption titled 'War Against Sleaze'. Closer to home, on the same day as it reported a jail sentence for a top banker accused of stealing a million rands, the *Sunday Times* blared 'South Africa has become a target for money laundering by crime syndicates,' and the *Sunday Independent* hoped that 'something tangible will somehow be achieved to prevent the wave of crime and corruption from escalating to Nigerian proportions.' A study by an audit firm reported that fraud losses in South Africa had reached R2.9 billion the previous year.

Angus wasn't any help either, showing no interest when I tried to discuss these things with him. All he said was, 'I wouldn't fret about it, old girl.'

'But I do. And you were the one who opened my eyes, remember?'

'Water under the bridge,' he mumbled, turning his head away against the pillows. It was one of the bad days when he had not felt well enough to get out of bed.

'Angus.' I touched the cold hand on which blue veins meandered like trails of watery ink. 'I can't help being concerned about that second deal with Jumbo and Hugh Softley, when you asked me to carry messages to them. Did you manage to resolve the problem?'

I thought I'd put it rather well and hoped he would reward me with some juicy insider gossip. But all he said was, 'Oh, that. All under control. Paid 'em in squeaky clean dollars. Profits snug in the Cayman Islands. Everybody happy.'

Persistence is my middle name; at least, that's what I call it. Mother accused me once of having the drive of a battering ram coupled with the hide of a rhinoceros. I said, 'And the maggots?'

There was a stillness, then, 'What are you talking about?'

He had forgotten that he'd brought them up in the first place. Was it the general debility that results from serious illness, or the cancer invading his brain? That would be his ultimate horror.

I murmured, gentle where I would once have been caustic, 'You said of me when I first met Dexter, "She's liable to start digging around in the compost heap and uncovering maggots best hidden," and Dexter said, "Some of the maggots Oom's talking about are getting ready to hatch, and they're not butterflies." Ergo, there are questionable secrets still festering in your dung heap.'

His chest gave a small hiccup of laughter and the once majestic head, now shrunken to a skull fuzzed with silver down, turned back towards me. 'You call my affairs a dung heap now? What vile calumnies have you uncovered in your researches?'

Now was not the moment to discuss my qualms. 'Nothing vile about you; plenty of dirt about others.'

'Who?'

'You know that I have two student researchers beavering away? Yesterday they chanced on a legal matter that never went to court, involving a timber company headed by…'

'Donnington-Black.' The name was out before he could stop it. His thought processes were as quick as ever; no cancer in that sharp brain.

'The very same. And his directors. It seems that in order to launder the ill-gotten gains they had skimmed off profits on timber machinery imports, they each bought an insurance policy and then cashed it in after a few months. This meant taking a loss but being able to bank a legitimate cheque from an impeccable source.'

'Nothing new.'

'Except that the insurance companies have a patent way of tracking down collusive scams now, and they nabbed them.'

'Aha. This I didn't know.' He looked pleased.

'The money was forfeited to Inland Revenue and the insurance companies hushed the whole thing up.'

'Hushing up is standard procedure. Wouldn't do for the general public to get ideas. So the perpetrators got off with a stiff fine and a slap on the wrist.'

'But the word's around. There's a fat file on them in the Business School library.'

'And the watchdogs have been alerted. First Lowing and now D-B. Well, well. How are the mighty fallen.'

Striking while the iron was hot, I said, 'Since I'm not the general public, would you give me some ideas?'

'About what? Do you wish to delve into my innermost secrets, oh pestilential hag? Is there no peace for the wicked?'

I played along, glad that the news had cheered him up. 'The short answers to your last two questions are yes and no. It's the first one that presents a difficulty. Since I'm not sure what you've been up to, I can't specify what I need to know.'

'You're coming at me from two directions,' he grumbled, 'my hatching maggots and Donnington-Black.'

'Is there a connection?'

'No fear. Wouldn't touch the bastard or his cronies with a bloody barge-pole.'

'That's a powerful indictment, coming from you.'

'Don't be pert.' His eyes blazed with a sudden blue intensity that startled me. 'This is serious. D-B's not just surfing the money markets like I am. He's bad news.'

'How bad?'

'I've heard whispers of links with the heroin trade and other nasties from the Far East and South America. Timber's a useful import. Its sheer bulk can conceal many sins. So steer clear there, right? No digging, no questions, no sniffing around. He's been known to strong-arm nosy journalists.'

That solved the mystery of Mitch Kincaid.

But Angus didn't stop there. With the black frown that had once sent erring employees skittering, he emphasised, 'I mean it. Wouldn't like you to end up in concrete gumboots at the bottom of Boksburg Lake.'

I thought of Brian saying only the day before, 'If you want to live dangerously and delve into some of the scams going on today, you could score a couple of yachts like Mitch Kincaid or end up with no kneecaps.' And shivered.

'You've had a previous warning?' I nodded. 'Who from?'

'Brian Lapidus. He works for…'

'Vanguard Trust. Know the fellow. Good reputation. Had much to do with him?'

'I've met him a few times.' I tried to make it sound casual. 'He approached me some weeks ago with a query about my research and we found we had mutual interests.'

'You didn't tell me.'

'There are lots of things I don't tell you.'

I must have said it with too much asperity, because it attracted a keen look. 'First you agree that he warned you, then you say he approached you with a query. Explain.'

I was going to prevaricate; I hadn't told Angus about Brian because I wanted to keep him in a separate compartment of my life, unshadowed by illness and death. The preceding months had taught me that a person can have many private lives, not just the paltry one I had given myself. But lying is impossible when you're talking to a friend who is leaving on a journey with no return ticket. While I could try and keep things from Angus, I couldn't tell him deliberate untruths.

I said, 'Brian phoned out of the blue with questions about my new book. When I refused to answer them, he asked for a meeting which ended quite amicably. The day I met Dexter – remember? – Brian phoned again to warn me that people were putting a wrong construction on my book and there was trouble brewing.'

'Wrong construction? Trouble brewing? Don't be pompous. A pox on academics. What was the warning?'

'He said that there were rumours my book was an exposé about stock market and foreign exchange fraud, and that certain individuals were threatening reprisals.'

'Ah. So that was the reason for the sudden press release by your publishers. I wondered.' Angus looked relieved, which made me wonder too.

'Brian said it would avert a potential crisis and it must have, because I heard nothing more. I think it was a storm in a teacup, if you must know.' Striving for the casual tone again. 'The rest of the book's on hold at the moment while I concentrate on getting you down on paper. Not an easy task. I'm hoping to have something to show you by next week.'

But he wouldn't be diverted. He said, 'Tell me more about Lapidus. What sort of a fellow is he? Clever, I know, but with good legs?'

'Good legs!' I felt laughter bubble up and explode, reverberating round the crowded bedroom, bouncing off the wardrobe's bevelled mirrors and fading at last in the long shadows beyond the tall bookshelf near the window. 'Angus,' I said when I had wiped my eyes and could look at him again without chuckling, 'I have no idea whether he has good legs or not. They've been covered by trousers when we've met.'

Angus was lying against his pillows with half-closed eyes, an exhausted sultan willing himself to be amused by his favourite concubine. His pallor had a tinge of yellow that day, sign that his liver had been invaded by the cancer though I didn't realise it yet. He'd felt nauseous for several days, Beverley had reported, though it hadn't stopped him from demanding a nightcap the evening before. 'I gave in without a fight. It didn't seem right to go on resisting him. It's too late now.'

Too late. I said in sudden anxiety, 'Angus? Are you all right?'

'I'm fine.' With an effort he pushed himself up against the pillows and mumbled, 'Wine-tasting term, d'you know? Good legs. Means that a wine will last well in the cellar. Worth laying down.' He stopped to draw breath. 'Meant, is the fellow dependable in the long term?'

It was an odd question. Why should Angus concern himself with a young businessman he had never met? 'He seems dependable, as far as I can tell.'

'Good. Good. Sound operation too, Vanguard. Good choice.'

He went on muttering and I wondered for the second time that morning whether his mind was wandering. He was self-administering more and more painkiller, Beverley had warned me, which combined with the anti-nausea and other drugs, could affect his thinking. 'I've noticed that he hallucinates on some evenings; sees people in the shadows. He shouted once, "Uncle Ernie! Let me go!"'

We were speaking in low voices in the living room. 'Will the drugs hurry things up?' I had queried, unable to ask straight out if they would kill him.

'If he's lucky.'

'And will he be able to stay on here, as he wishes?'

'We may have to take him into Hospice for a few days at a time to stabilise his condition as it deteriorates, but I don't see any reason why he can't be allowed to die in his bed.'

She had said it unfazed by the grim finality that daunted me. In the months after Angus died, just thinking about Beverley's infinite kindness was enough to lift my sadness.

'Got to plan ahead. Got to plan.' Angus spoke with sudden urgency, raising his head and peering round the bedroom. 'Faith? You there?'

I leaned forward so he could see me. 'Right here. What do you want to plan? I'll help you.'

'Farewell party. Go out in style, what?' He turned towards me, a skull lit from within. 'Show the punters that Angus Quain doesn't fade away. Only vanishes in a puff of smoke and fire. Forked tail and all.'

'But…' It was an appalling idea.

'No buts, woman!' His attempt at a roar faltered, though the words held all the old force. 'I want a party before I go. What's the use of a bloody wake? Not there to enjoy it.'

'Angus, you're not well enough.'

'I will brook no opposition. Do you hear?' His gesture of command was a weak flap now. 'This is what I decree. Beverley will pump me up with her magic drugs. Prunella will draw up a list and extend the invitations. Praise and Boniface will handle the logistics. The Club staff will provide the catering expertise and the venue. And you, old girl, will co-ordinate a farewell feast to set even Joburg tongues wagging. Right?'

He collapsed back against the pillows, his pyjama jacket damp with sweat. He's really ill now, I thought, and made a mental note to phone Hannah when I got home, urging her to come as soon as possible. In the meantime, I would try and stall the party.

'Right?' he croaked, fixing me with the basilisk glare he had remembered from his childhood.

'If it's what you really want.'

'It is. And you're to help me.'

'When is this morbid festivity to take place?'

'Friday.'

That left four days. I said, 'Impossible.'

The hand lying on the sheet embroidered 'AQ' made an irritable gesture.

'Got to be soon. No time to waste. Might not last much longer. Fully compos, anyway.'

My eyelids prickled as I took his hand. 'I have never known you anything less than fully compos, Angus.'

'Comes a time,' he said, eyelids sinking with exhaustion. 'Last request, this. A party. Friday. Benjamin ... the music. Hannah ... '

He drifted off. As I tiptoed out I thought I heard him mutter, 'Loose end ... trust the fellow...' but when I turned he was lying on his back with his mouth open, silent and still.

Having evaded any further mention of his maggots, I realised as I creaked down in the lift. Mortally ill as he was, he remained a master of subterfuge.

Prunella was on the phone at nine the next morning with a list of thirty-seven guests to be invited. Fifteen were corporate colleagues; fifteen were Club members, including Dr Mkhize; the others were Dexter and his wife, Tom and Leo, Beverley Grant, me and Mrs Nesta Ngcobo-Patterson.

'Do you know the latter person?' Prunella fluted, annoyed at having to ask. 'There's nobody listed under that name in Mr Quain's address book.'

'I bet there isn't. But don't worry, I know her. I'll ask Praise to deliver the invitation.' And Mama Nesta would come, too, advancing through the Club's main doors in robe and headdress, more than a match for anyone who dared to ask if she was there by invitation.

'Very well. Do you need any help with the other arrangements, Mizz Dobermann?'

I said, 'No thank you, I can manage.'

'Does Mr Quain want me to come in early on Friday?'

'I'm sure he will. He likes his cohorts marshalled about him when he goes into battle.'

There was a pause, then an apprehensive, 'What do you mean, cohorts?'

'He's hatching a plot, Prunella. I have the impression that Mr Quain is going to do something controversial at this party. Try to find out what it is and tell me, will you?'

There was a righteous gasp. 'Certainly not. That would be a breach of confidence.' Her receiver rattled into its cradle.

The cocktail party had a silver lining, however. There would be a thirty-eighth guest: Hannah, who had promised during our conversation the night before to fly out as soon as she could get a booking. 'By Thursday morning, I hope.'

'He has an odd gleam in his eye. Don't be too long about it,' I said.

32

When Angus told Beverley of his plans, she whisked him into the Hospice's palliative care centre for what he called 'a retread,' and it worked wonders. He emerged looking better than he had for weeks: clear-eyed, his pain under control, and though his skin was now ivory, full of gusto at the thought of the party.

On Friday morning he had everyone hopping. Praise was sent to meet a delayed Hannah at the airport and bring her straight to the Club. In the kitchen, the chefs were working on preparations for the buffet. Mr Barkin, looking wan and smudged about the eyes but determined to take up his duties again, was selecting the wines with Boniface in the cellar. In the cocktail room on the second floor, Angus sat giving Prunella and me directions from his wheelchair.

The private rooms where members entertained had been designed to impress. The cocktail room had tall teak and glass double doors, antique tables, gilt chairs, an elegant bar salvaged from a demolished hotel, custom-woven carpeting with repetitions of the Club's crest, and panelled walls hung with portraits of members trying not to look too pleased at having distinguished themselves. Over the fireplace, already laid for the log fire which would warm and cheer the room later, a record kudu head surveyed the scene, as poised in death as he had been in the last startled moment of his life.

The Prune and I checked and rechecked the buffet table layouts, flower arrangements, bar supplies, wines and the menu. Everything was to be of the finest, Angus had decreed, from the French champagne to the single malt whiskies and Hamilton Russell vintage reds, from the whole sides of Scottish smoked salmon to the port-laced English Stilton.

'Got to show the buggers how it's done,' I heard him mutter.

'What was that?' Prunella bent over him, a solicitous question mark.

'Swan song, you know? Got to be good. Memorable. Parting shots on target.'

'Parting shots?' Alarm puckered her forehead.

'Fusillades of 'em. There's plenty of ammo. Just a question of directing the fire where it can be most effective.'

She gave him an uncertain smile. 'You're being mysterious again, Mr Quain. I don't quite understand.'

'Never mind. Tell me who's coming and who isn't,' he commanded, and she picked up the invitation list with a minuscule sigh and began reading.

The number of invited guests had doubled. 'To accommodate more odds and sods,' he had explained on the phone the day before. 'Want to put people on the spot, you know? Hear how they try and wriggle out of saying they'll miss me.'

'That's ghoulish,' I'd protested. 'This whole party is unseemly.'

'So is dying, dammit.'

'Angus, you can't…'

'I can do anything I like. Any bloody thing!'

It did not bode well. I had spent the intervening night dreading the scene which I was sure he was planning. Now I looked away from the Prune's raven coiffure bent over the list and saw Hannah come through the doorway and stop, her eyes on Angus.

I went to her and we embraced like old friends as she said in quiet dismay, 'Oh Faith, he's so frail and thin. I hardly recognise him.'

'He's a whole lot better than last week. For the past few days he's been in the Hospice getting a boost.'

She pulled away. 'What does that mean?'

'Drips to stabilise his electrolytes and pump in some glucose. Adjustment of pain medication. Blood transfusions.'

She looked stricken. 'It sounds so final. I should have come earlier, but I've been preoccupied with an exhibition and didn't realise how much he'd gone down. You promised to keep me informed.'

'I thought I had. When you see someone every day, though, it's hard to gauge the extent…' I trailed off. She wasn't listening; by her expression I guessed that she was castigating herself and I couldn't assuage her guilt. So I left her to greet Angus and went to consult with Praise in the passage over his next assignment.

Prunella came teetering out a few minutes later, saying with false brightness, 'I'm going back to the office. Not needed for the rest of the day.' Her shoulders sagged under their jutting foam pads.

She's losing her power base, I thought, and feeling sorry for her said, 'I hope you'll come early to help with the final arrangements?'

Her head snapped up. 'Of course. Mr Quain asked me to.'

Of course. The King had given her an order, for what could be the last time. I hoped that one of his partners – the admiring Cameron, perhaps – would take pity and keep her on as his secretary in another posh anteroom, but feared it would-n't happen. Office dragons are out of fashion today; brisk young women with so-cial and technical as well as business skills are in. Prunella was a doomed species. I hoped she had amassed a good pension and some staff shares.

When I went back into the room, Hannah was bending over Angus with her hand on his cheek, smiling as she spoke to him. He looked surprised, then gave a whoop of delight. 'It's a boy? Wonderful. When?'

'Yesterday morning. That's why I was delayed. Em wanted me to tell you in person rather than on the phone. He's a big strapping fellow, nine pounds, with bronze hair and the biggest tackle you ever saw – truly enormous.'

'Like grandfather, like grandson.'

They both laughed, then seeing me hovering in the doorway, he called me over to share the moment. Hannah rummaged in a big leather sling bag and fished out photographs of a crumpled goblin in a hospital wrapper being cradled in his proud mother's arms. 'He's to be called James William Angus. Rather a sonorous name for such a little scrap, but I expect he'll grow into it.'

Angus pored over the photographs, then raised his head with a valiant smile. 'Jamie. Most suitable. Wish I could hold him too.'

'Em said she'd bring him out as soon as she could,' Hannah lied, blushing under her moth fur.

'Thoughtful of her.' Angus's long slow blink was a new habit; it made him look sleepy and judicial. 'And how did she pull through?'

'Very well indeed. She went into labour on Wednesday morning early, and...' Hannah dumped her bag and drew up one of the gilt chairs and began to give a blow-by-blow account of the birth.

After a few minutes, when I could find a loophole, I said, 'I'm off now. Could you...' But it wasn't for me to tell a wife how to manage her ex-husband, so I changed it to, 'He'll need a sleep after lunch,' and headed for the door.

'I'll make sure he has a good rest. See you later.' She waved me away, engrossed in her narrative.

'No later than five, old girl,' Angus decreed. 'I want to discuss the order of the proceedings with you before everyone arrives.'

That stopped me. 'Proceedings? Are there going to be speeches?'

'One. Mine. A farewell oration. I had Prunella type out the salient points for me.' He tapped his shirt pocket. 'Want to make a good exit. Something to set the tongues wagging.'

I remembered his threat, not so long ago, to bring down the temple when he went. 'You're not going to make mischief, are you?'

Hannah turned in consternation. 'What do you mean?'

They were both looking at me in a way that made me uncomfortable: as if I

284

were a troublemaker intruding on their shared joy over their first grandchild. So I said, 'I don't suppose it matters now,' and went away.

Whatever Angus was planning to say, there was nothing either Hannah or I could do about it. He had always been a law unto himself and approaching death wouldn't change that. I just hoped that he wouldn't let any dangerous tigers out of the bag. Donnington-Black had been one of the names on Prunella's invitation list.

To my surprise, Brian Lapidus had been asked too; one of the 'odds and sods' Angus had slipped in at the last moment. He was among the first to arrive, coming up behind me in the doorway where I stood surveying the room and checking that the waiters were ready to circulate with trays of welcoming champagne.

'Hullo, Faith. You look good enough to eat.'

I swung round at the familiar voice. 'Brian!'

'You didn't expect me?'

'I saw your name on the list, but…'

'Didn't think I'd come or wasn't sure why I was invited? Nor am I.' He ran his hand over his short brush cut as if bracing himself for an ordeal. 'When Quain's office called yesterday, I thought it was a last-minute effort to make up the numbers.'

'Angus never does anything off the cuff.' I turned to look at him, seated in his wheelchair in a far-too large dinner jacket with Hannah standing at his side in serviceable grey and pearls, the ubiquitous sling bag dragging at her shoulder. They were talking to Bob and Moira Snerton, who looked more like a stick insect than ever. 'He's up to something, and it worries me.'

'What do you mean by "up to something"?'

'He's going to make what he calls a farewell oration and he's asked some curious people to this party, including Gerard Donnington-Black.'

'D-B? He's spoiling for a fight, then.'

'An over-statement, surely?'

'Not at all. When corporate Joburg forgets its dignity and reverts to the old mining town days, anything can happen.'

Though the fire had been warming the room since early afternoon, I shivered.

He laughed. 'Don't worry; we're all gentlefolk here. Vulgar outbursts are unlikely in this setting.'

'You said once that Donnington-Black was dangerous.'

'Long-range, not in company. Watch him working the people who matter tonight, and you'll see a master of the art of suave bullshitting. He can charm vultures out of a circling pattern over a newly dead carcass.'

It sounded familiar. 'And if Angus provokes him?'

'Could be instructive, specially if everyone's half pissed. Speaking of which, will you join me in a glass of champagne or do you have to stay here at your post?'

He stood jingling the change in his pocket, soberly dressed for once in a charcoal suit with a fine pinstripe, his Patek Phillippe just showing under a white cuff, his round glasses glimmering. It was a uniform intended to convey the gravitas of discreet ambition, and it succeeded. This was a new Brian, more businessman on the make than friend. Why was Angus giving him a leg up in the rarefied corporate network: as a favour to me or for a more devious reason?

I pushed the thought away and said, 'I'll join you in a while, when most of the guests have arrived. Can't leave everything to the dreaded Prunella.' She was busy directing activities at the bar, dramatic in royal blue taffeta set off by an array of matched diamanté jewellery: necklace, earrings, bracelets and a mini-tiara anchoring a cascade of black ringlets.

Brian eyed her. 'Secretary?'

'Angus's own, and mortified by the prospect of imminent relegation to the typing pool. Or worse still, retrenchment.'

'Poor old thing,' he said as he moved away, a more sympathetic version of what I had been thinking. The Prune had donned her finest feathers and pluckiest smile as she braced herself for her loss of both employer and status.

Which thought braced me for the arrival of two of Angus's elegant fowls: Sonya in blonde suède and gold chains, returned from the Caribbean and statuesque as a Miss Universe contestant, and Felicity on the arm of her hotelier husband, both built like hippos but full of dimpled smiles. I watched all three being swiftly introduced to Hannah, which forestalled any embarrassing intimate gestures in front of the assembled guests… All of whom had positioned themselves so they could observe Angus in his wheelchair to gauge the extent of his illness and make covert guesses as to how long he had left.

The estimates must have been out by weeks. Gaunt as he was, he looked in splendid form: hailing newcomers, cracking jokes, telling stories of past business coups, joining in conversations without seeming to be aware that his sitting position was a public admission of grave illness. He appeared to be knocking back the champagne too, until I noticed that he barely sipped from each glass before giving it to Hannah and taking another from the next waiter – and that his hand went under his jacket at surreptitious intervals to administer more painkiller.

By then I had joined Brian for a glass of my own and we had begun to circulate together. Benjamin, dressing down for the night at his father's request, wore a plain white kurta and his blond curls tied back as he played a subdued guitar in one corner. Mama Nesta had arrived in ruby silk and a demure wig in place of her usual tribal splendour, then tucked herself into a corner on a chair to watch the proceedings without being observed.

'Wouldn't want to frighten off my customers by being too obvious,' she chuckled under a fistful of knuckle-duster rings when I introduced her to Brian as the owner of the Midnite Club.

'Are there others here besides Angus?'

She surveyed the groups of dark suits, then said, 'At least half have been through my door.'

'Do you remember everyone?' What a potential for blackmail, I was thinking.

'Never forget a face.' Her shrewd upward look said, And I'm not stupid, girl. Try anything on these powerful fat cats, and my club would be closed down the next day. I patted her massive arm and we moved on.

Cameron Greenacre gave a complacent whinny when he saw me and introduced us to his wife, a chestnut filly with the fine nervous head and lean flanks of one bred for competition. As they turned to hail another, more important, acquaintance, I murmured, 'Bet she leads him a dance.'

Brian nodded. 'I've heard about Cyndi Greenacre. It's a classic case of second-wife syndrome. He dumps the first, marries a younger, more glamorous version and is flummoxed by her need for constant attention. Specially in the light of the old incumbent's stoic ability to get by with very little in return for the usual perks.'

'So the young stallions move in. Identifiable by their keen good looks, flowing manes and cellphone bulges. I've spotted several here tonight, though it's hard to tell them apart.'

'God, you're cynical.' His voice was admiring.

'I've sat at the feet of a master. And you're no slouch yourself.'

We exchanged smiles. The event I had dreaded was starting well. A waiter offered more champagne and we moved on, watching and listening.

The talk was of the new foreign exchange rules, union problems, gold futures, privatisation, the falling rand, golf handicaps. The crowd swelled and it became harder to thread through the gaps. Hugh Softley and Jumbo Urquhart arrived with other members of the Business Initiative board, whom they used as a barrier between them and Angus after paying him their briefest respects. Rory St Clair Brown posed in the doorway for a while so people could admire the line of his jaw above a double-breasted suit in crumpled beige linen, then finding himself unnoticed, collared a waiter and demanded tomato juice.

Dr Mkhize caused a stir when he came in; a subtle shifting of stances so that people were facing him, hoping to be recognised. I heard someone whisper, 'Is that Motlana or Ramaphosa?' and the answer, 'Neither, it's Tshabalala.'

When he bent over Angus to greet him with a sympathetic hand on his shoulder, there were raised eyebrows. When he stood up and approached Moira Snerton with a hearty, 'Moira, my dear,' while giving her husband a curt nod, there were sideways glances. Brian nudged me. 'What is going on there?'

'I'm not sure, but you know that the doctor is also a sangoma? Perhaps he's treating Moira for anorexia and has decided that Bob's wandering eye is the cause.'

'You seem to know a lot about life at the top.'

'I've been around these past few months with Angus. Going to miss the excitement, if I must be honest.' I stopped to face him. 'Confession time. I've always seen myself as an academic, high-minded and hardworking and superior to the rest of humanity – specially those who grub for money in the marketplace. I never thought I'd turn into a social butterfly, and worse still, enjoy it.'

His crack of laughter made heads turn. 'Stranger things happen in this town.'

And indeed, stranger things happened that night. It was an occasion that became a benchmark of who had made it on the corporate scene: 'Were you at the Quain farewell? No? Pity. It was quite a show. Night of the long knives.'

Rumpelstiltskin was there, only Brian called him The Goat, murmuring tales of a sexual urge that needed satisfying several times a day. 'Hence the need for a regular supply of partners. He wears them out.'

'You're kidding.' I watched the awful little man move in on Cyndi Greenacre and thought, Poetic justice.

'I'm not. He keeps at least half a dozen women and running accounts at up-market escort agencies all over the country.'

'Dangerous in this day and age.'

'The Goat isn't a billionaire for nothing. He pays well over the odds for quality and an up-to-date certificate of good health, and he'll take a calculated risk when he's desperate.'

'How do you know all this?'

'I have my sources.'

'Who don't need up-to-date certificates of good health, I trust?'

He waited long enough for me to regret the way it had slipped out before saying, 'That's a very personal question.'

'Sorry. I retract it, of course.' I looked away, flushing. I was finding increasing difficulty in drawing the line with Brian. One moment we could be chatting like old friends and the next, one of us would trespass on a sensitive area and we'd find ourselves pulling back in dismay. It's not easy making friends when you're older and wiser and have managed to erect skillful defences against being disappointed by others.

He put his hand on my arm. 'Don't go quiet on me. I'm the one who should be sorry. I was teasing you.'

My face burning, I looked down at lean freckled fingers, the nails clipped short, the sparse hairs glinting like threads of copper wire. 'I'm a klutz at things like this. Not enough practice.'

'Let's move on and forget it, then. Forgiven?'

I nodded, but it took another glass of champagne in a quiet corner before the flush of embarrassment subsided enough to resume our circuit. The cocktail room was humming now. Brian introduced me to Sonny Prinsloo, shooting star of the business press since his takeover of Westridge Investments, who told us several times that we wouldn't be sorry if we bought his shares because we'd be in the pound seats by this time next year. Guaranteed. We stood basking in his reflected glory until he moved away to pass his message on to more lucky punters.

'Guaranteed?' I asked Brian. 'Shall I commit some of my cash reserve to Westridge shares? What vibrations are you getting on your spider web?'

'Positive, but with an odd little hiccup I don't like. Hang on for a couple of months.'

'So a guarantee from Sonny Prinsloo isn't worth a row of beans.'

'Assurances are one thing, performance another. I don't have to tell a canny investor like you, surely?'

There was mockery in his eyes again, and I cringed. It was not done to fish for professional advice at a social gathering. The once high-minded historian had been contaminated – there was no other word for it – by the atmosphere she was butterflying about in. I mumbled, 'Oops.'

'What's that for?'

'Asking for free advice. Here.'

But he only said, 'No need for scruples. How do you think the really useful information is passed in this town?'

My awkwardness was soothed by Dexter Schoombie who ushered his wife towards us with his arm round her ample shoulders. 'This is my Aleesha. She's been dying to meet you, Faith. They've had all your books in her book club.'

She was a quiet dark shy woman with a bulging mole on the side of her nose. Saying hullo, I gave her the special smile I reserve for people who buy my books in hardcover instead of waiting for the paperback or getting them free out of the library. 'It's good to meet a faithful reader.'

She bobbed her head. 'Aangename kennis, Mrs Dobermann.'

'Faith, please. And it's been Miss for a long time.'

'Ag, sorry, eh?'

'It's all right.' What could I say to relieve her mortified look? 'A lot better than being Mrs. Marriage didn't suit me.'

Her eyes turned dubious. 'You don't say.'

Oops again. I'd offended a career wife and mother, not to mention a faithful reader. Beside me, I sensed Brian struggling to keep a straight face and blurted, 'I hear you have a lovely family, Aleesha.'

'Plus she's a great cook too.' Dexter seemed oblivious of my attempt to flatter by invoking unknown kids. 'Aaask Oom any day.'

I looked across at Angus who was talking to Mr Barkin, gesturing as if giving an order. Mr Barkin nodded and moved away to talk to Boniface. What was going on? I raised eyebrows at Hannah, who shrugged and shook her head. Angus was playing his cards close to his chest.

Suppressing a niggle of worry, I turned back to Aleesha and Dexter. 'Angus really enjoys your Sunday lunches because they remind him of home. Smoorvis is his favourite, he says.'

Aleesha managed a contained smile but said nothing. I hoped I hadn't lost her literary allegiance. It's an uncertain business, meeting readers; you never know if they'll be encouraged or put off by the discovery of the banal person who masquerades behind the glamorous title of author.

Dexter was saying, 'For me it's curry, any day. The hotter, the better.'

Shades of Kurt again. Perhaps it was the recurrent painful memory that precipitated my next remark. 'I meant to ask you: any sign of the maggots hatching yet?'

Dexter shook his head. 'Nay, Faith, you won't get anything out of me tonight. I'm not one for drink and loose talk.'

'It was worth a try. I don't like being kept in the dark.'

'But that's where maggots hatch, nè?'

Angus-trained like Praise, he had trapped me in logic. As we talked on, my eyes kept being drawn to Aleesha's mole, wondering why she hadn't had it removed. It was a mesmerising sight: large and brown and warty with two stiff black hairs sticking out like tiny antennae. Perhaps it was a listening device that Angus had had implanted to eavesdrop on conversations?

I pushed away the facetious thought, sparked by an incident from the previous week. Dexter's laptop had been stolen from his car, and he and Angus had been muttering about industrial espionage.

Angus had sat fidgeting with the controls on his wheelchair. 'We haven't finalised those nominee deals yet. Someone could be poking around.'

'I'm sure it was just some street kid who took his chaaance,' Dexter had said. 'I should have been more careful. But of course I've got backups. Never fear, Schoombie's here.'

'You've pinched my motto,' Angus had grumbled.

'Maybe Oom can leave it to me as a special favour when he goes, then?'

Having grown up in a slum, Dexter didn't shy away from talking about death as I did. I envied him his ease with his patron and thought again that a protégé has a much easier time of it than a child: there are no blood ties or skew family genes to blame.

After the Schoombies had moved on, Brian asked, 'What was the joke back there?'

'Just a silly thought. Tell you some other time when I'm not on edge.'

'Ah. That must be why you're looking so marvellous tonight,' he went on in the same voice. 'Sparking like an electrical short.'

It didn't sink in at once. I looked towards Angus again and caught him turning his head away as though he'd been watching us. He was definitely plotting something.

'Are you expecting someone else?' Brian asked.

'Something. There's going to be drama when Angus starts talking.' Only then did the words register: 'You're looking marvellous tonight.' Stupid with astonishment, I turned back to Brian. 'What do you mean by "sparking"?'

'You need a second definition? How like an academic.'

We were standing under one of the wall sconces that grew out of the panelling on graceful brass arms, and his ginger bristles and eyelashes and pale freckled skin were almost translucent under the direct light. Like the angel with fibre-glass hair who had presided over the Christmas tree when I was little, I remembered in one of those sudden shafts into the past that illuminate the present. She had reigned high above my head, glowing with promise: presents and sweeties for good girls, the baby Jesus snug in his crib and all well with the world. It had felt so safe then. Was it just that I had been young and gullible, or had life changed so much that promises were no longer to be believed? Or even expected?

'Let me think precisely what I meant by sparking,' Brian teased. 'Fizzing with dangerous energy? Flashing warning signs? Take your pick. My intention stands. In the short time we've known each other, I haven't seen you look so alive. This edgy anticipation suits you.'

'I can't ... you mean...?'

'A simple thank you would do.' His voice was as dry as the champagne in our glasses. 'You should learn how to accept compliments without displaying such patent disbelief in your charms.'

'I ... thank you,' I said, bemused.

'That's better.'

We exchanged smiles again, standing in the cone of light sealed off from the cocktail babble around us. Brian was the first to look away, saying, 'I hate to break this off, but something's about to happen.'

Across the room Hannah was bending over the wheelchair, arguing with Angus. I saw him shake his head and reach inside his jacket for what looked like a folded letter of several pages. To their right, Prunella positioned herself where she could watch him, diamantés glittering, tense hands cupping her elbows.

Mr Barkin stood by the buffet table, its imported delicacies already half-plundered, and tapped his fork on a glass. 'Ladies and gentlemen.'

His voice didn't carry far and the social chatter went on. Heads turned as Gerard Donnington-Black arrived, tall and athletic-looking with tight grey curls and an even tighter mouth. He made his way, cleaving through the crowd, to Hugh Softley and they stood with their heads together, conferring; Angus registered the arrival and the lack of courtesy with a quick glance, then looked away, his expression unreadable. Some of the few wives present had gone into a defensive huddle near the fireplace. Beyond them I saw Tom and Leo being handed glasses of beer across the bar; catching my eye, Leo signalled hullo with his free hand before raising his glass for a long thirsty pull. Moira Snerton and Dr Mkhize were now talking with their backs to Bob, who stood stroking his goatee and trying to look as though he didn't mind being ignored by a potential cabinet minister. He had bought so many in the past, Brian murmured, that he was unsure how to handle an honest man.

Mr Barkin was tapping again and said in a louder voice, 'Ladies and gentlemen, please!' When heads began to turn and conversations abated, he extended one hand and announced, 'Ladies and gentlemen, your attention for Mr Quain.' Then he gave a little bow and moved away.

Somebody said 'Shhhh' and the few people still talking stopped and turned with everyone else to see Angus push a switch on the wheelchair's arm and move forward a few paces. Those standing nearby fell back, leaving him in a cleared circle with Hannah standing behind him. For a long moment the silence was absolute. The guests were still, the limited space between them seeming to swell with anticipation of a significant event.

He began with a smile he must have practised before a mirror: it had an exact shading of regret, gallantry and bravado. 'Friends.' He looked round. 'Rivals.' His gaze skimmed past Gerard Donnington-Black and Hugh Softley. 'Fellow members, old and new.'

His eyes moved from the senior clubmen present – elderly white doyens of Johannesburg society – to Dr Mkhize's poised and confident black presence, savouring the irony.

'Not forgetting the audacious women … who chose to run … the double gauntlet…' he paused to draw in a slow breath '…of perilous city … and male redoubt … to attend my farewell party.' He acknowledged each of us, using the time to regulate his breathing.

There was no sound but the crackle of the log fire. 'You all know that I have … terminal cancer. The Grim Reaper is calling … earlier than expected. In short … I'm saying totsiens.'

After he had spoken the last word, his eyes roamed the faces of his guests as if seeking out those who would be joining him soon. Nobody moved a muscle. He went on in short bursts, pausing often and between sentences.

'I thank you all … for coming. Your presence means a lot to me. Specially that

'... of my former wife Hannah ... who flew in from England this morning...' He raised his chin as he always had when making an important announcement, though it was a weaker movement now, '...with news of our first grandson ... born yesterday.' There was a spurt of clapping which he stilled with a gesture. 'I am indebted to Hannah ... in more ways than I can say. Her steadfast friendship ... has been one of the mainstays ... of my life.'

As heads began to turn towards her Hannah lifted her hand to tuck in stray wisps of hair, her mothy face raw with grief. I saw their assessing looks: 'So that's the wife? Not much to look at. Dressed by Oxfam. But she's a potter, of course. What can you expect? No presence. No wonder he divorced her. Totally out of place.' And I seethed for her and all the unsuitable wives trapped in the corporate searchlights, to be judged by their appearance and ability to put up with (and shut up about) even the unreasonable demands of jobs they had not applied for.

'This is not, however ... a purely social occasion.' Angus waggled the folded pages in his hand. 'I'm an accountant ... trained to balance books ... before signing them off. And I have debts to settle.'

There was an uneasy shuffling. I saw Donnington-Black glance sideways at Hugh and jerk his thumb signalling, Let's go. Hugh shook his head: No. His mouth was drawn down in a sneer, as if jeering in advance at what Angus had to say. A few paces away Jumbo nuzzled at his whisky, oblivious of nuances. Other faces were alternately intrigued, alarmed and amused.

After another pause to breathe, Angus said, 'I have to inform you ... before I begin ... that there's no escape ... from my parting soliloquy.' As people swung round to find Boniface and Mr Barkin standing in front of the now-closed double doors, his old laugh rumbled out with more than a touch of malice. 'You are all my prisoners ... till I choose to let you go.'

'Watch D-B,' Brian breathed in my ear.

He had begun to edge towards the doors. Angus called, 'Gerard! Please don't go. You've only just arrived ... and I haven't had the pleasure ... of your condolences yet.'

'No reason to stay. This is bloody ridiculous.' He began to push through the crowd with more purpose.

'Is a few minutes ... of your valuable time ... too much to ask for?'

All heads turned to Donnington-Black who stopped, unsure whether to continue blustering his way out or to confront the deathly-pale adversary who sat in his wheelchair, already at an unassailable advantage.

'He's got him by the shorts,' Brian muttered.

'Have your say, then.' Donnington-Black planted his feet and folded his arms in a pastiche of the naval captain bracing himself on the bridge of a destroyer heading into a black storm.

'Thank you.' Angus reached into his pocket for his glasses, put them on, unfolded the typed pages and looked down. 'I'll be brief. No alternative. Run out of air … if I carry on too long.'

Hannah bent over him and said something, but he flapped his hand in a gesture of dismissal and she stood up again.

He went on, 'Want to say first of all … that I've been inspired … by the cathartic process of the … Truth and Reconciliation Commission…'

Apprehensive glances were exchanged.

'…and I wish to make a clean breast … of certain transgressions of the law … in which I and others have colluded.'

'Hang on, old chap.' Cameron Greenacre moved forward with a pained smile. 'Perhaps we should discuss this first at board level.'

'Not a board matter. My conscience. Would you deny me … a chance to salve it?' Angus impaled him with the famous glare.

'Of course not. But if it involves the firm…'

'Doesn't. Only me. Angus Quain, sinner. Full stop. Stand back, Cameron. Time's getting short.'

His hand shook as he lifted the notes again. Hannah started forward, then checked herself.

'Item number one: insider trading. Item two will cover … foreign exchange transgressions. Item three…' He looked up, a grinning death's head. 'Item three … is plain stealing from shareholders.'

The atmosphere crackled with shock as the men in the room, cream of the Johannesburg business world, realised that one of their number was breaking ranks and they had been trapped into witnessing the event. To try and leave would be an admission of guilt compounded by the physical problem of having to push both Boniface and Mr Barkin aside to get to the closed doors. To stay would be for the guilty to risk exposure and humiliation, and the bystanders to be forced to acknowledge misdemeanours they had preferred thus far not to notice. The cards Angus was playing were trumps.

For several minutes, stopping often to draw breath, growing visibly exhausted as his voice blurred and faded and his audience hung on every word, he itemised and dissected his financial sins, naming no-one and not needing to, for all those present – even the non-culpable majority – knew exactly what and who he was talking about.

'I admit to … manipulating share prices … for gain. In particular … Amalgamated Couplings. My partners and I…' Hugh and Jumbo squirmed under the hostile looks that found them '…made a mint there. So did others.'

More widespread squirms.

'And I apologise … to those who were caught … with a warning … to be more circumspect … in future. Sheep should be wary … of predators. Ignorance is no excuse.'

Paper crackled in his hands as he turned to the second page.

'I further admit … to insider trading … using knowledge gained … during annual audits. Easy pickings there. Though I don't have to tell … most of you.' He stopped talking and lifted his head. 'Never been a conviction yet … for insider trading. Something for you to attend to … Vuyo? Potential predators coming up … in your ranks too.'

Dr Mkhize gave a curt nod. 'Point taken.'

'Now to … foreign exchange transgressions. Common practice … among those of us … wishing to protect our assets. Hide 'em from the taxman … in Jersey or Switzerland … and who's the wiser?'

He hadn't mentioned the Cayman Islands, I noticed.

'I plead guilty again … along with most of those present.' Feet shuffled, sideways glances were exchanged; more than one face turned red. 'It's not playing the game …eh, chaps? Even if it's your own … hard-earned money. Taxes are owed. Nobody is beyond the law. Even the gods of commerce.'

For a moment he looked like an ageing Jack Nicholson: balding with spiked eyebrows and a diabolical smile.

'But to the third item … stealing from shareholders…' his voice strengthened '…I plead innocent. I may have been a market buccaneer … but I've never knowingly stolen … from anyone. There are limits … and they include … milking company funds … and dealing in drugs. No need to point fingers here. You all know … who the bastards are… '

He did not look at Donnington-Black, but others did. There was utter silence in the room. Nobody moved a muscle.

His last sentences were spoken in a whisper. 'In the spirit … of our new democracy … I have chosen to confess to the Receiver … and pay my fines … before I go. The Nelson Mandela Children's Fund … has also received … a donation. I'm not Harry Oppenheimer…' he paused for the knowing laughter '…but it was a large donation … by any other standard. All of us here tonight…' he raised his eyes and looked round the circle of uneasy faces '…have debts to pay. And I speak as one … who started with nothing. As I go. Accounts balanced … debts and taxes paid … family provided for…'

Dr Mkhize's deep, 'Bravo, brother,' made heads turn, then move back to Angus as he spoke his closing words.

'…conscience at peace.' His smile was a rictus of pain. 'Bottom line … can't take it with you. I've had … a bloody good innings, though. Bloody good. Over and out…'

As his voice petered out and the hand holding the typewritten pages dropped into his lap, the paralysed silence erupted into farce. Groups of dark suits split apart and there was a stampede for the now-open doors, led by Rumpelstiltskin and Donnington-Black, closely followed by Hugh Softley and Jumbo Urquhart. Those who stayed stood watching the leavers with amusement that grew into hilarity as the last back disappeared.

There was a general move to congratulate Angus who sat exhausted, wearing a look of sardonic relief. He's achieved his confession, I thought; I hope he finds absolution in the response. When Hannah insisted quite soon on wheeling him up to bed, he acquiesced with a weak wave towards the bar and the buffet. 'Enjoy ... the rest of the party ... my friends...'

I stopped them briefly at the door and put my hand on the sleeve of his dinner jacket, trying not to flinch at the terrible thinness underneath. 'Goodnight, old thing. That was neatly done. Reputations unravelling all round.'

'Old thing, is it? How have ... the mighty ... fallen.' His head lolled against the backrest. 'Did you spot ... my maggot breeders?'

'This is no time for a chat,' Hannah said firmly and pushed him through the door and away towards the lift. I stood looking after them, thinking, Friendship can survive divorce.

'Penny for them?' Brian had come up behind me.

'I'm amazed. Didn't expect this at all.'

'Quite a guy, King Quain. A charming scoundrel.'

'How can you say that?' I swung round, ready for anger.

For once his eyes weren't mocking. 'It's the only description for his combination of charisma, intelligence, self-confidence and disrespect for the laws that bind others.'

It was true. 'You've left out the sense of humour.'

'That too.'

'He's been a wonderful friend. For all his sins.'

'So I see. Quite a guy, as I said.'

'Unique.' I had tears in my eyes.

The party went on without him, though his presence dominated every conversation. People talked and speculated and caroused, making wilder and wilder guesses as to who had cheated at what. A well-known director of mining companies flirted with me; another said hopefully, twirling an elegant moustache, 'Looking for a new friend when Quain goes?' When I shook my head, he said, 'Pity. It could have been fun.' Brian overheard and laughed himself silly.

With the finesse of long practice and the excuse that the kitchen staff had to go home, Mr Barkin and Boniface eased out the bitter-enders at ten o'clock, including Brian and me. I had had too many dizzying compliments and too much champagne to drive; he took me home and kissed me in the car for a long time before he would let me get out and stumble up to bed. I say 'kissed me' but have to admit that I responded with equal enthusiasm. It was that sort of night: a defences-down, thank-God-we're-alive and maybe-all's-well-with-the-world-after-all night. I fell asleep with a spinning head, wondering how to retrieve decorum.

Angus had planned his farewell with the meticulous care to be expected of a good accountant. It was an occasion that was to go down in the annals of corporate Joburg as a crucial turning point in the debate over business ethics.

'Were you at the Quain farewell? No? Pity. It was quite a show. Night of the long knives.'

Night of an extraordinary confession and final public act of his life. He was not strong enough to sit up next morning and did not leave his bed again.

33

*M*y hangover next morning was less acute than I deserved. I put on the answering machine and got stuck into my research material, resisting the impulse to pick up the phone when Brian rang. He left a curt message: 'I rang to tell you that I'm going away for a few days. Back by next weekend. See you then.'

Peremptory, I thought, feeling put out that he hadn't told me he intended going away. It was the pattern Angus had established: when he was around, the friendship was on. When he went away, it was in limbo. Maybe this was how ambitious, driven men preferred to live their lives – neither tied down nor beholden to anyone? I decided that the kissing had simply been a result of too much champagne.

Someone (several someones, according to journalist friends) blabbed to the newspapers about the confession. Angus had known they would, which is why he had timed it for the beginning of the weekend, to give those who needed it a few days' grace. The old-boy network code states that one does not drop colleagues – even the ungodly – in the composting bin without an escape hatch.

By Sunday morning the witch-hunt was on. *DYING FINANCIER'S DRAMATIC CONFESSION* ran the main headline in the *Sunday Times* over a report of the cocktail party, the names of guests who had departed in a hurry and some interesting speculation as to their reasons for doing so. Under the headline *HOW COME THEY GET AWAY WITH IT?* the editor of *Business Times* ran a list of malefactors who had amassed and exported fortunes by fraudulent means and were living like sultans in countries that had no extradition treaty with South Africa. The *Sowetan's* Monday morning lead was a strongly-worded plea to the government to investigate 'the pernicious gravy trains of the rich and unscrupulous which run on hidden rails, carrying the wealth of our people to secret bank accounts in other countries'. *City Press* trumpeted: *HOBBLE CASH COWS BEFORE THEY STEAL ALL THE MILK!*

Some managed to get away with the cream.

Hugh Softley called a removal company early on Saturday morning, packed up all his beautiful belongings and was gone by nightfall. People said he had slithered into a crack he must have prepared well in advance; Europe, Canada or Brazil were the favoured guesses. He was not seen again.

Jumbo Urquhart was more canny than anyone had suspected. By Sunday evening he had cleaned out his safe of a million pounds in bank notes accumulated over the years in travel transactions, flown with his family (all on new British passports) to Zimbabwe and boarded a flight for Heathrow. Within a year he had set up a chain of Astra Travel agencies in Scotland and was being written about in the British business press, somewhat sourly, as 'yet another of the up-and-coming South African entrepreneurs in our midst'.

Others were too greedy to abandon the non-portable portion of their precious assets.

Gerard Donnington-Black was arrested at midday on Monday, still trying to make frantic arrangements for containers to ship out his fleet of investment cars. (He was later convicted of drug dealing, foreign exchange fraud and tax evasion, and jailed for twenty years). Two export agents, a rare manuscript dealer and a stockbroker were arrested on Tuesday morning.

By Wednesday three firms of importers had gone into liquidation and a metal dealer had been caught red-handed at the City Deep Container Depot trying to ship out gold ingots disguised as silver with a layer of aluminium paint. When questioned how this scam could have gone on for three years unnoticed, smuggling an estimated R75 million out of the country, a police spokesman revealed that between five and ten percent of South Africa's gold output – twenty tons, worth R1.5 billion – goes missing every year. *GOLDEN GOODBYE!* howled *The Star* headline in the afternoon edition. The Reuter news report went on to say: 'Gold smugglers have infiltrated every South African mine... Moonlight flights over the border, ships unloading cargo by night, forged papers and Swiss bank accounts could be part of a movie, but this is real life.'

That evening at Johannesburg International Airport, alert customs officials hauled off for questioning a bogus priest whose hollowed-out Bible was found packed with Kruger rands, and two couriers; X-rays revealed that each had stuffed a package of uncut diamonds up his rectum, housed in heavy-duty condoms.

General press comment was that the Fraud Squad must have been leaned on from a dizzy height to move so fast. The Commissioner of Police responded that the Office for Serious Economic Offences had been watching the miscreants for months and hoped that the courts would make sure the jail sentences were served in full this time, with no remissions for wealthy white-collar prisoners who expected to buy their way out.

'Set the cat ... among the pigeons, eh?' Angus mumbled as I put down the Thursday *Business Day* after reading him their tongue-in-cheek report on the number of pressing overseas appointments that had filled the first and business classes of every plane leaving Johannesburg International from Saturday evening.

'Don't you feel any sense of betrayal?'

'None. Buggers deserved ... what they got.'

'I have to admit that I never saw you as a white knight.'

'Dark horse, rather.' A weak laugh. 'Enjoyable night's work. Feel like ... a new man.'

'Half Joburg is after your blood.'

'Untouchable now. Foiled anyway.'

'What do you mean?'

He lifted his chin so his eyes could find my face; they were chips of dark blue slate now, compacted by pain. Beverley Grant had just been in to give him a morphine injection and I was trying to divert him until it started working.

'Dexter ... a maestro.' His voice was becoming more indistinct as the cancer invaded his lungs, robbing him of breath.

'I don't understand.'

'Tucked away ... untraceable assets.' A ghost of the card-sharp's smile tugged at the corners of his sunken lips. 'Don't tell. Our secret.'

Dumbfounded, I sat looking at my old friend. Even at death's door he was hedging his bets: hiding things in different compartments, letting people know what he chose to reveal and playing us off against each other. I wondered what he said to Hannah when they were alone, and what he would say to Indigo (arriving next morning from London) and Benjamin, back in his good books now that he was gainfully occupied. The professional men, Dexter and Leo, tapped for their loyalty and expertise, would also have been given their own edited versions. Which begged the question: Had I too? Had Angus really opened up to me, or was I imagining that he had appointed me his privileged confidante and biographer?

I said, 'How many more are there?'

'What?'

'Skeletons rattling in your cupboard.'

'One or two.' His blink lasted several seconds. If he admitted to one or two, there'd be more. It was only then that I fully grasped Angus's life wasn't like the attics I had been exploring: a matter of old furniture and packed-away trunks that could be opened and their contents examined with a cool historian's eye. His life was a cave labyrinth whose devious inner recesses no one would ever be allowed to plumb. Secrecy was as necessary to him as the air he breathed.

I said, 'Has your right hand ever known what your left is doing?'

'Knows. Doesn't tell.' He moved the hand to touch mine where it lay on the sheet embroidered AQ. 'Last words: don't give … everything away. Always keep ammo … in reserve. May need it … one day.'

'Something to fall back on, you mean? My mother was always harping on about that. You Depression children carry such scars. It's different today.'

'How so?'

'We try to be more open with each other. The word is transparency.'

'Bugger that. Obfuscation … a far better policy. Keep 'em guessing. Remember?' His weak frown demanded a response.

'I'll remember, but don't agree.'

'Contentious hag.' His head fell back, limp with the effort of trying yet once more to convert me. 'At least … hide an ace … up your sleeve. Quain has spoken.' His heavy eyelids closed as the painkiller spread its narcotic peace through his collapsing veins. 'Hear me.'

When Indigo came, she and Hannah and I were able to spell each other so that one of us was always at the bedside or near at hand if Angus called. 'Need you now,' he mumbled. 'My graces.'

Hannah and Indigo were sharing the Club's twin-bedded guest bedroom; a special concession, Mr Barkin had said, for the dependents of a long-standing and valued member. 'But neither of us is a dependent,' Indigo fumed when she heard, over sandwiches and tea in the living room of Angus's suite the day she arrived. 'I can't stand being treated like a clinging vine.'

'It's a kindly-meant effort to save us from having to shuttle back and forth to an hotel.'

'You're far too charitable.'

'Not so. I'm being pragmatic.' Hannah turned to me. 'I don't know how you see relationships between men and women, Faith, but I deplore the current hostility in western society: women marching and shouting under the feminist banner and men hitting back below the belt with accusations that they're being emasculated. It's so confrontational. Angus and I were never enemies, just two people who agreed to disagree.'

I was about to answer when Indigo cut in. 'You're being simplistic, Mum. Product of your time, I suppose. I'm proud to be a feminist. Male condescension, however kindly meant, makes me boil.'

Hannah said, 'Men of my generation and older were brought up to believe that they would be the head of their families. They want to protect, not insult, you. That's how your father feels. There's no comparison with your generation's very different attitude towards women.'

'Don't you believe it.' Indigo sat glaring at us. 'The British male is insufferable, whatever his age. I had an argument with my boss yesterday before I left. His exact words at the end of it were: "If you don't be a good girl and toe the line, Mizz Quain, I'll have to put you in the corner." I resigned on the spot.'

'So you're jobless?'

'Temporarily. I can stay as long as you and Da need me.'

'And there's always your trust fund.'

'That doesn't make me a dependent!' Indigo's furious blue eyes were so like her father's that both Hannah and I flinched. 'It was Da's idea, not ours. I have my own savings put away.'

'I'm sure you do.' Hannah had not quite expunged the irony from her voice. 'You've always been a good manager. You should have been the son, not Benj.'

'You see? There you go again. That's exactly what most of the members of this antediluvian club would say.'

'But I didn't…'

'The ability to manage is not sex-linked,' she went roaring on. 'Women simply start off at a historical disadvantage. In fact, it's been proved that they are better managers than men. More sympathetic to people's problems, for one thing.'

Hannah looked at her and sighed. 'Angry and headstrong too.'

'Don't keep passing judgments like that!' Indigo's voice rose.

'Shhh. You'll wake Da. I don't mean to…' Hannah faltered, then went on, 'I don't mean for us to fight, darling. It's a bad time we must try and get through by guarding our words and being gentle with each other. Right?'

'Diplomacy rules,' her daughter muttered.

'That's a mother's home ground.' Hannah's smile was wan. 'I apologise if I've offended you. Pax?'

'Pax, of course.' Indigo turned to me. 'Sorry. This is most unedifying.'

I said with a lump in my throat, speaking to both of them, 'If you only knew how much I have missed a mother I could argue with like that. She always decreed, and we never ended up making peace afterwards.'

'Da taught us to say pax.' Indigo's irritation was receding with the memory. 'He always said it's all right to disagree – as vociferously as you like – so long as you stop before arguments cause irrevocable hurt.'

I saw that this was another reason why he had needed my company over the years: he got a kick out of pushing a controversy to the limit, then pulling back at the brink with a solacing 'Pax'. He and Indigo shared a passion for wrangling with ideas which he had passed on to me, and I was finding it again in Brian. Perhaps life wasn't the straight line I had always thought it to be, but a series of circular patterns.

And Angus's allotted span was reaching full circle with his tying up of loose ends, his completed business and gathering family. The Hanseatic trader had reached his home quay after his last voyage. This concept of a robust life being rounded off was easier to accept, came the thought, than a pallid continuation of the freed spirit amid harps and heavenly choirs.

Quite often after that, the three of us would sit chatting in the living room if he was asleep or round the bed if he was awake. Benjamin filled in when he could take time off from practice and recording sessions; he would sit holding his father's hand and telling stories of his travels, his new friends and musical discoveries. Their growing closeness pleased Hannah and gave Indigo wry pleasure.

'It's about time Da gave Benj credit for his real talents, instead of hoping for mercantile miracles,' she said one afternoon as we sat at a pavement café in Melville, having left Hannah dozing while Angus slept.

'He may well achieve a miracle if he ends up starring in a successful rock group.'

'Wouldn't that be a scream? While you and I toil away over our word processors, worthy but modestly paid. Always assuming I find a new job, of course.'

'You haven't thought of staying on in South Africa?'

'Can't. My publishing contacts are in London and New York. I may try freelance editing; perhaps set up my own agency. Or even write that book I'm always on about. Talking of which, how's your Joburg book going?'

'Slowly. I find it difficult to work in spasms. Plus, I'm finding Angus very hard to write about. My feelings for him as a friend keep interfering with what should be an impartial assessment. I also find myself wandering off to look at related issues: the problem of corporate fraud, for example.'

'Related. He hasn't changed his spots, then.'

'He...' What could I say? The spots were the same but he had tried to make amends as far as he could. I wondered where Dexter had tucked away the assets – and if he would ever tell me about the maggots.

As though reading my mind, Indigo said, 'You don't have to be diplomatic like Mum is. Em and I know the score, though I'm not sure about Benjamin. He's always had his sights fixed on some musical nirvana; never questioned the source of his financial support.'

I said quickly, 'I'm not insinuating that all your father's wealth is ill-gotten. Just...'

'Some of it. Tell me what he's been up to. I won't pass it on to Mum and the others, but I think someone in the family ought to know.'

'In confidence, then?'

'Complete.'

I told her what I knew about his wheelings and dealings, though I left out the untraceable assets. He had stipulated that it be our secret and besides, I didn't want her to think too badly of him. Whatever his reasons for overstepping the bounds that honest men set themselves (poverty as a child, his need for conspicuous success, or a simple lust for the power money confers), he had been a good – if absent – father to her. And friend to me. He had succeeded where we were concerned, and that was what mattered that day. His transgressions were his affair, not ours.

In one of the paradoxes of the new South Africa, he had also succeeded as far as the media were concerned: his confession was held up as an admirable example of truth and reconciliation, and he was credited with precipitating the arrests of his fraudulent peers.

It was to be expected that the business community's reaction would be mixed. The majority applauded (at least in public) and the minority moaned that he had done irreparable damage to their image, reinforced the government's paranoia about capitalists, given the unions dangerous ammunition, and worst of all, closed off lucrative avenues for the enterprising buccaneers of wealth creation.

Angus laughed at them all. 'Hypocrites!'

34

Angus was his own cryptic, pugnacious, domineering self to the end. During the lucid intervals of the last week of his life he held court in the vast mahogany bed, propped up by pillows, nourished by a drip and taking small sips of honeyed tea. Imperious as a ruined potentate who refuses to acknowledge that his palace has crumbled round him, he pulled out all the stops: made last-minute *pronunciamentos*, called Leo to add minor bequests to his will, demanded that we read him news reports and savoured the gossip his friends and colleagues brought him when they visited to say goodbye.

Organised by Prunella, small groups came from Quain & Associates: the staff, the messengers, his partners to shake hands with gruff regrets, Cameron Greenacre whinnying farewells, the Prune herself in a houndstooth check suit with subdued shoulder pads and the raven curls scraped back by tortoise-shell combs. He asked Hannah and me to leave them alone and when Prunella came out she looked ten years older, her ashen face streaming tears.

Hannah got up from the sofa and went to her. 'Are you all right, dear?'

'I'm fine.' The shoulder pads squared with visible effort. 'Mr Quain was very decent to me. He's upped my pension to retirement age.'

The corollary was written in the ash: And now I'm redundant. No use to anyone. Finished.

'Do sit down and have some tea before you leave.' Hannah put an arm round her shoulders, urging her towards the sofa. 'I've been meaning to talk to you about the retirement options we have in England. It's quite remarkable what can be achieved if you're still young enough.'

'I'm not young any more. And no tea, thank you.' Prunella tried to shake off Hannah's arm but her legs buckled and she subsided into an empty armchair.

Hannah gestured, Leave us, please, and I went in to Angus saying, 'Poor Prune. She's very upset.'

'Losing a great boss … like me … never easy.'

'Losing a job at her age, rather.' It was a tart comment, regretted the moment it slipped out. I was finding it hard to treat Angus with kid gloves after the years of enjoyable sparring.

A gurgle was all he could manage by way of a laugh. 'So it's not … my magnetic … personality?'

His head was a skull now, all hollows and shadows, set on a skeleton from which the skin drooped in crepey swags where it had once swelled. His sunken face was showing signs of cyanosis in the progressive purpling of lips and eye sockets. Yet his adamant spirit lived on in the intense blue of his eyes and the concentrated force of his words, spoken so slowly now from the alert mind trapped in the failing body.

'That too,' I conceded. 'She's been in love with you for years, of course.'

His mouth made a dry sucking sound when he began to speak. 'Stew the prunes. Fixed her up … though.'

He looked so pleased with himself that I didn't have the heart to say that an improved pension was small compensation for redundancy, and that Hannah was busy trying to pick up the pieces next door.

With some success, she told me later. 'I suggested that Prunella offer her services to a charity or one of the NGOs working with underprivileged people, and she went off with a gleam in her sad red eyes. It's appalling how middle-aged people in our society are cast aside when their usefulness is over. Thank God I have my pottery. It's a far better bet than a lover: more rewarding, less demanding, and I can go on till I'm too feeble to pack my kiln any more. Which is not to say…' she gave me a sideways glance '…that I haven't had a few dalliances. Arty men can be very creative in bed, specially potters.'

The reminiscent smile on her face was identical to Angus's when he'd said he liked women. Perhaps it was catching? I thought, and said, 'I don't know any potters besides you.'

'They tend to shed bits of hardened clay all over the place – worse than crumbs in bed – but with all the heaving around and kneading and throwing and firing, they're not daunted by big women like me. Don't you find as you get older, though, that good men are harder to come by?'

'Oh, yes.'

It must have sounded more heartfelt than I intended because she said then, 'I'd stick to that chap with ginger hair if I were you.'

'Brian? Oh, there's nothing going on there. He's just a friend, like Angus. Somebody to see and chat to once in a while.' I was proud of myself for not blushing. 'I've a circle of friends like him.'

'Ah.' She looked unconvinced.

I was thinking, echoing Angus, Stew the Brians. He hadn't returned from wherever he'd gone; his answering machine took messages but gave no information.

It became more difficult to communicate with Angus as his condition deteriorated. He dozed often and when awake seemed not to want to talk, preferring to listen. We took turns reading to him: Hannah from the newspapers, Indigo from books of poetry she had brought, Benjamin from an account he had started writing about his quest for musical roots. I read excerpts from my research notes about Joburg businessmen and my findings in the attic, and did not mention my dilemma over the book's focus. He'd make a sound low down in his throat to indicate interest or amusement; a slight movement of one of the bony claws lying on the paisley eiderdown would show disagreement.

Once when I was alone with him, he looked up at me and mumbled, 'Have I ever ... thanked you?'

'Often.'

'My faithful friend. I wish you ... great happiness.'

'And I wish...'

'Sleep. So ... tired.' His falling eyelids could have been made of latex, flexible and transparent with the oily sheen of life on them, but not for long.

The Club members came to say goodbye one by one, dropping in when Mr Barkin spread the word that Angus was awake and able to cope with a visit. Most of the farewells were brief and formal: an expression of regrets, a hearkening back to better times, and a salute from the doorway. The older men came out either with watery eyes or a stern expression to hide the relief that it was not them lying there this time. The younger men (all successful in their fields or they would not have been elected members) came out with that cocky bounce in the step that marks its owner as a believer in his own probable immortality ... or fame at the very least.

The waiters and cleaning women came in a group led by Boniface and sang a farewell song in Zulu, their voices blending in a low sweet harmony that floated along the passages and down the grand staircase, arresting everyone who heard it. Unable to speak when they had finished, Angus gestured his goodbyes: a dying chieftain signalling a job well done. He had arranged a legacy for each according to length of service but they didn't know that yet. The song was for the man who had been courteous to them and shown approval of their efforts, not forgetting his origins. It was yet another paradox: Angus never failed in courtesy to people who served his physical needs – Mr Barkin, Praise, Boniface, the Club staff – yet at work he could reduce a lazy manager or a dithering secretary to shreds with a few harsh words.

I was sitting with him when Monty Steyn came in, preceded by the fiery nose that was a monument to Old Brown sherry. He came shuffling through the doorway wheezing, 'Yer decent, Quain? No strumpets in there?'

'Hardly.' It was a whisper.

'Who's this, then?' Leering at me.

'A friend.'

Eyes like grapes with noble rot wandered over me. 'Bloody good-looking tart. Nice pair of tits.'

I heard the noise that passed for a chuckle. 'Not bad.'

Monty Steyn would not have been out of place standing in line at a soup kitchen. His hoary tweed jacket sagged off his shoulders, his stomach sagged over a straining belt and his shoes looked as though they had been bought off the shelf of un-fixables in a repair shop. I never saw him without scabs flaking off his ears and a flaccid cigarette hanging from his lower lip, shedding ash and tobacco as liberally as the obscenities he rained on anyone who entered his radius. The staff loathed him and Boniface refused to serve him, saying he was *thakathi*, bewitched.

Now he rasped, swaying at the end of the bed, 'Come to say that the place won't be the same without yer.'

'Kind words.'

Monty Steyn was staggering drunk. 'Kind, hell. Yer the only fucker who doesn't talk down to me. Poncey shits. Treat me like a bad smell. Maybe I am.' He let out a noise that could have been a laugh or a fart; it was hard to tell. 'Fuck 'em anyway. Fuck this stinking town. Yer doing the dead right thing, buggering off.'

'No choice.'

'Place has gone to pot. Fucking muggers and beggars everywhere. Can't walk in the street for dug-up paving and rotting fruit. Break my bloody leg one day.'

'Join me...?'

Monty Steyn's mouth widened into a drooling grin as he jabbed his nicotine-stained thumb at the floor. 'Down there? Not fucking likely. Couldn't stand the heat. Yer on yer own now, Quain. Good luck, you hear?'

'Need it.'

'And bloody well done for stirring the pot last week. Too many turds spoil the broth, eh?' With a brief wave he stumbled out again.

Angus croaked, 'Crazy ... bastard. Makes a career ... out of being ... the Club embarrassment.'

'Why does everyone go along with him?'

'Can't get rid ... of fixtures. Been here ... too long. Like me.'

He drifted off as he was doing more and more often, slipping in and out of consciousness. Beverley's drug regime kept him largely pain-free when he was awake but there were prolonged periods of sleep. 'It'll only be a few days now,' his doctor had told us.

Mr Barkin was the last of the Club staff to say goodbye. Hannah and I were sitting quietly together in Angus's bedroom during the afternoon when the day nurse took an hour off, and his apologetic knock at the door was an unwelcome intrusion.

'May I come in?'

When Hannah turned, the afternoon light from the long windows glistened on tear tracks. 'Who is it?'

'Barkin. I'd like to pay my respects.' His head with its smudged eyes and thinning hair appeared round the door, followed by the ubiquitous black cloth jacket. 'Mr Quain has been so good to me. A real gentleman.'

There was a croak from the white face against the pillows. 'Barkin ... mad.'

'Come in,' Hannah beckoned. 'He's recognised you.'

Mr Barkin came in and surprised us both by dropping to his knees on the faded carpet next to the bed and putting his hand on Angus's still arm. 'I want to say a special thank you, sir, for your moral support. Most of our gentlemen are not easy to deal with. They call me Old Barkin and discuss my shortcomings in my hearing, and think I don't care. You have never condescended, and for that I am more grateful than I can say.'

'Nothing...' Angus struggled to get the word out, then tugged at Hannah's hand on the sheet. 'Tell him.'

'What, dear?' She bent her mothy cheek close to his gaunt stubbly chin, her ear to his lips.

'Railway ... shoes.'

'Ah. Yes.' She sat up. 'He wants me to tell you, Mr Barkin, that his father was a poor man who worked on the railways and couldn't afford to buy him school shoes. At the end of the school year on prize-giving day, he wore his father's only pair of good shoes so he could collect his prizes decently dressed, while his parents stayed at home: his father because he was shoeless and his mother so as not to shame him by her shabbiness. There is no higher place for him to condescend from, do you see?'

Angus indicated his approval with a nod.

'I see, but can't agree.' Mr Barkin put his hand on the bed to lever himself upwards and straightened his back from its usual submissive curve. 'A gentleman is born, not made. I thank you for your courtesy, Mr Quain, and for your kindness to members in trouble like Mr Steyn and Mr Linklater. You will not be forgotten. I'll see to that.' His chin went up too then. 'When the Club Annals are published – with Miss D's help, I trust...' he favoured me with a proud smile '...you will be on the roll of honour. Farewell, and Godspeed.'

He bent forward from the waist, stood up again, restrained himself from snapping a military salute, and marched out of the room.

'How infinitely touching.' Hannah's tear tracks were a network when she turned back to the bed. 'I had no idea you were such a force for good, Angus.'

'Good... in parts,' he managed, but the old smile was beyond him. 'Mostly ... bad.'

'I don't think so.' She covered his claw with her strong potter's hand. 'You're a brilliant, secretive, deeply flawed man – as we all are, deeply flawed – but there's always been that wonderful core of kindness and loyalty. Not so, Faith?'

She was deft at including me, the kindest of women herself. I said, 'Absolutely,' without a trace of shame and put my hand over the claw nearest me. 'Without question. Indubitably. Assuredly. Indeed.'

His lips moved. 'Bravo ... old girl.' It was the last time he spoke to me.

He only lived another day. We were called together in the bedroom, dusky with evening, by Hannah on the doctor's advice. When I demurred at joining the family, she said, 'Nonsense, he'd want you here, specially as Em can't be.'

'But I'm not...'

'No buts. Come quickly.'

In his last hour, she sat on one side of the bed with Benjamin next to her, hands joined, their faces thrown into relief on one side by lamplight like an old master painting. Indigo and I sat opposite them; she was holding one of the photographs of Em and tiny Jamie as if willing them to be there in spirit. Tom and Leo and Dexter stood at the bottom of the bed, completing the circle.

The room was quiet and close, the growl of home-going traffic muffled by the drawn velvet curtains. The medicine trolley having been banished next door, being of no more use, the familiar tobacconist's aura of sandalwood and cigars had crept back. Angus was dying in his lair as he had wished, with his best friends and most of his family round him. Only the slight whisper of oxygen from the transparent plastic nose tube and the slits of dull blue under his eyelids showed that he was still with us.

The death mask on the pillow made an infinitesimal movement and said something I couldn't hear, though Hannah understood. 'We're all present and correct, love,' she said in a low voice, then turning to the rest of us, 'Join hands.'

We leaned and clasped, then she began to sing a lullaby; it must have been one she had sung them as children, because Indigo and Benjamin joined in and Angus's lips moved as though he was trying to say the words. I watched his face as the song was repeated; by the end of it, his eyelids had closed for the last time and his face was still.

His breathing stopped a few minutes later. We were still holding hands round him, silent in grief.

Hannah said over the whispering of the oxygen, 'He's gone,' and wept.

Outside in the street, the sudden blare of a car alarm tolled his passing.

35

ngus was not a religious man though he would admit sometimes to believing that there must be a guiding power in the universe.

'It's too damn neat and well-ordered to have just happened,' he'd say, then turn round and contradict himself in the next breath by roaring that we live 'in a random bloody universe with no rules,' which immutable fact gave him the right to do exactly as he pleased.

I still don't know if he died believing in or doubting the great managing director in the sky. That agile mind could encompass conflicting ideas at the same time, giving each a Quain-like twist that brought them into line with his current thinking. If he had been less driven and impatient with fools, and more willing to toe the legal line most people abide by, he would have been a great man. But his life had been an unrelenting struggle to succeed that had demanded many compromises, and he had evolved a morality to match: anything or anyone that served Angus Quain well was to be nurtured and cherished, and if necessary, pursued; anything or anyone that stood between him and his goal was either charmed out of the way, or bulldozed. And he kept his secrets like bankers hoard their gold reserves, locked in impenetrable vaults and closely guarded.

Yet there were also his good qualities: the humour and the generosity and the intelligence and the infectious life force and what Hannah called 'that wonderful core of kindness and loyalty' that had survived the depredations of the struggle. It was these qualities that captured my allegiance and made him my best friend for fifteen years... not to mention the undoubted cachet of being associated with a man who commanded fortunes and rolled about in a chauffeured Bentley. I learnt during the months Angus was dying that I am not immune to glamour, flattery, party food and fine feathers.

So much for the academic, sceptical, discerning Faith I thought I was. Though

I must add in my defence that I managed to resist his bribes. While he was alive, that is. In his will, Angus left me a BMW Cabriolet and a large parcel of Vanguard Unit Trusts.

At Hannah's request, Leo read out the will to the main beneficiaries in the living room of Angus's suite the morning after he died. The family bequests were straightforward and dealt with first: since he had established separate trusts for Hannah and his children after the divorce, it was a matter of adding to them and creating a new trust for Jamie and future grandchildren. Specific sums were not mentioned but from the look on Indigo's face, she would have a problem convincing herself in future that she was self-reliant. I was relieved to hear that no constraints had been placed on Benjamin's trust. In his dying weeks, Angus had begun at last to trust his son's instincts.

He had also established a trust for Dexter's family, a multi-million rand fund for school, college and university bursaries for disadvantaged children, left shares to Tom and Leo and the Bentley to Praise. Besides the legacies to Mr Barkin and the staff, a substantial amount had been bestowed on the Club 'in recognition of its services to a deeply appreciative member'.

Leo looked up. 'The next bit is about Faith. "To my good friend Faith, with thanks for her unstinting companionship and cast-iron scruples which denied me the pleasure of gifts while I was alive…"'

'Oh no.' It burst out of me. 'I only wanted his friendship.'

'This is not about what you want.' Leo gave me an austere look. 'Allow me to finish, please.'

My convertible was to be bought from Praise, so I'd be the first customer of the BMW dealership he would purchase with the proceeds from the Bentley. The clause about the Vanguard Unit Trusts stipulated that they were not to be added to my share portfolio, but used in the quest for zero defect.

Hannah turned to me. 'What did he mean by that?'

'Oh, it's just a running joke we had.' When she kept on looking, I added, 'It's what he called his campaign to find me a boyfriend.'

She nodded. 'He told me he had unfinished business. Loose ends which bothered him.'

Me and the maggots, I thought, making a mental note to quiz Dexter again before he left. He was sitting on the sofa with Aleesha, both looking stunned at the idea of having a trust fund of their own.

I said, 'I was dragged round the business entertainment circuit for a few months. After a while, all the single men fled screaming when they saw us.'

Beside me, Indigo hooted. 'I know exactly what you went through. He tried it on me every time he came to London, and you have no idea how many scaly executives cruise the circuit over there.'

'Do you mind?' Leo was looking daggers. 'A will is a serious matter.'

'Da would have enjoyed the joke. Quest for zero defect, indeed.' Indigo doubled over, starting me off. Then Benjamin and Dexter began to chuckle and even Hannah managed a smile.

'Please,' Leo said, desperate to finish, 'show some respect.'

I pointed a shaky finger at him. 'You and I were two of Angus's loose ends, only we refused to get knotted.' I put back my head and roared, joined by Indigo who held on to my arm and laughed until the tears came.

'Enough, now,' Hannah said after a while. 'Let poor Leo finish. Loose end or not, he has a job to do.'

He looked at her, and then me. 'I'm not a loose end any more. The last time I saw Angus, he encouraged me to resign my job and join the staff of a new birding magazine as a photographer. I'm moving back to Cape Town next month. I dislike, with a passion, both Nelspruit and being a lawyer. So I'm off to do my own thing.'

'Sounds fairly loose to me,' Indigo murmured.

'Not at all.' Leo was looking down his nose like Angus had in his heyday, with the arrogance of the new convert who believes that others will never be as committed as he is. 'Bird photography means hours – sometimes days – of patient stalking and waiting. I'm going into a far more demanding profession than law.'

'That's wonderful, Leo.'

Hannah spoke warmly and he relaxed in his chair. He's been psyching himself up to tell us, I thought, and wondered why it had taken him so long to admit to having inherited his father's talent, and whether his new profession would heal his childhood wounds. Angus had not been entirely wrong about us; given time and no meddling, Leo and I liked each other enough to have become friends; perhaps good enough friends to marry. There are no Mr Rights, I realised, only Mr Maybes. Indigo would agree, I was sure.

And she did, in several long conversations before the funeral during which we became fast friends. Angus would have liked that – perhaps he plotted it from the time he realised he was going to die? Indigo, of course, was his most challenging loose end and remains one still, despite having become London's most acclaimed poetry editor.

'Found any interesting talent for me?' she'll say when she comes to stay for a few weeks during the worst of the English winter. And I'll parade my selection of eligibles, carrying on Angus's plan of action to find a suitable mate for his eldest daughter. I've become a canny potential weaver of loose ends myself.

Though Dexter takes the crown when it comes to scheming. Angus had taught him well.

I bullied him into a corner while the others were chatting over coffee after the will reading. 'I hope you're going to tell me about the maggots now.'

'Have a heart,' he said, looking evasive. 'I'm really busy this week, helping Leo with the financial side of winding up the estate.'

'Now,' I insisted. 'You and Angus dangled them like bait in front of me, and I think that as his biographer, I have the right to know.'

'You still going to put Oom in a book, then?'

I nodded. 'A book of his own, after I've finished the one I'm working on about financial fraud in South Africa. That's another reason why I must know about the maggots: I don't want to implicate Angus.'

'Yirrr, but you persistent.' He shifted from one foot to the other. 'If I say they've all hatched and flown away to a better place, is that enough?'

'No.'

'And that they turned out to be haaarmless in the end?'

'Not nearly enough. Tell. And I want to know about the maggot breeders too.'

'The what?'

'The last thing Angus said to me on the night of his cocktail party was, "Did you spot my maggot breeders?"'

'Oh, them.' Dexter shifted feet again. 'Listen, if I tell you, it doesn't go any further, right?'

'I can't guarantee that.'

'You must, or my lips are sealed.' He clamped his mouth closed, pulling a ferocious face.

With reluctance, I agreed.

'Promise? Cross your heart?'

'Promise.'

Which is why I can't specify the maggots or how they hatched, though I can say that Angus and Dexter had found a loophole in Stock Exchange regulations that allowed them to use nominee companies to buy and sell shares at a substantial profit, tax-free and unreported. The maggot breeders had been clients of Quain & Associates whom Angus had roped in to provide confidential information, telling each that he was the only one privileged to participate. No wonder there had been so many red faces on the night of his cocktail party, though they needn't have worried; he didn't mention the maggots. 'Left 'em … in the rotting corpse,' he told Dexter afterwards. 'Not my problem … any more.'

Like so many of his activities, the deals had been both brilliant and borderline – and none of the profits had gone into his own pocket, Dexter said.

'You're kidding.'

'Honest to God, I'm not. He called it the Quain version of affirmative action, and sometimes railwayman's revenge.' Dexter's brown eyes were full of glee. 'It's why I respected him so much; why I helped him. He never tried to chaff anyone he was a laaanie. And when he got rich and famous, he didn't forget where he came from.'

The ill-gotten gains had gone in anonymous donations to charity. It was the thrill of the chase that spurred Angus on, not the quarry. He loved beating the odds and bucking the system: enjoyed surfing the money markets with an optimist's scorn for tempestuous waves, underlying reefs and the safety of the far-off beach.

He had had time to plan his final arrangements in detail, and Hannah made sure his wishes were carried out.

A month before he died, Dexter was empowered to purchase and organise the demolition of a block of warehouses in Newtown, the run-down area to the west of Joburg's business centre for which many excellent upgrading plans have been formulated, though little besides the Market Theatre and MuseumAfrica complex has been accomplished. The block was to become a city park with trees and benches and a playground, and Angus asked to be cremated and his ashes buried in the park under one of the trees – 'Preferably indigenous, like me.'

'As a long-standing member of the Inner City Forum, I wish to donate a green island to the city that has been my home for four decades, in the hope that this will encourage intelligent redevelopment,' his letter of intent stipulated. 'Nothing would please me more than to be laid to rest under a tree that shelters children and lovers and old people sitting peacefully on benches.'

'Tramps snoring off last night's cheap wine, more likely,' Indigo murmured when Hannah told us. 'Da's ashes will be dancing a perpetual jig of rage. You know how he was always fulminating against won't-works.'

'He mellowed a lot towards the end.'

'Yes, he did.' Her smile was a carbon copy of his, though gentler. 'I think he'd have made a benign grandpa.'

We exchanged smiles. Everyone made an effort to smile during the two days between his death and his funeral, knowing how much Angus would have hated weeping and wailing and gnashing of teeth. He had also decreed a secular memorial service followed by a private cremation with only the family and close friends present, who would then repair to his suite for what he called 'a proper Irish wake with sentimental speeches.'

The service was held in the open air at the Country Club, on a beautiful early summer day with a breeze rustling in the oak trees. The Johannesburg business community was there in force: rows of dark suits listening to brief eulogies from a temporary dais by colleagues and fellow Club members, the president of the Chamber of Commerce, the Gauteng premier, several MPs, metropolitan councillors and friends, the last of whom was Dr Vuyo Mkhize.

315

He said: 'My friend, Angus Quain, was a man who rose from lowly origins to great heights, a man whom today's impoverished youth could well emulate, if they have the brains to do so. He was by no means a perfect man, but he had the courage to make public confession of his errors and to pay the dues he felt were owing in recognition of his many privileges.'

He paused, his ironic gaze travelling over the well-fed white faces turned up to him. 'Dues, gentlemen. Not just the rates and taxes you all complain about so bitterly, but the dues you owe for three centuries of lording it over us. In memory of Angus Quain, I ask you to search your consciences as he did and make what personal reparation you can. In a country where the richest ten percent earn more than fifty percent of the total income...'

There were murmurs of dissent, and he paused again before going on, '...more than fifty percent, it's true, there is a stink of greed somewhere.'

Someone muttered, 'He's making a political speech.'

And someone else, 'Politics at a funeral. Not on.'

Dr Mkhize was concluding, '...and so, gentlemen, I urge you at this moment of a great man's passing to give serious thought to the principle of reconciliation expounded in his farewell speech. And I say goodbye to Angus Quain in the Zulu way: sala kahle, umfowethu.'

'Reconciliation, hell,' the first voice muttered again. 'It was guilt money. I hear Quain made a bloody fortune on the side.'

'Talk about not seeing the beam in your own eye.' The last was Brian's voice. He must have worked his way through the crowd and come up behind me.

I gave him a wary look. He'd been away for a week and I didn't know what to say about the kissing.

'Miss me?'

'Some.'

'You could show more enthusiasm.'

'At Angus's memorial service?'

Dr Mkhize had stepped down and Hannah had stood up to thank people for coming. There were sprinklers chip-chipping on the lawns and the banked flowerbeds, and a rich smell of wet earth.

Brian took my elbow. 'I know you're upset and sad. I just thought...'

'You presume too much.'

Hannah was saying, 'Our son and daughter and I are most grateful for all your kind wishes.'

'You seem to think I'm an upstart who wants to take his place.' Brian had leaned closer. 'Wrong guess. I expect to play a far more significant role in your life.'

'That won't be easy.'

'It will if you can shake the Quain habit you seem to have picked up.'

The service was over and Hannah and Benjamin and Indigo were standing to-gether on the dais, talking to Dr Mkhize. Below them the rows of dark suits stirred, wanting to leave because the day was warm and collars were growing limp and business appointments beckoned, but not wishing to show disrespect by being the first to go.

I turned to face him. 'What do you mean?'

'Dividing your life into compartments: one for work, one for friends, one for your solitary travels, a special fur-lined cocoon for Angus, and the secret place where you withdraw to brace yourself against loss. Like now.' There was a hard white line round his mouth. 'If we're to be friends – more than friends – I don't want to be put into a compartment. I want to be part of a whole.'

I thought about it. He was right. I'd learnt early to label and tidy away into their separate niches the different aspects of my life, and perhaps my attraction to Angus had been motivated by our similar predilection for logic and secrecy. But habits are ingrained; could I change? More importantly, did I want to? I mumbled, 'It's hard for old dogs to learn new tricks.'

'That's what crusty old farts say!' He spoke in a furious undertone. 'If you'll pardon my pointing it out at this particular juncture, I think you've been asso-ciating outside your age group for too long.'

'How can you say that when Angus is hardly gone?'

'Look around you.'

People were lining up to talk to Hannah, solemn with condolences. Several of the dark suits had sidled away and were walking with purpose towards the shady parking lot full of Mercs and BMWs and sleek 4 x 4s. Others had clotted into murmuring groups. Someone's cellphone rang and he clutched his pocket look-ing mortified and hurried behind one of the trees to answer it. Benjamin, Indi-go, Brian and I were the only ones in the crowd under fifty-five. Joburg's whizz-kids were no longer under any obligation to pay their respects to the doyen of Quain & Associates.

'The old order changeth,' Brian said. 'Time to look to the future.'

'What do you want from the future?'

'It's quite simple. I look forward to the day when I can say, "Never fear, Brian is here" without you bursting into mocking laughter.'

I felt my eyes prickling. 'Or tears. That was Angus's idea of a joke.'

'And I'm adopting it as a legacy, like Dexter did. It's one of those sayings that can't help having a ripple effect because it's so positive.'

'You could always weave it into your next management meeting.'

He shook his head. 'I'm done with gambling other people's money.'

'Am I hearing you right? Mr Vanguard himself?'

'You are. I want to gamble my own now. It's the wine farm or bust.'

317

The words slipped out before I could stop them. 'And the nubile wife?'

'I was hoping that you'd...'

Appalled by my lapse of caution, I blurted, 'But you can't!'

The hard white line round his mouth intensified. 'Let me finish what I have to say before you answer.'

'I'm not – you can't – I'm not...'

'Listen,' he commanded, gripping my arm. His stubby fingers burned through my thin sleeve. 'My criteria have changed. Nubile wives are out. Waste of time. I'm looking for a partner with brains and guts and a passion for making things grow. It'll be a small beginning and it'll take years of work before any results show.'

'A partner?' That stopped me.

He nodded. 'Contracts signed, equal investments of cash and labour input. I know that you're honest, hardworking, self-motivated and financially sound, which makes you an ideal partner.'

I remembered Angus asking if Brian had good legs, and the explanation that followed: 'Meant, is the fellow dependable in the long term?' And, 'Sound operation, Vanguard,' he had said.

In a shaky voice I said, 'You're after my money, then.'

Brian shook his head. There were grey bristles among the ginger that I had not noticed before. 'Not only. You must know that. I like you more than anyone I've ever met, Faith. I hope in time that you could reciprocate. A permanent partnership would be a bonus.'

'You mean...?'

'I mean, we've got something good going between us, and I'd like to build on it. I also think you're as ready for a change as I am.'

'You're talking radical change.' My lips were so numb that I could only get a few words out at a time.

'Up to a point. Your work is portable. Writing should make a good fit with wine-making.'

'Trampling out the vintage has a certain appeal.'

It was a defensive answer and drew the equivalent of one of Angus's black frowns – only Brian's was an unnerving scowl. 'You're evading the issue.'

'And you haven't blinded me with specifics yet.' Why did it sound so hostile when that was the least of my confused emotions?

His hand tightened on my arm. 'I've found a farm on the Berg River near Paarl with a wine quota and good buildings and some elderly equipment, but very run-down vineyards.'

Another mystery solved. 'So that's where you've been. And you accuse me of secrecy?'

'A successful unit trust manager checks his sources personally, with due care.

And I am obliged to warn that this potential investment carries no guarantees. A lot of money and effort will need to be pumped in before the first new shoots appear, let alone actual grapes. A drinkable wine could take five years or more to materialise for marketing. So the proposition needs careful thought before you respond. Would two days be enough?'

I gave it two minutes, watching the clots of dark suits break up into single corpuscles hurrying for their cars to join the humming bloodstream running back into the city along its tarmac arteries. Watching Hannah and Indigo turn to Benjamin and be gathered into a consoling hug. Remembering the time Angus had said, 'You have to learn to reach out and grab opportunities, or you lose them.' He was reaching out from the silence beyond death to remind me, reinforced by the generous provision in his will. Was this the end of the quest he had begun with the intention of leaving his irregular lunchtime companion neatly tidied away and accounted for?

Brian was trying to keep his enthusiasm throttled down and not succeeding. 'There's also the question of lack of know-how. I've consulted the Cap Classique experts and they say that the slope and the water supply and the soils on the farm are good but they're not sure if a rank amateur should even consider trying to make a classic bubbly.'

I said, 'What about two rank amateurs?'

'That would make a crucial difference.' The white line round his mouth disappeared in the sudden boy's smile.

But I didn't want him to see me as a pushover. I said quickly, 'It's an appealing investment and I'm ready for a change, as you say.' We were equally wary of making mistakes, I thought. Two of a pair in that respect: burned by previous relationships, tentative about making new ones, cautious about dropping our guard. I added, 'As to a more permanent partnership, shouldn't we proceed with what you call due care?'

'Certainly. Contrary to appearances, I'm a patient investor. It's long-term growth I'm looking for.'

'The buy and hold strategy,' I murmured.

'Nail on the head. You could show more enthusiasm, though.' His fingers were biting into my arm.

I was going to say something clever but the way his smile was pinching in stopped me. Hell, I was tired of being clever; of puns and word games and trying to outwit people before they outwitted me. And I liked him tremendously too.

So I took my third uncharacteristic plunge into the unknown and gave him what was probably a foolish grin and said, 'Just try me.'

'That's good,' was all he said, but the quiet satisfaction in it was enough. The hand on my arm relaxed and slid down to hold mine as we began to move towards the Quains on the dais under the oak trees.

This is Angus's book, written too late for him to be able to exercise a veto. But I think that it's fair and objective, and having met and become an honorary member of his family now, that there's nothing in it that will inordinately embarrass them. I have called it *The Telling of Angus Quain,* but since it is also – by default – about me, it could equally well have been called *Joburg Renaissance.*

In memory of a rare old-fashioned friendship which gave birth to what I hope is a lasting new one.